CW00951906

THOSE YOU KILLED

CHRISTOPHER BADCOCK

BLOOD
RITES
HORROR

Those You Killed by Christopher Badcock
Originally published 2021 by Blood Rites Horror
First edition

Copyright © 2021 Christopher Badcock
Cover design © by Ruin Reel
Edited by Nick Harper

All rights reserved. No part of this book may be reproduced
except for the purposes of reviewing or with the express
permission of the author.

Any resemblance to real-life people or situations is coincidental.

The following is a work of fiction, but heroin and other hard drugs are not. If you're living with a monkey on your back, or know somebody who is –

Talk.

Seek out the services which are here to provide help and support. Take that first step.

THOSE YOU KILLED

Dear Amanda,
Stay out of the
woods.....

CHRISTOPHER BADCOCK

For Aubriella

Chase your dreams, my love.
They can be caught.

CHAPTER ONE
LAST HIT

Was he like that raindrop?

He watched it trickle down his car window, and conceded that yes, he was. On a downward course and dribbling toward the finish line, that was him. That was Elwood Cathis.

He wondered what might be waiting there for him at the bottom. Like the rain, would he just disappear into the great gutter of the world? That place which so many called *rock bottom*.

End of the line.

That's what they'd say to him when he touched down in that place, those who'd fallen off the wagon of life, finding their homes in subways and back-alleys, cardboard boxes and derelict buildings.

Coffins.

He snapped his attention back to the road as the lights turned to green; cars in front began to slowly shift forward through the downpour toward scattered suburbs that held the promise of a small town somewhere up ahead. Elwood turned onto Crescent Road, and sped up as he left what could barely pass for traffic behind him.

That wasn't all he was leaving behind though; this trip was make or break for him. Either he continued down the window, like the raindrop, or… well, he didn't know what, but something needed to happen, that much he was sure of. Something needed to change.

The prairie landscape, which had flanked him on both sides for the last hundred miles or so, abruptly turned to dense woodland, the change marked only by a battered and bullet hole-riddled sign at the side of the road.

Welcome to Misstonville Forest – Home of Lake Chance.

He squinted through the torrent, straining to make out the rest of the words.

Drive safe. Swim safe. Hunt safe.

Faded red graffiti advised he should *fuck safe*, rather than *hunt safe*.

The road lived up to its name and held a perfect crescent as it swept through the wooded landscape. Elegant in shape, its form left much to be desired; potholes and cracks littered the street which, like the sign, had clearly seen better days.

The sky overhead darkened gradually as the evening drew nearer. Elwood glanced at the dash and saw that it was approaching six o'clock; he'd been driving for almost nine hours. He could have taken the train, even flown, but he needed the space. He couldn't be around people right now. The crowds made him anxious, jittery, and when he got that way, he needed to fix it. That was what he was running away from, though: that medicine, that *fix*. It was ruling his life, had completely changed his life in fact.

Had changed *him*.

As he drew the car around the curve of the road, he passed another sign on the right. This one hung crooked, a small mountain of empty beer cans spread out on the dirt beneath it. He could still make out the words through the rain:

Lake Chance Villas – Homes away from home, by the water. Next 4 miles.

And beneath it, barely readable:

Woodland Tourist Centre. General Supplies. Trails – 4½ miles.

He hoped he wouldn't need to go into town to pick up anything, and decided he'd visit the store in the morning; he had enough snacks and rum left over from the journey to see him through the night. He'd yet to open the rum – the last thing he needed was another DUI, plus the bottle was earmarked to help get him through this.

Well, get him through the first night at least.

Elwood passed a narrow, gravel road leading off to the right. A stubby wooden sign beside the road marked the turnoff as *No. 1*.

He continued along the road for less than a quarter of a mile before reaching another turnoff, and another sign, this one reading *No. 2*. He guessed he only had another two miles or so to go; the friendly ghost had given him *No. 9* for a week.

He'd read somewhere that it could take between seven and ten days to get over it, to get it out of your system and be free of it.

Casper had initially agreed to a week, among other stipulations, and that he was to call him on the seventh day and let him know how he was doing; if he needed an extra few days then maybe that would happen, maybe it wouldn't. You didn't negotiate with Casper Stevens, you accepted whatever gift the horse was offering, and you were sure to be gracious as fuck about it, even as you deliberately steered your gaze from its mouth.

No.3.

He couldn't remember the last time he'd gone seven hours without a fix, let alone seven days. And who did he have to thank for that? The friendly ghost, of course.

No.4.

No wonder Casper had let him have this place without any argument. He felt guilty; he wanted to help, wanted to clean up the mess he'd made.

No.5.

As much as he relished the exercise of accusing others for his current situation, Elwood knew deep down that he only had himself to blame. Over the next few days he expected those buried feelings – and others – to be brought to the fore.

It was an expectation that terrified him.

No.6.

Yes, Casper had certainly helped bring about the downfall of Elwood Cathis, but he himself had been in the driver's seat. It had been his decision to put the pedal to the metal, it had been his hands on the wheel. Now, his knuckles tightened as he cruised through the forest.

No. 7.

The friendly ghost had just been a passenger, one who occasionally gave directions, all of them bad turns. Everyone knew how hard it was to steer a steady course with a backseat driver, someone in your ear, someone who made it difficult to concentrate. And so, this exercise in culpability continued as it always did. His ex-wife would come next.

No. 8.

And then perhaps his estranged sister. His father. Or that slutty fangirl he met in Charleston. Each had played a part in his ruin, it couldn't *just* be Elwood's fault.

No. 9.

He turned off of Crescent Road and onto a gravel lane that wound its way through the trees. The rain and cloudy skies were beginning to subside a little, and the evening growing brighter as a result, yet the thick woodland around him seemed to hold onto the darkness and distil it into an altogether different kind of gloom.

He could see shapes between the trees, figures. None of them real.

As a youngster he'd always enjoyed late walks in Bluebell Wood, a sprawling forest on the outskirts of his hometown. Smoking joints had been his release, and his wanderings along those dark paths had spawned many of the ideas which had later become international bestsellers. It was during those drug-induced jaunts that he'd imagined *things* standing in the darkness among the trees. It was easy to do – hell, take a walk through *any* forest at night and you'll see whatever your mind wants you to see out there in the dark. Trees become torsos, branches become limbs.

He'd always thought that was the key to writing good horror: letting your mind wander to places where there was no horror, and finding it there anyway. It was an art, seeing the terrifying that lay beneath the okay.

Elwood continued to follow the road as it snaked its way through the trees. He hadn't thought about writing in at least two years, maybe even three.

That's what it had been about at first, though; the writing. The weed had heightened his creative thinking as a youngster, and as an adult maybe heroin would have the same effect. It had been an experiment and that had made it okay. He wasn't a junkie, he was an explorer, a creative in search of great ideas, unlocking the full potential of his imagination.

Not a junkie, not him.

The road was heading downhill now – he could see it opening up into a clearing ahead – and there stood the lake house.

Like the signs on the road, it was a sad reminder of what once might have been great. The grand in decline. The two-storey redbrick sat amid overgrown weeds and wild bush, its façade crumbling in spots, a shutter missing here and there. But it still held itself with an air of pride – more than could be said of Elwood Cathis, that was for sure. The building's stone chimney still contained every brick, the porch steps all remained; it was a slow and dignified decline. Which, coincidentally, was also more than could be said for that of a certain Elwood Cathis.

A mixture of birches and maples created a perimeter around the yard, with a few firs dotted in between;

although he couldn't see any treetops beyond the house, this he assumed was due to the position of the lake on the other side. The building itself stretched lengthways across the entire clearing – Elwood didn't know why, but he'd assumed it would be much smaller; less house and more cabin. In fact, he'd been picturing the cabin from the Evil Dead movie. To the far right, the house formed an L-shape, with the porch and front door situated at that end of the property. There was a parking bay to the right of the porch steps, so he steered his car in that direction.

He suddenly realised what he might have let himself in for. The friendly ghost was a notorious party animal, a womaniser, a slob, dangerous. Essentially the sort of guy you wanted to remain on the right side of. Elwood dreaded to think what state the interior might be in, what vile surprises he might find.

Not that it mattered anyway; he wasn't here for luxury and relaxation. He was here to find himself, regain himself, even. Take back everything he'd lost.

He kept telling himself these things, but they were only words, words that meant nothing without action.

Elwood turned the engine off and removed his keys from the ignition. The rain had stopped completely now, but the clouds had darkened, signalling another imminent downpour.

He let his hands drop off the wheel, exhaled. Rubbed his knees. This was it.

He grabbed his sports bag from the passenger seat and unzipped the side pocket.

First came the spoon.

Then a lighter.

Next, a small bag of brown powder. It had been white, back when he'd started using. That was a standard that hadn't lasted long though. White was pure, white was expensive, and oftentimes white was harder to come by. Brown, black, or rose grey – these were the shades that all junkies eventually settled on, when the need for a fix outweighed any concerns for what they were actually putting in their bodies. Anything that wasn't white had been cut with God-only-knew what.

A tiny squeeze-bottle of lemon juice.

A ball of cotton, which he rolled up tightly between his thumb and middle finger.

And finally, a syringe.

He emptied some of the powder onto the spoon, added a drop of lemon juice to help break it down, then set the lighter to it.

'After this it's hasta la vista baby, see you later alligator.' He found himself speaking to the liquid that had now formed on the spoon. He paused. 'I mean it this time.'

Elwood let the cotton ball soak it up, and then he drew the liquid from this and into the syringe.

At least he was alone for this one, and had his own needle which nobody else had played with. He had lost count of the number of times he'd played roulette with HIV and Hep. C; sharing syringes was a dangerous game, but that had always been part of the fun too, part of the high, like fucking somewhere where you might get caught, or waiting until you could see the train before crossing the track.

There was still some left in the bag, but he stowed it

away in the glovebox – he wouldn't be needing it, but that didn't mean it had to be thrown away. There was a brief moment in which he considered rolling his window down and emptying the bag onto the wet gravel, but that would be stupid.

If things went wrong he'd need it. He'd need something to fall back on, something to tide him over until he got back to LA.

He set the syringe down in his lap and removed the belt from around his waist, then strapped it tightly around his bicep.

He went to his favourite spot – the skin irritation showing just how often he had visited – and pierced the flesh with the needle, before gently pushing it into his vein. He brought his thumb down, and with it, the heroin, skag, smack, helicopter, lifesaver – whatever he was calling it this time – entered his bloodstream intravenously.

And Elwood Cathis mainlined for the last time.

CHAPTER TWO
USSF MYSTIC

'We got him, we got him!' Anderson shouted feverishly over the comms link. With trembling hands, she managed to bring the lever down and engage the door, trapping the Captain in the airlock.

Durand had already escaped through corridor H as planned and now he doubled back on himself via the medical bay and labs. Moving briskly through zone two of the med bay, he forced himself to look at the examination tables; although main power was still down, the dim glow emanating from the backup lights was enough to show the bodies that lay beneath them, each covered with a white sheet.

All of them drenched in blood.

Durand had promised himself, promised all his lifeless comrades, that their deaths wouldn't be for naught. That he and Anderson would make it back to Earth, and make it back in time, with the payload intact. And by God, he was going to keep that promise.

He left the med bay and began to run along a darkened corridor which would eventually lead him back to Anderson and Olesk. Red lights flashed along the ceiling and on either side of the walkway as NAVI's robotic voice sounded throughout the now eerily quiet ship:

'Warning. Anti-gravity system shutdown in T-minus 13 minutes, 36 seconds. Warning. Oxygen circulation approaching critical status. Warning'

Durand ignored the monotone speech and moved as quickly as he could.

'Have you disengaged the outer-airlock controls?' he asked.

'Negative,' Anderson's voice crackled through his helmet speaker. 'We have a breach in the outer door – my guess is it's from that shitstorm earlier, we just haven't had time to get to it yet.'

They hadn't had time to get to many of them. There were still breaches all over the Mystic, but the captain needed to be neutralised. That had been their priority and still was, even now.

'Just,' Durand paused, breathless, 'just keep him in there. Don't let him do anything,'

Anderson cut in. 'You better get your ass down here right now, soldier. He's got a hammer. I think he's going to try to smash his way through.'

Durand quickened his pace. They couldn't afford a breach in the inner door, they might lose pressure in the entire west quarterdeck of the ship. He could hear Anderson screaming now, not through his comms link, but faintly through the casing of his helmet; he was nearly there.

'Don't you dare, Olesk. Just put it down. Put the hammer *down.*'

Durand took the final corner and found Anderson with her back to him, her nose pressed up against the window as she tried to reason with the captain.

'Anderson, get back and get your ass in a suit right now,' Durant ordered as he approached the door. The young lieutenant spun around. Her face was gleaming with sweat and her black hair was fixed to her forehead like silhouetted branches against a reddening sky. She looked at him, but said nothing. For a moment she only stared wide-eyed, exhausted.

Then she calmly began to make her way toward the lockers that lined the far wall. 'He's all yours,' she sighed.

Durand stepped up to the door and peered through the glass. He flipped the control panel on his left wrist and switched his helmet comms link back to *All.*

He paused for a moment, held his breath. Then spoke.

'Olesk, can you hear me?'

Olesk was facing the outer-door, but Durand could see the steel clawhammer in his left hand. The former captain of the USSF Mystic floated in the middle of the room. Slowly, he began to turn.

He was grinning from ear to ear, as though his face was stretched. His teeth were red with blood. Even from outside, Durand could see that he'd begun to chew off his lips. And he was making good progress too, by the look of it.

'Jesus,' Durand whispered, staring through the glass at the man he'd once called a visionary, an inspiration.

The man he'd called a colleague and a friend.

'You don't understand!' Olesk screamed, still smiling. 'It didn't hurt me, you idiot. It *killed* me.' He laughed, an evil cackle that tore through Durand's psyche like glass shards through tender flesh.

If he made it out of this alive, that laugh was going to haunt him forever. Shit, that laugh was going to wake his ass up every fucking night for the rest of his life.

'Enough, Cap, it's over. Put the hammer down and remain in your suit. We don't want to hurt you and we don't want you to hurt yourself. You need help. Shit, man, you need a *bunch* of help, but we can't let you jeopardise this ship and our mission.'

'Over? Over!' He laughed hysterically. 'It hasn't even started yet. Don't you see? It killed me. It actually killed me. And yet… I live.'

'It didn't kill you, Olesk, it fucked you up. Mind, body, soul, it fucked you up majorly. And you've done things now…' Durand trailed off, remembering the things his friend had done to the other crew members – crew members he'd also considered friends. 'Things you're going to answer for when we get you back home. Things you'll pay for.'

He looked toward Anderson, who was now almost suited.

'There'll be justice,' he added quietly.

Olesk shook his head like an insolent child. 'No, no, no,' he screamed. 'That wasn't my fault. They weren't ready, no, they *weren't!* Nobody is, nobody except me. People will see that, one day, yes… one day everyone will understand.'

'You really are off-the-fucking-chart crazy, aren't

you?' Durand replied. 'Maybe I should just release that outer door, throw you out into space – how would you like that, huh? *How would you like that, you son of a bitch?*'

He felt Anderson's hand on his shoulder as she muttered in his ear. 'Easy, easy.'

'Do as you wish. I am, after all, dead. As I said before. Dead, and yet living, immortalised through the primordial power of the dust bonding with my soul –'

'Shut up with that shit,' Durand screamed. 'Just shut up already! This was your life, your ambition. Your dream was to find EX9B, unlock its potential for the good of the planet. But look. Look where your *ambition* has gotten you.'

And he was right. Olesk's unrelenting ambition had ultimately been his demise, the fuel that had driven him into his current deluded state. The payload was good – Durand knew it, Anderson knew it, the rest of the crew had known it. There'd been tests, hundreds of them, everybody had handled the dust in one way or another; yet nobody had reacted in the same way as the captain. He'd gone completely mad, there was no denying it.

Olesk only laughed.

'I will, I swear to God, I'll open that fucking door and send you interstellar,' Durand shouted. 'Don't make me do it.'

He didn't want to, and he wouldn't, unless Olesk forced his hand. The captain had to answer for his crimes. That was only right, that was justice, and the crew deserved that much.

'I'm *dead*,' Olesk's voice came through the speaker calmly now, as though he were educating a young child on something as mundane as how to wipe his own ass. 'I can't be killed,' and just as calm as his tone, the captain held the hammer up before him and, with all his strength, swung it inwards.

'Holy fuck,' Anderson blurted. She was in her suit too and had joined Durant back at the window. Her eyes fixed on the horrific scene that now played out before them.

'Olesk, what the hell are you doing?' Durand called out, but there was no answer. Only the faint murmur of Anderson's breathing could be heard through his helmet speaker.

Olesk swung the hammer once more at his visor. This time a web of cracks appeared across its surface, distorting their view of the captain's face.

'Olesk, no!' Durand screamed, pounding on the window, but the captain once again held the steel hammer out before him, this time with both hands, and swung it into the glass.

The visor smashed inwards.

Flecks of shattered glass sparkled like diamonds as they spread throughout the chamber in all directions, turning the airlock into some sort of horrifying snow globe – complete with floating dead man.

Anderson and Durand both remained fixated on Olesk's corpse, which still hung in the air, blood floating up and out of his visor like scarlet dye in water.

That wasn't what held their attention though, no.

What had them gripped with terror was the smile. That demented, detached smile that still reached from ear to ear.

And then, more laughter.

CHAPTER THREE
FIRST NIGHT

He awoke in darkness. Dazed, confused, his head pounding.

'*Fuck...*'

He was still in the car.

He checked his phone: 3:14am. The rain had returned in abundance and it bombarded the roof of his car, bringing with it a cacophony of pitter-pattering.

'Fucking rain,' Elwood cursed. He reached for his sports bag and readied himself to step out into the deluge, wincing as the throb between his ears sharpened.

He glanced at the glovebox, knowing that the answer to his splitting headache was tucked away in there.

'That was the last time,' he whispered. And as if to bring the point home, he looked up into the rear-view mirror – his face like death on a bad day – and stared straight into his own bleary eyes. 'Last. Fucking. Time.'

Clutching his bag, he left the car. Locking the door

behind him, he began something between a fast walk and a light jog – the *cold turkey skip,* perhaps – but was still soaked through to his underwear and shivering by the time he reached the porch steps. He ascended awkwardly, rooting through the bag for his keys as he approached the top step.

He found them just as he lost his footing, slipping on the wet boards and crashing back down, hitting his head on the handrail along the way and finally landing in a heap in the wet dirt where he'd started.

Where he *belonged.*

'Fucking *fuck,*' he cried out, as much in pain as in exasperation.

He was still a little hazy from that last hit – that *last* hit – and for a moment found the position surprisingly comforting, like laying down in a bathtub for a cold shower. Without undressing.

He didn't try to understand why he seemed to find an odd comfort in this, didn't question it either. He just lay there, in the dirt, and let the rain splash his pale skin.

After a minute or so, Elwood snapped out of whatever it was he'd slipped into and pulled himself up out of the mud. He climbed to his feet, the back of his head aching from the knock on his way down. He rubbed at it tentatively, and with his free hand he retrieved the open bag from the ground beside him, the contents of which were now thoroughly sodden.

He started up the steps again, this time making it to the top without incident. He retrieved the keys along the way, which had slipped from his hand during the fall and landed on the fourth step up.

A wooden bench hung on chains to the right of the

front door, rocking gently in a breeze that coaxed the rain into the shelter of the porch. Elwood felt the cold drops hitting the back of his neck and, deciding he'd been out in the rain long enough now, quickly slid the key into the lock and let himself in.

He managed to find the light switch, after some fumbling in the dark and a lot of cursing.

The kitchen welcomed him with a stench. Awful and putrid, it hinted at the prospect of the friendly ghost having left something in the refrigerator. Apart from the foul odour though, the place looked nice enough – in a monotonous, uncared-for sort of way.

The floor was tiled with grey stone, and Elwood guessed it hadn't seen a mop in a few years. The pine cupboards were stained from years of being opened with dirty hands, the handles caked in layers of grime and dead skin.

He closed the door behind him, dropped his wet bag on the floor, and began to make his way around the kitchen, running his finger across the dusty worktops.

A pile of dirty dishes were stacked haphazardly atop one another in the sink, white ceramic cloaked in congealed sauce and God-only-knew what else. Leaning towers of wine glasses and whiskey tumblers, many of their rims sporting lipstick marks.

The smell grew stronger as Elwood neared the refrigerator against the back wall.

'Fuck me,' he gagged, bringing his shirt up over his nose as he reached for the handle. Inside it was fully stocked; a wide selection of meats, from steaks to burgers; sausages, bacon, salmon. Judging by some of the use-by dates, most of it would have been pretty tasty two years ago.

'Casper, you dirty bastard,' he slammed the door, dry-retching.

It didn't surprise him; the friendly ghost had never been one for this kind of thing, it was all just for show. Elwood guessed little-to-no eating had ever taken place here. But sex, hard drugs, and alcohol, and all the funky shit that came with that? Plenty.

To the left of the refrigerator, a wooden breakfast bar acted as a divider between the kitchen and dining area. He staggered along this until he reached the end, knocking over one of the metal stools on his way, still quietly cursing his friendly ghost.

'Make sure you clean up after yourself, bunnyman, leave it how you found it.'

That's what Casper had said to him. He always called him bunnyman, something to do with an old flick about a guy called Elwood and a giant bunny-rabbit. Elwood had never seen the movie, nor did he intend to; he'd never been enjoyed the black and whites. And he certainly didn't plan on cleaning up all of Casper's mess and leftovers, even if he ended up staying for more than a week.

He stepped around the bar and into the dining area, passing an open doorway on the left which led into a hall running all the way to a side-entrance at the far end of the property. He flicked another switch beside the doorway and the extra light revealed more of the villa's interior.

The place had the feel of a neglected show home or forgotten hotel; everything was generic and lacking in any sort of character; pictures of nondescript landscapes adorned the walls, all of which were egg-shell white, though smoke-stained for the most part. The table was laid out ready for a family meal; matching placemats and coasters were set neatly between knives and forks, all of them covered in dust.

Beyond the table, French doors opened onto a stone terrace. He pressed his nose against the glass and peered out into the darkness. The stonework quickly gave way to overgrown grassland, which Elwood assumed must have been well kept at some time or another.

Through the downpour and beyond the tangle of weeds and wildflowers, he was able to make out what looked like a small dock in the distance.

He remained there for a few minutes, staring at the lake, considering whether or not he might go for a swim at some point. He decided he probably would. He couldn't remember the last time he'd swam, especially in a lake. Pools were fine, but when it came to nature, he'd always been confronted with a degree of thalassophobia, suffering from some unnerving awareness of not knowing what might be swimming in the vast expanse beneath him.

There'd been a time when he had thrived on such feelings of apprehension – confronting your own dread and uncertainty could be an inspiring exercise for some, especially those who liked to read scary stories as he once had.

His mind was wandering. He decided the rest of the villa could wait; his head was screaming for the tranquillity of sleep, and it was likely he'd forget any remainder of the tour come morning anyway.

He moved toward a set of double-doors beside the

entrance to the hall, pushed them open, and sighed with relief when he saw the sofa in the middle of the room. There were probably beds upstairs, but right now, upstairs was a world away, and an expedition he really couldn't be bothered to undertake. The sofa would suffice. He'd slept on worse things.

He glanced around the room, which was clearly a lounge, smirking as he noted the enormous, fat-back TV straight out of 1995. More framed pictures lined the walls; most were unevenly set and depicted the same generic landscapes as those in the dining area. A stereo sat atop a wooden console against the far wall, and beside this was an impressive redbrick fireplace. For a moment Elwood entertained the idea of getting into the spirit of his locale and setting a fire to fall asleep to. Like most ideas, though, that didn't involve a needle, this one quickly fizzled out.

Another set of French doors behind the TV looked out onto the same overgrown terrace, and he assumed that an additional door on the opposite wall would lead him into the hallway.

He shuffled toward the sofa, removing his boots and coat along the way. He emptied the contents of his pockets onto the glass coffee table – his phone, lighter, and a crumpled pack of smokes – then collapsed into the leather, kicking up a cloud of dust upon impact.

He choked on the particles in the air, coughing repeatedly as he wriggled and writhed into a comfortable position, half-asleep and already oblivious to the dust he'd disturbed.

He'd left the lights on in the kitchen and dining room, but that was okay, Elouise was scared of the dark and the light from the hallway made her feel safe.

Elwood's eyes grew wet then as he realised he was forgetting where he was, and for just a second remembering a life he'd left behind. She wasn't here, neither of them were. It was just him – just Elwood Cathis, his guilt, his shame, and the monkey that sat heavy upon his shoulder.

He cried himself to sleep.

CHAPTER FOUR
THE VILLA AND THE FRIENDLY GHOST

Elwood awoke to a choir of birdsong. Sunlight permeated the dirty, cream blinds drawn across the French doors, bathing the room in a piss-yellow glow.

He groaned, suddenly aware of an excruciating headache that had been waiting for him to wake up before it kicked in the back door of his skull. This wasn't from his fall on the porch steps, though, this was something else – something like iron filings moving at a snail's pace through the soft tissue of his brain.

'Fuck,' he sat up and held his head in hands, running his fingers through his hair in some futile attempt to rub away the pain.

This wasn't breaking news, though; he'd expected this. He'd done his research.

Headaches were one of the first withdrawal symptoms an addict could look forward to when trying to get clean, and for those masochistic enough to forego the methadone and go cold turkey, the pain was amplified.

He'd never imagined anything like this though.

A saw. If only he had a saw, or even a machete. Any large blade would do. He was certain that if one was nearby, he'd use it to cut his own head off without a second thought.

Anything to stop the pain.

It wouldn't be easy. He tried to imagine how a person might do it and supposed it would probably come down to the type of edge. A serrated blade would be easiest; messy, but swift. A straight blade would take time – lots of slicing, hacking, cleaving – and could become tiresome fairly quickly.

He vaguely remembered a scenario like this in one of his books; one of the earlier works that hadn't bombed like his last few catastrophes. Self-decapitation… maybe he was wrong, maybe it had been in one of his final few. It sounded ludicrous enough to have been borne out of that awful period in his career, a time during which almost every word he'd typed had been conceived through intravenous inspiration.

For all he knew, he was thinking of some other author's work, or a movie. His memory was far from what it used to be. The needle and everything in it took more than just your money, your dignity, your family and friends.

It took it all. Your memory too.

He reminded himself again that he was here to find it, to take it all back. To remember.

In the absence of a worthy blade or any methadone,

he decided that rum and a cigarette would have to suffice.

After peeling himself off the dusty sofa and pocketing his cigarettes, Elwood shambled through the open double-doors and into the dining room, checking his phone on the way. It was 8:03am, and his stomach was growling for some breakfast, but he didn't feel all that hungry. Loss of appetite was another symptom of withdrawal, one of the early ones. One that – thankfully – didn't feel like a drill boring into your skull.

He retrieved his bag from the floor beside the front door and set it down on the breakfast bar, then moved across to the French doors and opened them as wide as he could to let in some fresh air. He'd forgotten about the contents of the refrigerator, and quietly cursed Casper as he began rooting through his bag, knowing full well that he wouldn't be able to stay here for any worthwhile length of time while that stench hung in the air. Sadly, ridding the place of it would mean cleaning up the friendly ghost's rotten leftovers.

He found the bottle and swiftly unscrewed the top like it was going out of business, taking a generous gulp – then another – before setting it down on the bar. Next came the cigarette, which he lit just as quickly.

Less than a minute later, he was stubbing out the remnants in the kitchen sink and lighting another. This was how it would be, because this was how it always was. Whenever he was down to his last hit and chasing the next baggie – which usually involved waiting around for Casper or one of his runners – the cigarettes kept his hands busy. He'd watched others chew off their nails whilst waiting for their next fix; some would scratch their skin until they drew blood; a few even pulled out their own hair. The waiting line for your next bag of skag wasn't a pretty one.

A few sorry souls even died in the queue.

This time there'd be no baggie at the counter, though. No magic dust waiting for him when he reached the front, because there was no front, there was no line. This was it; it was the rest of his life ahead of him, not just the next hit. It was life and everything that came with it, the most daunting of all uncertainties.

He needed to take his mind off it. If you didn't live from hit to hit, then what did you live from and to?

Aims. That was the answer. Milestones, targets, lists. You had a list of things you wanted to achieve or do. Life was never aimless, even when you didn't know what you ultimately wanted to do; there were still things you *needed* to do.

Elwood knew his cigarettes and liquor wouldn't last him the day at this rate, so he'd need to head out to a store. He could vaguely remember seeing a sign for one on his way to the villa. That was something he needed to do, something he could position in front of him and aim for. Like a hit.

There was this place, too. He'd not even been upstairs yet. The thought left him feeling a little uneasy, knowing he'd slept through the night without ever checking the rest of the property. It was an odd and specific nonchalance.

It was a junkie nonchalance.

The mind of someone who had lost the ability of well-considered thought, of seeing beyond the veil that came with the needle.

Elouise. That was it. She was his ultimate goal. His daughter. Once he actually took the time to think about it, the road ahead wasn't without its final destination, or stops along the way. He had a day of activities for now: finish his tour of the villa and get settled in, find the local store; restock. Now all he needed to do was fill another six-to-nine days with things that didn't involve getting jacked up.

Easier thought than followed-through.

His nerves did begin to calm though, his sinking chest rising with the knowledge that he might be able to at least get through today, make it to twenty-four hours without a hit.

He took another swig of the rum and lit a third cigarette before entering the hallway. The sun had risen over the lake at the back of the villa, leaving the front of the property cloaked in shade. The egg-shell walls appeared greyish in the dim light. Elwood passed the door which led into the lounge and continued down the hall, glancing out of the windows that ran along the exterior wall.

His car was still there. Right where he'd left it. Parked by the porch. Heroin in the glovebox.

Heroin. There was heroin right there. In his car.

He told himself again that it was off-limits. For emergencies only. *Just in case.*

Another voice inside screamed at him though, berated him for not marching out there right now and emptying the bag on the ground. For not doing it last night when he had the chance, when he was so close. The bag had been open; all he'd needed to do was roll his window down and tip. Instead, he'd chosen to stow it away. To torture himself.

He turned away from the windows and resolved to steer clear of the car – not to look at it, not to even think about it. He'd throw the stuff out of the window as he drove away from here a clean man.

A few feet beyond the lounge was another door. Elwood inhaled deeply from his smoke and took another gulp of rum before grasping the handle.

The closet was narrow. Clouds of dust danced in sunlight that poured in through a small window, set high up on the wall at the far end. Along the right-hand wall were hooks that held mops and various brushes and garden tools, as well as a fuse box and boiler. None of the tools looked as though they had ever been used.

On the left were two large shelving racks that reached from floor to ceiling; these were stocked with a wide variety of cleaning products, paper towels and other things that could either disinfect your shit or, at least, make it smell like roses. Like the tools, they didn't appear to have seen any action; caps were unbroken and plastic wraps remained intact.

A large butane canister and barbecue grill sat against the back wall beneath the window. Elwood made a mental note of those, deciding that a lonely barbecue might occupy at least an afternoon over the coming days, once his appetite returned. He'd never been one for red meat, but grilled fish had always been a favourite in the Cathis household.

He closed the door on the closet, and that memory.

Next came the stairs. Here the sunlight spilled in through a window on the small landing above, where the stairs turned back on themselves and continued up to the next floor. Two more doors remained past the staircase; the one at the far end of the hall which led outside, and one more on the right. Elwood opened the interior door and found a small toilet. The sight of it immediately brought on the need to piss, so he set his bottle down on the floor and relieved himself.

The last time he'd pissed had been at a rest stop a few hours away from Misstonville. He'd cried at the urinal. Some random Joe taking a dump in one of the cubicles had heard his blubbering and asked if he was alright, and Elwood had replied that yes, he was fine. But he hadn't been. It was at that rest stop that it had finally hit him. It had hit him before, many times, but most of those times he'd brushed it off because it wasn't *really* hitting him, not fully. For some reason though, it was then, staring at his pallid reflection in the grimy, white tiles of a West Virginia rest stop, that it had really, finally hit him.

Gracie had moved on, met someone else who cared for her, loved her. Loved her enough to marry her, even though she came with a plus one; their little girl, Elouise. That was a special kind of guy.

If Elwood didn't fix things, didn't fix himself, there might come a day when his daughter would move on too, and start calling somebody else *dad.*

It was this that had never really sunk in before, and he had no idea why it had come to him then. Maybe it had been the families he'd passed on his way to the toilet block, parents and their children picnicking at the tables by the parking bays. Maybe it had been a Tim McGraw song he'd heard on the radio a few miles back, and had all-but forgotten in his mind, but had held onto in his heart.

Whatever it had been, the memory of its impact was bringing it all back now, and he wasn't ready for it, not when there was no reprieve to look forward to, no final hit that would numb the emotions. Because the final hit had come and gone, there were no more resets on that front, no more escaping into the great nod that a needle of smack brought with it like some comfort blanket; a blanket that made you forget, not just people and things but feelings, too.

Once he was finished in the bathroom, Elwood unbolted the side door and stepped outside. Breathing deeply of the fresh morning air, he let the tears dry on his cheeks as he stared up into a cloudy sky that offered no sympathy, but instead a promise of brighter days ahead. They wouldn't shine as bright as they once had, but they'd shine.

If he could only get through this.

The side of the property – as with the back and front – was grossly untended, and he found himself waist-deep in weeds and thick grass that stretched all the way to the treeline. To his right was a dwindling stack of firewood, hidden beneath a veil of rain-soaked cobwebs that glistened, crystalline, in the sun. Beside this, semi-concealed amid all the greenery, was a chopping block and rusted axe. Elwood couldn't help but draw comparisons between himself and that corroded blade. What had once been useful, strong and reliable, was now diminished, stained, forgotten beneath something that had grown out of control. He gulped down more of the rum, hating this newfound desire for self-reflection – or was it self-deprecation?

He lit another cigarette and returned inside.

His head still throbbed, but the rum was slowly doing its job. The pain had been blunted, at least. He knew he needed more than rum, something like aspirin or ibuprofen, something more medically-inclined. He decided then that any trip to the store needed to yield a more acceptable form of pain relief, as well as the smokes and alcohol. Although he had no desire to drop the liquor from his feeble cold-turkey survival kit, he needed to remain mindful of the risk of drinking himself into a stupor, and replacing his *junkie* status with that of *alcoholic.*

He let his fingers run across the wood-panelling that made up the walls in the stairwell, stopping on the landing for a brief moment to peer out at the lake and take another swig from the bottle – that was already south of the halfway-empty mark – before turning around and continuing up to the first floor.

As was the case with the ground floor, a hallway ran along the front of the property, with rows of windows overlooking the overgrown yard and gravelled area.

To his right he found a door which led into a small bedroom; a single bunkbed against one wall and a basic dresser and wardrobe against the other, with a window that looked out toward the lake.

Both beds were made up neatly, adorned in navy blue bedding and – like everything else – a layer of dust. There was no way Casper would have made up the beds to the military standard they appeared to be. Elwood thought it likely that the beds were just as they'd been on the day Casper had bought the property, and had never been slept in or even laid upon.

He turned left and began to make his way along the hall. The next door led into a bathroom, much bigger than the one downstairs and complete with a bathtub and separate shower cubicle.

Beyond the bathroom was what he assumed to be the master bedroom, and quite possibly the place where Casper and his guests had spent most of their time. The bed was made up, but not to the same standard as the bunkbeds in the smaller bedroom. The layers of dust were noticeably thinner too, especially on the duvet and one of the bedside tables. Just as he began to close the door, Elwood saw a large spider appear from beneath the double wardrobe against the wall to his right. The hairy arachnid scurried across the floor and disappeared beneath the bed, and it was only then that Elwood noticed the dense web that was strung up in the gap between it and the bedside table. He saw other shapes in the web, other spiders; a whole nest of them by the look of it. There were other things too. Things that no longer moved, wrapped in silken shawls and waiting to be eaten.

'Nope.' He closed the door and swiftly moved on, taking another generous guzzle from the almost-empty bottle. He wasn't a huge fan of spiders, nor of the idea of sleeping in the same room as them, but if they stayed out of his way, he'd be sure to stay out of theirs.

The sight of that cloudy web had alerted him to the possibility of more though, and as he continued down the hall he began to notice other, thinner webs hanging in the corners of the windows. He was sure that if were he to go back now and check the other rooms he'd already seen, he would find webs that he hadn't noticed before, had been completely blind to because he wasn't really *here* – not entirely, anyway. As much as he hated to admit it, his awareness was shot, and he was closer to the walking dead than the mindful living. The sight of that ugly spider moving beneath the bed had served to heighten his senses though, and ground him just a little more in the present time and place, as opposed to his memories, or that place inside himself, that mirrored interior where he hated all that was reflected.

Elwood passed beneath an archway shrouded in more webs, and the hall opened up onto another lounge space above the dining room. Another set of French doors led to a balcony overlooking the lake; a small sofa-bed, console table and dead plant were all that occupied the area.

He tried the last remaining door. As with the first, this bedroom appeared to have never been used. The same navy-blue duvet was spread neatly and tucked in tight all around the mattress. A dense layer of dust had settled on top, but Elwood noticed a what appeared to be tracks and a trail of raisins running across the foot of the bed and up near the pillows.

Rats, or mice. Maybe both.

He attempted to recall the expiration dates on the food in the refrigerator; had they been a year old? Maybe two. Two years, long enough without the patter of human feet for things like spiders and mice to feel safe, safe enough to come out into the open, to settle down and make homes without the risk of being squished beneath a heel or having their neck broken in a trap.

It was as much theirs now as Casper's.

Elwood closed the door, leaving the room to whatever unseen guests had already claimed it.

After checking beneath the sofa bed, opening the drawer on the console table, and inspecting the plant pot, he decided this area would be basecamp. It showed no signs of life, save for a few ostensibly abandoned webs in the corners of the room. He'd fold out the sofa bed, which he assumed would be more comfortable than the couch downstairs, and wake up to what was probably the best view the villa had to offer.

He pulled his phone from his pocket and tapped into his recent calls list as he pulled the balcony doors open and stepped outside for a better look at the lake. Beyond the stone terrace below, a semi-concealed paved footpath cut its way through the overgrown grass for perhaps forty feet, flanked on either side by the forest, which appeared to act as a natural border between each of the villas that ran around Lake Chance.

At the end of the path was the wooden jetty stretching out over the water from the shoreline; from here he could see a few of the loose-hanging boards, but no boat. In fact, there were no boats at all by the look of it; from his current position, Elwood had a comprehensive view of the entire neighbourhood. To his right, he could see the eight villas he'd passed on his way here, the rooftops of each one visible above the dividing coppices of trees; to his left, the same again, each rooftop shifting away and back to the right as they followed the arch of Crescent Road, until the remaining few villas came into full view along the opposite side of the lake. Here, the line of holiday homes gave way to a dense forest that stretched off into the distance, gradually sloping upwards to meet the clouds.

Elwood assumed that somewhere in that thicket beyond the final villa, Crescent Road ended at the old store he'd seen signposted on his way in.

No boats, though. No jet-skis, no canoes, nothing. And away from the water the story was much the same: windows and doors were all closed; no joggers, no dogwalkers, no people, nobody. The only sounds Elwood could hear were those offered up by nature – birds chirping, a faint breeze that rustled the leaves, and apart from that, silence.

It wasn't the off-season, surely. Autumn was still a few weeks away, and no doubt summertime still had plenty of scorching tricks up its sleeve. And although summer was probably the busiest time for this neck of the woods, a place like Lake Chance would surely play host to some of its property owners across all seasons. Elwood imagined families skating the lake at Christmas, hiking the trails through a forest that turned from green to shades of red and auburn during the fall, and tending to their yards in the spring.

So why, then, did the place feel so empty?

He'd relished the thought of isolation, of coming to a place where he could shut himself away and mind his own business – rehab had never been like that – and not be disturbed. Now that he was here, though, his only company thus far the spider and the guilt that felt like lead in his heart… he wasn't so sure anymore.

He hit *call* and tapped the loudspeaker icon in an attempt to drown out the silence, taking a final swig of rum and setting the empty bottle down on the floor. While he waited for the friendly ghost to pick up,

Elwood lit his fourth cigarette in about as many minutes, affirming within himself the need to stay calm. The last person he wanted to run off his mouth at was Casper Stevens.

'Bunnyman? It's not even six in the fucking morning yet. What do you want? You fixing to score already?' The friendly ghost began to laugh, a mocking chortle that rapidly descended into a coughing fit, crackling through the loudspeaker and disturbing some birds in a nearby tree.

Elwood watched the tiny flock cross the water and disappear into the forest on the far side of the lake. He berated himself for forgetting that Casper was back on the west coast.

'Shit. I'm sorry Casper, I forg–'

'Too late now, bunnyman.' And then, a little quieter: 'Hey, hey, wake the fuck up, go get me a cold one.'

'Casper?'

'Yeah, I'm here. So, what do you want, huh? My guys don't take the Big H out of state, bunnyman, you know this.'

'I know, I know. I just...' Elwood wasn't sure. Now that he was on the phone, disturbing quite possibly the biggest heroin dealer in LA, he was drawing a complete blank on why he'd even called in the first place.

'You just *what*?'

'I... I guess, just, thanks again. For letting me stay here.'

'Come on, bunnyman, you didn't call me up at six in the fucking morning to thank my ass. What do you want? Did you run out already? Are you high right now? You sound fuzzy as fuck.'

'No. No, I'm not high.' He was well on his way to comfortable numbness though.

'Then what are you? Wait. Wait a minute. Are you… are you fucking lonely?' Laughter again. 'Are you fucking lonely right now? Is that why you're calling me, bunnyman?'

'No. Of course not.' Elwood was acutely aware – and abashed – of his defensive tone, but the question had served to remind him of why he had, in fact, felt the need to call Casper. 'I wanted to ask about the place. Like, when were you last here? There's a tonne of expired shit in the kitchen that stinks something rotten. There's dust everywhere. I saw rat shit in one of the rooms. And I think you might have a spider problem.'

'Spider problem? What are you talking about? That's it, sugar, set it down there for me. There you go, now bring your ass over here.'

'I mean, there's a nest in one of the rooms – and there's webs everywhere, man. I'm expecting Peter fucking Parker to drop down on my face at any moment.'

Casper laughed. 'Since when has that sort of shit bothered your junkie-ass? I've had no complaints before. You said you needed this, so I gave you what you needed. The place is fucking dead, has been for years. Nobody's gonna bother you.'

'But what about the food in the refrigerator?'

'What food? Whatever's in there ain't mine. I never did much eating when I used to stay there. Only thing got eaten was a hell of a lot of pussy.' He laughed to himself. Elwood had never found Casper's brand of crude, demeaning humour in the least bit amusing.

'So, where did the food come from?'

'Probably the last sorry shit. See, I'm a nice guy, bunnyman, and I make the mistake of letting friends hang out there – only my special friends though – and you, you're a special friend. I did you a favour. You aren't forgetting that, are you?'

'No, not at all. No, I do appreciate it, I really do. Just… I don't know. Just getting some bad vibes, that's all. It's real quiet here, does it get busy?'

'What, you getting scared? Mr Stephen Cunts horror-writer getting a squeaky ass because he's all alone out there? Yeah, that's it baby, keep doing that.'

'Casper, what are you doing? And what do you mean by all alone? There are others, right? Other people staying at the other villas?'

'What? Of course not, you moron. I told you. Don't you fucking remember?'

'Remember what?'

'Bunnyman, I told your junkie-ass this whole story. How many fucking hits you had in the last two days, huh? Shit, I bet you were in outer fucking space when we had our little chat. You junkie-fucks are all the same, you act like you're listening and you don't hear shit. Hey, hey. You stupid bitch, slow the fuck down.'

Aside from Casper's guttural west coast accent, there were other, more questionable sounds Elwood could hear in the background, and he was trying damn hard to keep the image of whatever was going on out of his mind.

'I'm sorry, my head's been all over the place these last few days, what was it you said?'

'I said you'd have the lake to yourself. Place is pretty

much closed down, has been for fucking decades. Some fucking hardhats have been buying up all the other properties, keep pestering me for mine, but I ain't stupid. I'm holding out for a fat pay day.'

'Why's everyone selling up?'

'Got a bad rep. Some shit went down way back and the snot-nosers who owned the villas didn't much like the vibe. It's how I got it so cheap back in... shit, I forget... ninety-one? When did Rodney King get his ass kicked by those racist blue-blood motherfuckers? Ninety-one, right?'

'I think so, I'm not really sure –'

'Hey – hey, bitch – was it ninety-one when King got fucked up? You don't need to take it out of your mouth to answer me, just nod. Hot fucking dog, I knew it. Ninety-one.'

Elwood failed, the image taking centre stage in his head now; Casper sprawled out on his bed whilst some poor lady worked between his thighs.

'What sort of shit?' he asked dimly.

'Oh, stop being such a pussy. Nothing serious – just, people have died there before, or got themselves killed. But that shit happens everywhere, bunnyman. You live in fucking LA. Get over yourself.'

'Damnit, Casper. You know I'm going cold turkey, you know that comes with a cocktail of crazy, and you send me to some place with a *history*?'

This was the last thing he needed. Elwood was fighting his own demons, staying somewhere that might fuel his anxiety and create undue tension wasn't going to be constructive; if anything, it would be compounding.

'Hey, relax, man. You need to remember two things. The first is that I did you a favour – me, Casper fucking Stevens – so show some gratitude. Second, you're Stephen Cunts, the big shot horror junkie. You should *thrive* in a place like that. Write a fucking book or something,' he laughed, another raspy gurgle that quickly turned to fits of phlegmy coughs.

'Not funny, Casper.'

'Alright, okay. I'm kidding with you, bunnyman, just pulling your little pecker. Don't go getting your panties all twisted up.'

'Fuck you. This isn't a joke. This is my life.' Elwood felt regret sink into his chest as swiftly as the words had been spat out. People didn't talk to Casper Stevens like that. Even if he punched you in the face, or bragged about sleeping with your sister, you didn't talk to him like that. You smiled, and you said thanks a bunch.

The line had gone quiet.

Elwood fumbled to light another cigarette.

'Casper? Casper are you there? Look, I'm sorry, I didn't mean to get –'

'Enough. I'll let that one slide, bunnyman. And I'll let it slide just this once. You run your mouth off like that again, and I'll cut you off. You fuck things up out there, like you have done at every fucking rehab in LA – and you know I don't just mean falling off the sober bus again – , you won't be getting your shit from me. And you know what that means, don't you? It means you won't be getting your smack from anyone in this city, you got that?'

'Yes, yes… I've got it. I'm sorry, Casper, really I am. I didn't mean any disrespect.'

'Good. I'm glad to hear that. Now, don't bother me again unless you're on your way back and need a fix. Understand?'

He hated how pitiful Casper made him feel, how small, how subjugated. It was a power that all dealers held over their customers, especially when the product was something like heroin or crystal, something potent.

'Yes, I understand.'

'And don't you forget nothing else I told you, either. I don't want you showing your face around town. Folks in towns like that ain't used to junkie-mugs like yours, it'll bring attention. I don't want attention on my shit, you hear?'

'Sure, I hear you, Casper. Loud and clear. I'm not going anywhere.'

'Then we have an understanding. Now, this bitch has me by the balls, literally,' he sniggered, 'and you don't want to hear what happens next, so, peace out. And good luck. Rooting for you, bunnyman.'

The line went dead before Elwood could feel any more demeaned than he already did.

Silence filled the world and he was once again left alone, only now the loneliness felt better; there was a comfort to it that hadn't been there before the call. Perhaps it was the assuredness that nobody was there to see how much he was trembling, to hear how laboured his anxious breaths had become, and to notice that, within his eyes, tears of shame had begun to swell.

CHAPTER FIVE
THE OLD STORE AT CRESCENT TIP

After wasting the rest of the morning – and the best part of the afternoon – feeling sorry for himself, drinking half a bottle of whiskey and inhaling his way through twenty or more cigarettes, Elwood decided it was time to haul himself back up the ladder and stop wallowing in his own self-pity.

He'd brought his bag upstairs and set it down beside the sofa bed, which he folded out and made up, using some sheets and a pillow scavenged from a cupboard in the smallest of the three bedrooms.

He found some comfort in this exercise and the distraction it created; there was something almost ritualistic about preparing one's area of rest, something which he'd always assumed had appealed to those who chose to camp in the great outdoors – a pastime that had never quite clicked with him.

It was a little past four when Elwood hesitantly decided it was time to break Casper's decree and venture out to the local store he'd seen signposted on the way in.

Having drunk a considerable quantity of liquor, he decided it would be a sensible idea to walk to the store. He couldn't actually remember the last time he'd taken a stroll along something that wasn't a concrete sidewalk. And aside from the need to clear his (now completely inebriated) head – though not too much, the liquor had numbed the ache after all – the thought of walking among some trees was one that appealed to him.

Only a small part of him though, a part that had existed long before the heroin. A younger version of himself, one whose only addiction had been the unbridled passion to whittle his darkest thoughts into words on a page. And those thoughts had come to him in the forest near where he'd grown up; he couldn't remember what it had been called now, all he recalled was that it had been named for the flowers that grew in abundance across the untrodden parts of it.

Elwood felt a pang of sadness at this forgotten detail from what had been a formative period of his childhood. Maybe it was the heroin again, clouding his mind and memories, or maybe it was just the years that had passed. Addiction could take a lot from a person, but so too could time.

Rather than make his way back up the gravelled driveway to Crescent Road, he thought it might be better to follow the shore of the lake. There were no fences that he'd been able to see from the balcony; if he followed the shoreline to the last villa, he figured he could simply walk through the yard and up the driveway and find himself near the end of Crescent Road, and much closer to the store.

Locking the front door behind him, Elwood cautiously descended the porch steps, remembering his fall the night before. He glanced at his car, his eyes drifting over the glovebox compartment, just inside the window.

It was starting to creep back in, that feeling, that need for it.

He realised then that he was the one who decided when things had gone wrong, when the fix was needed. He could, if he wanted to, just decide right now that things had gone to shit – this was no use, better to just give up now – because the pain he'd felt thus far was a mild inconvenience compared to the agony that was yet to come.

He could have his fix now. And nobody could tell him otherwise. Nobody would *know*.

But that was wrong, and he knew it. Because *he* would know. And in a roundabout way, Elouise would know too, sweet little El – she'd know, because she'd never see her daddy again.

He tried to think of something else, failed, and chose instead to light another cigarette as he moved through the bushes and brambles that dominated the front of the house. He reached the far side of the villa and turned right, passing the half-hidden chopping block and side door on his way.

As he stepped out onto the paved terrace at the back of the villa, he tripped over an uneven brick and stumbled forward.

'Shit.' He fell forward, barely managing to bring his arms up and avoid kissing the stonework.

Elwood climbed to his feet and dusted himself off, trying to ignore the heavy pain in both of his elbows. He glanced back and grimaced at the uneven brick protruding above its neighbours, as blatant as a wet floor sign in a store.

'What the fuck is wrong with me?'

He knew exactly what was wrong with him, though.

He was strung out.

Stupefied.

Desperately trying to focus on anything other than what his body was screaming out for.

It felt as though he was drowning beneath a surface that was ablaze. He could come up for air, there was nothing stopping him, but if he did, he would burn and sink.

What he needed to come to terms with was the knowledge that he could hold his breath for as long as it took for those flames to die out.

Until he could see and embrace that idea though, the battle would rage on within him, claiming his strength, dimming his senses and adversely affecting his ability to function. He knew there were more uneven bricks ahead of him on this path to redemption, and he knew he wouldn't see many of them, not until he was closer to the end at least.

He found his still-smoking cigarette on the ground and retrieved it.

The terrace gave way to a meandering gravel path that snaked its way through the grassland separating the house from the lake. Elwood followed this trail, lighting another cigarette with the meagre remains of his previous one.

His legs brushed through masses of crabgrass and goutweed that invaded the path and claimed it as their own, before finally reaching the shoreline and beginning his trek around the lake.

As he made his way around the lake he was afforded a better view of the villas, and he was able to see that most of the windows were boarded up. Some of these had become canvasses for bored locals, while others had been partly torn away. All of the properties suffered from the same level of neglect as Casper's place; weeds and plant life had reclaimed much of the land and the buildings themselves all shared the same shabby, forgotten aesthetic.

By the time Elwood reached the last villa on the other side of the lake, beads of sweat were not only forming on his brow but running down his face; he guessed it couldn't have been much more than a mile over flat ground, but his body ached and complained as though he'd been trekking for hours across mountain peaks.

He stood for a moment, hands on his hips, catching his breath as he stared back across the lake.

The summer sun would hold dominion for a few hours yet, though the day had visibly dimmed over the course of his journey and the sky was painted a golden hue. The surface of the lake gleamed like honey, and for a moment the world seemed almost too beautiful to be real. Like a sunset backdrop straight out of *Gone With the Wind*.

The sun, which had risen on this side of the water, now cast its light on the front of Casper's place, leaving the rear of the property in a creeping shade that had so far managed to reach the balcony. Elwood's eyes passed over the windows that had taken on a tinted appearance in—

It was then that he noticed the movement.

Not on the shore. Not in the water, nor even amongst the trees. On the *balcony*.

Casper's balcony. The same balcony Elwood had been standing on earlier today.

There was someone there.

He squinted against the receding light, wiped the sweat from his eyes and blinked.

They were still there. A lumpy silhouette standing on the balcony. No... that wasn't quite right, because whoever they were, they weren't *standing*. They were moving. Not walking, though, or swaying. Just... sort of *floating*.

It couldn't be right, couldn't be real. People didn't float, Elwood thought. And even with a hunchback, the figure shouldn't have been so bent over and deformed.

And aside from the inexplicable shape and movement of whoever it might be, Elwood was supposed to be alone.

He looked around, as though searching for someone – some previously unseen companion – who might agree that *yeah, that right there is a deformed person on your balcony, and they sure as shit* are *floating like a damn astronaut.* Or, simply: *no, Elwood, you're losing your shit, seeing things that aren't there, because to put it quite bluntly, friend, you're strung the* fuck *out.*

There was nobody around, of course. He was alone. And when he cast his eyes back toward the villa, he saw that he really was, because there was nothing there.

Just something in his eye, perhaps. Or maybe it had been a trick of the light, or lack thereof. A shadow. Aside from the Bible, most contemporary art, and the Looney Tunes, shadows were arguably one of the most frequently (mis)interpreted things in the world.

Yes, that had to be it.

He passed through the derelict grounds of the final villa and hurried up the driveway to Crescent Road. From there it was less than half a mile to the store – a sign at the side of the road told him as much – where the road eventually crumbled away, replaced by a gravel parking lot, flanked on all sides by a dense and encroaching treeline.

To his right, Elwood saw a small opening in the trees, a path leading off into the forest. A crooked sign nailed to a post marked it as the start of *Hobson's Trail*.

On the opposite side of the clearing was the store: a rickety old shack that wouldn't have looked out of place in an Eastwood spaghetti western. Elwood's heart sank a little at the sight of it, hopes diminished a little. Buildings as fragile as this one looked were generally not the sort of places that housed luxury items like liquor or painkillers. And given his newfound knowledge concerning the desolation of the lakeside properties, he guessed that the store might not see a lot of footfall.

Were it not for the light on inside, and the two trucks parked in the lot, he might have presumed it derelict.

As he made his way toward the building, the light

flickered off. A bell chimed as the door creaked open and an elderly man stepped out. He closed the door behind him, apparently oblivious to Elwood's approach, and began to sort through a bunch of keys.

'Hey there,' Elwood called out. 'You still open for business?'

The man turned to face him, adjusting his spectacles as he looked cautiously upon the approaching stranger.

'What sort of business you looking for?' His drawl was typical of the area, spoken through a loose jaw with plenty of room, but apparently none for things like closing g's or f's.

'I was meant to close up at five. Already late and the lady'll have my balls if I don't get my ass in gear.'

'I was hoping to find some liquor and cigarettes. Painkillers too, if you have any,' he replied.

The old man laughed. 'I'll be damned if that don't sound like the sort of party we don't need round these parts, son. You buying for yourself, or for them young ones I seen kicking it out here from time to time?'

'No, no. Not at all,' Elwood offered shakily. 'Just for myself. I can assure you I'm not buying anything for any minors. And I don't plan on throwing any parties either.'

The old man continued weighing him up, clearly trying to judge whether or not Elwood had trouble written all over his face. 'Well, with a shopping list like that, if you ain't partying, what are you doing, huh? Looking to kill yourself, that it? If you are, I don't want no part in nothing like that.'

Elwood could already feel himself getting flustered, his face heating up.

'Jesus, no. No, nothing like that. I just, I don't feel so hot, that's all.' He wanted to tell the man it was none of his business, but was he was an out-of-towner and this was the first local he'd met. If he was going to see this through, the last thing he needed to do was piss off a local on day one.

The old man spat into the gravel. 'Well, makes no difference anyway. I can't help you – not unless you're fixing to do some hunting. Which case, we got some basics. Not much, mind you, we're winding down now.'

'Winding down?' Elwood asked.

'Closing. For good,' he replied, returning his attention to the bunch of keys. 'Yeah, last restock we had was… oh, I forget now. But it was the last. Ah, there he is,' the old man picked out one of the keys and jammed it into the lock. 'We don't get many visitors out this way no more.'

Elwood watched patiently as the old man turned the key stiffly, muttering to himself whenever it caught in the keyhole.

'So… pick your vein, boy,' he said, turning away from the door. He stepped out from under the lean-to, grinning inquisitively.

'Excuse me?' Elwood asked, thinking he might have misheard. Then the bunch of keys caught his eye, and his jaw dropped.

They weren't keys. Not anymore.

The old man was holding a bunch of syringes. They rattled and jangled on the large key ring, just as keys should do – only they weren't keys, they were *syringes* – each filled to the brim with a liquid he recognised all too well, a golden liquid that dripped onto the old man's boots.

Elwood took a step back, sweat stinging his eyes. His chest suddenly felt as though it might erupt like something out of a Ridley Scott movie, his face felt like a heat lamp, and he was pretty sure that any moment now he was going to faint right there on the gravel forecourt. For a brief moment he considered lunging forward, tackling the old man to the ground and taking the syringes from him – what the fuck was this old timer doing with so much smack anyway? – but he managed to refrain. Reason (currently occupying a small corner of his psyche) managed, somehow, to win out, and he found himself taking another step back. Telling himself that this couldn't be real, that it was senseless even.

The short space between them suddenly felt like a canyon. The jangling of the needles echoed loud like church bells in Elwood's skull and he gripped his head in a futile attempt to block out the thunderous din.

He looked up and saw that the old man was staring at him, eyes apprehensive. The bunch of keys in his hand were now just that: keys.

'What did you say?' Elwood asked, his voice groggy and far away.

'I asked what's your *game*, boy. What brings you out here? You don't look like no hunter or hiker to me. They's the only ones we get out here these days, except for Bob Scotchni and that mutt of his. That's his rust-bucket parked over there.' He nodded towards one of the trucks parked nearby and pocketed the keys. The tolling noise subsided.

'I…' he stumbled, his voice still distant. 'I'm here on vacation… staying down at the lake.'

'The lake?' the old man asked, his expression now more quizzical than suspicious. 'You at number nine then, I assume?'

Elwood nodded.

'Been a while since I seen anyone out there. Least a year, I'd say. I take it you know the fella who owns it?'

Elwood nodded again, not wanting to speak now – not wanting much of anything really, other than to be somewhere else entirely.

'Yeah, he don't show his face round here no more. Just sends his guests every now and then, and they mostly mind their own business. Never hang around too long neither, which don't surprise me none. Place ain't ever been the same since the murders.'

'Murders?' He had Elwood's attention now.

'Oh yeah,' the old man replied, adjusting his cap, 'been a few out this way over the years. Last ones were back in… oh, seventy-nine, I'd reckon it. Punk kids on vacation broke into one of them properties, killed the ma and pa. Bambinos, too. Terrible, terrible shit. Must've had a taste for it too, they done three others that summer, all families, all dead.'

'Jesus.'

'Well, it's funny you say that. Cops got 'em in the end. Said they was Satan worshippers, can you believe that? Here in the Ville… God-damn devil beggars. Folks ought to leave that sort of trouble at the county-line, but they don't, they bring it into our community. Been the same ever since the damn place was built. Problem is the out-of-towners always brought their money with them, too.' He moved toward his truck and brought the keys back out from his pocket. Elwood didn't dare look to see if they were still just keys.

'Can't complain, store's done me good. Never was the same after all that shit in seventy-nine, though. Place went to piss after that whole mess. Folks started selling cheap – and I mean *real* cheap – shit, some kids from A-State turned one of the villas into a damn frat house.'

Elwood kept his distance as the old man clambered into his truck, half-listening to what he was saying and half-contemplating why his mind seemed to be unravelling so quickly. First the shape on the balcony, now the syringes.

It hadn't even been twenty-four hours yet.

The old man didn't seem to notice though, closing the door behind him and rolling the window down before continuing with his history lesson.

'Place turned into a God-damn cesspit in the eighties, got worse when your buddy bought number nine. Parties, drugs, you name it. Dumb kids having too much fun. Few of them drowned in the lake, lot of them went missing out in the forest too. Number nine's always been trouble. If your buddy wasn't there causing all kinds of shit, he was renting it out to some other animals.'

'He's not my buddy,' Elwood said. 'And I'm not like that, I'm not here to cause trouble.' He had been, though, once upon a time less than twenty-four hours ago. And for that reason, his statement was nothing but hollow insincerity, and the old man knew it.

'Sure,' he replied, politely enough. 'But you come out here looking for liquor and painkillers… well, folk like myself might be forgiven for thinking otherwise.'

'That's fair, I guess.'

'Anyway, some outfit's looking to do something with it, Lord knows what. No point competing with those fancy condos they got over at Arkin's Lake in Bowles. And they got more out near Granville too. But they've been buying up all the plots here anyways. You ask me, they just need to flatten the whole damn place and let it turn wild again – ask any other folk round here too and they'll agree. Had a lot of problems with trespassers over the last few years. Drifters breaking in, punk kids vandalising and fraternising. Sheriff Tims don't take no shit though, I can tell you. You'd be wise to remember that while you're here.'

'Like I said, I'm not here to cause any trouble.'

'Yeah, I heard you,' the old man started up the engine. 'There's a ConveeMart on the other side of town. Be your best bet now, I'd reckon it. Place is open day and night and they'll have what you're looking for.'

'Thank you,' Elwood replied, still reeling and scarcely managing to keep up the pretence of a sane and sober man who *wasn't here to cause any trouble*. He was ready for the old man and his doubtful gaze to be gone, ready for this conversation to end, ready for all of this to end.

This wasn't what he'd had in mind when Casper had told him it would be peaceful here. He was already dancing with his own shame, his own guilt, his own demons. The last thing he needed was to be in a place that might give rise to more tension, more anxiety.

He turned to leave, wiping the sweat from his brow, eyes still stinging, as the old man reversed away from the store.

As he stepped back onto the road, the truck came up

beside him and the old man leaned out of the window. 'Sorry I can't offer you a ride, but… well, with all respect, you don't look so good, fella.'

Elwood only nodded. He couldn't blame the old man; as much as he knew within himself that he was harmless, he also knew he looked like shit, and not the *I need help* kind of shit, but the *I'm out of my damn mind* kind of shit.

The old man stared at him a moment longer. 'You keep yourself out of trouble now. And keep to the trails if you decide to go wandering. Woods is big out there, folks can get lost real easy. It happens.' He set the truck back in motion, and in less than thirty seconds he'd disappeared around the long curve of Crescent Road.

Elwood fell to his knees, and for reasons that were unclear to him – perhaps it was the need for a fix; the gravity of his situation; the environment, the fucking *hallucinations,* his burden, the unease in the old man's eyes, the simple fact that he hadn't been able to get a drink, some pain relief, some damn cigarettes, or all of the above – he wept.

CHAPTER SIX
CLEAN-UP ON AISLE FOUR

The sun had almost set by the time Elwood made it back to the villa. The sky moved steadily through shades of purple and blue as he paced back and forth across the terrace, smoking his way through a final pack of cigarettes, waiting for the dark.

It came.

It was almost ten, and although he was grossly over the legal limit, he felt as though he'd sobered up enough not to draw any unwanted attention. As much as a sizeable part of him wasn't comfortable with the idea – or thrilled to implement it – there was no chance of him surviving the night. Not without any more cigarettes, not without a drink, not without some kind of relief.

He could taste the night in the back of his throat, the air warm and heavy with rising moisture from the downpour the night before. As he reached for the driver's door Elwood paused for a second, remembering what was in the car, what was in the glovebox. He wrestled with the idea of taking it inside and leaving it in the villa, or better yet, throwing it out of the car window into one of those gutters he never wanted to find himself in.

He climbed in and shut the door behind him.

He was taking it with him. If he somehow managed to summon the courage to toss it out, he'd need it close by, at that exact moment. Any delay in following through would only mean more time to talk himself out of it.

And what if something happened? What if he got stranded in town and couldn't get back to the villa? He might wind up needing it if things got too bad, if things got on top of him. That could happen, even when you least expected it. The world could turn against you in ways you never thought possible, and it could happen on your way to the store to buy smokes, liquor and painkillers.

Anything could happen.

Having the smack with him meant that he was ready for either scenario. It meant that he was ready for anything.

That he was safe.

Slipping the keys into the ignition was proving difficult though, and after a few failed attempts he realised why. He was shaking. Not just his hands; his entire body was gently convulsing. He looked at himself in the mirror, both mortified and disturbed by the sight of his own head nodding back and forth – not the motion itself, but the unawareness of it, the fact that even now, as he looked upon his own reflection, he could not feel himself moving.

It took all of his concentration to eventually jam the key into the ignition. As soon as he did, he was on his way, skidding onto the gravel lane that wound its way back up to Crescent Road.

He dialled up the air-con, still dripping with sweat. His clammy hands were slippery against the wheel. Aerosmith blared through the radio; Steven Tyler was asking some girl what it would take to let her go.

There was light somewhere up ahead. Beyond the curvature of the road, a pinkish, green glow filtered through the trees. The main road and the edge of town were still a fair distance away, too far to throw any light over this neck of the woods.

As he rounded the bend, the source came into view; where the welcome sign had been the day before, there now stood a grotesquely lavish neon display. Letters as tall as Elwood, formed in shades of hot pink and emerald green light:

The Big H! Fill your needle with Noise!

The surrounding trees and roadside were awash in the pinkish-green glow of this enormous sign, one that wouldn't have looked out of place on the Vegas strip.

He sped through the glow, which promptly vanished. A quick glance in the rear-view mirror showed the same *Welcome to Misstonville Forest* sign he'd seen the night before.

'Fuck,' he cried out, bashing the steering wheel with both hands.

He began to laugh hysterically, noticing more light up ahead that was certainly not of the traffic-signalling kind.

'You've got to be kidding me. Come on…'

As he approached the end of Crescent Road, the lights at the junction changed to red and Elwood brought his car to an abrupt stop beside a pylon at the side of the road. The thing was at least fifty feet high, and it hadn't been there yesterday. At the top, flashing yellow lights invited him to *Come on down for the best brown in town!*

A vast syringe, constructed in lines of neon white, spat blinking amber light into the dark.

He turned back to the road, teeth gritted, patiently waiting for green and trying his damnedest to ignore the incessant buzzing of the lights above. When he saw amber he didn't hang around, putting pedal to the metal and turning onto the main road leading into the town.

After a few minutes he began to see houses; a mix of craftsman bungalows and ranch-style homes, sitting upon substantial plots scattered across the dim hills that crept away to his right. On his left, the dark forest gave way to neat rows of Tudor-style redbrick abodes, and finally the more impressive, sprawling Queen Annes that stood behind locked gates at the ends of impressive driveways.

Within five minutes he had hit the town proper, and it was like the Vegas strip for junkies. The lights were almost blinding; every store window flashed with tempting invitations. Huge signs supported by towering pylons stretched across the road and formed great archways of light.

Ride the Galloping Horse!
Take a ride on the A-Vein Baby!

Elwood gripped the wheel like his life depended on it. This was like a rollercoaster, one with no brakes, no safety bar, and one apt to loop-de-fucking-loop at any moment.

'This isn't happening,' he told himself. 'This is *not* happening.'

Find your forever vein!

Capital H on tap!

Lights blazed ruby red, pink fuscia and cobalt blue.

Get jacked Smack Daddy!

Flashes of lime green, bumblebee yellow and heavenly white.

Inject some POW into your life!

And the buzzing. Dear God, the *buzzing*. Like that of some incomprehensible multitude of bees, the noise invaded his ears, creeping into his skull unfiltered and settling on brain tissue that seemed to vibrate under the cacophony.

'Enough,' he yelled, thrusting his palms against the steering wheel, slapping his face, wanting so badly to tear off his ears, poke through his eardrums and scoop out his head like a pumpkin. Anything to stop it, anything to bring about an end to it all.

He reached for the glovebox.

Paused.

It would help, he knew it would. That last hit was calling out to him, almost as loud as the buzzing lights. It offered him succour; he didn't need to hurt himself, he didn't need to put himself through all of this pain. All he *needed* to do was ready a dose, find his favourite vein, find peace.

He screamed. Not just at the noise and the light, but

at everything. He screamed at the world, at himself, at Casper, at the baggie in the glovebox and everything that came with it. Screamed for it all to stop.

And then it did.

In the blink of an eye the blinding neon and ceaseless buzzing was gone, replaced with a collection of dimly lit store fronts, ordinary flickering streetlamps, and the silence of the night.

The sudden change in ambience shocked him, so much so that he momentarily lost control of the wheel and swerved into the oncoming lane. Luckily for him the road was empty, but for a moment he wondered what might have happened if it hadn't been. He heard horns blaring in his head, buckling metal and shattering glass. Screams. Would he have been able to swerve out of the way in time?

Would he have even tried?

Elwood passed by closed shops and diners, a few bars – he wasn't paying attention now, his focus on the asphalt ahead. The old timer had said the store was on the other side of town; if he just stuck to this road, then he'd get what he so desperately needed. A drop of something golden from a bottle instead of a syringe, a fresh pack of smokes... God, he needed a smoke right now.

'No, no, no. Not again...'

More neon up ahead in the distance. He felt a lump in his throat, a weight on his chest.

Dread.

He continued regardless, suddenly aware of how dry his throat was. He tried to find some saliva in his mouth, but it was like sandpaper in there. He couldn't remember drinking anything all day except for the rum. He wasn't known for drinking whole bottles of hard stuff so fervently; the syringe had been his passionate companion. Now he was alone though, relatively sober and absolutely dehydrated.

As he neared the sign he was able to make out the words:

24 Hour Groceries. Liquor. Tobacco.

'Finally,' he yelled, feeling a little light-headed.

He turned into the forecourt. Artificial light poured out from the glass frontage, trolleys lined up neatly next to a blinking ATM. Three cars were huddled together near the entrance. Elwood parked up in the shadows at the back of the lot and shut the engine off.

The night was silent, save for the occasional car that rolled by on the main road. The town was certainly in the latter stages of winding down for the evening.

He forced himself to look at his reflection in the rear-view again and wondered how he'd ever let it get this far. He wondered if Gracie had seen this same face before things ended. Jesus, had El seen him like this? He hoped not. He looked like death on a splurge: his face white as chalk, eyes stretched wide and sore from all the rubbing he'd been doing. Beads of sweat still trickled over his brow, stinging on arrival.

He took a deep breath and rolled his window down, leaned out, and proceeded to vomit down the side of his car. He gagged, his back rising and falling as he coughed up stomach fluid and bile that gathered slowly in a puddle on the concrete below. The stench only served to encourage more retching, a sickly-sweet scent that was nothing but liquor and shame.

Once he was sufficiently unburdened, he slumped back in his seat and rolled the window up, his eyes moist from the strain of it all.

The world was slowly fading. He wiped his chin on the back of his hand and looked up at the mirror again, his reflection now a blur. But there was something else too.

Someone sitting in the backseat. *Something* sitting in the backseat.

Something lumpy and misshapen.

Elwood blacked out.

He awoke dazed and confused, the taste of whiskey and vitriol at the back of his throat. He wiped the drool away from his chin and sighed, glancing around, trying to determine where he was and what he was supposed to be doing. The memory suddenly slapped him in the face and he whirled around to check the backseat.

Nothing.

Not anymore. But before, before he blacked out, he was sure there had been somebody – something – sitting back there. Watching him. That lumpy, distorted thing that had been floating on the balcony back at the villa.

He shuddered, his skin gooseflesh. Not at the memory of that figure, nor the lights which had plagued his journey here. It was more the thought of what was yet to come. He knew that over the next few days the hallucinations would only intensify.

It still felt like too much, though. Too much, and too soon.

Beyond the empty seat behind him, the parking lot

was now deserted. The store was still open, though some of the lights had been turned off.

He checked his phone: 1:57am.

He was starting to make a habit of blacking out in his car. Better than the habit he was trying to kick though, and at least this time it wasn't down to the shit going into his veins, but the shit coming *out*. He realised then that he'd passed a significant milestone in his battle – had slept through it, in fact.

It had been over twenty-four hours since his last hit.

His first twenty-four hours without a needle since… well, since Gracie had threatened divorce for the seventh time. The final time.

Elwood didn't allow himself any more time to savour the small victory. Instead he removed the keys from the ignition and slid outside into the cool early morning.

One half of the automatic doors slid open and the scent of cinnamon and industrial strength floor cleaner greeted him as he crossed the threshold. A loud *beep* alerted any staff to the arrival of a junkie.

He shielded his eyes against the light, squinting as he tried to take in his surroundings. A bank of empty checkouts stretched out ahead of him; to the left was a separate kiosk and cash register for the tobacco and cigars, also unattended. He moved off to the right and walked down one of the aisles, deciding he needed to find alcohol and painkillers first, then worry about finding someone who might serve him.

He passed fruits and vegetables, cereals, oats and porridge, granola. The fact that he had no food back at the villa never entered his warped mind.

As he moved further away from the checkouts the light grew dimmer. At the back of the store, the lights were shut off completely.

When he reached the end of the aisle he turned and looked back. He could've sworn he'd heard the door *beep* again. Nobody appeared; however, the checkouts were now nothing more than a pin prick gleaming on a distant horizon, the grocery aisle a vast plateau stretching out for mile upon mile of desolate vinyl. Elwood felt a pang of vertigo at the sight and had to steady himself for a moment against a display of tinned beans that were on offer at 2-for-1.

He turned away from the vista and began to feel the turning in his stomach subside. It was just in his head, that was all he had to remember. None of it was real. An easy enough mantra to get on board with, if not for the very *real* effect it was having on him: the sickness; the sweat; the nausea. The fear.

He pushed himself away from the beans and ambled off to the right, along the back aisle and toward the windows facing out onto the parking lot. He looked to his left and saw more aisles tucked away at the back, these ones heading across the store as opposed to up and down it. Incandescent light crept out from beyond the corner of the last aisle, the source of which he assumed was the refrigerators that held all of the beer.

As good a place as any to hope to find liquor.

Here the store was dark, the overhead lights shut off, the silence broken only by the squeak of his trainers on the vinyl floor.

The glass-fronted refrigerators ran along the back wall of the last aisle, providing just enough light for him to determine the contents of the bottles on the shelves opposite. He picked up a bottle of vodka, then another two before moving on.

Tequila next, just the one. Relief washing over him in shots now.

Whiskey, two of.

He found rum at the end of the aisle; next to a door marked *STAFF ONLY.* He took two, and began to wonder desperately why he hadn't thought to pick up a basket at least.

The refrigerator lights began to flicker, though he paid little attention to this, his focus now on juggling the eight bottles of liquor he had cradled against his chest.

As the flickering quickened though, it began to claim more of his attention; the flashing – which wasn't chaotic at all, but seemed to have some sort of rhythm to it – began to stir within him a peculiar sense of foreboding. He wasn't sure why, but as he stood there – now motionless, almost hypnotised – he believed that were he not there, this wouldn't be happening. It was for him.

More cold-turkey bullshit perhaps. It had to be.

But why, then, was there a voice whispering from some unknown recess within him? A voice telling him this was different. This wasn't supposed to be happening.

This was something to *fear.*

This warning was quickly drowned out by the monotonous hum of the cooling systems, which had been quite inaudible before the lights had begun blinking but now buzzed noisily inside his skull.

The strobe-effect intensified, the light growing brighter, the intervals between each burst shorter, until the flashing was almost imperceptible. Only light remained. Intensely bright to the point of near-blinding, the hum of the refrigerators rising toward some terrible crescendo –

One of the bottles began to slip through his arms. He tried to grab it, but succeeded only in pulling off what looked like a clumsy dance move – the junkie jive – and the bottle fell to the ground and shattered, scattering glass across the floor and soaking his trainers in vodka.

The lights shut off completely as soon as the bottle hit the ground. Elwood was left in the dark, frantically trying to secure the remaining seven bottles in his arms.

'Great,' he complained, glass crunching loudly beneath his feet as the scent of vodka reached his nose.

He fumbled in the dark, expecting a store clerk to appear at any moment and ask him to leave. Nobody showed up, though, and he was beginning to feel the same sense of loneliness he'd experienced back at the lake. There had to be some kind of buzzer at the checkout, some way of alerting somebody to his presence. If he could get to the tills he was sure to find somebody, anybody. There were cameras – for all he knew somebody might have eyes on him already. Staff in a back room huddled around a grainy monitor perhaps, all of them laughing at the junkie, the scared little junkie shitting his pants because the lights went out.

Mortified at the thought of this, Elwood straightened up, held his head high in some weak attempt at dignity and began to walk back the way he'd come at a brisk pace.

As if to affirm his belief that someone might be toying with him, the nearest refrigerator blinked into life the moment he passed it.

Then the next.

And the next.

All seemingly in sync with his steps. There was something comical about it, like some well-timed Mel Brookes bit. And were it not for his desperate need for a smoke, a gulp from one of the bottles, and to be gone from this whole situation, Elwood might've found the routine quite amusing.

He didn't, though. His embarrassment quickly turned to anger and he stopped in his tracks, as if in defiance of whatever game he was being subjected to.

The lights didn't stop with his steps. One by one, the refrigerators came back to life, replacing silence with the steady hum of the cooling systems.

His eyes followed this chain of illumination until it ceased, abruptly, about halfway along the aisle. He stood, waiting for the next refrigerator to turn on, as annoyed as he was terrified, but nothing happened. His gaze drifted toward the windows that looked out onto the parking lot at the far end of the aisle.

Somebody was standing there.

'Clean up on aisle four,' Elwood joked, wanting only to break the silence.

The figure didn't respond, though. Didn't move.

Elwood took a step forward, just one.

'Look, I'm really sorry. I'll pay for the bottle.'

Whoever it was remained silent, still. Elwood squinted, beginning to doubt himself; had there been some kind of display back there? Was he talking to some cardboard cut-out – a happy customer, or a brand ambassador wielding a tube of toothpaste and showing off their gleaming pearly whites?

As if to answer his thoughts, the person turned their head.

'Hey, listen, friend. I'm not looking for any trouble. I plan on paying for all of this,' Elwood indicated toward his pockets with his chin. 'My wallet's in there, you can check it if you like, I have money to pay. I look like a waster, I know, but trust me, please.'

Still no response.

Elwood took another step forward.

Another.

'Can you hear…'

He was beginning to see the figure more clearly now, and he stopped in his tracks.

Whoever it was, they appeared monstrous; a bulbous head sat neckless on shoulders that were far too wide. Their arms and legs looked as thick as small tree trunks.

Security, perhaps, Elwood thought.

'Look, I don't know what your deal is, but like I said, I'm not looking for any trouble.'

The figure began to move forward and it became apparent just how malformed they were. Their body was distorted, lumpy and misshapen in places it wasn't supposed to be.

It was the same figure he'd seen on the balcony back at the villa, and later in the backseat of his car.

Surprised by the sudden advance of the shape, and just as dazed by the realisation, another bottle slipped from his hands. It shattered on the floor and Elwood scowled at his own mishap; the figure was unflinching though, continuing its advance in awful silence.

'Fuck,' Elwood cursed, trying to keep hold of the remaining six bottles as he stumbled backward.

There was a strange, somewhat comical eeriness about the figure's gait. Between each step, it seemed to hang in the air for just a moment too long, as though sprinting in slow motion, or walking on the moon perhaps.

A third bottle slid between Elwood's cradled arms. Unable to comprehend what now confronted him in this half-lit convenience store, he stood motionless in the middle of the aisle, aghast.

An astronaut.

The visor on the helmet was cracked and ruined, a jagged maw reminiscent of a razor-toothed grin that gave way to nothing but darkness. An abysmal, unsettling blackness unlike anything Elwood had ever gazed into. Blood seeped through the cracks and crested the jagged tips of glass fragments, trickling down the white suit and leaving trails of crimson. More blood was spattered across the chest and arms.

The lights in the refrigerators began to flicker once more, and each one shut off completely as the astronaut passed by. The aisle grew darker as it closed the gap between them.

Another bottle fell to the ground and Elwood followed, losing his footing and landing ass-first in a puddle of liquor and broken glass. He dropped the rest of the bottles down and let them roll off to the side, shuffling away from the approaching form. He winced, pulling himself along, shards of smashed bottle piercing the soft flesh of his palms while others sought to tear him a new asshole.

'Shit. Shit,' he cried out. 'This isn't real, this can't be fucking real…'

There was no denying the pain though, no denying the aroma of spilt rum and vodka in the air. Whatever kind of messed up cold-turkey hallucination this was, it was becoming a little *too* real.

He couldn't move quick enough. The astronaut bore down on him now, arms outstretched, reaching for him. Still, he saw no face. Elwood stared straight into the darkness beyond the shattered visor and saw only that: darkness. Blood continued to trickle out through the cracks in the glass. A single droplet fell through the air and landed on his cheek.

He felt it. Cold and coagulated upon his skin.

Still he refused to believe it. Refused to accept that this wasn't just a side-effect of the heroin deprivation. Astronauts didn't just wander into convenience stores in the middle of the night to torment poor little junkies.

There was something within the gloomy interior of that suit though, something that was speaking to him, goading him. It wasn't the sort of voice you heard through your ears – no, this voice came from within, as though whatever it was had used some secret back door into his mind – and it was talking to him now in tones that only he could hear.

It told him he could suspend belief as much as he liked, it wouldn't help him, wouldn't save him, not now. Now was the time to *believe*. The time to accept, to stop fighting and submit himself.

Elwood fought desperately to pull his gaze away

from the blackness inside the helmet. He was sure that whatever was speaking to him was only able to do so while the dark held his attention. All he had to do was look away, to simply ignore it all and get on with his life –

The trickle of blood abruptly turned to a steady flow, as though in response to Elwood's dissenting thoughts. No longer bound by the rules of gravity it began to float, a glossy slither of crimson that snaked its way upwards and above the shelves.

He jerked back as the astronaut's gloved hand came within inches of his face. The close proximity of the thing was enough to coax him out of whatever it was he'd been trapped in – a trance? – or perhaps the immobilising effect the unexpected often brought with it. Whatever it was, he didn't care now; all he cared about was getting away from this thing. Real or not, it was freaking him out like a bad trip, and the last place you ever wanted to be on a bad trip was in public.

He scrambled off to one side and backed up against the refrigerators. Slowly, he began to edge his way along the glass frontage, his eyes darting between the torn patch of stars and stripes that hung blood-spattered from the astronaut's left breast, the chunky eggshell boots, the control panel on the wrist – anything but that chasm behind the broken visor. Anything but that.

The astronaut tilted in the air, following Elwood's movements until it floated almost horizontally in the middle of the aisle, boots brushing gently against bottles of whiskey and brandy that lined the top shelf on the opposite side.

By the time he reached the end of the aisle, the

astronaut had turned a full one-eighty degrees and was in slow pursuit; no longer stepping, just moving silently through the air toward him. The flow of blood from inside the visor was a waterfall, pooling into a vast globule of crimson in the air above.

Elwood paused at the corner, glancing toward the front of the store; no longer a speck on the horizon, it was now a well-lit refuge less than a hundred feet away. His gaze flickered from the shelves to the approaching astronaut and back again. It was time to go, but not without what he came for. He snatched up two bottles of whiskey in one hand, two vodkas in the other. Then ran.

He didn't look back. All he knew now was that he wanted out of this damn store. Wanted to get back to his car, back to the villa, even though both were places where the astronaut had already shown itself. Jesus, was he safe anywhere? Was there anywhere he could run to? Some place that might provide sanctuary from this storm.

The answer was no, and he knew that. It was a storm he had to weather. Needed to weather. But he wasn't ready to endure this, to confront it.

Not yet.

He reached the checkouts, breathless and wiping sweat from his brow as he looked around for a store clerk. He glanced back toward the darkness at the back of the store. The astronaut had yet to reach the corner of the aisle; a faint light flickered beyond, indicating that the refrigerators were whirring back to life, a sign perhaps that this particular episode had now come to an end.

He set the bottles down on the counter at the tobacco kiosk and pushed a button marked *Assistance*. Nothing happened.

He pressed it again. Still nothing.

The thought of leaving without paying was something he briefly entertained as he stood there waiting, his frustration increasing. He decided against it; he couldn't leave without cigarettes, and he'd have to go behind the counter to get them. That was... well, that was taking it too far. That was asking for the kind of trouble he didn't need right now.

He set off along the line of checkouts and breathed a sigh of relief when he spotted a store clerk a few aisles away. The young girl was loitering around a magazine rack at the far end, a mop in one hand and a comic book in the other.

'Excuse me,' he called.

The girl didn't acknowledge him.

'Hey.' Still nothing. 'I'm in a bit of a hurry, so...'

As he drew closer he noticed the girl was wearing headphones, the guttural growling of Cannibal Corpse faintly audible between his still panicked breaths.

'Excuse me,' he called out, louder this time. While there was still some distance between them, he didn't want to startle the girl by suddenly appearing by her side.

It was enough to catch her attention and she turned around, her eyes widening at the sight of him. She slotted the comic back into its slot on the rack and pulled her headphones out. 'Uh, hi... is there something I can help you with, sir?'

She looked stoned and spoke slowly – contemplating

each of her words before speaking, taking every effort to say the right thing.

'Please,' Elwood replied, as jovially as he could manage. 'I'm in kind of a hurry, you think you can ring up a few bottles of liquor for me? And some smokes?'

'Sure.' The young girl stood the mop back in the bucket and took a tentative step forward, pausing as she looked more closely at Elwood's face. 'Oh – I, uh... I'm sorry, please, after you,' she motioned for Elwood to take the lead.

The girl's apprehension was obvious, and as much as he hated having this effect on a young girl, Elwood obliged without defence, remembering how awful his reflection had been in the rear-view mirror.

'What's your name?'

'It's Arla, sir.'

'Nice to meet you, Arla. And you can drop that *sir* nonsense, my name's Elwood.'

'Sure.'

They reached the tobacco kiosk and Arla unlatched a swing door located at the far end of the station. She stepped behind the counter and closed the door behind her; there was an audible sigh of relief.

'So, what can I get for you?'

Elwood felt something then. He wasn't sure what; probably shame. Perhaps a morsel of self-loathing. She undoubtedly thought he was trouble; she was probably expecting him to try something too – pull out a gun maybe, or God only knew what else.

It was possible he was overthinking things – placing the blame entirely on his condition – when in fact it was quite possibly circumstantial. It was, after all, the early hours of the morning, and regardless of gender, she was still young, still – seemingly – all alone in the store. Would she appear so uneasy at three in the afternoon? Perhaps not.

He wondered how his daughter might react if she could see him now. Would she shield herself from him? Would she take one look at her father's deathly-pale complexion and feel nothing but trepidation?

'Excuse me. Uh, Elwood, sir? Hey, you still there, man?'

'Yeah, sorry,' he murmured, unaware that he'd momentarily drifted within himself.

The store clerk stared at him, her face a mixture of impatience and weariness. She pointed to the shelves behind her.

'The smokes. You said you wanted smokes, man. What did you want?'

'Of course. Erm, yeah, give me four hundred of those lights right there, please. Yeah, those ones there, thank you.'

She scanned the boxes and then the bottles, frequently glancing up at him as she did so.

'Want a bag?'

'Sure.'

Arla placed the bottles and the cigarettes into two separate bags.

'Is there anything else I can help you with this morning?'

'Actually, yeah, there is,' Elwood glanced back toward the back of the store. 'I might've had a little mishap back there. Dropped a few bottles that'll need cleaning up.'

Arla sighed. 'Seriously? What the fuck, man.'

'Hey, easy, easy. Listen, I can pay, okay? I can pay for them. It was three, I think. Or maybe four. Alright, just charge me for another four bottles of the whiskey. I don't want to make any trouble, it was an accident.'

'Whatever, man,' she hit a few buttons on the register. 'That'll be $224.96,' she said, recoiling ever so slightly. 'That going to be okay with you?'

'Of course,' he replied. 'Listen, Arla, I might look like shit, but I'm not a guy who doesn't *have* shit. I can pay.' Elwood pulled out his wallet and passed over his credit card, stealing another glance toward the back of the store, but seeing nothing.

'Hey look, I'm sorry, but I have to ask. No disrespect, but you look kind of fucked up, man. And if I have another runner my boss'll tear me up.'

'Just swipe it, please.'

She did.

Declined.

'Sorry, man.' She didn't look surprised.

Suitably embarrassed, Elwood held out his hand. 'Alright, alright, give it here. I must have given you the wrong one. I've got it covered, trust me.'

He returned the card to his wallet and produced another, hoping this one had some money left on it. Failing that, he had two others he could try.

He passed the card to Arla and this one was accepted. Elwood saw relief wash over the young girl's face, felt it himself too.

'Thanks,' she handed the card back to him. 'Was that everything?'

He picked up the bags. 'Yeah, that'll be all −' he

paused, remembering that he needed painkillers too. 'Actually, no. There's one other thing I need.' He looked at her closely, wondering whether or not he should ask. Not about the painkillers, but about something else, something he thought might be more effective and was quite certain this girl would have – or, at least, she might know where he could get some.

He knew it hadn't been legalised in this state yet.

'What are you staring at?' She took a step back. 'Seriously dude, you're barking up the wrong fucking tree if you're thinking about the kind of shit it looks like you're thinking about.'

'No,' he replied, appalled. 'No way. I need painkillers. But you look like you took your last break with Cheech and Chong, so maybe you can help a guy out with something a bit more… let's say, *natural*.'

She looked confused. 'What the fuck's a Cheech and Chong?'

'Seriously?' he grinned. 'You smoke weed, right? And you've never heard of those guys? Shit, maybe I'm as old as I feel.' He sighed. 'They were comedians, smoked a bunch of pot, they're, like, the most famous…'

She was clearly none the wiser.

'Forget it. Look, I can see you enjoy a little smoke. All I'm asking is, can you help me out? Either sell me a little, or point me in the direction of someone who can. That's all.'

She shook her head. 'I don't know what you're talking about.'

'Oh, come on. Arla, wasn't it? Look, Arla, I'm not going to tell anyone, it'll be our little secret. Just like the bottles back there,' he nodded toward the back of the store.

Still shaking her head: 'No way, man – for all I know, you're just some off-duty cop from out of town. Or – let me guess – you're buddies with Tims, right?'

'Tims?'

'Sheriff Tims. He send you out here to test me or something? Catch me out like he did with Chloe.'

'Listen, Arla. I don't know who Chloe is. And look at me. I mean, really fucking *look* at me. Do I look like a cop? Do I look like cop-*friend* material to you? You said it yourself, I look fucked up, because I am.' He sighed. The last thing he wanted to do was to spill his life story to this teenage girl. In fact, the last thing he wanted was to be arguing with a teenage girl in an attempt to buy drugs from her.

There were always new lows to be explored, it seemed.

'Full disclosure, okay. I'm a recovering junkie, and you can italicise the shit out of the "recovering" part of that. It's hard, really ha–'

'Not my problem, man.'

'I know, I know. It's not your problem. But look,' he set the bags down on the floor and pulled his wallet out. 'I have cash, I have,' he counted up all the notes, 'I have just over a hundred dollars here.' He folded it up and held it out. 'I'll give you all of this. All of it. If you can spare just a few joints. That's all I'm asking, please.'

He cringed at the desperation in his voice. It was pathetic. *He* was pathetic.

He wondered for a second what might come next. What if she still refused? Would he get down on his knees and beg?

Maybe.

There was hope though, a hint of it in the way she was no longer looking at his face, and looking instead at the money in his hand. Small-town girl on a convenience store wage. A hundred unexpected bucks wasn't a thing to frown at.

'Please,' he placed the money on the counter and stepped back. 'I'm on a rough ride here. Some pot would…' He sighed. 'Some pot would just make this whole thing a little more bearable.'

She eyed him ruefully for a moment; her eyes flitted to the money on the counter, then back to him, and back to the money. 'Fine,' she said, snatching up the cash and stuffing it into her pocket. 'Meet me out back in five minutes.'

'Thank you,' he picked up his bags. 'Thank you so much'. He turned away, not wanting her to see the shame now glistening in his eyes.

New lows. There were always new lows.

CHAPTER SEVEN
BACK AT THE VILLA

Elwood didn't see a soul – nor any dazzling neon installations – on the ride back to the house, and he was glad of it. He'd decided to open one of the whiskey bottles as he drove back; the trip had taken its toll.

He took another sip and set his glass back down on the balcony handrail. He felt better for having it; for the cigarettes; for the joints he'd managed to procure from the store clerk. Most satisfying of all, though, was the sense of a small amount of control having been exercised successfully. He had obtained things he needed; things that weren't heroin.

It wasn't much – and to a sober person, might have been completely inconsequential. To him, though, it was a step forward.

He gulped down the rest of the glass and poured himself another. The night air was still, and Elwood tried to embrace the peacefulness of it all and forget about all of this shit. All of *his* shit.

Try as he might, the desire kept returning. That deep, painful need for what had become normal. He couldn't remember when that had happened, when it had all become *normal*. Those parts of his life were gone now; there was no blurry recollection of that lost time, no vague memory, just the pointed end of a needle.

He remembered parts of his life that had come before, parts of the man he once was; an author, a husband, a father.

He thought of Elouise and began to cry. He brought out his wallet and gently pulled a worn polaroid from the back. The three of them at the beach.

'I...' he trembled. 'I couldn't picture your face. I couldn't remember what you looked like, my sweet little girl.'

He caressed the photo, guilt coursing through him. He'd give anything to be back there now – back with them, back on that beach – wherever and whenever it was, he couldn't remember now, but he knew it had been better than this.

He looked up at the stars, looked for answers or consolation in their twinkling light, but like the memory, they too were in the past.

'I'm sorry El, I –'

He sighed.

'I messed up. I let you down, I let your mom down.'

He wondered where they were now, what they were doing. He knew they lived somewhere in Illinois; they'd moved there when Gracie had remarried. And Elouise, she'd started elementary school two, maybe three years ago. That was as much as he knew, or as much as he'd cared to keep up with.

He had slowly, without ever realising it – or ever truly trying to fight it – become entirely apathetic toward himself and his life, which included those he loved. Getting high never solved your problems, it just made you care a little less about them; and over time, he'd begun to see his family as a problem. His wife, his daughter – both were problems he could do without. So, he dove deeper into the rabbit hole, injecting more and caring less.

He had no idea when the dial had switched, but it had. One day he'd been a man who still loved his wife and daughter but was struggling with an addiction. The next, there was no love, no struggle; *only* addiction, raw and relentless in its demands.

He felt ashamed that he couldn't recall the exact circumstance. His wife deserved better than that, Elouise even more so. He imagined her finding him in twenty years' time, a young woman curious about her absent father. She'd want to know why, of course. She'd want to know why he was so weak, why the heroin had been more important to him than his own daughter, why he'd stopped writing bedtime stories just for her, why he'd never come back, even after realising the error of his ways, *why, dad? why? why did we never see you again?*

'Fucking bastard,' he cursed himself miserably. This was worse than the pain, worse than the cramps and the sweats. It was the brutal truth fighting its way through the haze of his drug-soaked memory; it was the fog clearing.

It was remembering.

And it *hurt.*

He retreated to the upper lounge and snatched up a clear plastic bag from the sofa bed. Inside were the nine joints Arla had sold to him. He took one out and returned to the balcony and his whiskey, wiping tears from his face as he walked.

He lit up and looked out over the lake. A ripple in the still water caught his eye, near the shoreline to the right. He couldn't see anything in the water, but now that his eyes were drawn in that direction, he noticed there was somebody standing in the woods.

He gazed for a few moments, waiting for it diminish into branches and leaves, as would most figures and shapes that people thought they could see amid shadowy woodland; it remained though, the same bulky, misshapen outline which had confronted him at the store.

The astronaut.

Even from this distance, Elwood knew that the darkness inside that shattered helmet was looking right at him, calling to him.

Stupid, he thought. It wasn't calling to him; he was calling to himself. That's what all of this was, the lit-up signs, the astronaut, it was all in his head. None of it was real.

Why then, he thought, was there another voice? A voice that screamed, its volume muffled somewhere in the depths of his psyche so that it reached his conscious mind as nothing more than a whisper. It told him this was something else, something greater – *darker* – than himself, something twisted.

Something real, and insidious.

'Leave me alone,' he cried. His protest broke the

silence for only a second, and just as fleeting as its presence, so too was any indication of it ever having happened, like a pebble thrown into the water that left no ripples in its wake.

He didn't know who he was shouting at; the figure he thought he could see at the edge of the trees, or the voice he thought he could hear in his head. Had he even voiced the words out loud?

He hadn't been prepared for visions as vivid as these, or for them to come on so soon into his sobriety. He didn't like how they felt either: the buzzing of the signs that he'd felt within his skull; the trickle of blood from that smashed visor that had landed on his cheek; and the air right now – it was too thick, too metallic.

Elwood backed away from the handrail, afraid that he was starting to lose his grip on reality, afraid he might do something stupid like dive headfirst over the boundary, kiss the stone below, and call it a day on this whole thing called *life*.

He kept his eyes on the form at the edge of the woods, expecting it to begin its approach at any moment. One giant leap, he thought. That's all it would take. One giant leap from its position near the shore, and it would float through the air, a silhouette against a lunar backdrop – floating, floating, floating – until it landed on the balcony next to him.

And then what? he wondered.

Elwood stepped inside and slammed the doors behind him, drawing the curtains as though they were some sort of heavy-duty bunker door, a barrier that would prevent the outside world from getting in. Perhaps the inside world, too.

He sat down on the sofa bed and stubbed the joint out in an ashtray on a nearby console. Eager to forget about the visitor outside, he leaned over and rummaged through his bag until he found a bag of chips, then laid back on the bed. Crumbs gathered on his chest as he ate. He knew this wasn't sustainable; perhaps this was his next milestone, something else to focus on, to mend. He needed a proper meal. Proper nutrition.

He decided that, come tomorrow, he would go out and find another store somewhere in town. A store where he could buy something healthier than the chips and cookies he had in his bag. He had no intention of returning to the ConveeMart, not after everything that had happened there.

Stocking up on suitable food supplies was an exercise that would occupy some of his time. It was something that might help him get through one more day of abstinence.

Then, he hoped, there would be something else he could do. Because, much like the devil, the needle waited patiently for idle hands.

This line of thinking was a welcome reprieve. He'd all but forgotten about his guest out by the lake when his eyelids became heavy.

Within a few minutes, he was asleep.

It was still dark when Elwood was stirred awake by what sounded like the faint crackling of an old radio that hadn't been tuned properly. Although it sounded distant, it wasn't *that* far away; the downstairs hall, perhaps.

He propped himself up on his elbows and listened intently, wondering if it might be the stereo he'd seen in the lounge.

Or maybe it was Casper, he considered. That made no sense at all; there was no reason for him to have travelled all the way out here from LA. Surely the man had more important matters to attend to.

Elwood sat up, eyes trained on the corner of the room that gave way to the hall. No, it couldn't be Casper – it had to be the stereo, on a timer perhaps.

Anything but the astronaut. He didn't want to imagine that dead thing and its darkened recesses moving around in the villa beneath him, floating from room to room in the dim morning light.

A thud from the kitchen, directly beneath him. Another. A pause, a moment of silence –

Again.

The sound changed positions, as if someone was down there with a broomstick, prodding the ceiling.

No, he thought. It's the helmet.

It was the helmet of the suit, bumping against the ceiling below as the astronaut moved around the room, searching.

Searching for him.

He wondered if it might be a good idea to stay right where he was, rather than go downstairs. He suddenly recalled what the old man at the hunting store had told him – right now, of course, being the worst possible time to remember such things – about the kids. The murderous, Satan-worshipping kiddies.

The lake had a history. And for all Elwood knew, it was being played out once again. A crazed teenage cult had broken into the villa and at this precise moment, the little knife-wielding children were downstairs in the dark, big smiles on their faces, searching for their next sacrifice.

Maybe the astronaut would be better.

He worked himself up into a quiet panic as he heard more movement below in the dining room. A cupboard opened and closed in the kitchen.

That thing wouldn't open a cupboard, would it?

Elwood swung his legs out of the bed and placed his bare feet gently down onto the cold wooden laminate. He had no idea what he'd do, but he stood up anyway, and began to tiptoe across the lounge toward the hall.

Confrontation had never been something he'd faced willingly – nor successfully, for the most part. So, what if it actually was an intruder?

He refused to consider this point, and instead continued slowly down the hall, telling himself that this was all in his head. It was all just part and parcel of the withdrawal process.

He reached the top of the stairs and waited a few moments, hearing nothing and hoping it would stay that way. The silence was soon broken by a familiar crackling sound; was there a voice, too? He was sure he could hear a voice, like that of someone talking through a walkie-talkie that was just at the limit of range; distorted and fragmented.

He descended nervously, stopping at the landing halfway down the stairs to peer around the corner into the hallway below.

Nothing there. But he could still hear that same noise coming from the kitchen. Shifting around the corner, he took a tentative step onto the lower stairway, wincing as it creaked loudly beneath his foot.

Before he was able to take another step, the noise abruptly ceased.

He froze, his bare foot shaking only millimetres above the next step as he listened, waited. For what, he had no idea; for anything, another break in the silence perhaps, something that might indicate he wasn't the focus of attention.

He set his foot down carefully and continued to the bottom. When he reached the final step, he positioned himself against the wall and glanced around the corner. He could see the edge of the breakfast bar and the dining table through the open doorway at the end of the corridor. It remained silent, save for the wind picking up outside and slapping the taller weeds at the front of the house against the window.

His eyes lingered on the mass of wildflower swaying in the breeze, and with each gentle tap Elwood tried to convince himself that this must have been it. What he thought was a crackling radio or helmet bumping the ceiling had, in fact, just been the rhythmic *tap-tap-tapping* of tall weeds on glass.

Stupid, he thought, turning back toward the stairs.

As he turned, he glimpsed movement from the corner of his eye. Something had passed across the doorway at the far end of the hall. Something that didn't walk, but *floated*. A dark, lumpy shape that had moved far too swiftly for something that should only have existed in zero-gravity. It sped from the kitchen and disappeared into the dining area like a scene on VHS in fast-forward – too jerky, too distorted.

'Fuck,' he blurted out, darting back up the stairs as fast as he could. 'This isn't real, Elwood, this is all in your head. Your stupid, fucking head –'

He tried to calm his nerves, but it was no use. There was only one thing that would calm him now, and it was sitting outside in the glovebox of his car.

One hit, he thought. That one hit would end all of this. Sure, there was a creepy astronaut floating around between him and it, but if he *absolutely* had to he'd jump out of an upstairs window to get to what was his, to have his lifeline. To once again feel safe and secure.

To no longer care.

But that wasn't an option, it couldn't be. Not now, there was more at stake. There were things – *people* – he needed to remember. Elouise. His daughter. From her, the idea of her, the *reality* of her, he needed to draw strength.

Strength enough to get him through this.

It's all in your head, he reaffirmed – sprinting now, along the top hall and toward the upper lounge. He snatched up his bag and ducked into the bedroom above the kitchen. Hadn't he seen rat shit in here? He didn't care now. Rats, spiders, he'd take them as bedfellows any day of the week ahead of that thing floating around downstairs.

He closed the door behind him and cursed. No lock. He looked about the room and focused in on a chest of drawers beside the window that overlooked the parking bay. He dragged it across the wooden floor and positioned it against the door.

Breathless, his arms like lead columns, Elwood sat down on the bed beside his bag and pulled out his pack of cigarettes. Eyes never leaving the door, he waited. Listened.

There was nothing, though, only silence.

He attempted to light his smoke, but his hands were trembling. After a few failed attempts he gave up and spat the cigarette out, still staring at the door.

It would be hours before he was able to fall asleep again. And it wouldn't be restful. It would be a dark, disturbed slumber, the likes of which were reserved only for the most tormented of souls.

CHAPTER EIGHT
OJ

After waking from a rough few hours of something awful that had passed for sleep, Elwood had searched the entire villa for any signs of intrusion; a search that had turned up nothing, but had brought him to where he now stood, his t-shirt pulled up over the lower half of his face, a garbage bag in one hand, and the other reaching hesitantly toward the handle of the refrigerator door.

If he was buying food later, he'd need somewhere to keep it. He desperately needed a distraction too, something to help him forget that darkness, that pitch black void beyond the shattered visor of the one who floated.

The void that had spoken to him.

As he opened the door, the reek of putrefied meat and decaying fruit permeated the cotton of his t-shirt and jabbed him in both nostrils. He began to gag and retch, eyes streaming as he frantically shoved armfuls of rotten produce into the bag. After emptying the refrigerator of its rotting contents, he held the refuse sack at arm's length and walked briskly down the hall toward the side door.

Outside, he tossed the bag onto the ground next to the woodpile and fell to his knees in the tall grass, coughing wildly and throwing up thick mucus and vitriol that stunk of whiskey and nacho cheese tortilla chips.

This retching continued for a minute or two before subsiding, leaving him with nothing but an aching back and an awful taste in his mouth. He let himself fall back into the grass for a moment and simply lay there, staring up into that same unforgiving sky, where the sun seemed to shine just a little brighter now than it had before.

The heroin, he thought. It dulled everything; the enthusiasm, the interest – fear, love, even light. All of it.

The sound of an engine stirred him from this unexpected moment of existential awareness. Faint, but getting closer.

An engine, he thought. Engines came with cars. And cars came with people.

He rolled over and got onto his knees, then slowly poked his head above the tall weeds. Sure enough, he could see a car rolling down the driveway toward the villa.

The cops.

He ducked back into the overgrowth and began to crawl toward the door, cursing under his breath as he clambered through the grass.

It had to be the store clerk that had turned him in. Or perhaps the man at the old store. They were the only locals he'd engaged with.

Chancing another peek, he could see that the cruiser was now parked directly behind his car, blocking him in. The officer was talking on their radio and no doubt sharing his license plate with someone back at the station. He seized the opportunity and dived for the door, falling over the threshold and hoping he hadn't been spotted.

Easing the door shut with his knee, he stumbled clumsily along the hall on all fours like a drunken mutt, keeping beneath the windows that lined the front of the villa. When he reached the kitchen, he scrambled to his feet and pressed himself up against the front door.

He heard the sound of a car door slamming, followed by footsteps over gravel.

He looked down at the key in the lock, wondering whether or not he'd actually locked it the night before. If he had, then all he'd need to do would be to patiently wait for the cop to give up and leave. Yes, his car was parked outside, but wouldn't it be reasonable to assume that if he wasn't answering the door, then he was simply out for a walk? Perhaps. It would all depend on why the officer was here in the first place. If it was serious – like *buying-marijuana-from-a-teenage-store-clerk* kind of serious – then maybe the cop would try the door. And what then? Elwood wondered. He'd look pretty damn foolish – and guilty – when the cop opened the door and saw him standing right there.

A creak on the porch step.

It was too late now. They were too close. He wasn't

in the city anymore, a place where urban background noise might drown out the sound of a lock being engaged. This was the country, a place where you could cup your hand around your ear on a mild day and listen to two rabbits fucking in a bush a mile away. The cop would hear him for sure.

He closed his eyes and breathed. He just needed to play it cool. There was probably nothing to worry about. For all he knew, the cop was just making a friendly visit. Checking up on the lonesome tenant they'd heard about.

Three knocks in quick succession broke the silence.

They were firm knocks, too. The sort of knocks that suggested this was more than just a *hey, how are you* sort of visit.

Elwood took a few steps back into the dining area, silently, until he could see himself in the mirror that hung on the wall beside the lounge door. His reflection didn't fill him with any hope for a painless interaction with the law; his eyes were red, puffy and distant. His face was pale and clammy.

He looked like shit.

More knocking. 'Anybody home? This is the Sheriff's Department.' It was a woman; her country drawl made it sound like *Sure-if's Department.*

Clearly she wasn't going away, so Elwood stepped forward, this time making no effort to remain quiet. He turned the key in the lock and opened the front door.

The officer had her back to him, looking out toward the treeline, hands resting on her hips as she surveyed the surrounding woodland. She turned around casually and tipped her hat. There seemed to be the hint of a smile on her face, buried beneath a veil of formality and suspicion.

'Old man Kenner wasn't lying, huh? He told me you looked like a wet sack of scared corn. I didn't believe him, but by God, I do now.' She adjusted the collar of her shirt.

'Is he the man at the store down the road?' Elwood asked.

'That's the fella,' she stepped back and rested against the handrail that ran along the porch, the wood creaking as she thumbed her trouser pockets.

'I see.' He wasn't sure what else he was supposed to say, aside from enquiring as to what the hell a scared corn was supposed to look like. 'Well, is there anything I can help you with, officer?' He tried his best *nothing to see here* smile.

'How about we start with a name. I know you ain't that Stevens fella. He ain't been out here since I was a young one, but we know his face. Know his ways. He a friend of yours?'

Elwood cleared his throat, knowing the question was loaded and that his answer could affect the rest of this conversation. 'I guess you could say that. I mean, I know him. But that's all. I know him well enough to be able to stay here anyway,' he paused. 'And my name's Elwood. Elwood Cathis,' he offered his hand and she immediately took it. Her eyes were still suspicious though, still looking for more.

'Pleased to meet you Mr Cathis. Name's Janet, most folks round here call me OJ. I'll just cut right to it, though. I have two questions for you. The first is: what are you doing here in our town? And the second is… what in the hell is wrong with you? You look like my

Gramp Joe when he had the chemo.'

She moved her hand through the air and marked the holy trinity.

'Do you have the cancer in you?'

'No, I don't,' he replied, stalling while he searched for an excuse. A reason as to why he looked like a wet sack of scared corn – and preferably, one that didn't involve him telling a cop he was strung out.

'Then what it is?' she pressed.

'Well, it's just my luck, really,' he started. 'I come here for some peace and quiet – just to get away from it all, you know? And I get a real bad case of the flu on my ride here,' he shrugged.

She didn't believe him; he could see it in her eyes, still looking, still waiting. Waiting for this junkie-fuck to slip up and spill the beans. 'I know all about him. Your friend, that is. I've seen the trouble he brought with him. You aren't bringing trouble to our little town too, are you, Mr Cathis?'

Her eyes were demanding now, lips pursed. Elwood imagined it was an expression she wore often whilst minding the sort of troubles with which a small town like Misstonville was surely burdened: the town drunk swearing blind that he was sober enough to drive home while swaying on his feet; the husband looking puzzled when asked about a reported altercation in the home, blood still drying on his bruised knuckles; the metalhead teens in the park who insisted they had no idea what dope was as they stamped out the last embers of their burning butts in the dirt.

And now there was him, the mysterious out-of-towner who definitely didn't have cancer, but was certainly fucked royally in some way or another by the look of him. A lonesome lake-goer who absolutely didn't have any Class-A narcotics in the glovebox of his car.

'You won't get any trouble from me, OJ,' he replied calmly, and with an almost sincere smile. It seemed to him that being on good terms with this woman might mean the difference between a quiet break and a constantly interrupted one. 'I plan on keeping myself to myself,' he added.

She studied him a while longer, then her gaze began to drift over his shoulder, and she cocked her head to one side for a better view of the kitchen and diner behind him.

'How long you fixing to stay here with us, Mr Cathis?' she asked. 'Your friend coming to join you too?'

Her voice took on a different tone for that second question. It reminded Elwood of Gracie whenever she'd asked why he was so late, why he'd missed dinner, why he hadn't shown up to El's recital. Where all the *money* was being spent. She'd always been warm, genuinely – naively – curious; she loved him, after all, even if he'd forgotten that. But she'd always followed up with that unintentional tone of assumed disappointment: *you haven't been with Casper again, have you?*

And who could blame her? Back then she'd had a pretty good idea of the sort of person Casper Stevens was, and Elwood had always been a terrible liar.

Officer Janet clearly knew what type of person Casper was too, and almost certainly by virtue of that, knew all too well that just like shit and flies, undesirables such as he kept equally detestable friends and acquaintances. And she'd be right – to a certain degree, anyway. There was a time when she would have been completely right; hell, there was a time, no more than a few weeks ago, when he wouldn't have been nearly as polite as he was being now, a time when the smack would have been in his veins instead of the car, a time when he undoubtedly would have scrambled out of the back door instead of answering the front one.

But she didn't need to know that. He didn't want her to know that. Though her eyes clearly presaged her knowledge; she knew it well, he could tell.

And wasn't it always the eyes? Always the eyes that let the truth creep through, the truth of someone – not their soul, no, that was just a little too ponderous for junkie Elwood – but their intentions, yes.

'Well?' she asked impatiently.

'No. Just me,' he replied. 'And I'm really not sure how long. A week, I think. However long it takes, I guess.'

'However long what takes?' she asked, a crease forming across her brow.

And he'd been doing so well.

He scrambled for something. Anything. He was a writer after all – used to be, anyway. But then he'd always known that imagination wasn't a precursor to quick-thinking; the two, at least in Elwood's case, had always been mutually exclusive. Great ideas didn't come instantly; they were whittled out over days, sometimes months. Years, even. They required honing and refinement, a period of deconstruction and reconstruction, before the time came to allow others to explore them, investigate them, question them.

He would've been a shit conman.

'I…'

Her eyes never left his as he struggled to find the words, the right words, words that would allow this woman to walk away reasonably satisfied – satisfied enough, at least, not to feel the need to return.

Then it hit him. So simple. So obvious. And with a grain of truth to it, too.

'I'm a writer,' he offered.

'A writer, you say,' she nodded her head slowly, one of those *sure you are* kind of nods.

'Yes,' he replied, surprised by the conviction in his own voice. 'It's been a few years since I released anything, though.' And even longer since he'd released anything half-decent. 'I've been on a hiatus of sorts, you might say. I hoped this trip might help me find my way back to it though.'

'I see,' she sighed, turning to look out across the gravelled driveway again. This time, he saw her eyes fix on his car. 'I ain't never cared for all that nonsense, too much shit to shovel right here in the real world if you ask me.'

She leaned over the edge of the porch, as if trying to get a closer look at the car, and Elwood noticed a silver crucifix hanging from her neck. A sign, perhaps, that there was only one book she was interested in reading, and Elwood suspected she sang its contents every Sunday without fail.

'We get a few of the bookwormy-types now and then. They come to visit old Aubrey Christie's store. She's been selling books in this town since my Gramp

Joe was just a nipper; woman must be at least one-hundred-twelve years old by now.' She shook her head disbelievingly, still looking at the car instead of him. 'Anyways, her place is down on Gilead if you want to contribute to the economy of our little town whilst you're staying here, Mr Cathis. It's just around the corner from the all-night store.' She casually glanced back at him.

Elwood tried to compose himself, certain that she was looking for some kind of reaction.

'Well, I might pay that old lady a visit then,' he replied. 'I love to read, whenever I get the chance.' This was good. This was easier. He could play the part of the booklover, the *bookwormy-type,* because he'd been one.

Books had been his first addiction.

'I'm sure she'll appreciate that,' she tilted her head toward the car. 'Nice ride you've got there.'

'Thanks,' he replied, not wanting to talk about the car, where the heroin was currently tucked away. In fact, he didn't want to talk about anything, but if he had to, if he *absolutely* had to converse with this cop, then he wanted to talk books and appear as harmless as possible. He needed Officer Janet to know that he was one of the *bookwormy-types*, and not one of the *bringing-trouble-to-our-little-town-types.*

He had a feeling she'd already made up her mind, though. Had done the moment she'd laid eyes on him.

'My Pops loved his wheels. Loved tinkering with them, riding them – heck, he even loved taking pictures of the damned things,' she laughed to herself. 'He used to run the old garage out on seventeen. He spent more time at that damn garage than he ever did with his family.'

Elwood nodded in agreement. 'We all have our passions.' Regardless of her opinion of him, he was starting to feel as though he actually had some semblance of a handle on this exchange.

'I'm sure you have many, Mr Cathis,' she frowned. 'My Pops, though, he had eyes for wheels and wheels only. He never had him a drop of the drink, never hung loose with floozies or those bums over at Sykesport races, neither. But even with all those decades of sweat and grease and clean-living, my Pops would've never been able to afford a car like that. No way, no how.'

She looked at him, her lips pursed.

'But you can.'

'I did well enough, writing. But could I afford that car today? No,' Elwood replied.

'Your friend, Stevens… he had him a slick ride like yours. Impressed all the kids. Including my sister. Had a tonne of them out here to party with him. You know what he *did*?' She didn't allow him time to answer. 'He let the Sanders' daughter take it for a ride with her friends from Nilsport over in Bowles County – them and that bothersome Buxford boy. Next thing you know, we got a wreckage and five dead kids out at Jackson Bluffs.'

'That's awful,' Elwood said.

'Ain't it just.' She turned back toward his car and sighed. 'Your friend said they stole it from him, but we all knew different. He tarnished those poor girls – maybe not that little bastard Matty Buxford, but those sweet girls, they good girls. They were my friends.' She turned to face him, her eyes accusing.

'They had so much of that damn heroin in their veins, they were probably out of it before the car even left the bluff,' she shook her head.

Elwood didn't know what to say. He knew how Casper worked it, especially when it came to young ladies. He gave people a taste, a glimpse of the lifestyle: fast cars, liquor and late nights; music, orgies, and overflowing ashtrays. It was uncensored, uncivilised, and almost always ended in tears. Or death.

'Still,' she roused him from his thoughts. 'Ain't the first time we've had trouble out this way. Whole dang place is tainted if you ask me. And the only thing keeping it alive is your damn friend holding onto this place.'

She clearly didn't like the friendly ghost, and Elwood couldn't blame her. But Casper was coming up way too often in this conversation, so he attempted to steer it elsewhere.

'The man at the store, Kenner. He mentioned some murders.'

'Those devil kids, back in seventy-nine? Lot of folks say that was the start of it all. But you speak to the old timers – the Christie lady, Whiskey Bob – they'll tell you different.'

'Oh yeah?' he asked.

'Yeah, they'll tell you those Godless Injuns didn't like the place. All sorts of crazy hoohah that ain't worth the breath they waste on it.' A short laugh escaped her then – forced, Elwood noticed, and just a tad nervous. 'But as long as people listen, they'll keep on telling their tales.'

'Maybe I can get some inspiration for my next book,'

he mused out loud, attempting to remind her once again that he was a harmless author, nothing more.

'Maybe,' she replied, moving toward the top of the porch steps now. Hopefully leaving. 'Maybe not.'

She began to descend the creaky boards and Elwood felt a steady flow of relief begin to envelop the dull cramps he'd been feeling in his gut.

'You can spend your money in town. But we don't need more books about Misstonville, Mr Cathis,' she touched her head and chest again; this time, she clasped the dangling crucifix in her hand and kissed it. 'We've had plenty of you and yours, if you are what you say you are.' She raised an eyebrow. 'Curious folk that want to ask questions and write down the answers. Want to dig up the past. And we're sick and tired of it.'

'I don't want to cause any trouble. Like I say, I can keep myself to myself, and in a week or so I'll be on my way.'

'If you say so,' she returned nonchalantly, still lingering longer than was needed, longer than Elwood wanted. 'If you asked me, I'd tell you a week's too long and you'd be best getting on your way sooner. This place ain't a fucking rehab, no matter how many junkies your friend sends here.'

And there it was.

She reached her cruiser and turned back as she pulled the driver's door open.

'You're trying, I'll give you that much. But I see your face, and I see those scars.'

Elwood crossed his arms, suddenly embarrassed.

'We don't need more of your kind out here getting into trouble.' She ducked into her car and closed the door behind her, rolling down the window as she started up the engine. 'No servant can serve two masters, Mr Cathis; either he will hate the one and love the other, or be devoted to one and despise the other,' she fixed her eyes on his, grinning, and nodded her head knowingly. 'Luke, 16:13. You can't serve God and heroin.'

'I serve neither,' he retorted weakly.

'Oh, but you do. To serve God is to serve yourself, to love Him is to love yourself – and you ain't looking after yourself. Something else has your attention and I see it's reflection all over your face and arms.' She laughed as she started up the engine. 'Like I said, you'd be best to skip along sooner, rather than later. I'll be telling Sheriff Tims all about you, and Jo likes to stop by and meet any folks who come stay out here.'

That was the last thing he needed right now.

'Know why he likes to come out here, Mr Cathis?' she adjusted her sunglasses and rested her arm on the open driver's side window.

Elwood pulled the packet of smokes from his pocket, took one out and lit up.

'No,' he replied.

Officer Janet grinned.

'Because once he meets them, they leave and they don't ever come back,' she winked at him as the car rolled gently across the gravel.

He kept his eyes on her as the cruiser sped along the winding lane toward Crescent Road, then disappeared from view.

'Well, shit.'

CHAPTER NINE
THE LAKE

He lingered throughout the villa for an hour or so after OJ's visit, abstaining from drink and joints, but compensating with far too many cigarettes. Moving from room to room like an apparition without purpose, Elwood touched things, adjusted things, moved, rotated, prodded and poked things, for no reason other than just... well, *because*.

When he eventually pulled himself out of this apathetic autonomy, he decided it was time to do something sensible. He still needed food that wasn't sugar-coated and drink that wasn't hard. He was quickly approaching the third night of his stay, and he hadn't eaten a single proper meal since he'd arrived. The thought made his cramped stomach grumble in protest, so he grabbed his keys and headed back into town.

He decided against returning to the ConveeMart. Choosing instead to drift through town, he interrogated signs and billboards in search of something less *local –*

in other words, a store where nobody would care who the hell he was or why the hell he was there.

Were he to shop there again, he suspected the likes of OJ or Sheriff Tims would know what he was putting in the cupboards before he'd even gotten back and filled them. It wasn't like he was stocking up on painkillers and liquor though, not this time. This was a *sensible* shopping trip; no crying in front of teenage girls because they wouldn't sell him any marijuana.

No *astronauts*.

He'd been both amused and embarrassed by the notion that any sort of shopping trip which didn't involve the purchase of drugs or liquor should be considered *sensible*. It was a stark reminder of how far gone he was – but at the same time, his awareness of that change in perception was a good sign. Ignorance was bliss, and heroin was the spark that ignited that ignorance. These small, seemingly insignificant observations heralded the dying of that fire, slowly but surely, bit by bit.

Before long, he started seeing signs advertising Walmart.

Perfect.

He was guided through the town proper and spat out the other side onto the interstate heading south; from there it was only a few miles.

He took a trolley and, ignoring the concerned and sometimes cautious glances from some of the other patrons, he did what any normal, functioning member of society does: he shopped for groceries and essentials.

***

He made it home without incident, flicked on the kettle and loaded his groceries into the fridge.

His mind, although scattered, kept coming back to what OJ had said about the Sheriff. His potential visit hung over Elwood's cold turkey retreat like a suspicious cloud on the horizon. The threat of his calling was probably just scare tactics, but the uncertainty was palpable; dry and salty, it reminded him of the feeling he'd always had when his next fix wasn't guaranteed. He wondered when, he wondered how, and he desperately hoped it would happen sooner rather than later.

He'd already been on edge. But this had left him hanging over some black precipice by his fingertips, too weak to find the strength needed to pull himself back up, just waiting for some backwater Sheriff to come along and play *This Little Piggy*.

And he'd fall. Oh yes, he'd fall. Elwood Cathis would fall hard and easy, because he was gutless. Because he was *weaker now – you've lost your values, Woody, you've lost who you were, what you stand for –*

He heard Grace's tired and regretful voice in his head.

You aren't the man I married, she said, *and you aren't the father our daughter needs. That's, why we're leaving. Are you even listening to me, Woody? Hello?!*

Are you high right now?

That had been the day. He remembered it now for the first time as he sat at the dining table, sipping his coffee and taking his time with a cigarette. That was the day they left, the day he had let them go. The day they finally gave up on him and he did nothing to change their minds. And she'd wanted him to, he knew that now, she'd wanted him to *try*; she'd needed to see something, he was certain of it now. Gracie had wanted him to get better, wanted him to at least take a step in the right direction.

He felt the threat of tears again. That was the worst part of it; she was never angry with him, never demanded he stop what he was doing whole-hog and go cold turkey. No, she loved him. She'd loved him right to the end, and probably for a while afterwards too, without a whisper of arrogance or loathing. God, how close they'd been; kindred spirits, two peas in a pod and all the other clichéd bullshit people spouted when hearts were full and love was young and blind – but it wasn't *truly* bullshit, was it?

Elwood knew this, deep down; buried beneath the junkie exterior, deeper still beneath the anguished horror writer, failed father, neglectful son and one-time ball polisher at K-Bowles Tenpin Heaven – beneath all of that, was an old (and now hopeless) romantic.

That part of him was buried too deep though, drenched in heroin and drowned in ignorance. Hell, he wondered whether it had even been there at all by the time his habits had turned *hard*; had he just buried those parts of himself, or had he killed them completely?

It was only now, as the hazy smog of addiction began to clear, that he was able to ponder such things.

He peered over the rim of his mug as he gulped the last of his coffee. Like virgin snow demanding the crunch of footfall, the lake seemed to call out for its still surface to be disturbed. He suddenly felt the urge to swim out into those dark waters and wash away all the shit from himself.

Like a spa day, or a colonic. He grinned to himself. Yes, there was actual science in the benefits of flushing out your ass, and a hell of a lot of credence in the perks of sweating yourself dry in a sauna or having some stranger knead your back like pizza dough. As well as the physical benefits, activities like these also came with psychosomatic results – and right now, Elwood's mind needed help even more so than his body. The cramps and the shakes were painful – and more would come soon – but the things he was seeing, feeling… he needed to try something. Something that felt like a cleanse.

The more he sat there thinking about it, the more he felt it was worth a try. And what did he have to lose anyway? He'd either come back feeling a little refreshed – sharper, more focussed perhaps – or he'd return cold, wet, and shivering. Both potential outcomes felt far more desirable than simply loitering around the villa. He pushed his chair away from the table and stood up. 'Fuck it,' he announced.

He hadn't brought swim shorts with him. But a part of him believed – not that he'd ever held the conviction until now; or perhaps he'd always had it, but never had the need to exercise it – that if you were swimming for the sake of cleansing, then your Sunday best was… well, *best*, perhaps.

He checked all of the doors, made sure everything that could be locked was locked, and took a brisk walk along the winding path that led from the back of the villa down to the lake. He stood at the end of the short jetty, wondering how he hadn't managed to talk himself out of this already.

'YOLO, I guess.' He pulled off his trainers, his shorts, socks, and then his t-shirt, and finally his underwear, placing them all in a neat pile on the dock, his phone and the keys to the villa on top. It was a mild afternoon; he was sure the lake wouldn't be so mild, though.

Elwood sat on the edge of one of the wooden beams that jutted out from the end of the dock, legs hanging over the edge, toes only a few feet above the gentle surface.

Without hesitation, he placed his hands flat on the boards either side of him and pushed himself up and away from the dock.

For a split-second he seemed to hang in the air, weightless, like an astronaut.

Then his feet broke the surface, and as the cold rose up throughout his entire body, so too did an acute feeling of regret.

'Sh–' his cry was cut short; in its place, a sharp intake of breath as his chest was submerged. A fraction of a second later he disappeared beneath the surface, water flooding his nostrils, legs thrashing and arms flailing. He floundered his way back up; his feet hadn't touched anything which might be considered the lakebed, and for a split-second, he imagined there might not even be one. This brought on a wave of unfounded panic that fuelled his ascent back to the surface, leaving the dark and watery abyss beneath him, along with whatever hideous monstrosities that might dwell down there.

As he emerged, he burst into fits of nervous laughter. His hair – which had long been in need of a trim – drooped over his eyes like a fat slug. He brushed it aside and wiped his face.

He screamed, his voice cracked and trembling. '*Fuck*!'

It felt as though his ribs might snap at any second, his chest constricting so tightly that he found himself imagining each of the bones cracking and splintering under the pressure – the noise it would make, the pain he would feel as jagged points breached his lungs, his heart.

He planned on swimming out as far as he could manage, but refrained for a moment, cognisant of the fact that junkies – and even more so those trying to kick the habit like he was – were prone to convulsions and violent seizures. And right now, he felt as though he might be encouraging such an attack.

He tried to focus on his breathing, lips pursed into a tight circle as he inhaled shakily and exhaled just as unevenly. He carried on like this for a minute – the longest of his life, it seemed – before his breathing steadied and he felt his chest begin to relax.

Pushing his arms forward into a tentative breaststroke, he began to swim away from the dock. 'Okay,' he sighed. 'I'm really fucking doing this,' and after a few metres he began to pick up his speed and decided to flip over into a backstroke.

Clouds gathered overhead, blotches of greyish-white against the big blue. It didn't take long for the sun to get lost behind them, and the world noticeably dimmed in its absence.

Realising he'd managed to swim a fair way out from the shore, Elwood gave his arms a rest and allowed himself to drift. He closed his eyes, floating on so much more than water, floating on a wish, a wish for clarity. For change. He wondered if something might happen now. Did he need to will it, or would it happen naturally? Some profound moment perhaps, a cleansing of the soul. A flick of some junkie switch inside his brain from *fuck yeah* to *no thanks*.

He tried to clear his mind, something he'd never been good at. The heroin had helped with that. It had helped with a lot of things, actually, and killed others. He hadn't just lost his family, his life, his career. He'd lost himself too, but could he find that man again? Find him here?

Maybe, but it wouldn't be the same person, he was sure of that. How could he ever be exactly the same again? The heroin had left marks – and not just the hideous track marks on his arm, but ones that ran deeper, that would never be forgotten. Shame, guilt, these were feelings that had a presence in their own right, like a shadow.

At least he'd never be alone.

Why did he suddenly feel uneasy? That word, *alone*, it had stirred something within him. A realisation. He didn't *feel* alone, not right now.

He wasn't alone in the water.

He opened his eyes.

The air had taken on a metallic, coppery scent that he could taste in the back of his throat – could actually feel resting on his tongue like an old dime.

He noticed a dark patch spreading out around him, a gloomy, reddish blotch on the otherwise grey water. Stricken by the thought that it was blood – his blood – he began frantically checking himself, rubbing his arms, his torso, legs, face. Nothing. He couldn't feel any pain, but he was sure it was blood. The smell, the hue, it couldn't be anything else.

It was staining his skin.

This observation both horrified and sickened him, and he could only wonder how long he'd been away with his thoughts, blissfully unaware of the blood spill he'd been drifting in.

He could feel it on him, thick and cloying; there was a weight to it, it seemed. Elwood began to thrash forward, arms rising and falling in panicked strokes as he moved desperately toward the border of this crimson blemish. He needed to be out of it. Not just this particular patch, but the lake altogether – he needed to be back on the dock, back in the villa, fuck, he needed to be back home, back with Grace and El. Back where he belonged.

He slowed his frantic escape to little more than a paddle, turning back to check if he was clear of the murk. He was at least ten feet beyond the borders of the bloody patch, now warped toward the shoreline courtesy of his retreat. There was something unsettling about the trail of red he'd left in his wake though; it looked too rich, too substantial. There was no diminishing end to it which, he considered, could only mean one thing.

It was following him. Not the blood, but something else, something beneath the surface.

Something bleeding.

He picked up his pace again in the direction of the jetty. Heart racing, mind empty save for the intense and desperate need to get away, to get the fuck out of this lake and away from whatever wounded thing was stalking him through the murky depths below.

The dock was no more than thirty feet away now; he could see his clothes folded in a neat pile, and strangely felt an amusing and equally terrifying sense of regret at the decision to skinny-dip. He found himself thinking of the *Vandellia cirrhosa*, a parasitic catfish that could swim into your urethra and cause all kinds of unimaginable pain, and then death. He'd researched them for a book maybe a decade ago, and was now acutely aware that his penis was floating around down there without any protection. And although this was far from the Amazon basin, he couldn't help but wonder *what if?* What if one had escaped from some government lab or some nutjob anarchist had one as a pet and thought it'd pretty fucking hilarious to release that thing into the wild? What if it was on its way to a zoo or some bio research lab, and there was an accident along the way? What if it just rode the fucking rain all the way from South America?

He'd heard they could do that.

He was panicking, his body drenched in cold water and fear. Bottom line; he felt exposed and vulnerable and wanted out. *Now.*

Twenty feet.

The aches were becoming agonisingly painful. Any second now the cramps would set in. His body wasn't accustomed to this sort of exertion; muscles that had long been in hibernation were now awake and complaining profusely. He felt himself slowing down and knew that he was powerless to stop it, his arms growing heavier with each stroke.

He jerked as something touched him; a caress that tickled his Achilles heel, then the ball of his foot, as if something had tried to grab him but failed to secure any kind of grip. He pictured the claw-grabbers they had at A-Luck Arcade back home; he'd never wasted his money on them, but he'd watched others throw theirs away.

Ten feet.

Dumb kids and even dumber adults putting their faith in a shiny claw whose gangly limbs never seemed to grip quite as hard as they should. He imagined one of those below him now, some artificial, robotic claw ascending from the deepest, darkest depths of Lake Chance. Only this time, he was the prize.

Five feet.

He was approaching a wooden ladder nailed to the side of the dock, but before he could get close enough to reach out for the lowest rung, the ladder, the dock, and the world above the water disappeared entirely.

Something gripped his left ankle. A hand, soft but coarse. A gloved hand pulling him beneath the surface with such force that Elwood felt a painful, worrying *click* in his knee. Startled, he yelped, swallowing lake water before his cry could stir even a single bird from any of the surrounding trees.

A flash of white in a cloud of red. His drowning reflection in… glass?

Then darkness. He tried to claw his way back to the

surface but the thing, the bleeding thing that had him in its grip, wouldn't let go. He screamed, letting out the last of his breath as he thrashed and kicked and squirmed. He felt a pinch on the sole of his right foot, the mild sting quickly turning to hideous, searing pain, but the grip on his left loosened and he was able to swim back up toward the surface, teeth gritted, head pounding as he tried desperately to hold his breath.

The silence of the lake and surrounding forest broke as Elwood resurfaced. His laboured gasps and croaked curses disturbed the trees above him.

'What the shit, what the fucking shit is this?' He didn't know if he was seeing things or being attacked. It couldn't be the junk – no, this went beyond that, this was more than some cold-turkey mirage. Something had pulled him down. And not just deeper, either, whatever it was had pulled him back toward the centre of the lake – the dock was at least twenty feet away now. 'Shit,' he shouted. 'Shit shit shit sh –'

His lips kept moving but the words had stopped. Elwood stared, confounded, at the white form now rising through the murky depths beneath him. A cloud of red pigment preceded the lumpy thing, and a thick, metallic reek once again filled the air, invading his nostrils, settling on his tongue and spreading out to the back of his throat. He grimaced, but remained where he was, some small – arguably insane – part of him wondering if this was some kind of profound moment, as warped as it clearly was, maybe this was why he'd come out here. Maybe this was the cleansing.

His eyes widened.

The wounded thing continued its ascent toward the

surface, and as it did, the blood gathered on the surface of the lake began to rise slowly into the air. Drop by drop at first, but soon enough there were whole streams floating up and away from the water. This queer evaporation of sorts continued until entire puddles of blood had formed in the air above the lake, each of them constantly shifting like globules of liquid in zero gravity.

Elwood shook his head, disbelieving, as the dome of a helmet broke the surface a few feet away from him. 'No, no, no. This… this isn't happening.'

Now the shattered visor of the astronaut's helmet, and the endless black that lay beyond the cracked glass.

'Is this real?' he shouted. 'Is this really fucking happening?'

Now the torso, waist, legs. Finally, the boots, which now hung limply just a few inches above the surface of the lake.

He stared up at the astronaut floating above him, the helmet bent downwards, as though whoever – or whatever – was lurking in that shadowy interior was looking right at him.

'What do you want?' he demanded. 'What the fuck are you supposed to even mean?'

The thing remained silent as one limp arm moved like lifeless machinery on an assembly line, the gloved hand – he wasn't sure if there was even a hand in there – reaching across to the other forearm. Elwood could see what appeared to be a small control panel located there; lights blinked red and amber around the tell-tale grid of holes that suggested a speaker. He heard the faint stuttering of white noise as the plump, gloved fingers worked the buttons of the panel.

'Olesk?' he blurted out loud, noticing the patch stitched to the left breast. 'Olesk…' Something stirred deep within him, a memory. He knew that name.

Voices. Low, tinny and distorted, but he could hear them; they were coming from that control panel. The sound felt strangely obscene against the tranquillity of the forest.

A flock of Sandhill cranes erupted from the surface on the far side of the lake, their quiet assembly disturbed by what sounded like a recording of a heated exchange between a group of people. Elwood was easing away now, moving toward the dock, his retreat agonisingly slow as he kept his eyes on the floating spaceman, listening to the conversation with growing curiosity.

'Don't let him – *krrrsh krrrsh krrrrrrsh* – I repeat… do *not* let him in there. Do you hear me, Mills? Over.'

'Roger that, Cap, we got – *krrrsh krrrrsh krrrrrrsh*… Over.'

'Say again, Mills. I didn't *krrrrrrrsh.*'

'*Krrrrsh* override in place, Cap, he's not getting in. Over.'

Elwood continued to listen intently, his eyes fixed on the hideous gloom that lay beyond the smashed visor, wondering if either of the voices he could hear were that of whoever had once occupied the suit.

Olesk.

As though in direct response to this thought, the two speakers were abruptly interrupted by a third voice. Laughter at first; a sinister, swelling chortle, like that of a mad scientist overseeing the awakening of some abominable creation.

'*You'll regret this.*'

'Olesk, get off the – *krrrsh* – and stand down, I repeat, stand *krrrrsh* –'

Olesk.

'I will *not* stand down,' a merciless snarl now.

The interference ceased, as though that menacing voice had chased away all the distortion, and now Elwood could hear the recording with perfect clarity.

'You can't shut me out.' Ominous laughter rose once again. 'I'm the reason we're here. This is *my* mission. It's *my* power, *mine* to understand, *mine* alone to wield… you don't get to shut me away, forget about me, not now. Death, for all of you, before I let that happen.'

'What is this?' Elwood whispered. 'What the fuck is this?'

The darkness within the helmet seemed to have taken on a form all its own now. It was a *thing* – there wasn't a person in that suit at all, not Olesk, not anymore. There was only darkness, and it wanted him. It wanted Elwood. He could feel it, something in the air that clawed at his throat, his body. His mind.

The astronaut raised an arm; slow and without effort, it floated to attention, as though carried only by a lack of gravity. Thin tendrils of blood continued to seep and rise out of the darkened interior of the helmet, joining the now colossal globules of crimson in the air above.

A gloved hand pointed at Elwood, and whatever might pass for eyes within the gloom of its helmet were now surely fixed on him.

The speaker screeched into life again.

'You can't shut me out. You can't forget about me. I will *kill* you. You can't shut me out. You can't forget about me. I will *kill* you. You can't shut me out. You can't forget about me. *I will* kill *you –*'

The words repeated over and over again, like some macabre mantra delivered by an insidious hypnotist. Elwood couldn't even be sure if the words were emanating from the control panel or from within his own skull. He soon realised he was no longer retreating, no longer edging closer toward the safety of the jetty – no, now he was moving closer, moving *toward* the astronaut, toward whatever was lurking in the shadowy interior of that suit.

'What do you want?' he screamed.

'You can't shut me out. You can't forget about –'

'Just shut up, shut up, shut the fuck up,' Elwood cried, still approaching it, still drawing nearer – why? Why the fuck was he getting closer? This wasn't right. This wasn't what he wanted.

'You can't shut me out. Forget. You can't. Forget.'

The floating, dead thing continued its stuttering broadcast in defiance of Elwood's pleas. The air began to redden, the gathering pools of blood in the air above the lake becoming a filter for what little sunlight permeated the clouds, turning the world an ethereal shade of claret.

'Forget. Forget. Forget. You can't. Shut me out. You can't forget. Shut me out. You can't. Can't. Shut me out. Forget. Can't. Can't. Can't. Shut me out.'

It sounded like some artificial intelligence gone wrong. A robot with a few crossed wires, half a glitch away from taking over the ship and *cleansing* all of the crew. Elwood could still feel that thickness in the air though – something yearned for him, groping at his face and trying to claw its way into his mouth and down his throat – it wanted to be inside him.

Wanted to taste him.

Wanted him to come home?

'What the fuck…'

He didn't know what any of this was supposed to mean; hell, he didn't even know where the thoughts were coming from.

Come home?

'Can't forget. Can't shut me out.'

No, he thought. This isn't *home*. None of this is. Home isn't at the end of a needle. Home isn't a powder or a pill or something wrapped in a paper to light and smoke. Home is where the fucking heart is. Home is where you hang your damn hat and take shits on a toilet seat you feel comfortable sitting on. Home is love. Home is warm. Home is *Elouise*. Gracie.

He suddenly found himself back in control, no longer approaching the floating husk that was bleeding into the sky, but moving back toward the dock.

'Fuck this,' he screamed. 'Fuck you. Fuck all of this.'

The astronaut did nothing, just floated – the seemingly-glitched speaker system still blaring out its deranged intonations as Elwood turned away and sped up his retreat toward the shoreline.

For a second he was sure he could he see them, Gracie and El. Standing expectantly at the end of the timber outcrop: Gracie's hand resting on El's shoulder, the girl's head tilted into her mother's waist; both waving lazily. He almost cried out to them, but before he could, they changed.

THOSE YOU KILLED

They weren't his ex-wife, nor his daughter. No, they were death: two standing corpses, grey skin stretched thin over their bones – not waving, but *beckoning*.

Before he could panic enough to begin to flounder, they were gone, and he was able to continue only mildly perturbed. He had bigger fish to fry right now, fish he could still see floating behind him, fish that wore broken spacesuits and drifted around supermarkets and lakes in their spare time, terrorising poor defenceless junkies who were just looking for a clean break.

After what felt like an age, he finally clasped the first rung of the ladder and lifted himself out of the water. The claret shade faded away from the world and the day turned bloodless once again. This abrupt switch was jarring though, and he missed his footing, nearly tumbling back into the water. His shin cracked against the rung below and he let out a pained grunt. He scrambled for purchase, clawing at the boards and only barely managing to avoid falling back into the lake. At that moment, as he pulled himself over the edge of the dock and collapsed in a naked heap against the hard wood, he didn't think he'd go into any body of water ever again for as long as he lived.

Not a damn toe, he decided.

Shuddering, breathless, and feeling like he'd swum a mile in concrete flippers, he reached for the towel beside his clothes and sat up to dry himself off. He looked out to the lake, wrapping the towel around his shoulders and clenching it tightly across his chest.

He was alone, and the lake was just as it had been before he dove in. Quiet, calm, devoid of things that floated and bled.

Some cleansing, Elwood thought. If anything, the ordeal had cleansed him of his sanity.

He'd known there would be hallucinations. He had spoken to enough junkies in his time who were trying to shake the monkey, and had watched dead babies crawling across the ceiling in *Trainspotting* more times than he cared to remember.

This felt different.

He wasn't sure how – he'd never been here before, this far beyond the starting line. And in that respect, could he even trust anything he was feeling?

Still, he couldn't shake the thought of this place, of Lake Chance – the thought that something didn't feel quite right about it; in fact, something felt intrinsically wrong.

There was every chance it was him though – he had brought the wrongness with him like some disease, one that was seeping through his skin and infecting the world around him.

He knew what the answer was. Knew what he truly needed right now, the only thing capable of washing away this uncertainty, this madness. He needed a lifeline, a remedy for what ailed him.

He needed a fix.

And in that moment, he forgot entirely that he'd found strength in his own mantra back there in the water, his own meditation on home, on family, and how neither could be found at the end of a needle. Because although neither of those things could be found in a syringe, peace could. And he needed peace.

He'd come this far – what was it now, day three? That was further than he'd ever gone before, which

133

meant he could do it again.

Just one more hit. And then he could get back to this spot, back to day three, it'd be easy. And next time there'll be a day four, he told himself. And a day five, and a day fucking six-six-six...

All the days.

He'd go all the way. Next time.

But for now, he needed a hit. A last fix, just to get him through this shit.

He finished drying himself off and got dressed, trying to remember where he'd left the keys to the car.

CHAPTER TEN
WHISKEY

He descended the porch steps three at a time and started across the gravel drive in desperate strides, fumbling with his keys as he moved. He dropped them as he neared his car but didn't curse or sigh; he just bent down, picked them up and carried on. He was in a junkie trance now, gripped by a single-minded focus on one thing and one thing alone: the hit.

'Last one. Last one,' he repeated it like so many of the lies people often told themselves. He opened the passenger door and ducked inside, not bothering to close it behind him.

He sat for a moment in self-inflicted anticipation, licking his lips, staring at the glovebox, knowing what was inside, and that it was all his.

'Last one.' His voice was a woozy whisper now, carried away on winds of craving.

His arm jerked forward – more of a muscle spasm

than a reach – and he yanked the glovebox open.

The first thing he saw was the plastic folder containing all the paperwork related to the car. Next, a short stack of Iron Maiden discs he never listened to anymore, an empty cigarette packet, a small LED torch, a pair of broken ear buds, and a disposable lighter.

No heroin.

'No… no, no, *no*.' This wasn't happening. Not now. Not when he desperately needed it.

He pulled out the folder, certain he hadn't put the baggie in there; opened it anyway and dumped the contents on the driver's seat. He muddled through the papers, searching, cursing in hushed whispers.

It wasn't there.

He pulled out the stack of discs and began to open each of the cases one by one; the infamous Eddie the Great stared up at him from each of the album covers in a different guise, mocking him, that skeletal grin suggesting the absurd possibility that he knew where Elwood's fix was. 'You'll never find it, matey,' the skeleton jeered in an unsettlingly jovial British accent.

'Shut up shut up shut *up*,' Elwood gathered them all up in one hand and began to smash them against the head of the gear stick. '*Fucking shut up.*' The clear plastic splintered and cracked in his fist, discs snapped, and within seconds, a collection he'd owned since he was a teenager – a collection of things he'd once held dear – was obliterated.

He hardly spared a thought for this loss. Instead, he reached for the cigarette packet, opened it to check it was definitely empty. It was. He began to tear it apart, his behaviour now verging on something comical, cartoonish, as he ripped it into tiny pieces and discarded them in a flurry, turning the interior of the car into a snow globe.

'Fuck,' he screamed, looking back into the glovebox. He reached in and grabbed the torch, held it up in front of him, twirling it around and inspecting it. He twisted off the bottom and two batteries slipped out onto his lap; he closed one eye and brought the empty cylinder close to this face so he could look inside.

Nothing.

'I put it right there, right there.' He began to pound his fists against the dashboard. 'Right. Fucking. *There*. I put it *right fucking there,* damnit!'

He sat back in the passenger seat, tired, breathless, his chest rising and falling in rapid tides. He tried to cast his mind back to the first night; he was sure he'd put the baggie in the glovebox after that last hit, which was after he'd taken it from – where? Where had it been before?

His wallet. It must've been in his wallet. His thoughts began to race, fuelled by excitement, expectation. Ignorance.

He shifted his weight and reached into his back pocket to retrieve his wallet; with a few awkward tugs, it came free. He held it up to his face as an intrepid explorer might behold a long-lost golden idol, found deep within some forgotten tomb. He unbuttoned the clasp and checked inside. First the coin purse; nothing. The not-so-secret recess behind the coin purse; nope. The card slots, photo windows; all the same.

Sweet fuck all.

He opened up the back, that stretch of space reserved

for notes and receipts; no heroin there either. But among the stash of bills and paper he noticed the frayed edges of that polaroid again, the one taken at the beach. A small part of him, on that had been silent and submissive in the wake of the junkie taking control, spoke up now. It urged him to grab that photo, to pull it out of there right now and look at it – *look at it long and hard* – and think about what the fuck he was doing. The insistence was almost inaudible, the sort of inner whisper so easily lost in impassioned situations.

He did hear it though, acted on it too, reaching in and pulling out the photo with the same care and consideration as an archivist handling some ancient papyrus that might crumble within his grip. He stared at it for a moment – not thinking, just looking, as a child might idly stare at a family portrait purely because their parents had told them to.

But then he began to see. Slowly at first, the veil of addiction and thirst slipping from his eyes as he took in more of the photo.

The single dimple in Gracie's left cheek; she always smiled with the left-side of her mouth and Elwood had always found that cute. The strapless dress she was wearing, the one with the floral print. Faint tan lines visible on her shoulders.

Elouise in her bright pink t-shirt, the one with *My Daddy is a SUPERHERO* emblazoned across the chest in yellow, bubbly text.

Not anymore, he thought. Not now, sweetie. Daddy messed up, messed up big time. And superheroes weren't supposed to do that.

He felt the sting of tears once more; the lump in his

throat which threatened outright blubbering began to rise. Guilt, sharp and unwavering, swelled in his chest again until it cut through the walls of his heart.

They were on vacation. Miami.

'Miami,' he cried out cheerfully. 'I remember…'

Now, he cried.

'Holy shit, I remember. I *remember*. It was… Disney. We took you to Dis–' he trailed off, frowning, remembering a past he'd forgotten, but also the dreadful present that he alone had brought about.

Remembering. An act that felt so foreign to him now, an act reserved for those who considered and reflected on things, not those who stuck needles in their veins to forget. Remembering was kind of like riding a bike; you never forgot how to ride, but you could forget what it felt like.

He reached into his pocket and pulled out a pack of cigarettes. Retrieving one from the carton, he put it between his lips, lit it, and inhaled deeply. He breathed out a thick cloud of smoke and sighed, staring at the empty glovebox.

That had been close. Too close, perhaps. He'd lost control and let something else take the wheel, something weak and needy, but strong enough to possess him and disarm his moralities. And he hadn't been able to beat it alone – it had been the past, a *memory* that had reached into the present and saved him, pulled him back onto the wagon and set him straight again. For now. He held the photo close to his chest, clutched it tightly. The polaroid had become talismanic in some way, an object of power. It had brought him back. He tucked it into his back pocket and decided it would remain on his person for the duration of his stay. Hell, maybe even the rest of his life.

He puffed eagerly at the cigarette, his hands still shaking. It was fear that gripped him now. Fear that he'd nearly fallen off the wagon, that he'd almost let himself down. Fear that he'd almost let his *family* down. Even though they seemed lost to him now – and in a way, they *were* lost – they were more important than ever before.

He needed a drink. Perhaps even one of those joints. There was an edge to him now, a jagged edge that needed to be taken off, and whiskey would help with that. He could fix himself some dinner too; that might help, might give him something to focus on. And later, he could take the time to find out what he could about this place – the lake, the town, and anything else Casper had neglected to mention.

He took a last draw on the cigarette and stubbed it out in the ashtray, retrieving another from his pocket and lighting up before climbing out of the car. The sun had disappeared behind the villa and was setting on the far side of the lake, leaving the driveway in a shade that was steadily darkening. He closed the door behind him and started for the porch, walking tentatively as he tried to regain himself, as one might walk away from an especially dizzying fairground ride.

It was then that the barking began. An aggressive growling that was growing louder; no, closer. Elwood wheeled on his feet, turning to face the surrounding woodland, half expecting some Cujo-like beast to charge at him from the darkness, head bowed and teeth bared in a rabid snarl.

He couldn't see anything at first – and then a white dog burst excitedly from the treeline further up the drive; its back paws skidded on the gravel surface as it froze, haunches raised, looking him right in the eyes; then it started padding down the driveway toward the villa, toward him.

Elwood began to back away. The barks weren't quite as aggressive as he'd initially imagined, but still, this was a dog coming at him in the night – a dog he didn't know.

As it drew closer he noticed that, rather than the rabid scowl he'd envisaged, the dog in fact wore a wide, dumb smile; its tongue lolled from one side of its mouth, thick tails of drool swinging from its jowls. He thought it looked friendly enough – less Cujo and more Beethoven, perhaps. Still, he backed away, hands raised in front of him.

'Easy doggo, easy…'

'Bullseye,' a shout from the woods. 'Bullseye!'

The voice was stern, aged. Elwood glanced up from the approaching hound for a second and spied movement amidst the darkened woodland further up the drive. His heel struck the bottom step of the porch as the dog waded through the thicket of weeds that had claimed the area to the front of the villa. He sat down roughly on the steps and braced himself for the imminent impact; in his peripheral vision he could see a shadowy figure walking briskly down the drive toward the house, still calling after the dog.

'Bullseye, God damnit, get back here.'

The accent was thick: *Bullsah, Gad damnit –*

Then the dog's front paws came down on his chest

and Elwood's world abruptly turned to so much hot dog breath and drool.

'Bullseye, you son of a –'

He couldn't see the man now; the dog, Bullseye, was stood on his hind legs, pawing excitedly at Elwood's chest as he licked at his face.

'Bullseye. You leave that man alone now.'

Elwood still couldn't see the man – he was too busy making a fuss of the dog now, who was starting to calm down a little. 'Good dog, easy now. Good boy.'

'Sorry about that, friend.' Elwood looked up and saw the man was standing near the car. 'Bullseye. Come on now, get off of him.'

The dog stared at Elwood for a moment longer, gave him a final lick across the cheek with a tongue that felt like sandpaper dipped in wallpaper paste, then slowly backed away, using his front paws to push himself away from Elwood. Bullseye trotted sullenly back toward the man, who remained by the car.

'Why you gotta act stupid like that, huh?'

Elwood climbed to his feet and brushed himself off. His shirt was covered in dirty paw prints, and he could feel patches of cold moisture on his face. He wiped away the drool on the back of his sleeve and forced a smile for the man. 'No bother,' he offered, looking down at the dog, who was now laying at the old man's feet, leg's outstretched and tail wagging. 'We had a dog just like him when I was a kid. A Terrier, right? Staffordshire?'

'Sure is,' the man replied. 'And normally he listens – he listens *good* – but he saw the light, and we don't often see the light around here these days.'

Elwood frowned. 'The light?'

The old man pointed up at the villa. Elwood turned, saw that he'd left a light on inside.

'Oh, the *light*.'

The man was old, but spritely, his trim build and straight posture both signs of an active life; Elwood guessed the guy probably walked these woods daily, and knew them well. He wore a camo parka with the hood drawn down; a well-worn Mountaineers football cap sat limply on his head, and something in his mouth caught the light of the moon as he smiled. A gold tooth, perhaps.

'We don't get too many visitors round these parts anymore.'

'Yeah, I heard,' Elwood replied, with a sigh that didn't go unnoticed by the old man. 'I'm sorry, I don't mean to sound like an asshole, I mean, I didn't expect it to be so... empty. I wasn't prewarned about the situation.'

The old man nodded knowingly and grinned. 'Thought somebody was doing you a favour? Didn't your momma ever tell you there ain't no such thing as a free turd? Even those babies cost you time,' he chuckled to himself and knelt down to stroke the almost-sleeping dog.

Elwood laughed with him. He seemed nice enough. 'You bet,' he replied. 'It's one of the lessons I always seem to forget, though. I'm Elwood, by the way.' He started forward, hand outstretched ready to shake. The old man stood, still smiling, but there was something in his eyes that Elwood didn't much like. Apprehension, perhaps. He cringed with embarrassment, hating the idea of this seemingly nice man being weary of him, even afraid. He didn't want anybody to feel that way about him. 'I –' he stumbled. 'I'm not a bad guy, honestly, just…' he sighed.

How did you tell a stranger about all of your shit? How did you not mention heroin, even when it was written all over your face?

'I just took a wrong turn, friend, and now I'm trying to find my way back. That's all. I'm not a bad person, at least I'm not trying to be. Not anymore.'

The old man studied him momentarily, his eyes searching for any hint of insincerity; there was none. His gait shifted and he relaxed a little. He stepped forward and offered his hand, much to Elwood's relief – and pleasure, in fact; like his feeling of normality in the supermarket buying essentials, he now felt a sense of civility, friendliness. Junkies didn't shake hands with their dealer or with fellow addicts, they exchanged, they stole, and sometimes they hurt. The old man saw the joy clearly in Elwood's face though, the joy in this so often dismissible formality, and his smile now turned to a frown of mild guilt.

'Don't mind me. If you'd been walking these woods long as I have, you'd understand my prudence.' He knelt back down and resumed stroking the dog. 'Name's Bob, folks round here call me Whiskey though.'

Elwood decided it might be a good idea to invite Whiskey in, get his information the old-fashioned way – through word of mouth, if the old man was willing to talk. He considered briefly whether it might also help ease the minds of the local law enforcement too. People talked in towns like this one, and maybe a good word from Bob would find its way to the right people, and possibly delay a visit from Sheriff Tims. Hell, maybe even prevent one.

He knew he still looked like shit, the lake hadn't helped with that; he wasn't even sure if the lake had helped in any way at all, save for scaring the shit out of him.

Olesk.

Right now though, he needed to be friendly – he needed to be hospitable as *fuck* if he wanted this to work. He needed to be himself; not the junkie, not even the recovering junkie, just Elwood.

'Pleasure to meet you, Bob,' he said.

The old man shrugged this off. 'Call me Whiskey, son. Like I say, folks round here call me that, and right now you're one of those folks. You might not be forever, but you are for now. My Jeanie always said you should treat people like there ain't nothing either side of them, you know? She was my wife, God keep her.' He marked the holy trinity. Elwood thought of OJ again.

'I think I get that,' Elwood replied. 'No past, no future, right?'

The old man smiled, his attention still on stroking Bullseye. 'You got it. I ain't talking to who you were, and I ain't talking to who you're going to be. I try my best to remember that, it's what she would've wanted. Lord knows she reminded me enough of it while she was here.'

'She sounds like a good woman,' Elwood offered. 'I'm sorry for your loss.'

'Oh, no need for that, going on a decade and a half

now since she passed.'

That settled it. He'd invite the old man to stick around. He was clearly the forthcoming type – the naturally friendly type, the type that didn't judge. Elwood needed that now more than ever.

'Say, it's pretty lonely out here, and so far the only guest I've had is Officer Janet.' Bob's eyebrows perked at that. 'Would you join me for a drink? I'd like to find out some more about this place, and you seem like the right person to talk to. Honestly, it'd just be nice to talk with a welcoming person. It's been a while.'

The old man considered this momentarily.

'I've got coffee,' Elwood added. 'Pepsi, too. And whiskey,' he said, hoping the latter might sway him. It was the man's moniker, after all.

'He'll be needing his chow soon,' the old man patted the dog's pink stomach. Bullseye was pretty much fast asleep now. 'Still got to walk back to the old store at Crescent tip too, I don't like to leave my ride there too late – damn kids take their girls out there and cause all kinds of trouble. I can't say much, though,' he tittered. 'I was one of them, once upon a long time ago. Took my Jeanie out there when we were courting. Kiss my tip at Crescent tip, that's what we used to say.'

Elwood couldn't help but laugh at that, although he was somewhat disappointed with the brush-off. 'I understand,' he replied.

Perhaps the disappointment was clear on his face, or in the tone of his reply; either way, the old man looked at him thoughtfully. 'You said you have whiskey?'

'Sure do,' Elwood smiled.

The old man pondered this. 'How about vodka?'

'Half a bottle of the Goose in there.'

'Well,' he grinned. 'Since you *caught* the Goose, I may as well stick around some.'

A few minutes later the two of them were settled on the terrace out back. Elwood had borrowed a couple of chairs from the dining table and found an old, rusted iron side-table laying in the overgrown grass. This decaying-yet-ornate piece now stood between the two of them; Elwood poured vodka into two glass tumblers perched crookedly on its surface. The terrier had mooched off into the tall grass and weeds beyond the paved area, and the two men sat and sipped as the sun began to set behind the trees on the far side of the lake. The clouds had taken on pinkish, purple tones, scattering to reveal a glorious amaranthine sky that was quickly darkening as the night drew ever closer.

'So, what's with the name?' Elwood asked. 'I offer whiskey to Whiskey and he sits here drinking vodka.' The two of them sniggered at this.

'Well, my granpap and *babcia* came from Poland. They were getting away from all that *Kulturkampf* bullshit Bismarck cooked up, and like most folks they brought their name with them too – which is *Scotchni*.'

Bullseye appeared from the jungle of weeds, panting gently and looking relatively satisfied with his exploration of the area.

'Come here, boy,' the old man said. The dog ambled over to where they were sat, sniffed at Bob's knees briefly, and then lay down on the paved stonework between his feet. 'Lots of them Poles settled in Illinois, but my people came down here to Misstonville. My granpap worked the old quarry right up to the day it closed – everyone called him Whiskey, on account of the scotch in his name. My pa had the same nickname too, so I'm a third-generation Whiskey. Funny thing is, Poles love their vodka.' He chortled at this and affirmed his words by downing the rest of the glass.

Elwood joined him and offered to pour them both another.

'I think one more should be fine,' the old man smiled. 'Much obliged, Elwood.'

'You're welcome. Do you mind if I smoke?'

'Don't smoke myself, but I've never minded those that do. You go ahead, light on up.'

Elwood did. 'You've lived here your whole life, then?'

'Sure, we travelled – Jeanie and me – seen what we wanted to see, even went back to the old country, but we always called this home.'

'What can you tell me about this place?'

The old man laughed at this. 'What do you want to know? I ain't no historian or nothing.'

'Sorry, I mean the lake and the woods, I…' he trailed off, trying to find the right approach. Did he just come out and say it? Spill the beans to Bob on everything he'd seen so far, plus his fear that it might just be his cold-turkey-fried brain playing tricks on him? Or how he'd felt the astronaut's grip, actually *felt* it – and the cut, the short gash on his heel, surely he wasn't imagining that. He could feel it, for Christ's sake, he could feel it right now, a low sting that tickled the sole of his foot.

'The lake and woods, you say?'

'I guess – just your experience of the area, anything that comes to mind.'

The old man looked at him thoughtfully over the rim of his glass as he took another sip. 'You see something out here, Elwood?'

Still pondering. Still deliberating on how much he should share. Elwood didn't want to lie to this man, this kind-natured man who'd sat down with him and had looked him in the eyes with something that wasn't disgust.

'You mean what you said before? About not judging a man,' he asked.

'I try my best, and that's more than can be said about most folk.'

'So, if I told you some things, things about me… things I've seen. You'd keep that to yourself?'

'Of course, a man's business is his business. Ain't for nobody else to talk about.'

Elwood believed him. Wanted to believe him, anyway. Bob seemed like a nice man, a man he could trust. He'd known him less than half an hour, but he was certain of that much.

Or did he perhaps just want to believe this old man could help him in some way? Was he desperate enough to risk Bob going away from here and telling people the guy staying out at the lake by himself was stark-raving mad (and a nervous wreck of a junkie to boot)?

Fuck it, he thought. He had nothing to lose. If the old man talked and that talk brought suspicion, trouble even, then he could leave. He wasn't a prisoner, after all. At least, not of Lake Chance.

Elwood threw caution to the wind and proceeded to spill all to this stranger. He told Whiskey about Grace and Elouise, the heroin, the divorce. He told him about the first appearance of the astronaut on the balcony, then at the ConveeMart in town, in the kitchen in the villa – and just an hour or so before, out on the lake.

As he talked, he recalled smaller things too, those so easily forgotten – like a road sign you only notice at the last second, just as you drive by. Fleeting things that don't stay in our lives long enough to sit anywhere else but within our subconscious.

He mentioned the trip to the old store at the end of the road – *kiss my tip at Crescent tip* – and the jangling syringes Kenner had held.

He told him about the pale figures waving at him from the end of the dock.

The one thing he neglected to mention was the missing heroin. He knew he'd put the baggie in the glovebox, he was certain of that. But he didn't think Bob needed to know about it – not out of fear, or nervousness, but *shame*. He'd told this man he was trying to clean up his life, trying to find his way back to the right path, to his family. He didn't want to tell him that he'd also brought some *just-in-case* skag with him.

It felt good to lay it all out on the table, to tell someone. Even if that someone was a stranger – hell, maybe that made it better, maybe it was easier this way.

Elwood swigged the rest of his vodka and began to pour another. 'Think I'm crazy yet?'

The old man was contemplative, his expression one of quiet consideration. He too drank the last of his vodka and placed the tumbler gently back down on the table.

'Another?' Elwood asked, still holding the bottle.

Bob shook his head. 'It's a long walk back to town –

if I have another, that's what I'll be doing. I wouldn't frown at a cup of coffee though, if it ain't too much of a burden on you.'

Elwood returned a few minutes later with a mug of sugarless white, as requested, having left the old man out on the terrace to ponder over what he'd shared.

'Thank you kindly,' Bob said, as Elwood set the mug down on the table for him and fetched another cigarette from his pack. The old man picked up the drink and held it below his chin, blowing into the steamy brew to try and cool it down a little. His face was still one of calculated thought as he took his first tentative sip. 'You say you don't know if what you're seeing is just your mind, or that stuff – the drugs – playing tricks on you, or if this place is just plain old haunted?'

'That's right,' Elwood agreed.

'I say it's probably both,' Whiskey proffered.

Elwood felt the hairs on the back of his neck prickle.

The old man took another sip of his coffee and held the mug in his lap. 'I've heard a lot; shit, I've probably seen just as much too. Bad folk doing bad things,' he laughed a little. 'Even some good folk doing bad things too. Most would tell you that shit happens everywhere, and they'd be right.'

He stared out across the lake, his eyes pensive. Steam rose thinly from the mug he now cradled in both hands.

'This place is different from most, though. Not bad, not exactly, but… wrong, in some ways. It's hard for me to explain. I ain't never been into all that hippie hooha, but when those tripped-out kids talk about essences and auras, and all the *vibes*, I think maybe this place has some of that. A lot of it. But it ain't right.'

'Why do you still walk around here, then?' Elwood asked. 'I mean no disrespect, but your average Joe doesn't normally choose to go walking in haunted woods, right?'

Bob laughed knowingly. 'I guess I just always had that idea that if you don't go looking for trouble, then trouble ain't going to come looking for you. I know that isn't always the case, but here, I think it is.'

'What do you mean?' Elwood asked. He downed the last of his vodka and lit another cigarette. He decided against pouring another. He'd had one more than Bob now and that was enough; carrying on would only mean him getting drunk with a sober guest, and Elwood figured that would be pretty damn rude of him.

'Well, I don't know. I guess I'm pretty much a simple man, Elwood, to some degree anyways. I don't want for nothing. I don't desire. I ain't greedy, or bitter, or resentful either. I'm too old for all that nag shit.'

Elwood nodded and the old man continued.

'So, I come down here, but I don't come down here looking for nothing. When bad folk – folk with demons, folk with greed and designs and such – when folks like that come to some place like this, where there's... I don't know, vibes or whatever the hell it is. It works on them. It works on them like a blade whittling down a stick.' He frowned. 'My Jeanie was into all that hippie hooha – she liked to read a lot too, could've told you better than I. She talked a lot with that Christie lady in town too. Now that girl, Aubrey Christie, she'll tell you things you wouldn't believe.' He gulped down the last of his coffee. 'Main reason I don't mind walking these parts, though, is because nobody else walks them anymore. I like the peace and quiet. So does he,' he nodded at the dog.

'You think I'm seeing this shit because of both; my head *and* this place? Do you think it's the—' he stopped himself. He didn't even want to say the word out loud anymore. 'You think I'm vulnerable or something?'

'Probably ain't making it any easier for you, that's for sure.'

Elwood was still trying to process the idea, the absurd nature of it. *Last Chance Lake, a new nightmare from Elwood Cathis.* That was what this all sounded like, a fucking book, just another scary paperback lining shelves that were closing in on him.

'What have you seen? Any astronauts or dead girls waving at you?'

'No, nothing like that. What I've seen is quite a few of your sort though. Folks with their own demons – this place latches onto that.'

'The Deputy called this place a rehab, why would she say that? Do you always get guys like me staying out here?'

'Sure. Twice, maybe three times a year. They don't last long. Few days and we never see them again. They probably pack up and leave once they get a feel for the place. Decide to run back to whatever it was they were running from. Some folk have done bad things though, real bad things. Others have just gone missing, out there.' He pointed toward the trees.

'I'd like to hear more about those people. I can make you another coffee, and I'll be happy to walk back to your car with you.'

The old man chortled. 'Boy, you fixing to get your

tip kissed at Crescent tip? I'll be fine making my own way back.'

'So, does that mean you'll stay a while longer?' Elwood asked.

'Sure,' Whisky grinned. 'I'll take another vodka in that coffee though, if it ain't too much trouble.'

CHAPTER ELEVEN
DAYTON'S LAST RIDE

Dayton was torturing himself, seeing things that couldn't possibly be there. That was it. That had to be it. There couldn't be any other explanation, because the truth was harsh and unforgivingly simple; there was nothing else. You didn't go anywhere else after you died – there was no heaven, no hell, and you didn't stick around either to walk the earth and haunt those left behind.

The shapes in the shadows had been undeniable though, the whispers; things he couldn't explain, couldn't fit into a logical thought process that aligned with his long-held perception of the world.

He needed to know.

Were they all just manifestations of his own guilt? A guilt he didn't even believe existed – and why should it? He didn't feel bad, he felt *liberated*, free from the burdens that had shackled him to a place and a life he had no love for, no desire to be part of.

No, he wasn't torturing himself, but he clung to the thought in blissful ignorance, as the dying do, with their faith in those pearly gates.

Maybe he hadn't done it right. He wondered if he'd missed something, hadn't checked properly. And then what? Had they just followed him? Followed him back from whence he'd taken them almost eight weeks ago now, that quiet place in the nameless copse of trees about a mile south of the old Mills Ranch?

The place where he'd buried them.

He took the next exit and left I-19 behind him, moving onto country roads that snaked their way through moonlit creeks and hollers. He wondered what he might find out there; the dead? Or not?

The dead? *Or not?*

That ghoulish voice in his head began to recite the words with childish excitement; the dead? or not? the dead? or not? Like some nightmarish *loves me, loves me not* – but instead of picking petals from a flower to help him reach a conclusion, this tore away at his mind, his sanity, piece by piece.

But damn, it felt good. *She* felt good.

Dayton passed the sign for Warr Liveries again, the last operating and occupied homestead this side of the interstate, and began to ease off the gas pedal. The sign had changed since his last trip; apparently there were no longer any vacant stables, and the advice from Mama EJ, painted in black on a strip of wood and hung with chains over the sign, was to *Check Macintyre's off TR-5 West.* The car's headlight beams washed over the sign only for a brief moment; the words painted in black gleamed, as though Mama EJ might've walked away with her dripping brush only minutes before. Then the sign and the turnoff were both lost to the darkness.

Dayton recalled his last meeting with Mr Rodeo Dickweed Macintyre.

'When I see you again, Kakky Maccy,' Dayton sneered. He spoke out loud because it was what *she* wanted.

And *she* was in control.

'I'm going to hang you up and peel you like a fucking orange. I'm going to snip off your eyelids first, so you have to look at me while I do it. And you'll *look* at me, cowboy. Then I'll cut off your balls too, rip out some of your veins and feed it all to you like the spaghetti and meatballs your grandma use to make.'

He howled, thumping the wheel triumphantly. He looked in the rear-view and imagined Mr Rodeo sat there in the back seat, hands tied behind his back, dirty rag stuffed in his mouth, sweat on his brow and fear in his eyes.

'I'd take you somewhere, somewhere out of the way, somewhere dark and dead to the world. Maybe I'll bring your itty-bitty titty-sucking shitter of a boy too. Feed his fingers and toes to his dear old daddy.' Dayton was breathing heavily now, his shoulders rising with each laboured breath. The grin on his face began to wane.

Once again, he felt as though he'd lost himself for a moment. He had no idea he'd even spoken, remembering only that he'd passed the sign for Mama EJ's, which meant that he was close.

The sedan trundled along slowly, and he kept his eyes on the treeline to the left, knowing the next turn had his name written all over it. Theirs too, in fact, but only in his mind; nobody else would ever know. If he'd done things properly, that was. There would be no sign – *turn left here for the historic final resting place of Meredith and Laney Mitcham* – and there would be no gravestone, no marker, no epitaph to a *devoted wife and mother, cherished daughter, taken too soon, heaven now had two more angels* blah de blah de blah.

He wondered if his feelings about murdering his wife and daughter would ever be anything more than cathartic. Remorseful, maybe? Perhaps even sorrowful? Not while he was in *her* grip, *she* wouldn't let such diseases fester in his heart; not as long as he remained a willing vessel.

He tried to remain focused on the road and passing forest; any second now those trees on the left would give way to that same dirt road he'd driven along all those weeks ago, his lifeless passengers sprawled in the back seat.

Had they been lifeless?

He finally came upon the turning, speeding up just a little as he steered the car off the tarmac and onto the dirt. He followed the road for a few miles through pitch-black forest, then out into the forgotten pastures of the Kinawa Valley. He passed the turnoff for the abandoned abattoir – suddenly thinking of that idiot rancher Macintyre, though he had no idea why. He couldn't see the derelict buildings where so much blood had been spilled, not even their silhouettes, not tonight.

Tonight, the world was darker.

He followed the road for another fifteen minutes before reaching a dead end, and the entrance to the old Mills Ranch. He parked up in front of the chain barrier and climbed out of the car, leaving the headlights turned on so he could see what he was doing. Behind him, the engine thrummed rhythmically.

The branch, which he'd propped against the spot on the old gatepost where the steel chain was hooked, was now lying among the weeds at the side of the road. He couldn't recall any particularly windy days since that night, and even if the wind had knocked it over, it would've fallen at the base of the gatepost, not five feet away. He tried not to think about it too much. Punk kids maybe, a drifter.

Or maybe it had been *them*.

Dayton removed the chain from the post and set it down on the ground, then returned to his car and drove it in. After fixing the chain back up, he began to make his way down the long drive toward the farmhouse and outbuildings. As he approached, forms began to take shape in the dark: the chimney stack that sat atop the crooked roofline of the derelict homestead; the old Ford pickup that Isiah Mills had decided to park up against the barn one day in 1979 and never start up again.

The barn itself was imposing; the night made it feel cyclopean, something huge and hard to comprehend, a remnant of an old world that refused to be put down, refused to go without a fight. He thought of his wife and daughter again, thought he could see them in fact; their silhouettes moving without motion, as though some hidden conveyer belt was carrying them away from the barn, onto the trail which led through the back pastures and toward the woodland beyond. Their heads bowed as they moved slowly, like some nocturnal funeral procession.

He stalled the car and cursed out loud. They weren't there, they couldn't be there. People didn't move like that, he told himself – unless you were the prince of fucking pop or Nosferatu, people just didn't move like that. It wasn't natural, wasn't right.

He started the car again and when he looked up the figures were gone, faded from his imagination.

'Enough,' he screamed. 'Just – *enough*!'

He was at the barn now, passing the old Ford. Weeds and tall grass jutted out from the rusted hood and shattered windows, swaying gently in the evening breeze. The farmhouse flanked him to the right, forgotten and crumbling. A wind chime still hung from the porch awning and clinked softly, melodically even, breaking the stillness of the night. The sound was like an invitation, a yearning plea to enter: *come inside Dayton, come into the darkness... be our guest, forever.* He thought of mermaids and their harmonic wails, drawing ill-fated sailors to the rocks to die. Those sea dogs were doomed without knowing.

But not him, no. Not Dayton Mitcham.

He continued along the road as it began to veer south. He passed more agricultural ruins as he drove; the same empty storage sheds, the dilapidated farrowing house, the old stable block and the fallen sycamore that had crashed down through its roof. The place was dead and forgotten, as were the things that resided here. Wasn't that why he'd brought them to this place? To be left to lie like everything else – left to rot, left to be forgotten.

Only they hadn't been, it seemed.

He reached the back of what might be considered the populated area of the farmstead. The gate which led out into the pastures – and the trail to the woods – was still closed, just as he'd left it. He decided this time he'd save his car the ordeal of the rough terrain beyond the rusty old gate. Last time, there hadn't been any choice in the matter; he'd had his cargo to consider. Carrying two dead bodies for at least a mile, along an uneven dirt track, in the dark… well, it just wasn't practical.

He followed the road as it looped back on itself and eventually opened onto a courtyard at the back of the farmhouse. On the left side of the yard there was an empty carpool; the roof had given way at one end of the shelter and now slanted toward the ground. It looked as though there was just enough space for him to park under it without scratching the roof of his car, though.

He heard the faint clink of the wind chime again as he killed the engine and stepped out into the night. Across from the carpool, on the opposite side of the dusty, overgrown courtyard, was a much smaller barn. This one didn't have a hayloft, and felt considerably less imposing than the behemoth out front. Only one of the plank doors remained, hanging like a dislocated appendage from one hinge and rocking gently in the intensifying breeze. Fallen roof tiles peppered the weedy stonework of the yard; crushed beer cans and joint ends littered the steps of the back porch and he wondered just how forgotten this place truly was.

What if he'd been seen? Some dumb kids from St Crane, or Ellis Ford High over in Brocktowe; out here getting stoned, drinking beers, getting their fingers wet, then they see headlights. What if some punk kid saw him? Saw what he did?

For all he knew, the police could be out here waiting

for him, camped out in the woods and playing the long stakeout, knowing his head would be screwed and he'd be driven back to this place at some point in the future. Wasn't that a thing on the cop shows? Killers always returned to the scene of the crime. Sometimes for souvenirs, or to gloat.

Sometimes, to check that whoever they'd killed had actually stayed dead.

A ridiculous thought, but he entertained it nonetheless.

If somebody had seen him, and that somebody had told the police – maybe even caught his plates – he'd be locked up in county already. Shit, he might even be standing before a jury right now. Things could move pretty quick when kids and their mothers were being murdered.

The stick. What if the stick at the front gate had been moved this very evening? A gang of teens just looking for a good time out at the old Mills place. They would've heard his car before they saw him, they would've had time to hide, maybe duck into the darkness of the farmhouse, or the barn, huddled in a shadowy corner. Dialling mommy and daddy for help, or 911.

He breathed in deeply; no marijuana or tobacco, no cheap perfume. Nothing.

He crossed the courtyard and peaked inside the barn for good measure. It appeared that only leaves, dust and at least two used condoms called this place home. More empty beer cans were gathered in a far corner, and someone had sprayed *CB luvz JW* in neon green paint against the back wall. He wondered if *CB* and *JW* had seen him that night, witnessed what he'd done, heard his car while they were bumping uglies in the corner of this decrepit barn.

He stepped away from the open doorway and headed back across the courtyard toward the dirt road, reminding himself again that he hadn't been arrested, nobody had asked any questions, and nobody had come for him.

Yet.

He walked back briskly the way he'd driven, hands stuffed into the pockets of his navy parka, jaw pressed tightly into the collar. He could see his breath escaping in misty plumes as he moved arduously up the hill. The ranch sat on a gradual incline to the south and summited at the back of the property, where the open fields and pastures began. He was gasping for air by the time he reached the gate at the crest a few minutes later, the first beads of sweat beginning to gather across his brow. He cursed them both again for doing this to him. When he and Meredith had met he'd been an impressively trim one-hundred-forty-four pounds, but romance, more often than not, bred contentedness, and contentedness was only a mask that laziness wore. By the time Laney was born he was almost one-ninety, and the last time he was weighed, which had been that appointment with Doc Wintrell, he'd clocked in at a whopping two-thirty-nine.

Yes, they'd made him content all right; made him lazy and made him fat.

He passed through the gate and crossed the barbed wire borderline between the farm proper and the fields beyond. He stood for a moment and surveyed the route ahead; unkempt grassland descended steadily for almost a mile toward the south, before hitting the black mass of nameless woodland. The large copse of trees looked like an inkblot on the dark horizon – solid and uninviting, it revealed no glimpse of what might lay within. He knew, though; knew they were waiting. Dead or alive they'd be waiting for him, waiting in the dark.

He retrieved his phone from his breast pocket and turned on the lens flashlight. He'd need to see where he was treading; the terrain ahead was lumpy, beset by canyon-like scars left by decades-old John Deere tracks. He took his first cautious step, eyes on the ground; the last thing he needed right now was a sprained ankle or a twisted knee.

It took him the better part of twenty minutes to descend the field and reach the treeline. There'd been some rainfall since his first visit, turning much of the path to sludge and puddles, which made the going slow. The path continued to follow the perimeter of the field along the edge of the woods, fading into black only a few feet ahead of him; he assumed it carried on around the entire field and eventually led back to the gate he'd entered through – not that it mattered though, he'd never be walking that trail, he had a route and he was sticking to it. Corpse disposal, he'd learned, was a pastime that required not just careful planning, but a steadfast desire to stick to the plan. To the fucking letter. If you went off script, started improvising and taking unnecessary risks or indulging in flights of fancy, you were apt to find yourself meeting old sparky, and doing your very own rendition of the electric jig.

Listen to yourself, he thought, sounding like a
regular John Wayne Gacy. He laughed to himself in the
dark, inexplicably pleased by the comparison he'd
drawn, and seemingly forgetful of the fact that returning
to the Mills ranch had never been part of the plan, had
never been part of *her* plan. But she was letting him
anyway.

He shone his torch across the treeline, searching for
the opening through which he'd entered through last
time – a spot where the barbed wire fence had been
flattened, as though some giant perhaps wandered these
forgotten lands, a giant that probably ate wild deer for
breakfast, slept on sweeping riverbanks, and perhaps
watched, and saw things, saw Dayton.

He thought of that troll movie Meredith had insisted
they watch some years back; he'd hated it, but he
remembered those trolls now, imagined casting his
torch beam along the treeline and revealing a giant,
hairy foot, toes as big as his sedan. The ankle and leg
would rise up into the darkness like some ancient
sequoia tree. The foot would slowly lift up, pulling earth
and roots with it, casting a great shadow over him and
disappearing into the night for just a brief moment
before appearing again, and the last thing he would ever
see would be the mud-stricken sole of that foot.

He guessed this was some sort of fucked-up
metaphor for his life, but he didn't dwell on it. He
pushed giant troll feet to the back of his mind and placed
them on the same shelf where the dead faces of
Meredith and Laney lived, next to his relationship with
his mom, and just a little further down from that one
time he and Kirk had *experimented* in college.

He came across the spot he was looking for soon enough, gasping as he cast his torch over the area. Did he just see someone? He could have sworn he had, a trailing arm on the other side of the barbed wire, as though someone had crossed the threshold less than a second before he shone his light there. Had it been a woman's arm? A child's maybe? And had he seen something glint? He had. Something had caught what little moonlight there was out here, something metallic, serrated…

'Fuck you,' he called out, having no idea what he was expecting in return.

But then a reply came.

A reply that made his skin crawl, made him want to tear his ears off and bury them in the sludge beneath his now-shaking feet.

It was his wife. His dead wife. She was calling out to him from the trees:

'Dayday… Dayyydayyyy… Dayyydayyyyyyyyy…'

The pet name she'd so affectionately bestowed upon him didn't have quite the same ring to it when it became a haunting wail in the night.

'Dayyyyydayyyyyy,' the voice was ethereal – distant, but too close.

Dayton tried to home in on where exactly it was coming from, but he couldn't; it was everywhere. He was sure she was in the woods. No – further along the path, perhaps. Wait, that wasn't right either, now she was behind him, in the field somewhere –

Then a whisper in his ear. '*Dayday.*'

He flinched, startled not just by her voice, but by the breath he felt on the nape of his neck, hot, dead breath;

prickly, it reeked of rot and betrayal.

'You shouldn't be here, Meredith,' he called out weakly. 'I killed you.'

Now the playful laughter of a young girl permeated the darkness.

'Laney?' he cried. 'Laney, is that –' a hand brushed the back of his knee.

'Tag, you're it, daddy.'

He cried out, turning quickly to face her – to face his dead daughter – but there was nobody there. Only the field, the darkness, and more chuckling, faint now and growing fainter.

This was getting out of hand, seeing or hearing things was one thing, but *feeling*?

The torch beam had become jumpy and unstable. He realised he was trembling all over.

Dayton took a few moments to compose himself, casting his torch back along the fence. He found the spot again; it appeared clear this time, no trailing arm or glint of a blade in the darkness, only the barbed wire, flattened and gesturing him in like an open-armed host.

And in spite of his confusion and growing trepidation, he pressed hesitantly onwards.

CHAPTER TWELVE
REFLECTION

Elwood couldn't sleep. He'd been drifting in and out of wakefulness for the better part of two hours; Whiskey had left him with plenty to ponder on. Thoughts and theories swam through his restless mind. Dreams, dark and disturbing, plagued the fleeting periods of slumber he was occasionally able to fall into. He could never remember what he saw, only that whatever it was scared the holy shit out of him on some deep and unexplainable level, a level that he was still trying to find his way down to.

What he'd found his way to though, and what he did know, was that heroin addiction and cold turkey were the same thing. Both were a shovel. One piled on the dirt and buried everything you once were. The other dug it all back up; thoughts, feelings, memories, even morals and virtues. But perhaps it was unearthing something else too, something he hadn't brought with him, something that had been waiting for him here, at

Lake Chance.

He recalled a story Bob had told him about Celia Dawes, the teenage daughter of a wealthy New Hampshire couple, Lyle and Claudia Dawes. They vacationed at the lake during the Golden Age of capitalism – what some considered the lake's heyday – the conservative fifties. Whiskey had been a student at the time and had spent several of his summer breaks working out at the lake as a sort of unqualified handyman. Whiskey Senior had always called him a *thisandthatter*, and that's exactly what he'd done: a bit of *this* and a bit of *that*. Mowing lawns, pruning bushes, cleaning cars, waxing boats, even cycling to and from town to pick up groceries for some of the older and lazier out-of-towners.

From fifty-one to fifty-five he served the seasonal residents of Lake Chance: some he would meet only once; others who returned year on year would come to know him by his nickname, and Celia had been one of those. Her folks had never known him – they'd talked to him, given him jobs to do, crossed his palm with greenbacks in exchange for services rendered – but they'd never known him, never called him Whiskey. They'd been what Bob had always thought of as the worst kind of money; not the kind that looked down their noses at you and scoffed, but the kind that didn't notice you at all. The type of people who were blissfully oblivious to anyone that didn't shop where they shopped, or attend the social gatherings they so often graced with their presence.

Celia had been different though, and over the course of her vacation that first summer in fifty-one, she and

Bob had become good friends. It had never been anything more than that; he'd hastened to add that he was already a couple of years into his courtship with Jeanie at the time and very much in love with her. But they talked, walked in the woods sometimes and shared a secretive beer or two on occasion. Her parents were prissy, but she certainly wasn't. She would regularly sneak away during the evenings and join the local teens up at Crescent Tip. Bob had seen her there a few times, always loud and having a good time, just like any other kid letting off some steam – and yes, he'd also heard that she'd kissed her fair share of tips out at the Tip.

Whiskey hadn't been the only kid who worked out at the lake during those barmy summers though; Wesley Levant, an African American boy from Earlswood on the south side of town, also earned his weekend spends as a *thisandthatter*. He and Bob became friends; truth be told, Bob had never known of the boy before that summer. There was a special school over in Earlswood for all the African American kids and they all pretty much kept to themselves over on that side of town. Bob had never been one for all that segregation-bullshit, but he'd been a kid at the time, and it was the fifties, and… well, that's just how things had been.

Celia and Wesley got close though. And it turned out she did more than just kiss his tip at Crescent Tip during that first summer.

The following year the Dawes family returned to Misstonville and Lake Chance. Celia had changed, though. Whilst Bob had been studying back at college, and Wesley had been working out at the warehouses they had over in Keeling, Celia had been throwing up,

171

having mood swings and periods of dizziness. Her parents were furious when they found out she was with child, and a swift termination had been arranged out of state – well out of state, far enough that nobody would know of their daughter's scandalous behaviour.

Bob saw less of her that summer, and never saw her away from the lake. But on the few occasions he did happen upon her, she would always talk of her daughter. Apparently, a sex had never been determined, things had never gotten that far, but she was certain it had been a girl. Knew it, in fact. She swore blind that her baby was right there, at the lake, calling out to her each night from the trees – only she wasn't just a baby, she was a fully grown woman, older than Celia herself, as though she'd been born and lived her life into adulthood. She would call out every night. Why? Why had Celia killed her? Why had she allowed her parents to force her into the abortion? Why did she *listen* to her parents? Why were her parents still alive?

Why didn't she *kill* her parents?

It got darker.

Local Misstonville PD were called out to No.4 on the last Wednesday of the family's vacation. Neighbours had reported hearing loud screams coming from the lake house well into the late evening.

The police found Lyle and Claudia Dawes in their bedroom. Both looked as though they'd been tied down on their bed while they slept. Both had been gutted. Their stomachs were gaping, empty holes, their intestines strewn about the room like party decorations.

The cops followed a trail of blood leading away from the villa and into the forest. Eventually they caught up with Celia, almost a mile away. She was walking with one arm outstretched, her hand clasped as though she were holding someone else's and being led somewhere.

Even though she was young, it had taken three officers to subdue her and bring her in. She was sent to Hope Sanatorium in Granville to live out the rest of her days.

There weren't too many left, it turned out. It was only a few months later that she decided to force-feed herself her own gown, stuffing the cotton garment down her throat until she choked to death.

It had been the biggest news story to hit Misstonville since the Jackson Bluffs landslide of twenty-nine, even making national press – and in Bob's opinion, had been like the appearance of iron or nickel in the centre of a star. Once it was there, that was it, there was no recovery, no remission. Only inevitable death, a death which came slowly, and not without pain.

Elwood wondered if the heroin was like iron to him. He knew many addicts *did* manage to kick the habit, forge new lives, sometimes even better ones. But too many followed the path of the stars; unaware or uninterested in their slow demise, destined to explode into supernovae, then fade into the endless blackness of space.

Elwood decided to get up. Sleep, no matter how hard he tried, was not going to come easy, not now, not while there was so much to think on.

He wore hipsters and nothing else, a foolish move given the fact the air had grown considerably colder over the course of the evening, and he'd yet to figure out exactly how he was supposed to heat the place up.

Had he seen a boiler in the closet? Perhaps; he couldn't recall, his memory was far from what it once was. But he hadn't even thought about heating, that was the real issue. It was cold, but heating the place up hadn't even entered his mind as an option until now. And this was another sign, a positive sign that he was coming back, affording consideration to everyday things like the heating. It was an odd thing to consider positive, or even to highlight, but for those in the grip of a smack addiction, such basic considerations were forgotten, replaced with that inexorable focus on the next hit.

He climbed out of the sofa bed, teeth chattering as the cold air hit his skin. He noticed now that he certainly hadn't helped matters by leaving one of the balcony doors slightly ajar. He sifted through his bag at the side of the bed, found his hoodie and some jogger pants and got dressed. He crossed the open landing toward the balcony, picking up the half-empty bottle of whiskey and his crumpled pack of smokes from the console. He pushed the door open and cursed as his bare foot touched the cold stone floor. He lingered for a few seconds though; after the initial shock, the freezing discomfort soon turned to a cool soothing. The cut on his foot was still sore, and had been burning gently ever since his ordeal out on the lake earlier that afternoon. Like the heating in the villa, he'd ignored it. Hadn't even tended to it, as any normal person would.

He felt ashamed. And incompetent to boot; he didn't even know where the first aid box was, didn't even think this place would have one, now that he *was* finally thinking about it. He set the bottle down on the floor and his pack of smokes beside it, deciding now was as good a time as any to check out the damage down below, and at least give it a clean. He stepped back inside and crossed the open landing, pausing at the entrance to the hallway. He'd definitely used the bathroom before he'd gone to bed, but he couldn't recall whether or not he'd turned the light off.

It shone now through the open doorway about halfway along the dim hall.

Elwood turned the lights on and began his tentative approach, all the while telling himself that yes, he had in fact left the light on, he was quite sure of it. Convinced, even. Yes, it had been him. He grinned in spite of himself, suddenly aware of his own mind, and that he sounded like a character from one of his books. The one who was scared and ultimately doomed, but told themselves everything would be okay, there was nothing to worry about. The one who appeared in every horror story ever told, the one who almost always met with a grisly demise before the final page was turned.

He didn't hesitate when he reached the door, swinging it open and stepping straight into the empty bathroom.

Nothing.

No astronaut, no floating blood puddles; just the lime-green and orange tiles, which were arguably just as horrifying.

He breathed a sigh of relief and crossed the room to the sink against the far wall, above which hung a mirrored cabinet beside a frosted glass window. He opened the cabinet and was beyond astounded when he spied a small first aid kit on the bottom shelf. He plucked the green box from its resting place and perched himself on the edge of the tub, resting his wounded foot on his knee as he examined the neglected cut. The sole of his foot was caked in vermillion, crusted and congealed; he wondered what the inside of his sock or the bottom of the sofa bed looked like. Disgusted at what he saw, he once again felt shame rise within him, felt his face blaze hot in spite of his solitude. The wound itself was insignificant, but the mess around it served as yet another reminder of his inability to function as a normal human. What it showed was that he'd yet to wash – not just the wound, but the rest of his body too, everything. He hadn't washed since the morning he'd set off from the city, and it was now his third night at the villa. There was the lake, but that didn't count; it had washed away his sanity but left the dirt and grime, left a hell of a lot more too: fear, anxiety, a cocktail of dread and confusion.

He suddenly became aware of a sour odour in the air. The fusty aroma seemed to be all around him, engulfing him like some malodourous blanket or gas cloud. He hadn't even been aware of it before, but now that he was, he couldn't help but choke.

'What the fuck,' he declared, looking about the room, even glancing toward the toilet bowl. For a moment, he was like a dog confused by its own fart, then realisation dawned.

It was him.

And with that, the junkie decided it was time for a bath.

***

It was almost an hour later when he decided to pull himself out of the now-lukewarm water and dry himself off. He sat back down on the edge of the tub. Picking up his phone from the sink, he tapped his way to Google to find out how to dress a minor cut. Before the page had finished loading though, he realised he already knew. Remembered, in fact.

'Upshore,' he laughed. 'Chesney Upshore.'

He shook his head and grinned, the sort of half-forced, self-conscious smirk employed by those suddenly aware of their own forgetfulness. Chesney Upshore was a supporting character in his fourth book, *It Came to the Town in October*, and had fought alongside the hero and some others as they faced off against an unspeakable horror that was terrorising a small town in Colorado. Upshore was injured during a confrontation early on in the story, and Elwood had written a short sequence whereupon the hero's love interest had dressed the wound.

He tore open a pack of antiseptic wipes and cleaned the cut, after which he applied a gauze strip and carefully wrapped a bandage around his foot. All the while he felt a keen sense of wonder; that feeling of finding himself again, uncovering those forgotten things, no matter how small. It was as though the heroin had been a storm, knocking all of his books from the shelves. But now the storm was over, or at least beginning to clear, and he could see some of those books scattered about the floor, see them well enough to be able to pick them up and place them back where they belonged.

Optimism began to creep into the back of his heart,

not just the silly idea that he might actually write again; he knew that was a ridiculous notion right now – premature and perhaps even self-indulgent – but basic optimism was good, and it was something he hadn't felt since… well, he guessed maybe the release day of *The Dead at Night*, his last *good* book. The last one before the smack train came choo-chooing into the station with Casper Stevens at the head.

Feeling refreshed and smelling like mandarin and grapefruit, Elwood returned to the balcony, switching off the bathroom light as he left and making a mental note of the decision.

The night air cooled his bath-warmed skin as he lit a crooked joint, the silence of the evening gently broken by the soft smouldering of the blazing end. The moon shone like burning magnesium in the blackened sky, casting a vast, jagged scar of glittering light across the surface of the lake, which for a brief moment resembled floating snowflakes on the water. He unscrewed the cap on the bottle of whiskey as he looked out over this nocturnal theatre; a haunting stage set for an audience of one, an audience of Elwood Cathis. He wondered where the players were, the actors and actresses who starred in this matinee; El and Gracie, surely beyond the curtains stage left, *way* beyond. A few hundred miles beyond, in fact, in some other city, with some other guy, in another play entirely.

And Casper – stage right, perhaps? Or was he behind the scenes? The one directing proceedings? He was, after all, the one who had sent Elwood here, the one who had stuck that first needle in his arm and opened his eyes to another life, another world. Yes, the friendly ghost was almost certainly calling the shots backstage; this was his play, not Elwood's, and the poor junkie was simply a player – a now-unwilling player – desperately trying to find the exit.

And what of the astronaut? Where was that thing lurking right now? And the dead girls he'd undoubtedly seen on the dock earlier, their grey, pallid faces and lifeless eyes, the mechanical, mindless way that both had waved at him.

He gulped down the whiskey and let his mind stick with these apparitions for a moment longer. He wondered what they might mean – regardless of whether or not it was this place or his head, surely they had to mean something. Like dreams, were they born out of something buried in the depths of his sub-conscious? Perhaps, if they really were just withdrawal visions. But he wondered now if they even could be. From what little research he'd done on the subject of going cold turkey, he'd learned that in the majority of cases, hallucinations were expected about forty-eight hours after the final hit had worn off.

He burned the joint, inhaling deeply as a dense cloud of smoke swelled in the cold air around him, rising and dissipating on gentle gusts of wind that carried away the earthy, herbal stench.

Yes, it had been forty-eight hours, but when had he first seen the astronaut? He knew it had been at the supermarket, but that was *where*, not when. When had that been?

'The second night,' he uttered to himself, both shocked and confused by the sudden realisation. It hadn't even been twenty-four hours; much less in fact.

How could that be? he wondered.

He thought of the young girl from New Hampshire again. The papers had reported no prior history of mental disorder, either within Celia herself or the extended Dawes family. The *lunacy* – which was how national press had referred to Celia's breakdown – had likely come about as a direct result of the abortion, and not because of any curse or dark force at work; an idea that some townsfolk and even the local rag had hung their hat on.

Apart from a handful of accounts from people like Whiskey – none of them from Whiskey himself – there was no evidence to support the idea of a greater evil at work, even in Elwood's eyes. On the face of it, although extreme and downright depraved, the girl's reaction to her forced abortion at the hands of her parents was understandable, logical – some might say expected – or perhaps even *deserved*, if one was feeling particularly Catholic. Forced abortion could do strange things to a person's mind; it could twist it, cloud it, break it.

Either that or, rather than her being manipulated by some unseen force, she had been coerced by an actual person. By the Levant boy, perhaps. According to Whiskey, many of the Tribunes and Heralds of the south ran with that story, including artwork and imagery designed to incite a response. And a bad one, at that.

The Nilsport at Noon, in neighbouring Bowles County, ran with a drawing that showed a scared, adolescent white girl wandering the woods, à la Snow White. The evil black boy followed closely behind, whispering in her ear, cajoling her, his tongue snake-like and eyes brimming with mischief.

A pretty far-fetched theory; one that lacked any evidence at all but was steeped in racial fear and hatred. And in the fifties, in America, that was enough.

Wesley Levant was eventually brought in for questioning, but before any proper investigation could be conducted, a local posse saw to it that injustice was served. At the age of nineteen, the innocent boy was dragged from his cell at the town jail in the early hours of a sultry Tuesday morning. He was brought before a kangaroo court on the corner of fifth and Johnson – now fifth and Levant – and his beaten, charred corpse was found the following day, hanging from an old pitch pine that stood just a few feet away from the porch of the Dawes' villa.

The Civil Rights movement proper was still a few years away, but during the months that followed, residents from Earlswood staged a number of protests and boycotts, all of which garnered national attention. Before long, out-of-towners and even out-of-staters began to show up, all in support of the Levant family, most with nowhere to stay. The law tried in vain to keep the situation under control, but unofficial camping grounds began cropping up around the lake – others scattered about the forest – and people even set up vigils and slept at the murder scene. Most of the Lake Chance residents packed up their suitcases and cut their vacations short within days of the Dawes' deaths, and all but one packed up like it was the damn apocalypse when crowds of African Americans began appearing in the surrounding woodland.

According to Whiskey, the only one who stayed was a middle-aged man from Chicago named Ron Hilliard.

He was a regular renter of No.7 and had been for some years, but in forty-nine he purchased the title from the resort developers and began to spend almost half the year at his new lakeside retreat. Known locally as Lucky Hill, Ron enjoyed gambling, preferring especially games of chance to those that favoured any skill, and was seen frequently – most days, actually– shoving coins into the slot machines at Workman's Casino in Nilsport. He kept himself to himself for the most part – he was friendly though, and more importantly he was generous with his tips, especially on his *good* days, of which Whiskey recalled there were many.

The otherwise-unwanted guests around the lake didn't seem to bother Lucky Hill, who continued his daily ritual as though nothing had changed. Whisky continued his work too, and each day he would see Ron leave the villa at 9:00am on the dot. The man never took his car, choosing instead to hike through the forest on the other side of Crescent Road. There were trails in Misstonville Forest which ultimately crossed the county line into Bowles; the forest itself covered over a hundred square miles and straddled four counties in all.

Whiskey would never see the man return, but others would see him around Workman's sometimes as late as midnight, laughing to himself as coins spilled from slots and dice landed ever in his favour.

The lake and town continued to swell with protesters arriving from across the country; there were reports of fights breaking out between visiting supporters and local townsfolk, who saw the protesters as a nuisance. Whiskey swore he was never involved in these brawls, but he knew some who were – most, in fact – and he maintained that they were honest, good-working people. They didn't condone what had happened to the Levant boy, but they wanted their town back, and they were willing to fight for it.

There were also those who had taken part in the lynching, Whiskey knew many of them too, but he didn't spare a word in their defence. Some of these people, chief among them Gideon Poole of Poole Automobility Centre, would arrange for attacks on protester camping grounds during the night, setting tents ablaze and brawling in the stretch of Misstonville Forest that covered the area between Lake Chance and the town.

With all of this happening, it came as no surprise to local law enforcement when they began to see an increase in reports of missing persons. All of these reports involved protesters disappearing – always at night, and always from the forest around the lake.

Gideon and his people were never questioned; aside from him being a prominent figure in the community and influential member of the town select committee, the police just didn't care about the missing activists. The assumption reached in all cases was twofold; firstly, it was highly likely that the missing had in fact just returned to their homes, the novelty of the situation wearing off after a few nights of camping it rough in what was then becoming a dangerously cold winter.

Secondly, it wasn't a local problem. None of the missing were from Misstonville, so nobody cared. Whiskey talked of some small groups arranging searches; mainly the protesters themselves, but a handful of sympathetic locals joined in too, much to the disdain of Gideon and his cronies.

During his time working around them – oftentimes steering his mower around tents set on lawns – Whiskey heard talk of a demon. A white demon that stalked the forest, preying on the dark-skinned only, tempting them away from their groups until they were too far gone to be able to find their way back. On a few occasions, people had been sighted walking trance-like away from their camps. When confronted, these people would often struggle – not wanting to be stopped, believing they were being led to something greater, something more important that was for them and them alone. In some cases, the yearning to escape was so overpowering, so deeply entrenched, that their friends or fellow campers resorted to physically tying them down and restraining them in their tents if they couldn't be convinced to go home. Whiskey thought this a little extreme, but from what he heard, people allowed to wander off into the forest never returned.

Not all of those tempted away were so willing to go, though. Sometimes they were scared, confused, their feet taking them away but their eyes pleading for help, pleading to be stopped, begging to be saved.

Elwood saw the astronaut again in his mind's eye, tempting him, inviting him into that darkness.

He exhaled another plume of smoke and surveyed the forest; in the moonlight the trees were nothing more than a featureless black mass, beginning on the far shore of the lake and stretching for miles beyond that, cresting a hill in the distance, and then what?

He wondered perversely for a second what he might

find out there if he did start walking. If he just headed out into the wilderness in that general direction and didn't stop. He wasn't sure.

They did eventually solve the mystery of the missing protesters, but not entirely, not absolutely.

According to the old man, it was a callously cold evening in January of fifty-three when Emmet and Jacoby Laveau, two brothers from New Orleans, awoke to the sound of hushed voices outside their tent. These hushed voices soon turned into what sounded like a struggle, and the brothers, assuming somebody else was trying to wander off into the woodland, both got up to offer their assistance as they had done before.

Their makeshift camping ground had been near the old general store at Crescent Tip. What had been a chaotic mess of tents in a clearing at first had since evolved into an organised circle, fortified with chicken wire and placards. Their site had seen some action, courtesy of both Gideon Poole and the so-called white demon of Chance, but they hadn't lost anybody, and this was almost certainly down to the presence of the Laveau brothers.

Emmet and Jacoby were both boxers – semi-professional, but destined for far more than that. The two had grown up listening to stories of Jack Johnson, the first African American world heavyweight champion, who had died only seven years prior. He'd been known as the Galveston Giant, but would have had to look up at both of the Laveau brothers, who each peaked at well over six feet tall. Their size, coupled with their fighting skill, made them a big problem for anyone trying to bring trouble to the camp, and on that night, that bitterly cold Friday night, that *anyone* just so happened to be Lucky Hill himself.

By the time the cops arrived, Hill's face looked more like a cauliflower dipped in tomato soup than that of a man.

Upon exiting their tent, the brothers spotted Ron on the far side of their camp; the gambling man from Chicago was forcefully ushering a bound-and-gagged Raveena Dimaro beneath the chicken wire border.

The brothers crossed the campsite and Lucky Hill's luck finally ran out. According to Emmet and Jacoby Laveau, the man had pleaded with them at first, even offering them money to let him take the woman. Much of what he said had been nonsense, which the brothers couldn't understand or even properly recall when questioned by the cops later on. The word *demon* had been mentioned though, but whether Ron had referred to himself as the white demon, or the brothers had assigned him that title themselves, was unclear.

A few days later, after recovering from his injuries, Ron Hilliard was questioned by Sheriff Moir and his deputies for all but twenty minutes before they called in the feds. He confessed to the attempted abduction of Raveena Dimaro without even being asked, and went on to claim responsibility for almost all of the missing persons cases reported since the Levant tragedy. He gloated of others too: women he'd met at bars in Nilsport, and other towns that peppered the circumference of Misstonville Forest; children he'd taken from playgrounds in Brigdon and Spencer Creek, ramblers and dog-walkers from the forest trails, and a few hitchhikers along I-19.

It turned out Ronald Hilliard wasn't like most gambling men from Chicago, or anywhere else for that matter. He was a self-proclaimed mass-murderer, the likes of which the state hadn't seen in over a century. His self-purported kill list numbered in the sixties, and went as far back as 1944; some of his descriptions of the abductions eventually helped put to rest a number of unsolved missing persons cases across four counties.

Not a single body was ever recovered, though. Ron refused to disclose his motives, his reasonings, or his methods. The assumption then – and one still held by anyone who cared – was that he buried them somewhere out in the forest. Nobody would ever know for sure; there was just too much land out there and too little manpower for any sort of meaningful effort to be made.

Lucky Hill took his secrets to the gas chamber with him in sixty-one, just a few days after Kennedy had told everyone to ask themselves what they could do for their country.

Don't ever leave the trails, Whiskey had said. *Don't wander off, if you know what's good for you.*

Only Elwood had never really known what was good for him; he wouldn't be where he was now if he had. He was getting better, yes, but he was still finding himself, still trying to remember who he was. He'd yet to find his way back and in a way, he was already in that place, away from the trails.

He wondered now if that was why he felt this urge, no, this *battle* inside of him. The subtle argument between that glimmer of good – the old him, the father, the husband, the writer – and a voice. A voice that crackled through a comms link, but lingered in the air, even now. A voice that pleaded for him to step off the balcony, to take the stairs two at a time and not worry about closing the terrace doors behind him. A voice that was begging him to follow that path to the shore, to keep going until he reached the other side of the lake, to carry on past Kenner's old store, follow the trails – *yes, follow the trails* – but only for a time, only for a minute, because he needed to leave those trails.

He needed to step into the darkness, that blackness that was lush green but in the night had turned to an abyss, a finite stretch of darkened woodland like a stain on the earth. And beneath it, the infinitely possible, the endless terror of the undetermined. An abortion grown old woman, a white demon, an astronaut and some dead girls. A graveyard of Lucky Hill's dead.

Elwood took a generous swig of bourbon and drew deeply from his joint. He was trembling, not from the cold though. This was fear. It wasn't withdrawal, it was terror.

Was it, though?

He heard that quiet voice of reason again, the one that chirped up every now and then from its dark corner, reminding him that he was a junkie only days ago, and had been for years. His mind was tainted, and the purge wasn't going to be easy, no *sir*, it was going to be the motherfucking trip of a lifetime and all bets were off. He simply needed to buckle up and stop asking so many questions. You weren't *supposed* to enjoy the ride, only endure it.

There was something though, something more. He could hear it. Feel it.

He knew he couldn't entirely trust his own senses

though – not for a few days at least, not until he was on the other side of this rodeo – but that didn't change the history, the things that had happened here. Celia Dawes, Lucky Hill, and apparently everything else the bookstore lady had to tell. He'd need to visit her; perhaps tomorrow, after he'd called Casper again. Casper was top of his list right now. He needed to know what that son of a bitch knew. For a moment he contemplated calling the friendly ghost there and then – chances were he'd be awake too; shovelling snow up his nose or betting on the horses, pushing some poor woman's head down on his dick. Knowing Casper, probably all three. He decided the call could wait until morning; he needed to sleep, that, and he wasn't particularly looking forward to hearing the other man's voice. His eyes had suddenly grown heavy, and the fight to keep them open was one he was happy to be losing.

Maybe it had been that much-needed soak in the tub. The thought made him smile; he remembered how much Gracie had loved warm bubble baths before bed, and how she'd always said that a hot bath was foreplay for a good night's sleep.

He began to feel a throb in his crotch, recalling how there'd been room for two in their old tub, and how the two of them had put Gracie's idea to the test on more than a few occasions.

He let his hand drift toward his midriff as memories flickered in his mind; her body tensing, suds running between her legs, rolling over the mole that sat just above her lips, his tongue between them. Camomile and rosewood. His ankles resting on the rim of the tub, his hands working shampoo into brunette locks, her head moving slowly up and down between his legs. Vanilla and papaya.

He could smell the aromas, even feel the touch of her body, hot and demanding. He gripped the now stiffening bulge beneath his joggers and squeezed.

'Fuck,' he sighed. It had been too long. He couldn't remember the last time, but then he rarely did these days – that was, rarely remembered *and* rarely had sex. He'd never cheated on Gracie; his mistress had been the needle and everything that came with it. In the years that had followed the divorce there'd been a few occasions he was certain he could count using the fingers on one hand – he went to parties to get high, not to get laid – but he went to plenty of parties, and things sometimes *happened* at parties.

The ethereal hoot of a nearby owl broke the silence, and the moment. Elwood felt the weight of his eyes, suddenly reminded of his tiredness. He relit the joint and took a few more hits before dropping the roach-end into what was now an almost empty bottle of whiskey. Maybe he'd masturbate in the morning, he decided.

CHAPTER THIRTEEN
GROOVY KIND OF LOVE

'*Tag, you're it, daddy…*'

Elwood awoke suddenly from a satisfyingly deep slumber that had long been overdue. Morning wood didn't greet him as he'd expected, on either count; the sun was still hours away, and his dick was far from hard.

Something had touched him. Tapped him on the shoulder.

And a voice. The words already forgotten though, like so many dreams.

He stared up at the ceiling, not wanting to move, not wanting to perpetuate or encourage anything that might best be ignored.

During his teenage years, he was gripped on a number of occasions by what he later learned was sleep paralysis. At the time though, he hadn't known any better; he had in fact believed that somebody, or something, was holding him down. His coping mechanism had been to close his eyes and go back to sleep, to simply ignore it, as though to sleep was to protect oneself from the evils of the world.

The childhood instinct was creeping back in now, that urge to just close his eyes tightly and tense himself to sleep – not because of some Pathophysiological condition, one that actually caused many to believe they were either being abducted by aliens or had a demon sitting on their chest – no, the instinct was taking over because there was something here with him. It wasn't holding him down, but it was here; he could sense it, and he could still feel its icy touch on his shoulder.

Sleep couldn't save him now, and he knew that it never truly had anyway. The idea was so delightfully childish that it couldn't exist in the minds of those who've lived long enough to see how terrible the world can be, how awful people can be. Elwood imagined that throughout the history of the world there had been more than many innocent children who had closed their eyes against evil, wished for the safety of sleep, and never opened them again.

Why then, he wondered, was this naive notion sliding back into his psyche now?

As if in reply, a young girl's voice in the dark: 'Catch me if you can, daddy.'

He sat up and looked toward the corner of the room where the landing became the hallway. A figure, a child, standing by the window. Before Elwood's eyes could completely fix in on her though, she skipped impishly into the hall and out of sight.

Pigtails. As the silhouette had moved across the

landing, he was sure he'd seen pigtails bouncing with each skip.

'El?' He swung out of bed and jumped to his feet. 'El, is that you?'

He pulled on his joggers and started toward the hall, pausing when he reached the foot of the sofa bed. It couldn't be his daughter. Oh, sweet Elouise, baby girl, he missed her so much... but there was no way she could be here.

Laughter now, the sort of cheeky mirth you might expect from a kid playing hide and seek – or hide and scare the shit out of an unsuspecting parent.

'El?' he called.

He heard footsteps now, running away from him and down the hall toward the stairs. More laughter.

He knew it couldn't be her, but part of him wanted it so desperately that it was enough to make it completely plausible in his mind. For all he knew, Gracie had ditched whatever-his-name-was and come to find him. Through her enquiries she learned quite quickly – she knew who to ask, at least – that Elwood had come here, to Lake Chance, to this very villa in fact.

So, she brings El, he thought, because she figures a surprise visit from his gals might spur on Elwood's recovery; she also figures out how to get into the villa in the middle of the night, with a young girl – quietly, instead of knocking. But it doesn't end there, folks – see, she also figures that it's time her and Elwood gave the whole happy marriage thing another go. They could make it work, things could be just as they had been, before all the shit. Before the heroin.

'Stranger things have been happening,' he uttered to

himself, as he stepped beyond the corner and glanced down the hall.

He saw the shape of the young girl once again; she had gone beyond the stairs to the end of the hall and stood at the door to the smallest of the three bedrooms.

'Is that you, Elouise?' he said, his voice parental: loving, but with an edge of authority.

The girl laughed again and began hopscotching back along the hall toward him. Elwood reached for the light switch and the figure stopped abruptly at the top of the stairs, hands on her hips in childish protest.

He flicked the light on anyway. As he did so the young girl leapt gracefully onto the top step and out of view. But not before he caught a glimpse of her face.

It wasn't his daughter.

As far as he knew, *his* daughter still had both of her eyes, still had a left ear that wasn't smashed into a purple pulp. *His* daughter – he hoped – still had overly rosy cheeks, without the gaping maw that revealed rotting teeth and a putrid tongue.

Whoever this girl was – this poor, decomposing girl that was trying to coax him into a game of tag at three in the morning – she wasn't Elouise.

Consumed by fear, yet driven still by a kind of morose inquisitiveness, Elwood started down the hall in pursuit, without any intention or expectation; this time he simply let his feet carry him and didn't fight them, unlike the night before when he'd barricaded himself in the bedroom.

He likened this feeling to that undeniable urge to walk out into the woods – only that urge hadn't come from him, hadn't felt like it had anyway. It had come from somewhere else, something else.

This was all him, though. He didn't know how he knew, but he was sure of it. Whether it was a part of his subconscious or something greater that was propelling him forward, he didn't know, couldn't know. It wasn't like a gut feeling or a hunch; an *instinct,* or whatever else you liked to call it. It was different, something grander.

Destiny?

He wondered then if destiny was actually a force, rather than some destination or state of being that you had to arrive at. Might it not be the power that *got* you there instead? A force much greater than determination or willpower, tenacity, perseverance. A force you had to welcome without awareness, and hear without listening.

He tried to calm his thoughts. This wasn't the time or the place for his wandering mind to be in control. His writer's mind. A mind that had taken him to places his feet never could; to the distant past, the far-future, to shady government facilities… to space.

Something began to happen then. For just a second it was as though a door was about to open. A key being turned in a lock somewhere, and he could hear it, *see* it.

Space.

The door wasn't here in the villa though, it was in his head, buried deep down in Freud's *Id*; the lock was disengaging, and soon the door would creak ajar.

Space…

But did he want it to? Hadn't a great man once said there was nothing scarier than a door, slightly ajar?

Space.

But why was that so scary? Was it that it showed too much? Or too little? He didn't know which was more terrifying – knowing too much or not knowing enough.

'Spa–'

Before he could say the word, speak it out loud and give life to it – before he could open that door and peak at whatever hideous comprehension might dwell within – he heard the almost-rhythmic *thud thud thud* of dancing footsteps on the stairs.

Descending, then silence.

Elwood continued forward, abstract thinking aside, his focus now back on the game of tag he was being drawn into. He passed the bathroom. The light was still off, but he found little comfort in that fact.

He reached the top of the stairs and peered around the corner. His eyes followed the steps one by one, down to the lower landing, which stood empty and lightless.

Thud thud thud. Dancing feet again, this time on the second set of stairs that led down to the ground floor.

She was just around that corner.

Two feet now, firmly landing on the floor below. He imagined a gymnast making a perfect landing from the balance beam, arms stretched high and taut, a beaming grin.

Those rotten teeth.

He needed to catch her, wanted to see what would happen when he did. Would she tell him something? That's how it worked in the books and the movies. These sorts of things always belied some deeper meaning, some ultimate truth that the unwilling protagonist must confront.

Or maybe it would be like when they were kids; once he caught up with her, tag, *she* would be it.

And then *she* would come after *him*.

The thought was briefly unsettling, but he continued unperturbed, moving down the steps swiftly and around the corner to the top of the second set of stairs. He looked down into the darkness of the hall below; no sign of the girl, but he could feel a growing chill, as though a door or a window had been left open somewhere.

He couldn't remember seeing a wind chime outside, but he was sure he could hear one now – faint, but there. He wondered if it might be strung up outside one of the neighbouring villas, a remnant of past vacationers.

Elwood took the stairs two at a time and drew close to the wall. When he reached the final step, he glanced to the right and checked the side door. Closed. He crossed the step and put his back up against the opposite wall, allowing himself to look down the hall and into the kitchen and dining room.

Darkness. And a stronger sense of cold now – he could feel the breeze against his skin. He noticed too that the door to the lounge was rocking gently on its hinges, silently – back and forth, back and forth, back and forth.

He could hear music, low but rising. Someone was turning up the volume on the stereo in the lounge. Had to be, there was no other source for it. It couldn't be his car radio; it wouldn't sound as intrusively clear.

His eyes remained fixed on the door to the lounge, still rocking gently, back and forth, back and forth. No light came from within; only the sound of a lonesome piano, and then Phil Collins.

Groovy kind of love.

Elwood left the stairs behind and began to move slowly down the hall. His hand glided along the wall; a mannerism he'd never exhibited before.

He wondered if he really was just allowing his hand to glide over the wallpapered surface, or subconsciously looking for purchase? Some deeper part of his brain that still knew, still had the *good sense* to know that this situation was fucked up, was sending some kind of message to his appendage – telling it to grab on, ordering it to hold on tight to whatever its fingers came across and don't let go, don't let this fool carry on, don't let this idiot walk into that lounge and see whatever might be in there, whatever it is that likes listening to Phil Collins in the dark –

Gracie loved this song. It had been on their wedding playlist. He wondered if this meant anything, symbolised some deeper meaning perhaps. Shit, was Gracie in there? Was Gracie in the lounge? Maybe it *was* them, maybe they had come after all.

His pace quickened ever so slightly as he neared the open doorway. 'Gray? Is that you?'

He wanted so badly for it to be her, for it to be both of them – his girls, his ladies, the moon and star of his life once upon a sober night. But things didn't just happen because you wanted them to, that wasn't how life worked. It was how *writing* worked, sometimes. If he wanted something to happen on the page, he could make it happen, he could write it – and he wished so fiercely to have that ability now, to just be able to write them back into his life.

'Gracie? Honey?' he called out again.

This time it wasn't just Phil who replied. It was a woman's voice that echoed back at him.

'*Daydayyyyyy…*'

The tone trancelike, but invitational, even playful in an obscene sort of way. The sort of *come and get me* challenge a scantily-clad lover might throw at a horny partner.

'I'm in the lounge, Daydayyyyyy.'

It didn't sound right, though.

'Come find me, Dayday.'

It didn't sound like it belonged there at all.

'I'm waiting, Daydayyyy…'

He thought of obsessed stalkers taking images of their own roughly cropped face and editing them into photos of the person they were fixated on; creating the illusion of a happy life together, a life that didn't exist, a moment that had never happened.

This was like that, as though the voice of this lady, whoever she was, had been cropped from somewhere else, copied, and then pasted into Elwood's world to create a moment that wasn't happening, wasn't real.

And still the music played.

He reached for the door, his arm trembling but his body still propelled by that force, that need to know; that inexorable desire to find what was real, to find *himself* again.

He swung the door open and stepped boldly into the entranceway, surprised for a moment by his apparent courage, or stupidity.

The first thing he noticed was that the room was suffused in radiant blue light. Next was the open door into the dining room on his right, through which he could see that the French doors were wide open.

He decided to ignore this for now and turned his attention back to the lounge, back to the music. Phil Collins was making way for the instrumental. Drums, and strings of some kind; the strings of what, Elwood couldn't remember exactly – a cello, perhaps – but he remembered how Gracie had always called them the heartstrings.

'Gra–' he started to call out for her again, but her name became a whisper.

There was somebody else in the room with him.

The source of the blue glow was the LCD screen on the stereo system, which sat on a console against the left wall. The woman stood there, directly in front of the stereo, her back to Elwood. She wore a floral sun dress, the kind Gracie would wear – and maybe still did, for all he knew. An open CD case hung limply from the woman's right hand as she rocked from side to side, arching her back and bending her knees with each sway.

She was dancing.

Elwood remained in the doorway, fascinated by what he was looking at, terrified by what he was seeing. The patchy dress was torn and frayed at the hems; a dark stain ran down her back, beginning just below her left shoulder blade. That was where the hole was. At first glance it looked like a bruise, only at its core it was too dark, suggestive of some greater depth.

Then something crawled out of it, crawled out of the hole in her back and scurried across her spine – a centipede or millipede perhaps, judging by the shape. It swiftly disappeared into the tangle of mangy curls bunched at the nape of the woman's neck. She didn't react to it, didn't even seem to notice as she continued her dance, her knees bending lower now, until she was almost squatting with each sway of her hips. The dance was becoming erotic, sensually slow. The curvy mounds of her upper buttocks were noticeably prominent under the dress, as though she was presenting herself. Like a cat or dog in heat, she was inviting a partner, inviting Elwood perhaps; he was, after all, the only spectator in attendance.

He stifled a gag and steadied himself against the doorframe as the instrumental drew to a close and Phil joined the party again.

And still the music played.

A fly landed on his nose. He swatted it away and watched it return to a growing swarm circling the air just above the woman's head. He could see more of them on her shoulders too, landing on her bare skin for brief moments of sustenance, before spiralling back up into the throng. They were feeding on her – enjoying the sort of banquet never presented on a plate, but instead served up in coffins, or shallow graves dug haphazardly in secluded forests.

Elwood watched another fly descend upon the hole from which the insect had emerged. More followed, but they didn't spiral back up into the swarm like the rest.

Because they weren't just feeding on her, Elwood realised. They were burrowing into her, making nests of her insides.

Elwood began to feel queasy, torturing himself with the possibility that the fly which had landed on his nose might have already completed its expedition through the rotting interior of this dancing corpse. Treading the voids between her organs, climbing through arteries and exploring any regions that were still wet, still warm. Before landing on his *fucking nose.*

The song was nearing its end and he found himself hoping it was set to repeat; either that or it was an album with more to come. He suddenly dreaded the possibility of silence.

Before the song began to fade out though, he suddenly became aware of laughter, that same playful giggling from earlier.

It was her, the girl with no eyes.

He looked to his right, through the open doorway into the dining room, and the French doors beyond.

She looked at him from the doorway. The darkness in those empty sockets belied the sight she truly had, he was sure of it; he could feel her eyes, her darkness, on him. But it wasn't insidious – although grotesque in appearance, the girl didn't seem to mean him any harm – on the contrary, she just wanted to play, wanted to be chased.

He remained on the threshold of the lounge and hall, grinning awkwardly. The girl smiled, brought her hand up to her face and pressed her thumb to her nose, then wiggled her fingers and stuck out her tongue.

She called out to him. '*Too slow.*'

The music stopped.

It was the sudden dimming of the room that caught Elwood's attention though. He looked back toward the woman. The stereo was turned off completely, and he saw that she was no longer dancing, no longer facing away from him either. Her eyes, wide and glaring in the darkness which now filled the room, were fixed upon his.

Her lower jaw was chap-fallen; it hung loose and ever-so-slightly out of kilter with the rest of her face, affording her a look of deep exhaustion. Either that, or it was the face of a woman who had taken one hell of a knock in the kisser.

Blood spatter peppered the front of her dress, and a wider streak of it trailed down from a hole close to her left breast, which Elwood assumed was either the entry or exit wound to the one on her back. It must have been the exit wound, he realised, because it was the size of a teacup and the raw skin around it quivered as bugs moved across the sloppy bridges of tissue holding it together. As with that other unnatural maw, this one too was a hub of activity; flies buzzed around it, some disappearing inside, while other things crawled out – some scuttling beneath her dress, and others, those without legs, simply falling to the carpet, where a scattering of maggots was slowly building to a mound.

He drank in the situation in great laboured gulps, his throat suddenly as dry as sun-baked denim, his skin blazing as he breathed warm air out into the cold room. His head was a tin teapot with no handle; there was no respite, no cool purchase he could latch onto.

A fever. One brought on by his own sickness, that which he had for so many years injected into his veins, now seeping out.

Or was it fear? Yes, fear perhaps, that's what it was. But not fear of the woman, no. Nor the girl – this was a different kind of fear, a fear that wasn't his, and yet he felt it vicariously, swelling in his chest. This was someone else's fear, someone else's… guilt? That was it, whatever had happened to this poor woman, and her girl – for surely it was her daughter, the two shared the same slender, Grecian nose – he was feeling the brunt of it, or *fearing* the brunt of it. His was now the heart of another man – the mind, the soul, whatever the fuck else might be in there, it wasn't his, it was *his,* the one who did this to them – the husband maybe, the father, perhaps.

Once again, he found himself on the precipice of some awful revelation. But then she spoke, softly, her words coming from somewhere else. Words that couldn't be spoken so eloquently through a broken jawbone and fetid gullet, words copied and pasted from elsewhere.

'We've been waiting for you.'

She drew her arm up and pointed toward the door that led to the dining room, toward the eyeless girl who still stood out on the terrace where he and Whiskey had talked only hours before.

'Out there.' Her emaciated, mottled arm hung in the air like a dead branch, almost arachnoid in the darkness of the room. For a moment Elwood thought she might begin some hideous transfiguration: four more gangly appendages would rip through her skin; two feelers would tear through that chap-fallen jaw and extend out toward him; her abdomen would swell bulbous and white with eggs. Then she'd crawl toward him, spin a web about his person and wrap him like a burrito; string him up and save him for the babies that would eventually burst forth from that swollen belly-sac.

She spoke again, the broken silence a welcome reprieve from his own torturous thoughts.

'Go, Daydayyyyy.'

Her arm dropped back down to her side and she turned to face the stereo once again.

Elwood watched, confused. 'Dayday,' he said, the word not much more than a whisper on his lips. *Dayday.* He knew that name, he was sure of it.

Blue light illuminated the room once again as the LCD screen came back on, seemingly of its own accord; the woman hadn't stooped down to flick it back on at the socket as far as Elwood had seen. Her fingers moved over the buttons now though, selecting the same CD, and what followed were those same melodic keyboard tones heralding the return of Phil Collins' *A Groovy Kind of Love.*

She began to dance again, tilting her head this time and spying him from the corner of her widened eye. 'Go,' she repeated, her voice still coming from elsewhere but fading now. 'Go.'

Elwood remained in the doorway, wanting to go, wanting to follow this woman's command and get the fuck out of there, but what was she asking of him? To go outside into the dark and follow a girl with no eyes? Where? Out into the woods? At this time? Fuck that.

And why not? That voice again, that voice that wasn't quite a voice but more like a force. Not from him, from something else.

'Go,' the woman was still dancing, still watching him from the corner of her eye.

Sweat ran down his face in streams now, cresting his brow and rolling into his eyes. He blinked and she was gone, no longer dancing by the stereo – no, now she was right next to him. Now she was in his face, her hand on his shoulder, oh God, her dead hand; he felt it, felt it like ice, a searing cold that permeated his flesh and coursed through his veins like the flies and crawlies that had made their homes in her rotting corpse.

She spoke again, this time right in his ear – Jesus Christ, so close that he felt her nose against his hair; far too close for a first date, lady, all far too close for the dead and the living. Never should the two exist in such close proximity to one another.

'*Go.*' Her voice was no longer a fading harmony but a roar, a guttural cry that was desperate and furious. The shock of it knocked Elwood back and he stumbled into the hallway, legs tangling together. He went down, and it was a *hard* down too. As he fell, his head struck the sill of one of the windows that lined the front hall; he hit the laminate hardwood with a *thud*. A muffled groan escaped him as a dull pain undulated through his right thigh. He didn't look back at the doorway, didn't want to know how close the woman might still be; instead he turned over onto his hands and knees and scrambled away along the hall toward the kitchen, his head reverberating like church bells.

He was on his feet just in time to crash into the dining table. Bent at the waist and sprawled across its surface, he glimpsed the young girl out on the terrace – only for a second though, before she bounded out of view once again.

'*Can't catch me,*' her laughter moved around his head as though he were listening in surround-sound; she'd moved – at an unnaturally rapid pace - from the back terrace to the front of the property.

He pushed away from the table and forced himself

into an upright position. The room span for a few moments as he tried to centre himself. The back of his head throbbed, the bells inside still ringing loud.

He wasn't sure if brain palpitations were even a real thing, but right now they were all *too* real; he felt as though the force of the throbbing might at any moment push his eyeballs from their sockets. *Pop,* he'd be blind – but not like the girl, because she *could* see – for him it would be darkness, and nothing else.

He wiped the back of his head and checked his hand for blood. Luckily, the hit didn't appear to have broken the skin; the last thing he needed right now was a trip to wherever the nearest hospital might be.

The girl.

He stumbled away from the table and headed across the kitchen to the front door, making a point of not looking back into the lounge, or down the hall. In the corner of his eye, though, he was sure he could see the dead woman. She was still standing in the doorway, still watching him expectedly, still waiting for him to do as he'd been told and follow the girl.

He had no choice now. There was no way he was going back down that hall as long as she remained there; not until he'd carried out her request anyway, for fear of what she might do, what she might be capable of doing. Even if this was all in his head, the cut on his foot wasn't. The throbbing in his head, the pain in his leg – all were real, and he dreaded to think what other levels there might be in that particular tower.

Elwood flicked on the kitchen light, unlocked the front door, and stepped out onto the porch. He could see the eyeless girl standing further along the gravel track that led back up to Crescent Road. She waved to him, standing right at the spot where Whiskey and Bullseye had emerged from the woods earlier that evening.

He started down the steps and across the weed-infested gravel front, aware that he was still barefooted and topless, but unwilling to act on it; the trepidation brought on by the thought of having to pass by the dancing lady far outweighed the flaws in his current wardrobe choice. As if to compound this notion, he glanced back and saw that she was still watching him, her still form now occupying one of the windows that ran the length of the hallway.

No, he wasn't going back in there – not now, maybe not ever. For a second though, he wondered how following a girl with no eyes into the woods in the middle of the night was in any way a better option. Surely all that was left for him now was to just get in his car and leave. It was right there, after all. Right. There.

His keys, though. Christ, his keys were on the console next to the sofa bed, which was upstairs, back in the villa, back where the rotting woman was waiting for him.

He could leave on foot, just walk on out of here now. Sure, it was a few miles into town, he was out of shape and his wallet was back there in the villa too. But he could take his time, keep close to the roadside and stay away from the woods; once he hit I-19 he could stick out his thumb. Eventually, he would get home. Then he would worry about replacing the contents of his wallet: the credit cards, the bank card, the wallet itself.

Not the photo though, the polaroid of him and the

girls in Miami; that could never be replaced. It didn't exist in the Cloud or on some USB lying in a drawer somewhere. Gracie had always been good at that – moving with the times, backing stuff up to the Cloud and saving things on sticks. Elwood had always been a sucker for a good old fashioned photo album, something you could flick through instead of swipe through, turn instead of scroll.

Part of him wished now that he'd at least held pace with some of the technological advances the world had seen in recent years. Chief among them the ability to pay for things using your cell phone; had he done that, he wouldn't have to worry about hitchhiking all the way home at least.

He suddenly realised he was now standing on leaf-strewn dirt instead of gravel. When had he left the driveway and come into the woods? Had he been so away with his own thoughts that he hadn't noticed the change in terrain under his bare feet? Hadn't noticed the minutes that had passed by?

He hoped it was only minutes. Right now there was no way of knowing. He about-turned and saw nothing. No villa. No comforting light pouring out from the kitchen. No lake, not even a hint or glimmer of moonlight shimmering off the surface through any of the blackness that seemed to be closing in on him now.

Confusion struck him like a freight train. A coal-laden beast of iron and steel, its quarry black and ancient, departing Lack Chance and arriving at damned-if-he-knew. He faltered under the force of it, his mind so muddled that all he could think to do now was cover his face with both hands and cry.

This wasn't like anything a child might feel upon realising they were lost and their parents were nowhere to be seen. This was deeper; it offered no way out, no adult who might come to his aid, no security guard or employee to comfort him in some back room while a call sounded out over a PA system. He felt like a homicidal somnambulist, that poor soul who wakes from their sleepwalking only to realise they unintentionally murdered a loved one during their slumbering stroll.

Hopelessness. That was what he felt now.

There was no path in sight, no route he'd followed. He'd done what Whiskey had told him he should never do; he'd left the beaten trail and waded out into a sea of the unknown, lost in his own thoughts. No signposts, no North Star visible through the thick canopy of foliage.

Nothing.

Nothing but trees and darkness and more trees and shadows and... others.

He wasn't alone. There were others out here with him.

To his left, maybe thirty feet away, the lumpy silhouette of the astronaut floated in the gloom, the comms unit on the suit crackling indistinctly beneath the breeze that whistled through the dense thicket. The misshapen form drifted behind trees, then in front of them – behind, then in front again – edging closer, but never actually getting any closer. It was like an illusion of some kind, the effect dizzying.

Behind him, all but fifteen feet away, the rotting woman stood with her back to one of the black willows that dominated this particularly area of the woods, as opposed to the prevailing birches and maples that could be seen around the villa and lake. Her face was a picture of expectation and yearning. Lady Chatterley waiting for her lover to arrive. Only there was no dashing gamekeeper here, erect and ready for some frolicking in the undergrowth. Nope, only a pale-faced junkie running a high fever, confused, scared out of his wits and ready to get the hell out of there.

He continued his about-turn and saw the young girl ahead of him. She was skipping around another black willow, her arms raised whimsically in the air as she caressed the low-hanging catkins. The downward arch of the branches created a natural shroud like some opaque shower curtain; her form was visible but obscured, with an eerie ambiguity that hadn't been there when Elwood was able to properly see her, to see those childish pigtails and innocent smile. And the empty sockets where naïve eyes had surely once nestled.

He had no idea where to go from here. No idea which direction might lead him back to the villa, and perhaps his sanity. His tormentors were helping with that though, surrounding him on three sides and leaving a clear opening to his right.

Helping, he thought, or *herding*?

He began to move in that direction, feeling the dirt between his toes like sand – damn, he wished he were on a beach somewhere right now, a beach where it was warm and sunny and bright and there were people, *living* people.

He winced a little each time he set his injured foot down on a fallen twig, tensing his calf each time as a cramp began to work on his leg.

Not now, he thought, please, God, not now.

He moved away as quickly as he could, regularly glancing back to check if they were following or holding their positions.

They were following.

He tried to speed up but felt the cramp in his calf rising. Up ahead through the trees he could see an area of the forest that sloped down into a small gulley, the earth rising up on either side to reveal masses of tangled willow root, clay and sandstone. He made for this area, guided by a vague assertion that it might offer some form of safety from those that were now following him.

He was still confused, still upset – unable to process anything except the need to move, and even that was quickly becoming a challenge. His feet were growing numb; in fact, he was losing all feeling in his feet at an alarming rate.

Stumbling desperately toward the ditch that was now only a few feet away, he felt the ground underfoot begin to slant downwards as roots and ancient earth began appeared on either side of him. Soon enough he found himself below ground level, the gulley having descended a good nine feet into the earth.

The numbness had reached his knees now and he came to a halt, unable to take another step, no matter how much he wanted to. He turned to check on the girls and the astronaut, but even the simple act of turning around was now too much for him; he struggled to gain focus as the world carried on turning. His vision now a blur of darkness and shadows and yes, there they were, the three of them, the mother and the daughter blocking the path into the gulley, the astronaut floating in the air above them.

'Keep going.' He heard the girl's voice, oddly encouraging, and the shortest of the indistinct shadows began to move toward him. He couldn't move though, not now – as much as he wanted to, as much as he wanted to *keep going*, he simply couldn't.

He clawed at the side of the gulley, seeking purchase on any of the gnarly roots that curled in and out the earth, but it seemed his hands, too, were now devoid of any feeling. He tried to grasp on, but the roots only slipped through his flimsy fingers, his hands were now like the gloved astronaut's hands, those useless claw-machine hands that had grabbed at his ankles in the lake.

Pineapples? He could smell pineapple, and something else. Paint? That was it, pineapples and emulsion paint, an aroma so vivid he could feel it in his nostrils.

Lost time. Confusion. Numbness. Strange smells. And wait, something in his chest now.

He had just enough time to realise what was happening. Just enough time to regain enough coherence to remember one of the possible side-effects of going cold turkey.

Then he fell to the ground, and the seizure took hold.

CHAPTER FOURTEEN
CATHISTROPHIES

A dreamless dark was his world now. Empty of all thought, all feeling. But fading, slowly, the numbness subsiding. Cold – no, not cold, more than that, *freezing* – shivering, that was what he felt now. Sensations began to return in a tirade.

Elwood's back prickled against the bed of soil he was spread-eagled upon, the rough dirt and brushwood abrasive on his exposed skin. He felt it beneath his heels too. The dull ache in his wounded foot once again made its presence known.

'*Elwood...*'

A voice, tinny, as though from the far end of a long tunnel. A man.

'Elwood.'

He shifted his head toward the sound and groaned. His neck was stiff; his joints screamed. His shoulders, elbows, knees all felt like over-inflated lead balloons.

Worst of all was his head, though. Whatever he'd

been up to last night had left him with a hangover unlike any he'd experienced in his life. It felt as though someone had peeled back his scalp, opened up his skull, filled it with broken glass and set a rat loose in there. The pain seemed to radiate from the back of his head and flash through the soft tissue of his brain in jagged pulses, turning into an awful throb that settled between his eyes.

'Damn, son, what you get yourself into?' The voice was closer.

Something was being draped over him now, a blanket maybe. Whatever it was, it was thick and warm and woollen and welcome. He tried to open his eyes but couldn't; it felt as though someone had glued them shut and the more he tried to force them open, the more intense the throb in his brow became. He gave up.

'Don't fret now. Just wait, they'll open soon enough.'

Who was that? He knew the voice.

He became aware of a heavy panting to his right, a mess of quick, laboured breaths that didn't sound human. Then whatever it was descended upon him. He felt something like gloopy sandpaper or a wet-wipe peppered with sand. It ran up and down his cheeks, across his chin, accompanied by hot breath that reeked of tinned meat.

'Bullseye. Damn it, he don't need none of your slobbering kisses right now. Over there.'

'Whiskey? Whiskey, is that you?'

'You bet. Just rest easy, give it a few minutes.'

'What's wrong with me? I can't open my eyes. My eyes won't open.'

He felt a hand rest on his shoulder and pat gently. 'Easy now, don't panic. Looks like you spent most of the night out here sleeping in the dirt. Got yourself the 'junctivitis for your troubles too. Lucky you didn't die out here though, been a cold one. Give me a second.'

Elwood heard what sounded like a zipper, rustling, then a click.

'Right. Got some water here. I'm going to pour it over your eyes, okay?'

'Okay,' Elwood replied.

'Then what you're going to do is rub your eyes real hard and get rid of all the crusty gunk you got there – that's what's keeping them shut – you understand me, Elwood?'

'Go ahead.'

Whiskey counted down from three, then Elwood felt the cold water splash over his face and run down into his ears. He brought his hands up and began to rub the water into his eyes, feeling the crusty deposits between his eyelids begin to dissipate. He gently pried them open with his thumb and index fingers, as he found that tensing only aggravated the pain in his head.

'Jesus,' he declared, hissing like a vampire as he pulled himself up into a sitting position and shielded his eyes from the brightness of the world.

Whiskey laughed. 'Could be Jesus. Or God. Probably one of them that needs thanking for this fine morning. And probably both of them need thanking for letting you wake up to see it. You spend the whole night out here?'

Elwood Cathis let his hand drop away and blinked against the bright morning. Whiskey was down on one knee, Bullseye behind him, the dog's leg propped up and taking a piss against the sandstone.

'Here,' Whiskey offered him the bottle of water and Elwood took it.

'Thanks,' he clicked open the cap and began to chug, gauging his surroundings.

They were in a fairly deep trench. Rocky sides rose up perhaps ten feet or so above them; the gulley itself was no more than five feet wide. He looked to his right and saw that the base of the ditch gradually rose to meet the forest floor at least forty feet away. Beyond that he could see the forest, thick with birches, firs, and willows.

Willows. Parts of last night started to come back to him – fragmented though, distorted like reflections in a rippling pool.

Only one way, only one way to go, they're following.

'They were following me,' he uttered to himself.

'What you say?'

'Nothing,' Elwood replied, shaking off the memory. 'Nothing, just, trying to remember. Trying to…'he trailed off, his gaze now drawn toward the other end of the trench, the direction he'd been heading in last night.

Safe. He'd be safe down there.

'Elwood? You still with me?'

He felt Whiskey's hand clamp down on his shoulder, no gentle tap this time either; instead the old man began to shake him forcefully. 'Don't you be drifting off again now. Ain't no way I can carry you out of here.'

Elwood didn't look at the old man, only pointed. 'You ever been down there, Whiskey?'

The trench carried on for at least another thirty feet

before curving away and out of view. He guessed that it continued snaking through the forest like an old meandering river, eventually meeting a dry basin that was once a pond or small lake.

'No,' Whiskey replied abruptly. There was something in his tone though, something in the way he seemed to spit the word out.

'What do you know about this place?' Elwood still wasn't looking at him, his eyes fixed on the bend in the ditch. There was something down there. He didn't know what, didn't know how he knew. But there was, he was sure of it.

'Listen to me, Elwood,' the old man placed both his hands on his shoulders now and squeezed tight. 'Listen good. There ain't nothing out here worth looking for.'

Nothing.

'Hey, snap out of it.' More shaking. Elwood was aware, could hear the words and felt the hands upon him – he just couldn't act, couldn't draw his eyes away from that bend in the trench.

'I need to check what's down there. There's something down there, Whiskey.'

'There's *nothing* down there. Just a dry river is all.'

Bob Scotchni had spent his whole life wandering these woods – probably passed by this gulley on countless occasions – but Elwood knew the man had never followed it to see where it led. He just knew it.

Because it wasn't *for* him. It was for Elwood.

It was for Elwood and all the others like him.

'Like me?'

'Who are you talking to, Elwood? You hearing something I ain't?'

'There's something down there. Something I need to see,' he paused. 'I think they wanted me to come here. I don't know why, but they brought me out here... they were leading me to something.'

Whiskey was still hunkered down, but he shifted to his other knee now and glanced around, looking back up the trench and checking above them. 'Who?' he asked, gripping Bullseye's collar and bringing the dog closer to him. 'Who led you out here?'

'The astronaut. The woman and her daughter. They were with me last night. They were here, Whiskey. Right here. I'm telling you.'

The old man's shoulders slumped, and his face visibly eased. 'Ghosts, Elwood. They're just ghosts. Your ghosts.'

'My ghosts?' Elwood uttered, expecting them to take on some other meaning, and they almost did, something was there, something like a door – unlocked, but not open. 'My ghosts.'

'Come on,' Whiskey climbed to his feet. 'Let's get you up out of the dirt.'

He bent down and fixed a hand under each of Elwood's arms.

'I'll need your help on this one.'

Elwood's joints still complained furiously, but he placed his hands palms-down on the ground and managed to do his bit; once his ass was out of the dirt he leaned into the bedrock behind him and shimmied himself into an upright position. He couldn't help but smile briefly, ignoring the roughness of the sandstone against his bare back.

'Something tickle you?' Whiskey asked.

'Just a memory,' he replied. Noticing now that it hadn't been a blanket the old man had draped over him, but a coat instead. Still shivering a little he held onto it, clutching it about his person. 'I did a Baloo.'

'You did a what now?' Whiskey asked, grinning blankly.

'A Baloo,' Elwood replied. 'You know, that bear in The Jungle Book. El, my daughter, she loved the part when Baloo needs to scratch his back, you know? He does this kind of shimmy, up and down a tree. I'd copy it, and that girl would just howl, she found it so damn funny. It was… I mean, still is – always will be, I guess – one of the best sounds I ever heard.'

Whiskey grinned. 'Oh yeah, I remember that one, I was just a boy when that came out. My Jeanie, she loved those old cartoons. Had them all on the VHS. After she passed, and the player broke, I'd be lying if I told you I didn't go out and get all those cartoons on disc.'

They stood for a moment, just two guys laughing together in a ditch.

'You can put that on,' Whiskey pointed to the coat. 'Keep you warm until we get you back to the lake.'

'Thank you.' Elwood threaded his arms through. The woollen interior felt soft and comforting against his goose-pimpled flesh. He looked down at his feet and frowned.

'Yeah, can't help you with those,' Whiskey said. 'You'll just have to grin and bear it until we get back to my truck, I'm afraid.'

'How far's that?

'I'm parked at Kenner's. We ain't too far from the trail, but gosh, we're at least a mile and a half west of his store. That puts you at least two, maybe even two and a half miles from your villa.'

'Fuck,' Elwood blurted. 'I'm sorry. But... holy shit, that means I was out of it for, at least, what? An hour?'

'Couldn't say for sure, depends which route you took, but an hour's probably close.'

An hour. A whole hour unaccounted for. He cringed at the thought of himself wandering through the dark, alone, half naked. Had they been walking with him the whole time? What would someone have seen if they had just happened to be in the neighbourhood? Would they have seen him stumbling alone, his eyes glazed over, bumping into trees like some glitched video game character? Or would they have seen an astronaut and two dead girls shepherding him along, offering a gentle nudge in the right direction whenever an obstacle presented itself?

'Don't beat yourself up,' Whiskey offered, laying a hand on Elwood's shoulder, 'I told you this place has strange effects on some folk. The right folk. You ain't the first, sure as hell ain't going to be the last either, I'd set my watch on that.' He ushered him forward. 'Come on, let's get going.'

Elwood allowed the old man to lead him away, but not without taking one final glance down the gulley toward that bend, toward whatever was waiting around that corner. Because there was *something* there, he was sure of it. It was why they had brought him to this place; they wanted him to find whatever it was, but now, now this old man was leading him away and Elwood was letting him.

Come back.

That voice again.

That voice that wasn't a voice, it was more than that. It was a conversation through a crackling comms link, a game of tag with a dead girl. It was a signal, a low frequency broadcast that picked at his nerve endings as a guitar player does their strings. The strumming of chords translating into sounds. This was like that – at least, that's what he thought. The words he could hear were only words conjured up in his own mind, as a translation of whatever force was at play. Whatever transmission this forest was sending out into the world. He was receiving it.

He was the *right folk.*

But who was strumming the chords?

'Baloo.'

He turned back to Whiskey, suddenly light-headed, as though the word had pulled him back at the speed of light from a thousand miles away. The old man was staring at him.

'Sorry?' Elwood asked.

'Baloo,' the old man returned. 'Worked pretty good then, didn't it? Come on,' he gently eased Elwood along a few more steps. 'Come on, Bullseye.'

The dog had been clawing in the dirt a few feet back, but now he pitched his head up, eyes searching and tongue lolling, and padded happily toward them.

'What just happened?' Elwood asked, as they began to move up and out of the gulley. Bullseye ran ahead of them, circling trees and sniffing at underbrush.

'What happened is you started drifting again and I managed to get your attention.'

'By calling me Baloo?'

'No. Well, yeah, I guess. It was the memory more than the word. A little trick my Jeanie used to flip whenever we had a falling out. Which happened a lot. You don't spend seventy-two years with someone and not drift apart every now and then. Anyways, she said that sometimes, the right kind of memory can be like an anchor in a stormy sea. So, whenever we weren't ourselves, she'd throw out a word or two, something we both understood. Things like *Moira's forty-ninth,* or *Sandwell Beach, Tacoma Pie.* My favourite was *fart-burp.*' He chuckled to himself. 'She hated that one – always embarrassed her, me bringing that one up – but it made her smile too. It always helped us out of the rut. Out of the ditch, you might say.'

'You're a wise man, Whiskey.'

'No, I ain't wise, but I listen, and I remember. Always been good at that, and my Jeanie, she taught me a lot, God rest her.'

'Well, thank you anyway. And thank you, Jeanie.'

The old man tipped his cap. 'No bother. Trail's up ahead, other side of all that switchgrass,' he pointed ahead of them.

All Elwood could see was more trees, though, and a mass of wispy, tall grass that offered no hint of what might lay beyond. 'State paid for all the seeds back in… oh, must've been ninety-four, maybe ninety-six. Place has never had Rangers since the forest never made the Nationals, but a few locals – me and Jeanie included – walked all the trails and planted all the seeds along either side. I guess the state thought it would help deter folk from leaving the trail and they were too cheap to pay for fencing. It didn't work though – folk still wander, folk still don't come back.'

Elwood was only half-listening now; he was busy feeling something he hadn't felt in a long time. Gratitude. And not the sort of gratitude you felt for your dealer when they provided that next fix – no, this was genuine appreciation. The sort of gratefulness that restored one's faith in humanity, and resulted in a wildly different kind of high. This was the high you got from being the recipient of the pure and simple goodness of others, the kindness shown by a stranger who could so easily ignore whatever plight you might find yourself in.

He thought, then, that addiction actually had many faces. Most addicts were hooked on their own lives, their own goals and their own problems. They were addicted to finding some resolution, an end goal – meeting a target, buying that new thing they desperately wanted or getting to some place they felt they needed to be.

It wasn't always a drug. But in most cases, those addictions, those fierce aspirations, they took over, and they blinded people to what truly mattered.

He thought of the great Philosophiser, Alan Watts, and his analogy comparing life to song. You had to remember to stop and dance, and not let yourself be blinded by the anticipation of the crescendo. That was true.

But what Mr Watts hadn't mentioned was that when you did stop – when, for just a moment, you decided it was time to dance – you needed to be like Whiskey. You needed to take someone else by the hand and show them some moves.

THOSE YOU KILLED

***

It was almost midday when they got back to the villa. Both the front and French doors had been left wide open. Elwood found no sign of maggots on the lounge carpet though, or anything by Phil Collins in the stereo.

Keen to return more than just a word of thanks to the old man for saving his life no less, he insisted that Whiskey stick around so he could make them both some sandwiches for lunch. The old man graciously accepted the offer.

The two of them sat on the terrace and ate.

Elwood set down his empty plate. Bullseye was sprawled across the paving between them, content with the universe and everything in it, after enjoying a bowl of sliced ham and cold wieners.

Elwood had changed out of his dirty joggers and was now fully clothed.

Whiskey sipped the coffee Elwood had prepared for them (as what the fancy restaurants liked to call a *digestif*). Bob had scoffed at the word and Elwood had talked a little about his time as a successful writer, a time when he'd regularly frequented establishments that served *digestifs*.

Bob talked about the few restaurants they had in Misstonville township; The Slice, Jimmy's, and *Bistro @ the Ball Park*. All were the sorts of places where, if you asked for a *digestif*, you were apt to receive directions to the local pharmacy for antacid tablets.

Something had been playing on Elwood's mind since earlier that morning, though. Words that Whiskey had spoken, words that were still floating around in his head.

Your ghosts.

That's what he'd said when they had both been down in the gulley.

Your ghosts.

Elwood sipped his own *digestif* and teased a cigarette from his pack, casting a quick *do you mind* glance at the old man beside him.

Whiskey waved him on. 'Don't mind me.'

Elwood lit up. 'After you found me, and I told you about the…' he paused, not wanting to talk of dancing corpses and astronauts in the woods now that he felt reasonably *compos mentis*. 'About *them*,' he said. 'About what I've been seeing. You said they were my ghosts.'

Whiskey nodded.

'What did you mean? Is there anything else you can tell me about this place that might help me understand? Because I'm starting to think this has nothing to do with my own issues.'

The old man took another gulp from his mug and set it down on the table between them. He paused for a moment, remembering? Elwood wondered. Considering, perhaps? Maybe both. A moment later he spoke, confirming the latter.

'When you were staring down that gulley, you had this look in your eyes. That look reminded me of someone I used to know, someone from town. Jud Kennishaw. He had that look in his eyes.'

He scratched pensively at his beard, looking out toward the lake.

'Vietnam was a complete shitshow. But that wasn't

any excuse for the shitshow of a parade our boys got when they came home, those who made it home. Me, I was lucky. Ma and pa worked their asses off and used some of their savings to pay for a draft counsellor. Son of a bitch probably saved my life. I got my draft letter in sixty-six, see – I don't recall the exact date, but it was warm, so I guess it was maybe spring, probably summer, doesn't matter much. I was never a coward, let me be clear on that, I wasn't afraid of fighting for what was right. My pa fought in the Pacific and I always admired that. But 'Nam, that was different, and I didn't want no part in *that* war.'

He paused to sip some more of his coffee.

'I got the letter anyway. All because Johnson ended the marriage deferment the year before. Can't complain though, the counsellor told me what to do and I did it. He pulled a few strings and got me an appointment with the army shrink, told them I was unstable. So, I sat down with this doc, and he asked me two questions. He asked if I ever did drugs, and if I ever thought about killing myself. I told him yes – to both – and he disqualified me right there and then.

'Jeanie was waiting for me in the reception. I told her the news, and let me tell you, she never hugged me so tight in all our years, had me fit for bursting she did.'

He laughed a little, but his smile began to fade.

'Over her shoulder though, I see Jud sat on one of the chairs, hands in his pockets, eyes like a deer in headlights. He was there for his physical; no quack meet for him, his people couldn't afford a draft counsellor. And honestly, in that moment, I didn't feel pity or shame or guilt. I didn't feel inclined to help the boy, either – those things all came later, and they hit me hard I can tell you. Right then, though, I felt nothing but relief.' He paused again and swigged the rest of his coffee.

'Need another?' Elwood asked.

The old man checked his wristwatch. 'Got to be five o' clock somewhere right? I'll take a whiskey, if you still have any?'

Elwood fetched a couple of glasses and poured them both a moderate amount.

'I didn't see Jud again for almost three years after Jeanie and me left the draft office that day. He came home in sixty-nine, but he didn't come back the same, and he didn't come back alone. He brought his ghosts with him.

'He became a regular at The Quarry – not the actual quarry out at Jackson Bluffs, but this bar on the west side of town. I used to drop in from time to time for a drink with Gary, this guy I used to work with. We'd stop by after our shift for a cold one before heading on home; Jeanie never minded much, I didn't do it every day and I only ever stayed for one. She spoke with a lot of the other ladies in town, some of them had fellas who'd stay out till sundown, drinking away their pay, or losing it all at that damn casino over in Nilsport. And when their wives called them out, most were inclined to show those poor ladies the back of their hand.'

He took a sip of his whiskey.

'Ain't no place for that kind of behaviour, not then and not now.'

Elwood felt blood rise in his cheeks, remembering that time Gracie had tried to stop him from leaving the house. Tried to stop him from going to see Casper for that next fix he so desperately needed. He hadn't hit her – he'd never gotten that bad – but he *nearly* had. He'd raised his hand that evening, a momentary lapse in control fuelled by anger, desperation, instinct. He hadn't laid a finger on her, but for a split-second it had seemed as though he might, and to him, that felt just as bad.

She'd flinched, stumbled back and fallen down, hitting her head on a walnut console which they kept the telephone and car keys on. He'd walked out of the door, and hadn't looked back.

Elwood had spent most of that evening in blissful euphoria, strapped to a rocket ship fuelled by skag injection. Meanwhile, his wife, and Elouise – who was maybe two years old at the time – had spent most of their evening in the emergency room. Gracie had needed six stitches just above her right eyebrow. Questions had been asked, and she'd lied, lied to protect him.

The worst part about it though, was he never said he was sorry. What he wouldn't give now to go back to that time, to that moment in their hallway, he was sure he wouldn't raise a hand, not now. He'd let her embrace him, as she'd tried to do.

Elwood took a gulp from his glass, hoping to hide the fact that he was now fighting back tears. Whiskey had continued his tale, seemingly unaware.

'People made fun of Jud, pushed him around, teased him, but he was sure as shit they were out there,' the old man pointed across the lake. 'I remember one evening he was swaying on his stool, talking all kinds of crazy.

Saying they were out here in Misstonville woods, saying he found the entrance to their tunnels. That night he was chasing every drink with the same words, *Non Gratum Anus Rodentum*. He was hollering it like some priest doing one of those exorcisms, you know?'

Elwood shook his head. 'My Latin's very limited. I recognise *ass* in there though.'

'That's one of the great skills in life: recognising an ass when one presents itself.' They both laughed. 'I didn't know what it meant at the time, but I found out some years later, once guys started writing books about the shitshow. It means *not worth a rat's ass*. It's something the tunnel rats used to say, like a motto. You ever hear about the tunnel rats?'

Elwood shook his head again. He'd never paid much attention in history.

'Jud was a tunnel rat for pretty much the whole time he was out there in 'Nam. How he survived that long I have no idea, ain't no surprise to me he lost his mind either. See, the tunnel rats were little guys, and Jud was a real shorty – five feet and nothing much else. They were the guys who got sent down the tunnels the Viet Cong had dug; apparently, there were vast networks of these things underground. They were real small folk, so these tunnels were tight – I can't imagine what it must've been like to crawl into one of those things.

'I read about booby traps too, all kinds of nasty stuff. They had these things called punji sticks, like sharpened bamboo – real sharp, sharp enough to impale a guy. They had living traps too, used spiders and scorpions and snakes with the venom in them,' the old man shivered. 'The more I learned about the whole mess

231

later on, the more I felt like I should've passed on my advice to that young boy sat in the draft office. I should've just told him to act like a loon, then maybe things might've been different.'

'You can't blame yourself for the things that happened in that war,' Elwood offered. 'Or the draft office. You were young, younger than I am now. You had a wife.'

'Yeah. I try my best to forget about that day, but every now and then it comes back to me – whenever I drive down Sturdy Street and see the cemetery, I'm always reminded of what it all led to, an empty grave. But I'm sorry, I'm taking my sweet time explaining all of this to you – let me get to the point.'

'It's no bother to me. I don't have any other visitors scheduled in for today, unless the Sheriff decides today's the day he's going to pay me a visit.'

The old man's brow peaked at this. 'You got Sheriff Tims sniffing around?'

'No, but the Deputy said he'd stop by, said he always likes to come and speak with whoever's staying out here. Should I be worried?'

'He cares a lot for this town. Grew up here, knows all the history too. If he thinks you're going to add to that history, he'll get heavy with you. Remember when I said there's been guys like you before, staying here, getting themselves into trouble like you did last night? Well, like I said, they don't stick around too long, soon enough they're just gone. I think sometimes it's a visit from Jo Tims. A few words of encouragement, maybe more. He's known for getting rough sometimes.'

'Thanks for the heads up,' Elwood replied, deciding

then that he probably wouldn't be answering the door if this Jo Tims decided to stop by.

'No bother. But if you want my advice, I'd say get out now. Today. Before what happens last night happens again. It might not be me who finds you next time – might not be anybody, and then what? If Kenner would've seen you last night, he would've called the Sheriff for sure, I can guarantee you that. Wouldn't even surprise me if Sheriff Tims already has Kenner keeping an eye on you.'

Elwood saw the sense in leaving. A part of him had desperately wanted to leave last night. There was another part of him though, the part that wanted to see his daughter again, and that part was reminding him that he was getting clean. Regardless of whatever questionable shit was going on here, tonight he'd reach the seventy-two-hour milestone, a point he'd never reached in the comfort of his own home or any of the rehabs he'd run from.

'I'll try my best to behave,' he said.

Whiskey laughed. 'Well, okay then. Let me finish up here, I'm about done anyway, then I'll be on my way.'

Elwood poured them both another glass and the old man continued.

'Day after all that hollering at The Quarry, I came out here with Emelia. She was our first dog, looked just like Lassie too, God rest her. Anyways, I'm driving up Crescent and I see him walking along the side of the road in full military fatigues.

'I didn't know it then, but some folks had already called the cops. Apparently he'd walked all the way out from town like that, just marching along, pistol in one hand and a flashlight in the other. Couple of revolvers stuffed down his waistline too, even a bayonet. I mean, the guy was ready for warfare, no doubt.'

'Holy shit,' Elwood blurted.

'That's what I said when I pulled up alongside him. Kept the truck rolling, of course. I asked if he was okay, or if he needed a ride back into town. But he didn't even look at me. Hell, my guess is he didn't even know I was there. He had that same look in his eyes, the one you had this morning. And he was mumbling to himself too, same as you.

'He was saying he killed them all back in Củ Chi. Said they were all supposed to be dead, but they weren't. He said they'd followed him back, they were in the caves, they were waiting for him and he had to go finish the job. He had to go kill the gooks.

'I tried to get through to him, told him to get in my truck and we could go for a beer, but he just kept marching. I was tempted to pull over, maybe lay my hands on him. Truth be told, though, I was scared. I thought there was every chance he'd mistake me for one of those Viet Cong he was looking for, point that pistol square between my eyes and *bang*, that'd be all she wrote. So, I let him go.

'Apparently some vacationers out trekking the trails saw him a little while after that. They didn't even attempt to approach him, and why would they? They weren't locals, they didn't know Jud. They said he was shouting too, hollering that same motto – *Non Gratus Anus Rodentum* – then he left the trail and disappeared into the forest. They were the last folks to ever see him. I was the last who ever had a real chance at helping him.'

He drank some more whiskey and turned to Elwood.

'That's another reason I helped you out today. I didn't want you to be another Jud Kennishaw, and I didn't want to be that guy again, that guy who had a chance to help someone and was too God damn scared to do the right thing.'

Bullseye began to snore.

Elwood couldn't hear it, though. He was close, so close. He'd hoped hearing this story would be the push he needed to open that door all the way, that door in his mind that would open on… truth?

'Yeah. This place is good at drawing out your own demons if you're vulnerable enough. And I mean no disrespect by that.'

'None taken,' Elwood replied, still pondering, still trying to remember. 'Damn this shit in my veins. I can't think like I used to. There's something I need to remember, something about…' his eyes drifted toward the lake. 'Olesk. *Olesk*. How do I know that name? *Dayday,* too. I know it. I'm sure of it. Ghosts. You said ghosts. You said *my* ghosts. And Jud had his, those he killed. And Celia, she had the baby. What am I trying to get at, here? God damn it,' he gulped down the last of his whiskey and set the tumbler down roughly on the table. He remembered this breed of frustration during particularly dismal spells of writer's block. Characters couldn't just miraculously figure something out, that was stupid. There had to be a thought process, a path that led them to whatever it was they needed to know. He was on that path now, he was like one of his…

'Well, whatever it is, my advice would be to figure

it out as quickly as you can. For your own sake and sanity. I know you want that monkey off your back, and I wish you the best of luck with that, I really do. I think you stand a good chance of beating that demon, for sure. Just remember what I told you about memories in a stormy sea. Remember that big bear and how you made your girl laugh. The longer you stay here, though, the closer you'll get to something like Jud, or Celia, or any of the others who've come here over the years and lost themselves. You're a ticking time bomb, Elwood. A catastrophe waiting to happen.'

Catastrophe.

Only a word, a single word, but it had begun to illuminate that dark room in his mind. The room with the door that was open now. Wide open.

Catastrophe.

'Catastrophe,' Elwood muttered. 'That's it. That's what they called them, that's what they called my… only it wasn't that – not quite, no, no, *no*… It was…it was *Cathistrophe*. That's it.' Elwood turned to Whiskey, his eyes wide with implausible comprehension. '*Cathistrophies*!'

Bullseye jumped to his feet and started growling.

'That's what they called them. Holy shit, how did I not see it before? I should've known, I should've remembered as soon as I saw that fucking name badge on the suit – Olesk – I should've known then.'

But he knew why he hadn't remembered. He knew why he'd been so blind; it was the same reason he'd been so blind to his family for so long, to the things that truly mattered. The heroin. The burying of memories.

'Should've known what?' Whiskey asked.

But Elwood wasn't entirely there with the old man, not anymore; he was in his own mind now, crossing the threshold of that doorway and into a room that was no longer dark.

He'd nearly found the thought on the landing when pursuing the eyeless girl. And that dancing corpse, what had she said? *Dayday*, that was it, that's what she'd called him, only it wasn't him she was talking to, it was someone else – he'd known it then, but he couldn't get at the memory, couldn't grasp it. Like a speck of dust or fluff in the bathtub, any effort to retrieve it had caused it to slip further away.

But on the landing beforehand, something had helped him along; an idea, a memory of how he once wrote, and what he'd written. The memory had been like a key, opening a door that would ultimately lead to this realisation, this absurd reality that he hadn't been able to comprehend at the time.

Now, though, now the fog was clearing, and the right words had been spoken, laid out before him like breadcrumbs into his past, he knew. He remembered.

Olesk, the girl – her name was Laney – and her mother – Meredith – they were *characters*.

They were characters from the books that critics had referred to as his *Cathistrophies*. His final three, the worst three, because with each of those books he'd lost a part of who he was, the heroin claiming that which it always did, when given the chance.

And the characters, they were those parts of him, the parts of who he was, the parts he'd lost along the way, not just written out of his stories but written out of his life too, those parts he'd chosen to let go, to bury deep down and forget about. Those he'd killed.

Then a thought occurred to him.

Three. There were three *Cathistrophic* novels that had heralded the end of his career, the end of who he was. But only two had manifested themselves so far.

And he knew what was coming next.

CHAPTER FIFTEEN
ALWAYS

Ephraim stepped into the elevator and presented the card to the reader on the panel. The scanner answered with a beep and the thin LED strip bordering the panel glowed green.

'You've lost your fucking mind.' The surviving guard was being helped to his feet by Dr Streaver, hand pressed against the bullet hole in his left shoulder.

Ephraim couldn't recall his name – *Erickson? Henrickson?* – not that it mattered anyway; all that mattered to him right now was Always. He had to get to her, had to speak with her, before she was lost entirely.

If she wasn't already.

'Mr Comeroy,' Streaver bleated. 'Mr Comeroy, please. Don't go down there. It's not safe.'

The younger guard was on his feet now, searching for his pistol.

'You don't get to tell me what to do,' Ephraim said. You're lucky I'm not dragging your ass down there with me. You should've stopped this, you shouldn't have let it get this far.'

Streaver adjusted his crooked spectacles and grimaced. 'I tried to stop her, but you know just as well as I do how much this meant to her.'

'Well, you didn't try hard enough, Doc.'

Streaver winced. 'Please. Don't be a fool. We need to wait for Caruthers and his team. Like I said, they're already on their way here. They'll help resolve the situation.'

Ephraim scoffed at this. 'Resolve? We both know what that means, Doc. It means someone upstairs wants this whole situation to go away. Losses are about to be cut. My wife's not going to be one of them.' Ephraim pushed the button labelled *B3*.

Neoteny and Regenerative Biotechnologies –
Research and Development.

The speaker on the panel pinged and the doors began to slide shut.

'She's not your wife anymore, Ephraim. Ephraim, please, list–'

The doors closed.

A robotic voice from the speaker: 'Going down.'

Then the music started. The awful tune that Always had told him about, the sort of monotonous melody you heard in shopping malls. Neither uplifting nor downbeat, it reminded Ephraim of the last call he'd had with her. Well, the last time she'd actually spoken on a call. Her voice – her usually childlike voice, tinged with curiosity and wonder and excitement – had been apathetic. Almost inhuman.

He looked down at the pistol, and the blood that was

already on his hands. He hoped there wouldn't be more.

But it hit him, then. The thought, like a kick to the balls.

A green light blinked next to the button marked *A6* on the control panel.

Was he going to kill his wife? Was that what was happening here today?

A5.

Surely not, he thought. But what if it comes to that?

A4.

What if she really was so far gone there was no coming back? What if Streaver was right? What if she wasn't Always anymore?

What if she wasn't his *wife* anymore?

A3.

No, he thought. If they're smart enough to take things in one direction, then surely they can come back the other way. There'll be some way of reversing whatever she might've done. A naïve notion, but it was all he had right now, and he needed to remain optimistic, no matter what. Not just for Ally; for the baby, too.

A2.

He fixed the gun to his belt and breathed deeply, watching the lights blink beside each level on the panel.

A1.

He'd descend below ground level any second now… what was that smell? Something dank, wild, swampy rose in the air.

A0.

The stench grew in intensity as the elevator continued down. A deep, boggy scent with the fishy overtones of a seafood market.

B1.

Ephraim began to gag. He pictured crates overflowing with rotten trout and putrid squid. A marshy pond filled with dead leaves, mouldy driftwood and decomposing carcasses. Dear God, he thought. What am I descending into?

B2.

He let his fingertips rest on the pistol, wondering whether or not he should just leave it in the elevator. It might be better to need it and *not* be able to use it, rather than need it and…

'You don't have to shoot to kill,' he murmured.

The elevator slowed to a halt and the robotic voice spoke once again. 'You have arrived at level B3.' The doors began to slide open; a thin chute of water quickly turned to a torrent as it flooded in around Ephraim's feet.

'Shit,' he moved away from the doors and pressed himself against the back of the elevator. It was a futile move, though; within seconds he was almost knee-deep in murky water.

A gasp escaped him as he shifted his attention to the corridor. Although he'd never been down here, he guessed it didn't normally look like it did now.

The corridor itself was pretty much identical to the one in which he'd confronted Streaver and the guards: straight, clinical, with doors on both sides leading off into smaller laboratories. There were intersections at regular intervals too: more corridors, leading off in all directions, connecting with others, and so on.

A maze of white linoleum.

Only down here, much of the white was no longer visible.

The flow of water had subsided now, and Ephraim was left standing in what was essentially a stagnant canal, the surface of which swelled just above his knees. Duckweed and water lettuce floated about his thighs.

He waded into the corridor; red willows climbed the walls on either side, the low ceiling forcing them into a natural arch that blocked out most of the fluorescent strip lighting. These trees rose up from muddy banks that lined the hallway on both sides, littered with petty spurge, yellow nutsedge, sweetclover and melilot.

He stared down into the water itself. Beneath the surface, his legs passed through great thickets of water hyacinth and crystalwort. Clusters of spikerush dotted the water in various spots too, poking out like arrows from a quiver.

Ephraim jerked as he felt something slither past his right leg. He looked back, dumbfounded, and saw that the water was teeming with life.

Swarms of small crustaceans moved nonchalantly through the shallows, occasionally dispersed by a darting tadpole or other smaller fish. On the banks of the canal – because that was what this was; it wasn't a corridor in a building in Sacramento, not anymore – slugs and snails ambled through dirt that was being toiled by worms. Ephraim watched as one of these worms, long and slimy, lost its balance and began to barrel-roll down to the shore, eventually disappearing into the water with an almost inaudible *plop*.

'This is insane,' he whispered to himself, reaching out to touch one of the red willow leaves. It was real, no doubt about it. The smell was enough to confirm that absurd fact. The elevator doors closed behind him, and without thinking about it, he removed the pistol from his belt and clutched it with both hands.

'Ally,' he called out. 'Ally, can you hear me?'

A splash, somewhere far away in a distant corridor. Something big, falling into the water.

'Ally, is that you?'

No reply.

He noticed some writing on the wall, only partially visible through the groves that had terraformed this level of the building. He drew back some of the branches and learned that he was heading toward *Neo Labs 11-15C*, and that he needed to take the next left for *ReGen Labs 4-21F*.

When he reached the first intersection of corridors, he took the one on the left, remembering from their conversations that Always worked in Lab 19D.

He moved cautiously, conscious that he was now an intruder in a living habitat that wasn't his own. For all he knew there could be things down here which had teeth, had venom.

'Ally, I just want to talk, honey. Can you hear me?'

Another splash, closer this time.

'Talk to me, Ally. Please.' swamp

Ripples travelled across the water at another crossroads far ahead of him. Large ripples, not the sort that a tumbling worm might create.

He held the gun in front of him now, his finger poised on the trigger. He didn't want to shoot his wife, but for all he knew there might be gators lurking somewhere in this swamp. A ludicrous thought, but so too was the idea that an entire floor of a building, located almost fifty miles away from the nearest substantial body of water, could play host to a fully-formed, thriving wetland. It's like a giant aquarium, he thought, filled with all these tiny creatures. But where's the predator? Who, or what, is top of the food chain down here?

He tightened his hold around the pistol grip, almost certain he wasn't at the top of that list.

Ephraim looked back, hearing another splash somewhere behind him. Even closer this time.

More ripples broke the stagnant surface, spreading out across the intersection from which he'd turned only a few moments ago.

Something was stalking him.

'Ally, if you can hear me, shout up. I'm starting to get a little freaked out now.'

He came upon an opening in the willows to his right. A doorway, the branches and vines twirling about its border, suggesting someone – or something – was regularly passing through it, creating a well-trodden path.

19D was printed in block black vinyl above the doorway.

This is it, he thought. Her lab.

He stepped over the threshold and into what felt like another world entirely.

Out in the corridors there'd at least been some semblance of the artificial base layer that still existed beneath the boggy facade. In here though, there was nothing to suggest it had ever been anything but a wild habitat.

Moss blanketed the walls behind dense stands of red willow. Throughout the room, clusters of fat-bottomed cypress trees rose up like statues, showing decades of growth in what couldn't have been much longer than a day or so.

Mounds of dirt – he guessed there were desks or workbenches beneath them – played host to an eclectic mix of greenery that swarmed with insects and other creepy crawlies. Ephraim felt a tickling sensation on the back of his neck and released his grip on the pistol to quickly slap whatever it was. He brought his hand back down and found the squashed, bloody remains of a giant mosquito in his palm.

'Damn it.' He wiped his hand on his leg, obliterating the rest of the corpse and leaving a bloody streak of wing-bits and leg-parts across his thigh. 'Ally, are you in here?'

An intense alkaline scent had begun to invade his nostrils, settling at the back of his throat like a dollop of peanut butter.

Another splash, just out in the corridor now. It was close. Whatever it was.

He scrambled toward the nearest cypress tree and positioned himself behind it, hoping to get a glimpse of whatever it was that was following him, without it seeing him.

You're kidding yourself, Ephraim, he thought. It knows *exactly* where you are. He wasn't being quiet about things; water still sloshed and rippled in his wake.

As he listened intently for more movement outside, he became aware of another sound, this one much closer. It was a sort of echoed thumping – like your heartbeat when you drop beneath the surface of the water in your bath – only it wasn't rhythmic, and it seemed to belong to more than one heart.

Thump, thump-thump thump, thump…

It was coming from somewhere nearby, beyond a desk – no longer a desk – just a few feet from Ephraim. He stepped away from the tree, allowing himself a quick glance back toward the open doorway, where the water remained calm and still, and began to approach the desk that was no longer a desk, but instead a mossy tor of soil.

Thump-thump, thump, thump, thump-thump-thump.

It was getting louder now, he felt it in his ears like a heavy bassline. He looked back towards the doorway. Still no sign of movement over there.

Thump-thump-thump-thump-thump-thump–

Sweat stung his eyes. He could feel his own heartbeat quickening, racing in fact; were he anywhere else in the world right now, he'd probably insist on sitting down for a moment, worried that some sort of coronary malfunction was imminent.

He came around the desk, his eyes flaring at the sight of what was slowly being revealed to him. He had to set a hand down on the mossy dirt to steady himself as he tried not to puke.

It was a nest.

He was far from a specialist in any biological field, but he knew enough to know it was a nest, it was clear to see. Literally, in fact.

He stood on the perimeter of what was essentially a henge; a circular earthwork formed by a radial mound of dirt. This mound protruded above the water level, resulting in a closed, circular pool of water that was at least twenty feet in diameter.

He bent over and rested his hands on the bank, staring down into the water, struggling to comprehend what he was looking at. The pool was brimming with viscous sacs piled on top of one another; these spherical gelatinous wombs held some sort of larvae that looked all-too human, and at the same time not. They were bigger than anything in the photos Always had occasionally shown him, at least the length of his lower arm from fingertip to elbow. Their flesh was partially translucent, with a pinkish pigment that darkened at the head. Each had four appendages, and when he looked closely, Ephraim could see five smaller extremities at the end of each one. Fingers and toes, he thought. These things have fingers and toes.

He was mesmerised, so he didn't hear the disturbance in the water behind him, wasn't aware that something else had now entered the lab.

Their heads appeared almost as large as his clenched fist, their faces those of new-born babies – round and pudgy, but with dot-like eyes as black as crude oil. Protruding from each of their heads were six biramous gills – three on either side, extending out like hairy tentacles. The babies had a strange cuteness about them, and this unnerved him. They were an abomination, unnatural. Whatever they were, and however endearing they looked, they weren't supposed to exist. That was clear to Ephraim, as clear as the glutinous sacs which held them.

The larvae wriggled and writhed, bumping against the interior walls of their sacs and creating the chorus of thumping that had initially drawn his attention. The thumping, though, was slowing down; the peppy little things were becoming docile.

As each of them became still, Ephraim stood upright and took a step back from the circle. They had all slowly turned to face the same way. They were all looking at *him*.

Their beady eyes stared up and his sense of vulnerability deepened. He once again entwined both hands around the pistol grip and held it tightly, checking the safety was still disengaged. He expected at any moment that one by one, the uncanny amphibians might burst through their sacs and leap toward him like an army of frogs. Covering his body, his face, sucking at his skin, his eyeballs – shit, did these things have teeth? he wondered.

Things that were still growing in sacs or wombs didn't have teeth, did they?

Perhaps not, but that was nature and these things were far from natural, far from normal, with their amphibious torsos and round baby faces.

What little light there was suddenly dimmed. A shadow appeared, towering above his own, casting him and the babies into darkness. Then he understood, and the terrifying comprehension dawned upon him like the shadow that now loomed immense and gloomy.

They weren't looking at him.

Something else had caught their attention. Something else that induced unconditional devotion, something right behind him.

Their mother.

Ephraim turned to face whatever had been watching

him, stalking him, the thing that had silently approached and was now upon him.

It was her, yes. Always, Ally, his childhood crush come teenage sweetheart and later his wife. Mother to their three month-old baby girl. Doctor, scientist, Raiders supporter, lover of dystopian YA and unashamed Daddy Yankee fangirl. The sweetest, most kind-hearted person he'd ever known.

Now, a monster.

There was no coming back from this, there couldn't be. She wasn't even human, not now.

'What did you do, Ally? What did you do?'

The thing that used to be his wife raised its head and began to suck at the air.

He wondered for a moment if she was trying to talk to him – but only for a second, and then she moved toward him.

CHAPTER SIXTEEN
THE UNFRIENDLY GHOST

Elwood sat at the dining table, a mug of coffee turning cold in his hands. He'd been this way for the best part of an hour, staring at the car key next to a plate of uneaten toast on the table's surface. Deliberating, considering, pondering, whatever the hell you wanted to call it. Shrinks called it fight-or-flight, or hyperarousal; a dissonance within the brain that caused stress, anxiety, depression. Even death, in some cases.

He thought it strange that ultimately, the inability to make a decision might eventually lead to death. Wasn't there a level of Dante's hell reserved for the indecisives? It wasn't just a harbinger of death, but a sin to boot.

He had an itch. A couple, in fact. One of them he was sure could be relieved by picking up that key, heading out the door, jumping into his car, and driving away from this place.

The other itch, though, that required a needle.

He tried to focus his mind on the first – quite sure that the latter wouldn't help resolve the former, but almost optimistic that the former might eliminate the latter.

Why stick around? This was the question he needed to tackle – needed to wrestle to the ground and gain a clear understanding of – because right now, in many ways, the idea of staying at Lake Chance seemed like a complete folly. The place was clearly dangerous, for his sort anyway. The weak, the lost, the tortured. There was something out there in the woods, something that called to him and those like him from years gone by. Something that showed you things.

If he left now, though, wouldn't heroin do the same thing? Sure, he was doing well, he was four days clean, but that wasn't long enough; he still felt vulnerable to the call of the needle, and if he was back home, he was quite sure he'd answer that call.

But so too was he vulnerable to the call of Misstonville Forest. It had taken the others who came before him – the few that Whiskey had told him about, and probably countless more over the years. Poor souls who were caught in the snare of whatever it was out there; caught, brought out into the deep woods, and never seen again.

He was different, though. Yes, he was like them in most ways: weak, tortured, grappling with his own demons – the parts of himself he'd lost through his addiction, the characters he'd killed who now seemed to symbolise those parts of himself.

He had something else though, something he guessed the others hadn't had. The knowledge of the power of memory.

Baloo.

And not just any memory, but the sort that anchored you in a stormy sea. That was what Whiskey had said; the power of a good memory could do that, because good memories brought with them a sense of fortitude. They could save you.

If he could win this fight, he could win the other one, too. At its simplest, that was what this argument came down to: if he could stay here, focus his thoughts on figuring out what the hell was going on, then the heroin would fade into the background. He'd never been a man of faith, never believed in God or sat in the pews for anything other than funerals and weddings. But the Church was right about something, the devil *did* make work for idle hands. And if he left now, he was apt to become the embodiment of those words.

It was selfish, sure, but didn't most endeavours begin as self-serving? He had a family – well, he didn't have a wife anymore, that train had left the station and there was no return service. But he still had a daughter, and he'd never be able to help her unless he first helped himself. That was what all of this came down to; she was the reason for his being here in the first place.

She was old enough now to have some awareness of what was going on, to know that daddy wasn't around, and at some point down the line she was going to ask why – why he'd gone away, why he'd left them, and how he'd managed to find his way back.

Elwood thought of Whiskey again. The old man had

helped him, when ignoring him would've been far easier. He said it was what his wife would've wanted, his Jeanie. His actions were guided by that thought, the pure and simple idea of living up to the love or the memory of another. There was a time, before the dope, when Elwood had been that guy. It wasn't just his writing and success that had been fuelled by a love for his family, a need for them to be proud of him, to affirm his actions. It had been everything else too: the donations to hospices and schools in poverty-stricken neighbourhoods; the funding programme he'd set up for amateur authors; the free webinars, the time he'd dedicated to talking with fans, stopping for photos.

A time when he'd possessed helping hands instead of idle ones.

He had a chance to do good here, perhaps. He couldn't help those who'd came before him, but he might be able to help those who would almost certainly come after. There were enough in the world, that was for sure, others that Casper no doubt would send here for a little detox.

His phone, which he'd set down on the table, suddenly began to buzz like a dentist's drill. He looked at the caller ID and a somewhat bemused laugh escaped him.

FG is calling. 'Casper fucking Stevens,' he muttered, shaking his head.

It was as though the friendly ghost was haunting him, listening in on his thoughts somehow. He took a gulp of coffee, which had now become a frappé, then picked up the phone and answered.

Casper didn't wait for Elwood to announce himself.

'*Bunnyman,*' he exclaimed, like some old game show host announcing the grand prize, *a lakeside retreat!* 'Elwood, my main man, how the fuck's it hanging out there? God's honest, I didn't expect you to last this long,' he laughed.

'Actually, I was just thinking of you,' Elwood replied.

'Oh, really? Were you jerking off?'

'Christ, no. How many people have you sent here? Before me, I mean. How many others like me have you let stay here?'

Silence.

'Casper?'

Elwood checked the screen to make sure the call was still active. It was.

'Casper, can you hear me?'

A clearing of the throat on the other end. 'Yeah, I hear you. Why're you asking me that? You been talking to someone out there?'

'Just answer the question, Casper, please. How many?'

'Hold on just a second, bunnyman, I'm not a big fan of your tone right now. You haven't forgotten that I did you a favour, have you?'

Elwood wasn't the biggest fan of Casper's tone now either, he'd heard that tone before, those same words too in fact. It was a question normally reserved for those who hadn't paid up on time, hadn't paid what they owed and by doing so had purchased themselves a ticket to some back alley or derelict building, where they'd be left, beaten to within an inch of their lives, bones broken, teeth smashed in, and sometimes worse, if rumours were to be believed.

He needed to tread carefully.

He was getting better now, shaking off the timorous, cowardly veil that heroin threw over most junkies, but he was still just Elwood, a guy who'd been in so few fights during the course of his life that he could count them on one hand – a guy who'd never been capable of hurting anyone. But Casper, he was a drug dealer. And a pretty serious one too. He could be dangerous, especially if he didn't like you.

'No,' Elwood replied. 'I haven't forgotten, and I appreciate you letting me come here, Casper. I really do. The place has fucked with me a little, got me on edge, but it's done me some good. Done me a world of good, actually.'

'Good to hear,' Casper's tone was calmer now. 'So, you been getting out into those woods much? Breathing in that country air?'

Elwood recalled his nocturnal jaunt the night before last, and the swim in the lake. 'A little,' he replied. 'Actually, I plan on heading into town later this morning.'

'Town? What business you got there?'

'I hear there's an old lady who owns a bookstore. I want to talk with her.'

Silence again.

'What're you sniffing around for, bunnyman? Planning a book or some shit?'

'I don't know, maybe, one day. Right now, I just want to know more. I might be onto something here. The shit I've been seeing can't just be in my head, something's going on here, and I think I need to find out what.'

'The whole fucking world is weird, that place ain't no different. What exactly is it that you think you're onto?'

Elwood didn't want to go into the details, not with Casper. You didn't explain this sort of stuff to your dealer – ex-dealer, he hoped – who'd likely sneer at such confessions. You shared this sort of thing with normal folk, kindly old men like Whiskey who might impart some sincere advice or wisdom.

'Nothing major,' he lied. 'Just… I don't know. Just a chance for me to maybe do some good, I guess.'

'Do some good?' Casper scoffed.

'I'm being serious. People go missing here, Casper, did you know that? You knew about the murders.'

'They're big fucking woods and people go missing in them. So? People go missing every day, in towns, cities, and in big fucking forests like that one. How exactly is it that you think *you* are going to be able to change that? What? You going to paint a big sign? Do a song and fucking dance about the whole thing? And who are you hearing this shit from? Who you been talking to?'

He didn't want to bring Whiskey into this. He didn't want someone like Casper knowing who Whiskey was; it didn't feel right, didn't feel safe. 'Nobody, I… you know, I Googled some stuff,' Elwood replied. 'And I just want to find out what's going on. Maybe help if I can.'

'Help? Who the fuck are you? Do I need to come out there? Maybe bring a special delivery with me?'

'No,' Elwood snapped.

He took a breath.

'No, thanks,' a little calmer now. 'It's okay. I'm okay. Well, I'm not okay, but I'm getting there. I'm getting better. And whatever's going on here, I think it can help me. I think if I can help in some way, it'll help me too.'

He felt a surge of adrenaline then. His flesh tingled, not only at the words, words he thought he would never speak – *I'm getting better* – but the sincerity behind them, a truthful conviction that signalled a definite step-change.

'I don't want you doing anything stupid, bunnyman, like running your mouth. You hear me?' He didn't even give Elwood a chance to reply. 'Five-O down there already has it in for me, those fuckers *hate* me.' More coughing. 'Fucking backwoods barneys wouldn't know a Screwball from an El Diablo, but they can cause trouble. Any kind of light, and they're on you like a fucking moth.'

Elwood had never tried an El Diablo – heroin mixed with cocaine and marijuana – but he'd had his fair share of Screwballs and Primos, H-bombs and Dynamite doses. The Screwball had been his juice of choice, the classic pairing of heroin and meth. Just hearing the word had sparked a small fire somewhere deep within him, a fire that only a Screwball could douse.

And only seconds before he'd been sure he was getting better.

Was he really this susceptible? He silently damned Casper for even mentioning the word out loud.

The friendly ghost continued his rant. 'Don't you go talking to anyone, not about missing persons, not about anything. I don't want that kind of heat, and you shouldn't even be going into town. Did you forget what we agreed, you junkie-fuck?'

Elwood reached for the cold coffee, wishing it was whiskey, and took another large gulp. He fished his packet of cigarettes out from his pocket and quickly lit one, his hands trembling. Casper had a way of putting you down, reminding you of your place in *his* world.

'We agreed you'd keep to yourself and talk to nobody. We agreed you'd get supplies before you got there, so you didn't have to show your junkie face at any of the stores. We agreed you'd only walk in the woods, nowhere else. We agreed you wouldn't answer the door to anyone, or have any of your junkie friends come visit you. But now... now you're talking about swanning off into town like you're on fucking vacation, to talk to some old lady, to show your face. So, tell me, bunnyman, how many of our agreements have you already broken? Because that wouldn't be very nice, would it? That wouldn't be very gracious of you, would it?'

This was turning bad, and that was the last thing Elwood needed right now. 'None, Casper. None, I swear. I just – I didn't. I don't... I'm sorry I won't, I won't do it, I'll just...'

'Bluh bluh sorry bluh bluh,' Casper laughed. 'There's the bumbling junkie I know. Getting better my ass.'

Elwood felt himself sinking.

The tidal wave that was Casper Stevens continued. 'You get three more days, you hear me? That's the week we agreed on, no more. Do you understand me, bunnyman?'

'Yes, Casper. Yes, I understand.'

'Good. And in the meantime, you better forget about going into town to speak with some old lady. The only person you're going to be speaking with is yourself, or that little monkey I know you still have on your shoulder. And the only place you're going to is the other rooms in that villa, or the woods. Get out into the woods all you like, bunnyman, get lost for all I care, but stay away from town, and stay away from people. Do you hear me?'

'Yeah, I hear you, Casper,' he lit another cigarette.

'Good. I'm glad we have an understanding.' The line went dead.

Elwood stared blankly at the phone. Trying to process what had just happened.

He felt himself steadying, the shakes beginning to subside. He couldn't help but feel shame wash over him, though. All the hours of conversation with Whiskey, the deliberation, the clearing of the fog and the memories, the feeling that he was actually getting better – and all it had taken was a two-minute phone call with Casper fucking Stevens to bring him right back down.

Screwball. That fire still burned within him, raging toward a blaze now.

He knew there was only one way to douse the flames.

He picked up the car key and headed for the door.

Fuck Casper.

CHAPTER SEVENTEEN
AUBREY AND THE SHAWNEE

'*Some experts say social distancing could be introduced as early as next week, with a full lock–*'

Elwood killed the engine and the radio along with it.

Gilead Street had been easy enough to find. He'd tapped the street name into his phone and brought up a Google map of the area; there'd only been one possible route to take from the villa, so he'd fixed his phone to the holder on the dashboard and made his way into town.

Casper had been with him for most of the ride. A voice in his ear telling him he shouldn't be doing this, shouldn't be leaving the villa, shouldn't be talking to folks, *have a fucking Screwball.*

Screwball.

That fire still burned, but it wasn't spreading.

He'd hoped it wouldn't be too busy in town, and that

turned out to be the case. It was still early in the day; a few people walked along the store fronts, but they were the early birds, here with purpose. They weren't browsing, their interests were already promised to something else, something they absolutely needed to get this morning, so they could crack on with whatever plans they had for the day – likely involving said item of interest.

He watched a middle-aged fella in denim overalls and a baseball cap walk by, head low, a bag of nails in one hand and a couple of timber strips tucked under his arm.

DIY.

A lady in an ankle-length green coat hurried along behind the man, packs of what appeared to be flour and sugar held tightly against her chest.

Forgotten promise of a birthday cake.

A young couple holding hands, walking briskly toward the end of the road, where the local bank occupied the substantial corner property.

Mortgage appointment.

A young boy on a bicycle, newspaper bag slung over his shoulder and headphones over his ears.

No deliberation needed with that one.

Elwood climbed out of his car. There were only a dozen or so other vehicles occupying the parking area (two long rows of angled spots which ran the entire length of Gilead Street). An arched roof of bottle-green pine sat atop equidistant pillars of white stone, creating a shelter for the cars that were parked there. The street itself was a one-way system; you'd enter from Main Street, do a lap, and exit back onto Main Street. The end of the road was separated by a row of bollards from a paved pedestrian area, where a modest fountain quietly spouted water and played host to thirsty wrens and wandering chickadees.

Store fronts lined the road on either side of the arched parking area, creating a quaint little shopping precinct. Like that of the villa though, its charm was fading; many of the stores were open, some closed, but quite a few were derelict, their windows boarded up and turned into advertising spots for other local businesses that were still managing to keep their heads above the water. Large banners offered the chance to *Drive away TODAY! with fast finance at Poole's Autos*, or to *Help yourself at the Nilsport Breakfast Buffet for only $3.99,* and *Vote James Wright for Mayor – Wright has the Right Stuff!*

The buildings themselves were a mixture of red and yellow-brick townhouses, with a few white stones dotted among them – some even had turrets, and a few still showed the names of the original businesses that might have occupied them over a century before, painted in white and fading after decades of exposure to the elements. The ground-level storefronts of each building were clad in grey PVC, with sheltered doorways and external signs hanging above; tacky and garish when compared with the old-world feel of the upper-storeys.

He looked up and down the street, scanning each of the signs until his eyes came upon one that read *Tome is Where the Heart is.* He locked his car and crossed the street, heading toward the tiny outlet that seemed to occupy only a third of the building it was housed in –

the lion's share of which played host to the neighbouring *99 Cent Store.*

He stepped up onto the sidewalk and peered through the window onto a carefully curated display. Neat little stacks of books were accompanied by handwritten captions on yellow paper that included short biographies for the authors. He smiled as he read a few of them: *dark tales from Nilsport-born Michael Benavidez; spooky stories from the ghoul of Bowles County, Nick Harper.* There was also a small area dedicated to the shopkeeper's own works, *Non-fiction titles from Misstonville Historian Aubrey Christie. Trial by Rope: A History of Misstonville Township and County; How the Shawnee Shaped Misstonville; Being Black in the Backwoods.*

This well-ordered foreground was in stark juxtaposition to what lay beyond in the deeper interior. A heavenly chaos, the sort of disorderly establishment only the most vehement of bookworms could appreciate. Beneath the dim lights was a landscape of crooked paperback mountains, books upon books upon books, all piled precariously atop one another. Foothills of magazines and periodicals created pathways between these bookish ranges for the peppy explorers and collectors to tread. Any collector would have a field day in such a place. They'd almost certainly lose their mind too; hardbacks were stacked tightly spine to spine, horizontally, vertically, upside down and inside out from floor to ceiling in some places. A cornucopia of well-thumbed reads, torn jackets, broken spines, sun-bleached covers and frayed corners.

Elwood felt a tide of nostalgia wash over him. As a

young man, if he hadn't been getting high out in the forest, he'd been hanging out in caves of wonder like this one. A smile had managed to unfurl on his face without him realising. He couldn't wait to get inside.

That Screwball fire within him raged no longer, now nothing more than a collection of smoking embers – forgotten, like a campsite you left behind for pastures far more beautiful.

A bell above the door jingled as he stepped inside.

'That you, Felix?'

Elwood looked around but couldn't see anyone. 'Erm, no ma'am,' he replied.

'Just a minute then, hold on.'

Beyond the hills and mountains, he spied a wooden counter at the back of the store. Next to this was a short doorway which he assumed led into the back, where he fancied it was much the same as it was out here. He heard the whistle of steam and the clattering of crockery from somewhere back there.

'If you're sticking around for a nosey I'm making hot tea. Did you want a cup?'

Elwood was overcome by the aroma of musty paper, deep and aromatic, a wondrous scent that filled his nostrils. He closed his eyes for just a moment and imagined himself back in Ralph's Book Nook, one of the stores in his hometown where he'd spent so much of his time.

'Well? You want a tea or not, mister?'

He opened his eyes and saw an old lady standing in the doorway by the counter. She wore a pea-green cardigan over a navy-blue dress, and one of her hands rested on a walnut walking stick that looked more for show than actual necessity. Her back was hunched ever so slightly; her skin was timeworn, but her smile was angelic, vivacious even. Her liver-spotted face was the picture of stoicism. He was sure Whiskey had mentioned her age – ninety-three – perhaps, but there was just something about her that made Elwood sure she'd still be alive and kicking in another twenty years.

'Stare any longer and you'll make me blush.' She spoke with the same country drawl as Whiskey did, but with an ebonic twist that lent it a comforting quality.

'I'm sorry,' Elwood replied, feeling his own face heat up now.

She waved this off. 'I haven't had a man stare at me like that since seventy-four,' she laughed. 'So, what'll it be? I have lemon, and peppermint, and I think I have some camomile too if you like that? Does you the world of good, does a good cup of hot tea. No milk though, that stuff's for the pussycats.'

As if on cue, Elwood heard a meow from somewhere deep within the ravines and canyons of paperbacks.

'Alright, alright, we hear you Jeremy.' The woman looked back at Elwood, eyebrows raised.

'Oh, peppermint would be great, thank you.'

'Peppermint it is,' she nodded. 'Make yourself at home. I'll only be a minute, pot's already boiled.' She disappeared into the backroom.

Elwood approached the counter. On his way he passed Steinbeck-capped peaks, McCammon mountains and crags of King and Simmons; cliffs of Slaughter, Golding and Patterson; Herriot highlands; grand formations of Tolkien, Pratchett, Poe and Ahern. Gaiman and Straub massifs ran alongside tors of

Crichton and L'Amour. Although the store was modestly bijou, it felt vast with its literary multitudes.

He moved slowly – the walk of the awe-struck – taking it all in. A small, narcissistic part of him hoped to catch a glimpse of one of his own works in there, a beat-up Cathis paperback wedged between bluffs of Barker and Farris perhaps.

As he reached the counter, the old lady appeared through the doorway holding a tray with two mugs and a saucer laden with biscuits. Their eyes met and her smile broadened politely; Elwood was about to ask if she wanted a hand but thought better of it, she clearly didn't need any help and he didn't want to belittle her ostensible vitality.

She set the tray down on the countertop and passed him one of the mugs.

'Help yourself to cookies,' she said, pointing at the plate. 'Made them myself, oatmeal and raisin with pumpkin seeds. My great-grandkids love them.'

'Thank you,' Elwood replied, and proceeded to take one and dig in.

She watched, one eyebrow raised. 'Well? They're good, ain't they?'

'Delicious,' he replied, holding his hand up to cover his mouth while he chewed. 'Thank you.'

'It's no bother, but you're surely welcome. Take a seat,' she nodded toward a nearby bar stool.

The red leather seat rest was well-worn, shaped with grooves from a thousand asses and then some. People evidently loved to spend time here with the old lady. He perched himself on the chair and washed down the cookie with a sip of tea. The woman remained standing though, and Elwood noticed there was no stool on her side of the counter.

'Not seen your face round here before. You passing through?'

'No,' Elwood replied. 'Vacation, I guess.'

'You *guess* – well, I *guess* you must be staying out at Arkins over in Bowles then, right?'

'Lake Chance, actually.'

She paused before taking a sip from her mug. 'Really?' her brow furrowed. 'We don't get too many folks vacationing out there these days.' She took a drink, set her mug back down on the tray and picked up a cookie. 'You're not that Mr Stevens, are you?' she narrowed her eyes, as if to try and get a better look at him. 'I met that fella, but it's been a few years and my eyes aren't what they used to be.'

'No,' he replied. 'I know him... we aren't friends or anything, but he agreed to let me stay at his place for a short while. My name's Elwood – Elwood Cathis,' he offered his hand and she took it, the hint of abhorrence fading from her face and quickly replaced with one of pensiveness.

'Aubrey Christie,' she returned, her face still reflective. 'Cathis. Cathis. Where have I heard that name?'

She moved with surprising speed, disappearing into the paper hills and mountains behind him. Seconds later she returned with a small stack of paperbacks and set them down on the counter. Elwood couldn't help but grin, and hoped he appeared at least a tad sincere.

'These yours?' she asked, nodding toward the stack.

Elwood picked up *It Came to the Town in October*

and turned it over in his hand. He opened it up to the back page where his author photo had been printed in grainy black-and-white, and held it up next to his face.

'Guilty.'

Aubrey chuckled. 'Well, I'll be damned. We get authors stopping by from time to time but never any so famous… I'd be much obliged if you could sign these before you go, Mr Cathis.'

'Famous?' He was taken aback momentarily, unable to remember the last time anyone had asked him to sign anything. 'I'd be happy to. And please, call me Elwood.'

'So, what brought you to Lake Chance, Elwood? It ain't exactly a vacation hotspot anymore, you know? Working on a new book?'

'Not exactly,' Elwood replied. 'I had some issues I was dealing with, needed some time away to get my head straight. But you never know. The place has turned out to be a lot more interesting than I'd imagined.'

She scoffed at this. 'That's one word for it, but I can think of a few more. Got a book's worth over there in the front window.'

Elwood sipped his peppermint tea. 'I was hoping I could pick your brains on the subject, if that's okay?'

The old lady narrowed her eyes. 'Why? Did you see something out there?'

'Maybe.'

'Well,' the old lady sighed. 'Why don't you grab another one of these cookies and tell me all about it.'

He did. He told her everything, more or less. He told her about the astronaut and the dead girls, the call that echoed from the forest, how he'd lost time and lost his way, and how Whiskey had found him and showed him the way back. The stories Whiskey had told him: Celia Dawes; the white demon; Jud Kennishaw. The memory, *Baloo*, and how it had helped him, how it had been an anchor in a stormy sea. All of it.

Everything, except the heroin.

Aubrey stood and listened soundlessly, drinking her tea. Every so often her eyes would drift beyond him to the front window as she nodded considerately.

After he was finished, she made them both another cup.

'I wrote a book about the Levant lynching. Poor child, so young, and I wasn't much older myself back then. I remember it though, remember it well. We lived on the same street over in Earlswood, that's where they sent all the black folks back then. Some of the locals used to call it *Coalwood*, on account of it being so black. People could be cruel back then.' She paused. 'Well, people still can be, but times have changed, and things have changed with them. Not enough, but some.'

She blew into her cup before taking a tentative sip, grimacing at the heat of it before setting it back down on the countertop.

'It wasn't always like that, though. Before Lincoln's Emancipation Proclamation, that whole side of town was Shawnee. Folks forget that, or they choose to. But that's where the natives were rounded up and forced to live, until most of them moved into the reservations out west. For a time though, blacks and natives lived together as one community, united as outcasts. I have a little Shawnee in my blood, and I'm thankful for that.'

The bell above the front door jingled as a young man

entered the store.

'Felix,' she declared enthusiastically.

'Hey GG,' the young man approached the counter, he carried a duffel bag in one hand and a copy of *Sports Illustrated* rolled up in the other. 'MawMaw told mom you needed a hand with some stuff, I thought I'd drop by before practice.' He reached the counter and looked at Elwood. 'Who's your friend?'

Aubrey motioned toward the stack of books on the counter as she stepped in for a hug. 'This is Elwood Cathis. He wrote all of these books right here.'

The young man eyed him suspiciously over her shoulder as they embraced.

'Elwood, this is my great grandson, Felix. He plays football, but he writes too, just like his GG'

'Nice to meet you,' Elwood offered his hand and Felix took it. His grip was firm, a little too firm.

'Nice to meet you, Mr Cathis.' Polite, but the eyes were still searching, still sussing him out.

'Oh, enough of that, Felix. He's harmless enough and you're forgetting your manners.'

'No, it's okay,' Elwood said. 'I understand.' And he did; Aubrey was doing him a courtesy by not calling out his appearance. He was looking much better than he had been, but he was still clearly restless, still looked unwell, and had an air of dishevelment about him – all of which indicated a man afflicted.

'I'm just here to learn a little more about the town, that's all,' he offered.

'Sure,' Felix grinned, but his eyes were still considering. 'What did you need me to do, GG?'

'There's a few boxes out back that need putting in

the alley. I've marked them, so you know which ones to move. Make sure you put them under the lean-to though – rain's coming tonight, and I don't know what time Brooke and Keith are stopping by to collect them.'

'No problem,' Felix helped himself to one of the cookies and Aubrey slapped his hand.

'Hey! There's a tin out back for you and the girls, you can take it with you when you're done.'

Felix smiled as he backed away, his arms held up in surrender, speaking through a mouthful of oats and raisins. 'Thanks, GG.' He disappeared into the backroom.

'And don't you think I haven't counted how many are in there, I'll be checking in with your mom.'

'Yes GG.'

Aubrey turned back to Elwood and rolled her eyes. She took a sip from her cup and set it back down on the counter, sighing contentedly. 'Much better. Now, where were we?'

'You were just talking about the natives living in Earlswood,' he reminded her.

'Of course. Well, my MawMaw told us kids all sorts of stories from when she was a young'un. Truth be told, it was her who inspired me to write. She never wrote herself, bless her heart, she didn't know how – but she was a storyteller alright, and all her stories were passed down to her from her MawMaw, and so on, right back to the first Christie who rolled up on this town just after the Revolution. I traced them back once – my family, that is – spent a few years going at it. Got all the way back to the San Miguel de Gualdape colony too, if you can believe that?'

'You don't seem like the sort who gives up too easily, so yes, I can believe that,' Elwood smiled, feeling a little foolish that he didn't truly understand what she was talking about.

She waved him off. 'Oh, enough. I already gave you cookies and tea, what else do you want?'

They both laughed. It was easy to see why so many people stopped by this store. He recalled OJ talking of people travelling from far and wide, and he guessed they didn't just come for the books. They came for Aubrey.

'Anyway, the Shawnee and my ancestors shared stories about their history, their lands, and the forest out there,' she tipped her head toward the front window. 'That used to be a hunting ground for the local tribes, and their ancestors before them, the Clovis Paleo-Indians. They spoke of sacred caves too, where their ancestors performed rituals in supplication of the stars and constellations and such. We've never found any in this region of the forest – though truth be told nobody's ever really gone looking – but they did discover some caves over in Keeling County. They have a visitor centre there now, and you can go down into the caves and see some of the paintings and the tools. A fine gift shop there too. We could do with that kind of tourism here, I can tell you. I digress, though… let me get to what you want to hear.'

'I'm not in any rush to get back to the lake; please, take your time,' he snatched up another cookie and smiled as he bit into it. 'These are good.'

She smiled – the sort of contented beam worn by those who were happy to know that people cared to listen to what they were saying.

'The forest had always been a good place – sacred, safe, bountiful. But all that changed when the first settlers showed up. Most of them were Slavic, they came from eastern Europe, descendants of the Tribe of Boii. I don't expect you to know who they were, none too many do, but they were Bohemians; they belonged to the Gallic peoples that existed way back in Roman times. They brought their own stories with them, their own ways, their own religion – and according to the Shawnee, they brought something else with them too. Something old… and when I say old, I mean ancient. They called it a *dusios*.'

She took another gulp from her cup.

'But you or I, we'd call it a demon.'

'A demon?' Elwood whispered the word, as though giving it volume might give it power – or worse still, allow it to hear them.

'That's right, a demon. Apparently, this thing, this *dusios*, it would bring luck and good fortune for the people settling in this new world. So, these pilgrims, these Bohemians, they found a spot out there in the woods, and they held an unholy discourse. The Shawnee called it the *Mškwaawi Nikanikawe Waapa Hileni* – the black dance of the white man. And according to the local tribes, it worked. The colony thrived. Where others suffered disease and famine, the Misstonville settlement and its peoples lived healthy with stores overflowing produce. The settlement began to grow into a village and then into a small town. At the same time though, the tribes diminished. Natives regularly disappeared and were never seen again. More often than not they were taken by the settlers – the white men would come in large groups, steal away children or the sick and dying. Sometimes it was the hunters who went missing – groups would get split up, lose their way in woods they'd known like the back of their hand for so many years. They said the land had become tainted by a white demon.'

White demon.

He remembered what Whiskey had said about how lucky Ron had been at the casino, how he'd always seemed to win, and how he'd never told the authorities what happened to those he'd kidnapped.

'I don't recall the exact year, but it was sometime in the early eighteenth century. A group of Shawnee warriors made up from various tribes across the county all came together and decided enough was enough. They set upon the colony in the middle of the night, killed every man, woman and child in Misstonville – which at that time neared a hundred or so souls. It was an awful thing they did that night, made all the more terrible by the fact that it didn't even work. If anything, it made it worse. All they did was destroy the creator. That still left the *created*, still left it hungry and without a feeder. Some of the natives in more distant tribes – ones that didn't even hunt the land in Misstonville forest – started disappearing too. They held council and debated whether or not to vacate the land and settle elsewhere, but with the demon's reach extending beyond the forest, they were scared it might follow them wherever they went. They didn't know how to get rid of it, either – they had rituals for their own demons and blights, sure, but they didn't have any knowledge of European evils, no tried and tested method for dealing with a white man's demon.'

'What did they do?'

'Well, according to some descendants of the tribe, there was a great shaman named Tenskwatawa – you can look him up too, he was real, there's paintings of him out there somewhere… I don't recall where, but he was a person and he lived. He's the only part of these oral tales I could verify when I came to research this stuff for one of my books. There's no official accounts of him ever being in the Misstonville colony, but he spent a lot of time in the Appalachians, and we're right in the foothills, so it adds a speck of credibility to the oral history. Not that *I* need any convincing, mind you.'

She gulped down the last of her tea before continuing.

'The way they told it, Tenskwatawa gathered up all the medicine men from the tribes across the counties. He instructed each of them to bring a totem as a form of defence – do you know about totems, Elwood?'

'No, I know the word, and I can picture a totem pole – they had some kind of spiritual significance, right?'

'That's right. Totem poles were something for the whole tribe, but sometimes, individuals would have totems of their own, small things – normally carved out of wood, sometimes stone, but always an animal. For the Shawnee it was mostly wolves, bears, buzzards, snakes, horses – sometimes a turtle or a raccoon too. They'd carry their totems with them, and they had two purposes. They represented the spirit guide, a guardian that walked alongside you, teaching, guiding, protecting; and they represented lineage – they were supposed to be a reminder of your ancestry and memory. A way to remember the things that came before you, right back to the creation myths.'

Memory. Elwood recalled how the memory of his daughter's laughter had helped him, how the simple act of shimmying up out of the dirt had given rise to that memory, and the word, Baloo, had given it power. Baloo.

A bear.

'I see your cogs turning, and I know what you're thinking. You're thinking about the memory you told me about. The one that helped you. I guess that was a kind of totem, just without the object to back it up. Jeanie – God rest her soul – and I, we spoke about these things a lot, and I'm glad Bob listened, or you might not even be here right now. And I know that might sound melodramatic, but that's the truth of it.'

'Not at all. I just can't believe how close I might've been to death, or… whatever it is that happens out there. I don't think I want to believe.'

'Death is what it'll be. People who go missing out there never come back, and if it really is this demon, this *dusios* that the natives spoke about, then I wouldn't imagine it's keeping pets out there. I'd imagine it's feeding.'

'So, what did the natives do? I mean, they obviously didn't get rid of it if people still go missing – how were the tribes able to carry on living here?'

'They trapped it,' she shrugged. 'It was all they could do.'

'Was it the totems? Did they use those to trap it?'

'No, but the totems kept them safe, helped them

remember. The *dusios* relies on you forgetting yourself, preys on the weak and the lonely. That's how it takes you. But Tenskwatawa and his medicine men went out there knowing who they were. They convinced themselves they were stronger with the totems, because they were – it's not enough to just have something that anchors you, you need to know that it gives you strength too, that it works in that way – and they knew that. They somehow managed to herd it into one of the sacred hollows out there and trap it. Don't ask me how though.'

Elwood thought of the gulley again. Something had been just around that corner, he knew it. The voice, the call, it had been telling him there was something there, *it* was there, the *dusios*. It had been inviting him, he was sure of it.

And Whiskey had talked about Jud finding the *entrance to their caves.*

But had he actually found the entrance to *its* cave?

'You don't think there's a way to get rid of it for good?

'Oh, there'll be a way, for sure. Anything that can be summoned can be banished. But that knowledge is probably long dead – it most likely died with those first Slavic settlers. And if it does still exist, tracking it down will be tough. You have to remember, these people were nomadic. They didn't stick around anywhere long enough to etch their beliefs in stone. We know very little of the Tribe of Boii – they were a small piece of a bigger picture.

'There was a time when I was of the mind to follow that path.'

'What stopped you?' Elwood asked.

She frowned. 'Oh, another demon entirely, Elwood. Something else that was summoned up by just a few misguided souls, many, many years ago, and arguably more terrible than whatever it is out there in the forest. Racism. Don't get me wrong, I dedicated some time to it. I wrote a book, not that many have taken the time to read it. None too many care for the ramblings of a backwoods black lady. Especially when she's talking about demons in the woods,' she laughed. 'When I heard about the caves in Keeling I managed to get involved in the efforts to uncover the whole site. I did some digging – and when I say digging, I mean digging with a shovel. I thought for a time that it could be the cave from the story, but it's not. Those caves have been completely unearthed now and all the dead-ends have been reached. I firmly believe there's another cave out there though, *the* cave. The one that holds the *dusios*. Once they'd trapped it, the Shawnee buried the entrance so that nobody would ever go down there. But, at some point in time, someone, or something, uncovered that entrance. I'm of a mind to believe it was sometime just before – or during – the Civil War, on account of the pattern of missing persons in this area. I tracked it, you see. Even have a timeline in my book.'

She reached beneath the counter and pulled out a staple-bound booklet. The glossy cover depicted silhouetted woodland beneath a red sky, with the words *Disappearances in Misstonville Forest: An Unacknowledged Dark History, by Aubrey Christie.* She opened it up and turned to the middle centrefold. A horizontal line ran across both pages; vertical lines branched off at intervals, leading to years and bullet-pointed lists of disappearances or events.

'See here,' Aubrey pointed at a clear gap in the timeline. 'After Tenskwatawa and the others did their work, most decided to leave, assured that the dusios wouldn't be following them. For those who stayed, carrying a totem became a necessity; although the *dusios* was trapped and buried away, its power to... *show* you things... permeated through the soil, and as you've come to know, that power can easily twist a person's mind. The remaining Shawnee were wise to this; as you can see, there's at least a hundred years of no disappearances or tragic events, based on their oral history and the records that began to appear from new settlers moving into the area. But then, after the civil war, some of the vets started going missing out there – much like Jud Kennishaw and the Viet Cong later, there were men who believed the Confederates were hiding out there – so they went to find them, and never returned. Since then, there's been a steady stream of poor souls going missing. Not enough to draw attention, though. Hundreds of people go missing in forests and national parks every year in this country. Misstonville makes up less than five of the total number, sometimes less than three.'

'So, in the grand scheme of things, it's not much, is it? Not that I'm trying to downplay the issue – I guess, I don't know... maybe I'm looking for confirmation that me staying here, trying to do something, is worthwhile.'

'No evil should ever be accepted, Elwood, no matter how small or insignificant it might seem. Once we start on that path, we'll find ourselves in an entirely evil world soon enough. I'll admit I'm a little hypocritical in what I'm saying there, all I've done is create a record of this evil, but maybe that's what I was supposed to do, maybe that was the part I had to play in all of this. And maybe you have a part to play too.'

'What part do you think that might be?' he asked, wondering again how he, a recovering junkie born into the digital age, might hope to defeat an actual demon. The thought still felt absurd. Was there still a chance that all he'd seen had just been part of the cold turkey process, and the disappearances throughout time simply coincidental? Sometimes stories were created to convey messages – fables, like those in the Bible – was it the same with the Shawnee tales? Had historical events like the massacre of the first settlement simply been woven in to create a sense of legitimacy?

The old lady looked at him, ruminating. 'Honestly, I wouldn't hold it against you if you decided to leave right now and never come back. A few people disappearing in this small town every year ain't going to impact your life none. It knows you now, it's shown you things, but it can't follow you. Whatever prison they managed to trap it in has held up for almost three hundred years – and I expect it'll hold for three hundred more, and then some. If you're adamant on doing some good, though, affecting some sort of positive change here, there's only one thing you *can* do.'

'Seal it back up,' he said.

'That's right,' she nodded. 'Maybe you'll bring another hundred years of peace, and that ain't nothing to frown at, for sure. I don't know how you'd go about it… you'd have to find the cave first I guess.'

'After the other night, I think I have a pretty good idea of where it might be, or at least where to start looking.'

But then what? For all he knew, the entrance to this cave system might be some tiny crawl space, and a shovel and some tightly packed dirt might suffice. But what if it was something bigger? He glanced at the short doorway leading into the backrooms; even something that size would amount to a mammoth task without cement and bricks.

'Don't suppose you have a shovel somewhere back there?' he grinned.

She laughed at this and raised an eyebrow. 'As a matter of fact, I do. Snow falls pretty heavy around here come winter. If I don't take the time to clear a path and lay some salt out front and in the alley, it can get quite treacherous for an old girl like me.'

'Could I borrow it, perhaps?'

He wasn't confident it would be enough but at least it was something, better than venturing out there with nothing at all.

'Sure,' she tipped her head back toward the doorway. 'Felix? Felix?'

'Yes, GG.'

'Fetch me that snow shovel from the utility closet.'

'Okay, GG.'

She turned back to Elwood. 'I have something else you can take, too, something that might help you.' She turned to a series of shelves that lined the wall behind her. There were a few books here and there, but it was mainly curios, trinkets and other small odds and ends that occupied these shelves. She reached up and retrieved something Elwood couldn't quite make out from where he was sitting.

Felix appeared through the doorway, holding what looked to be something that was old enough to have been shovelling shit in the age of wagons and coaches. Like the old lady though, its aged appearance wasn't the sum of its parts; it had a durable quality about it, a sense of reliability. The blade appeared to be copper, extra deep and with a pointed tip, bolted at the collar to a thick teal shaft that culminated in a T-grip.

'What you need this for, GG?' Felix asked his great-grandmother, his eyes unashamedly fixed on Elwood.

'My friend here might be doing a little digging. That's all you need to know, Felix,' Aubrey turned back to the counter, shooting her great grandson a smile.

The young man set the shovel down without argument and leaned it against the side of the counter. He afforded Elwood one final suspicious glance before returning through the doorway.

'I don't know how helpful this old thing might be, but it won't hurt to have it with you while you're staying out there at the lake.' She set a small lump of wood down on the counter. Elwood picked it up and began to turn it over in his hands.

It was somewhere between the size of a baseball and a golf ball, and depicted the head of a grizzly bear in mid-roar. Elwood marvelled at the workmanship; a hollow had been carved inwards at the mouth, inside he could see a tongue and rows of individual teeth. It looked as though it had been set to a flame for a brief moment, so that a blackened, scorched muzzle sat beneath beady eyes. Delicate grooves were carved across the entire piece, creating the illusion of a wavy fur coat; the lines were so meticulous, so considered, that Elwood felt as though the tresses might at any moment begin to sway gently, swept by some breeze that didn't exist here in the store, but out there in the wild where this bear roamed.

'The bear brings protection and fosters courage and fortitude,' Aubrey said. 'You'll need a heavy dose of that if you want to walk in the footsteps of Tenskwatawa and his medicine men.'

'Thank you,' he turned the totem over and gazed at it once more before tucking the totem away safely in his coat pocket.

'You're welcome,' she returned. 'Just be sure to bring it back to me, along with the shovel.'

'I'll do my best.'

The magnitude of the task he'd seemingly signed himself up for was yet to sink in. He was still trying to get to the grips with the notion of demonic forces – the frightening, outrageous, yet seemingly legitimate reality of it. He still felt like a passenger, only now there was no driver, nobody steering the wheel. The course had been set and he was rolling with it; soon though, he'd need to shift into that driver's seat and take the wheel, or the shovel. He thought then how ironic it was, that ultimately he'd come to this place to unbury the parts of himself he'd lost through his addiction, but that soon he'd have to bury something much more insidious than heroin.

The old lady offered him a heartening smile. 'I hope you find what you're looking for out there, Elwood

Cathis, and I don't just mean the cave of the *dusios*, I mean whatever you came out here for in the first place. I hope you find that.'

After finishing up his tea and the last of the cookies, Elwood signed the stack of his books. He also purchased all of Aubrey's non-fiction works, and as he left, he found himself hoping that one day soon he'd be stepping back through that door once again.

He returned to his car, the bag of books in one hand, shovel in the other, and the bear totem resting against his heart in the inside-pocket of his coat. He glanced back and saw that the old lady had moved to the front window and was watching him leave. She raised her hand and waved, like a mother watching her child leave for war. Her face was one of apprehensive hope.

Elwood raised his hand and nodded a final farewell.

As he climbed back into his car and started the engine, he glanced up and down Gilead Street. The footfall had increased noticeably during his time in the store, and now the sidewalks weren't just reserved for the purposeful early birds. Elderly couples and families walked at a leisurely pace along the storefronts: window-shopping, pointing at various advertising signs and conferring with one another. Many of the benches around the fountain were occupied by humans as opposed to chickadees, and more than half of the parking spaces had now been claimed.

He realised then that he was being watched.

Not by Aubrey, though. The old lady had now disappeared from the window and was probably out in the back checking up on Felix.

The man wore a tan khaki shirt, black tie and bottle-green trousers. A broad-brimmed campaign hat sat crookedly on his head, pinched at the four corners, and beneath it a pair of Ray-Ban Wayfarers reflected the late-morning sun. He was leaning against the hood of a cruiser parked outside a derelict store further down the road in the direction of the fountain.

The word *Sheriff* was emblazoned in blue across the side of the car.

He was looking in Elwood's general direction, and although the sunglasses gave nothing away, Elwood was certain he was staring right at him. He cocked his head to the left and spat on the asphalt.

This was all Elwood needed right now. He waited a moment, expecting the Sheriff to make his way over any second now – tap on the window, introduce himself to this new face in town, and ask him what the hell he was planning on doing with a shovel out there at the lake.

Instead, the Sheriff tipped his hat in Elwood's direction. There was nothing friendly about it, no smile, his jaw rigid as he chewed what was probably tobacco, judging by the brownish puddle to the left of his boots.

Elwood raised a hand and smiled thinly, a feeble attempt at a *nothing to see here, officer* grin, started up the engine and turned onto the road, heading in the direction of Main Street, relieved that he was on the right side of the one-way system so that he didn't have to pass by the Sheriff. It was a shallow feeling though; beneath it was a deeper worry – no, a dismal certainty. It wasn't going to be the last time he saw him.

CHAPTER EIGHTEEN
LET ME LOVE

Elwood spent most of the journey back to the villa with his eyes fixed on the rear-view, expecting the Sheriff's cruiser to appear at any moment. It didn't.

Much of his afternoon and evening was spent in quiet reflection on the terrace, watching the gleam of sunlight on the lake gradually draw back as the darkness of night approached, keeping an ear out for the sound of tires on gravel, waiting for the Sheriff to pull up on the driveway.

He didn't.

Much like the call from Casper, the appearance of Sheriff Tims in town had served only to derail Elwood's thoughts. Where Casper had managed to knock him down a peg or two and fan the flames of an addiction that was finally dying out, the Sheriff had piled on the hay, creating a thick smoke that brought uncertainty and trepidation. Like Casper, the Sheriff had exercised a particular method of gaining control.

He wondered for a time what explanation he might offer for the shovel. Some light garden work perhaps, tidying up the grounds as a way of saying thank you to his friend – no, not friend, *acquaintance* – for letting him stay at his place. Sure, but why borrow a shovel from an old lady who runs a bookstore? Had he bought his own shovel from a local store, perhaps that story might feel a little more plausible, but he hadn't. Could it all just be happenstance though? He had a legitimate reason for being at the bookstore – he was a writer, after all, and he'd come away with a bag filled with the complete bibliography of Aubrey Christie. Maybe he mentioned his plans to her whilst he was there, and she'd been kind enough to lend him the shovel. Or perhaps he'd found a dead animal around the villa, wanted to bury it; he'd mentioned that to her and she'd helped him out, saved him the trouble of having to buy a shovel to only use it once. But what if he asked to see the grave? What if he decided to take the shovel and use it himself to dig up whatever carcass Elwood was adamant he'd buried? What then?

He wished he'd never accepted the damn thing now. If he'd walked out of that bookstore without a shovel then he wouldn't have this worry, this need to fabricate some bullshit reason for it. He'd have one less thing for the Sheriff to prod him with, one less thing to sweat over.

Ultimately, it didn't matter. The Sheriff couldn't arrest him for having a shovel – or for what sounded like a weak reason for having one – but Elwood, in his current state of mind, was unable to satisfy his paranoia with that conclusion. He'd decided the marijuana was probably doing him no favours in this regard, and threw the rest of the bagged joints in the trash, burying them as deep as he could.

That had been another step in the right direction.

Apart from these worries, he'd spent some time reading Aubrey's book, looking at the timeline in the centrefold, and pondering his approach. After all the novels he'd written – all the blood-soaked showdowns, action-packed climaxes and tense finales that saw characters face unspeakable evils in battles to the death – was he going to simply head into the woods with a shovel and fling some dirt over a hole in the ground? Was that the resolution of this story? He hoped it was. If he ever decided to write a book about this whole mess, then it wouldn't be the epic ending readers might expect or hope for. It would be real though, it would be *truth*, and the truth was often as mundane as taking a shit.

There was, of course, the possibility that it would be less straightforward; what if the hole was larger? What if there was no way he could bury the entrance to the cave? What then? Would he just give up and leave? Or perhaps make some half-hearted attempt at camouflaging it with a few branches? How long would something like that last? A week? A few days?

Minutes?

He'd considered explosives, considered talking to Casper about sourcing something he could use. That idea had been short-lived; given how the phone call had gone earlier that day, he hoped he'd never have to see or even speak to the friendly ghost ever again.

A quick online search showed him he could,

potentially, fashion his own explosive, if it came down to that. Although he had visions of blowing his hands off, losing his face, even getting himself arrested on charges of suspected domestic terrorism. There were options, though. Ammonium nitrate was still available at a few outlets. There were also instructions on how to turn nitric and sulphuric acid into potent bombs, and how to create picric acid from aspirin. Saltpeter, aka potassium nitrate, was easy to come by, as were charcoal and sulphur, which constituted the three key ingredients of black powder. And there was always gasoline and oils, propane, butane.

It was at that point – sufficiently concerned with how easy it was for any idiot out there to make their own explosive – that he went to check in the closet by the stairs, remembering something he'd seen in there on that first day. Sure enough, standing in the back corner next to the dirty barbeque was a 25kg butane gas canister. He gave it a laboured shake and found it pretty much full. Elwood couldn't imagine Casper presiding over a grill, a spatula in one hand and a beer in the other, smiling merrily in his *kiss the chef* apron.

That discovery gave him a fallback option, though; if burying the entrance to the cave warranted more than just a shovel and some dirt, he at least had something he could light a fire beneath. The force of the explosion would hopefully be powerful enough to cause a cave-in that ultimately blocked the entrance.

He was still struggling with the reality of the situation though. It was this turmoil that occupied his mind as he lay in bed, the day having drawn to a close and the moon now high in the night sky, its light creeping through the blinds in incandescent shafts.

It wasn't just the idea of a demon he was still struggling to accept – it was the fact that he'd somehow become a protagonist in the situation, in a story that spanned hundreds of years and had touched so many lives. Was he imagining this entire episode? And if it was real – if he truly was experiencing this, and was able to succeed in burying a demon – who would believe him? More importantly, would he even feel comfortable sharing such an irrational tale?

Would he ever be able to tell his daughter what had happened here?

Could such stories damage his chances of rebuilding a relationship with her? He was sure Gracie would be glad to hear he was clean, and happy for their daughter to start spending time with her father. But what if he started speaking of imprisoned demons, native American totems and characters from his books stalking him? Characters he was sure were representations of parts of himself, parts he'd lost somewhere along addiction avenue, tossed to the side of the road and buried with so many discarded needles.

His thoughts lingered on his family. There was hope in his heart that he and Elouise still had so much time to share with one another, joy, laughter, lessons, even tears. He imagined a day in the future when he'd be there to wipe the tears from her cheeks, console her, tell her everything would be alright and then be the one in her life that made sure it went that way.

Gracie was different. It pained him now to think of the love he still felt for her, and the love she certainly no longer felt for him, and would never feel again. He wouldn't try to win her back; that wouldn't be right, it wouldn't be fair on her or the new man in her life. David, that was his name – Elwood remembered it now, recalled it like all the other forgotten details he was unearthing. No, he wouldn't try to rock the boat in any way. In fact, he wouldn't even go as far as to assume that he'd be *able* to rock the boat; he'd been a complete fuck. And just because there'd been a day – years ago now – when Gracie had loved him, a day when she'd committed to him with the words *I do*, that didn't mean he held dominion in her heart still, or any influence.

It would be dangerously narcissistic to think such a thing, or seek to pursue it.

No, he would apologise, that was all. Any thoughts he might have, any feelings, they'd remain within. No matter how much that might inevitably hurt him, that was a pain that was self-inflicted, and one he'd have to live with. One he deserved.

As his eyes grew heavier, he welcomed the sleep which crept toward him like a shadow, hopeful that the slumberous shade might cool his now raging heart. Memories of Gracie flashed through his mind like a slideshow, her critical eyes perusing his first drafts. Her embarrassed smirk as she wiped wedding cake frosting from her bottom lip. Her strained, clammy, and never more beautiful complexion as she pushed their daughter into the world. And as sleep took its hold and carried him off into a peaceful abyss, he took with him one final image: that same sultry recollection that had risen in his mind – and his trousers – on the balcony two nights before. The bathtub, steam drifting around her in a dreamlike haze of lavender and vanilla, foamy bubbles barely concealing those intimate areas of her body he'd known so well. And her eyes – oh, her eyes – how they'd been so captivating.

And with that, he fell into those eyes, and a wondrous dream.

He awoke a few hours later to a thunderous rumbling in the skies above. Heavy rain thrashed against the balcony windows as jagged strands of lightning pierced the cloudy horizon beyond the forest. Each strike brought with it a burst of white light that flashed through the panes and illuminated the landing and hall.

The phone rested on the console where he'd left it: 2:17am. He lay back down, dazed, still half-in and half-out of a dream he was already forgetting. It had been something to do with Gracie, he knew that much, and he could guess the rest – not every part of him had been so quick to forget the details. Halfway down the bed, the sheet poked upwards like a tent, his blood-swelled pole standing to attention, and calling for it too.

'Damn it,' he sighed. This was another itch, one that couldn't be satisfied with a needle or by going to see an old lady, though he guessed both of those worked for some people.

This itch was something he'd long neglected, for no other reason than being too out of his mind on the skag to care about something as trivial as scratching it. But now that he was expelling the junk from his life, and from his system, perhaps it was time to show his own junk a little more attention. How else could he exercise some form of relief? Without the dope, and without the cannabis, there had to be something else, something that would help ease his stress in a way that liquor and cigarettes couldn't.

He slipped his hand beneath the sheets, squeezed. It didn't take him too long to find his rhythm.

For some intangible reason, he could feel himself blushing with embarrassment. Perhaps it had been so long that the act now felt alien to him, outlandish even, but he was alone; there was no need to feel uncomfortable with what was perfectly normal behaviour for ninety-five per cent of men. Had he, at some point over the last few years, drifted into that other five per cent?

He tried to push the unwelcome sense of shame aside and began to move his hand up and down the aching shaft, still squeezing and relaxing his hold in fits and starts. He closed his eyes and thought of her. He saw her in the bathtub again, only now she was hoisting herself up and out of the water. Swathes of foamy suds ran down her body in great, slow torrents, gradually revealing the parts of her which would entice his climax.

He quickened his motion, no longer loosening his grasp, but gripping tighter now, up and down, up and down, up and...

The image dissolved as he opened his eyes, disturbed by the sound of a creaking floorboard in the hall. Thunder still rolled in the sky above, and in the next flash of lightning he saw her there, standing in the entrance to the hallway, watching him.

It was her, the dancing corpse. He sat up and gathered himself against the wall behind him, pulling the sheets up to his neck like a frightened child. He wondered how long she'd been stood there with her eyes on him.

Another flash and he saw that no, it wasn't the dancing corpse after all. It was…

'Gracie?'

'Hey, handsome.' Another flash and he saw that yes, it was her. His ex-wife, mother to his child, here, now, watching him in silence as he jerked himself off. 'Looks like you could do with a hand,' she grinned.

This had to be a dream. That was it, he was still dreaming, still lost in some lustrous slumber.

She moved toward him, leaving wet footprints in her wake, but there was something majestic in her walk; she seemed to glide toward him like an angel sent from heaven, only this angel wore a strappy sun dress, one with a tantalisingly high hem that showed enough of her sleek thighs to keep his manhood firmly erect.

'How?' he asked. 'How are you here? Where's El?'

Maybe the questions were just part of the scenario, the roleplay. Why else would he ask, if this really was a dream?

'That doesn't matter right now. All that matters is that you're getting better, darling, you're beating it, and you're coming home, coming back to us. Because we still want you. *I* still want you. I *need* you,' she smiled.

The smile didn't reach her eyes, which swam with fiery lust.

'I don't understand,' he began.

'Ssshh,' she placed a finger over her mouth, her lip gloss sparkling in what little moonlight managed to breach the storm clouds. 'No more talk. Let me help you. Let me love you.'

She bent over and reached for the top of the sheet. He let her pull it down, revealing his still-rigid penis. Her teeth pinched her bottom lip, then a sassy grin began to spread across her face as her gaze moved back up his naked form, finally settling on his eyes.

'Let me please you.'

He stared up at her, not knowing what to say, not knowing if he believed that this was actually happening.

'Let me love you.'

Elwood shifted awkwardly, aware that he was naked and still standing to attention as she leaned in closer.

'Let me take away the pain.'

'Yes,' he whispered. 'Please. Love me again.'

She began to pull the hem of her dress up and he watched, enthralled, as she revealed the higher reaches of her loins. Her fingers found the waistband of her white lace thong and she pulled it down, turning away from him and bending over as she did so. He gazed upon her curves, two peachy mounds that met in a cleft that had seen little exploration. His eyes followed this south and settled upon the soft, pinkish flesh of her vulva, two foothills meeting to form lips that glistened dewy in the moonlight. He reached out and let his fingers glide gently between her moist gap whilst his thumb applied pressure to the darker area of her hood.

She began to moan with a quiet ecstasy, a sound that encouraged his fingers to move deeper, his motion to quicken. She moved closer to him, climbing onto the bed and positioning herself on her knees – his hand still between her legs, still working the now dripping wet ingress between her legs.

He was stunned by the vividness of this dream. The small part of his mind that believed it to be real only seconds before had now grown large and formidable, meeting that other part of his mind that knew it to be a vision and nothing more. The two notions warring for dominance only heightened the pleasure he was feeling. Like somebody who fucked in public and got off on the risk of being caught, he was getting off on the chance of this being real and not just in his imagination.

Still on her knees, Gracie reached around and seized his rock-hard member. She gripped it firmly and began to move her hand up and down the shaft, her grip tightening as she reached the base, then easing as she reached the tip.

Now it was Elwood's turn to moan. God, how he'd missed this, how he'd missed her, missed her body.

How had she gotten into the villa though? The doors were locked.

He pushed the question to the back of his mind; it didn't matter, she was here, somehow, and that was all he cared about right now. She was here, and he was here, and they were loving.

Why hadn't she knocked, though? Or at least called out to him?

These concerns were quickly forgotten as she took him in her mouth, panting heavily as her head bobbed up and down between his legs.

Soon enough, her fingers crept between his legs and she began to gently massage his balls. Rainfall continued its relentless barrage against the windows and roof above, but its noise now seemed like nothing more than a distant pattering.

She let him slip out of her mouth and began to run her tongue up and down the belly of his beast, which now sparkled in the moonlight, the flesh coated in her lip gloss and saliva.

He could feel the end approaching, but he didn't want this to end, not now, not ever. The part of his mind that still believed this to be a dream roared with protest. He couldn't let this end; if he succumbed to that yearning for release then the dream would be over. He'd wake up, he'd be alone again.

'Gracie,' he groaned. 'Oh, Gracie, I think I'm going to –'

She pulled away from him and sat up. 'Not yet,' she grinned. 'How do you want me? How do you want your wife, Elwood?'

He pulled her toward him. Their lips locked together. His tongue quickly found hers and they began the dance, over and under, twisting and rolling, pausing only for brief gasps of air. He moved his attention to her neck, kissing, biting, his hands squeezing her rump as he pulled her closer. He felt her fingers wrap around his shaft again. This time she guided him into her, a fresh wave of pleasure washing over him as he felt his throbbing end part her wet lips, and he heard her blissful sighs as she settled herself down upon him.

Above their moans, thunder continued to crash overhead, but the rumbling had grown louder, more intense, as though the planet itself now shuddered at the commingling of their bodies. Mountains shifting as their forms became one, oceans raging as their juices mixed.

She arched back and began to move her hips with

fierce intent; his hands cupped her breasts and squeezed, thumbs running laps along her areolas as he leaned in to lap at her erect nipples. She moaned. He moaned. The end was near.

He lay back, his hands resting on her thighs as he thrust upwards to match her rhythm, plunging deeper, harder, their groans growing louder now.

Lightning lit up the sky and for a second they were no longer in the villa. Darkness surrounded their entwined bodies and the sound of rustling leaves joined their sexual symphony.

Elwood felt himself falter for just a second and then they were back in the room. But he could feel the rain against his skin...

'Wait,' he said.

She ignored him.

'This isn't –' Gracie placed her hand over his mouth to silence him.

Lightning flashed again and the room transformed. He wasn't lying on the bed in the villa anymore, he was in the gulley out in the woods; he could feel the damp, coarse dirt against his bare skin, but Gracie seemed not to notice and she continued unperturbed, grinding down on him with even more urgency now. He could feel the rain hitting his chest, his face, wet and freezing.

They were back in the villa. Gracie was still on top of him, her hands clawing at his chest. There was no rain, but his chest, his face, he was soaking wet. More lightning.

The forest. Rain showered their naked bodies. How was she not reacting to this? There was a heat in this moment, sure, but her eyes were open wide and facing up into the sky – no, now the ceiling – now the sky again, the world snapping back and forth with each stroke of lightning that darted across the night. Her cries of passion became roars, savage and guttural.

It's a dream, Elwood, you're dreaming.

Fear suddenly began to swell within him.

No.

This wasn't a dream.

Lightning cut across the sky again, only this time it wasn't their surroundings that changed. This time it was Gracie. They were still in the woods, still down in the sodden trench, exposed roots knotting in and out of the walls of soil that rose up on either side of them. But it wasn't Gracie on top of him, not anymore. Now it was something else, something unthinkable. The monster named Always, her transfigured form riding his now flaccid manhood. The half-human half-axolotl abomination from his final book. Like the others, she was no longer confined to words on a page, she was right here.

She was fucking him.

Elwood screamed. She was more horrifying than he could ever have conveyed in written word.

Her head was too wide, as though the skull beneath had split in half and opened up like a coconut. Her pinkish, pallid flesh was stretched almost to the point of tearing. Her black eyes had shrivelled up like raisins and sat in hollow sockets unnervingly too far apart. Thick, caterpillar-like tendrils jutted out limply from her bald head – six of them, three on either side – wriggling and twisting like the snake-hair of Medusa.

Elwood's shrieking seemed to go unnoticed as she

continued grinding on him. He flinched with each sway of her hips, afraid that she might break the damn thing and equally disgusted by the fact that a part of him was still inside her.

He could smell her, too. Beneath the damp aroma of the rain, there was an awful, sickly ammonia-like stench, like oxidised fish. It caused him to gag and cough as he struggled to break free of her embrace.

Fuck.

'Fuck!' He cried out. Unable to shift from beneath her, *it*. Not like this, he thought, please God don't let me fucking die like this.

CHAPTER NINETEEN
ALWAYS AND THE GANG

Elwood reached for the console table, for the bear totem he'd left next to his phone, but his hand only found roots and soil. He was out here, out in the forest whilst a storm raged, out here with no clothes on. He needed to get back to the villa. Even if he somehow managed to survive this ordeal, this awful raping of his body and sanity, he wouldn't survive another night laid out in the dirt. And even if by some miracle he did, he wouldn't want Whiskey to find him, not like this.

Whiskey. What had Whiskey said?

Something about a memory.

That was it. He didn't have the totem, but he still had the memory, the memory of a bear. The memory of his daughter's laughter. He closed his eyes.

Baloo.

Just a single word, but so much more, because the

word was a ship in a stormy sea, and beneath its keel was the anchor that was his memory, the anchor that could save him.

'*Baloo*,' he screamed. 'Baloo Baloo Baloo!' he wailed. He remembered.

And then he felt something. For just a brief moment, less than a second, the appalling sensation of her body upon his was gone.

He opened his eyes and she was there again, still riding him. She wasn't looking toward the sky now though. Her lightless eyes were upon his and she made a sound that was somewhere between the hiss of a snake and the bleat of a seal.

'Baloo,' he screamed again. This time he saw her form flicker for just a second, felt the weight disappear from his midriff again.

Then she was back. Leaning down now, her lips puckered, ready to kiss his life away, ready to suck his eyeballs from the sockets, tear his nose and lips away from his face, just as she'd done to her husband in the book.

He needed to get out from under her, and quick. He screamed the word again, only this time he closed his eyes and saw nothing but his daughter's face, his sweet Elouise. He saw her face, heard her laughter in his ears as though she was right there with him.

The weight of Always upon him disappeared. As soon as he felt that shift, Elwood summoned what little strength he had left, and rolled off to one side.

The abomination flickered back into existence, only now she wasn't on top of him. For a moment she looked confused, staring down at the empty earth beneath her.

Then she turned and looked at Elwood, who was now clawing at the exposed roots and pulling himself to his feet beside her. She cried her complaint – that same repulsive, bleating hiss.

He didn't wait around to see what she might do next; he could guess as much. Instead, he turned and ran as fast as he could.

The rainfall had turned the ground in the ditch to sludge. His bare feet splashed and slipped in the cold slop as he tried to move as quickly as possible. The last thing he wanted was to fall down – not now, not with that thing following him.

He didn't want to look back, didn't want to see it. As he moved forward, though, he looked up and saw the astronaut floating above the edge of the gulley. The darkness behind that smashed visor watching him. Beneath the showers and still-rumbling thunder in the skies above, Elwood was sure he could hear that crackling comms unit. A frenzied voice pleading for him to *come back*.

He ignored it. He ignored the dancing woman on the other side of the gulley too. Great masses of creepy-crawlies skittered out from the hole in her chest, her arms cast wide as though inviting him into her decaying embrace. For a brief moment he had the appalling thought that he would've preferred her to have been on top of him. Her rotting body riding his erection. The lesser of two grotesques.

He could hear splashing behind him now. He tried to pick up his pace, but the slippery earth was treacherous beneath the bare soles of his feet. Despite his desperation he was physically unable to speed up. It was like running on the damn moon.

The ground was rising up now and he was moving with it. The wet earth beneath his feet was no longer visible; here the rain ran down into the trench like a river.

He reached the top and heard another bleating hiss somewhere behind him; still he refused to look, afraid that seeing the monster in pursuit would be enough to make him falter, enough for her to be able to pounce on him.

The ground was a little firmer here than at the bottom of the ditch, so he quickened his pace. He took long, loping strides across the forest floor, wincing each time his bare feet snapped through gnarled twigs or landed upon jagged stones in the loose dirt.

He vaguely recalled the general direction Whiskey had taken him in to get back to the trail; that was his main focus now. Once he found the trail he could follow it back to the store, and from there he could find his way back to the villa by taking the same route he'd followed – a lifetime ago – on that first trip to Kenner's.

His legs were already screaming though, his naked body drenched in icy rainfall. How far had it been? Two miles? Wasn't that what Whiskey had said? Two miles was a hell of a long way for a naked sprint in the rain. He was already struggling for breath, his chest constricting, legs like bottom-heavy lead rods.

He wouldn't make it. He was almost sure of that.

But what he was also sure of was that he wasn't going to stop, not for anything, not while he could still hear the squishy pattering of something pursuing him on all fours. Something monstrous that wanted to have its way with his body.

He moved through the underbrush, through curtained willows and across densely thicketed knolls, lightless beneath the canopy of rain-soaked leaves. He tried his best to maintain a straight course, though he had no sense of place now; he didn't recognise anything because it all looked the same. There were trees in the darkness, and there was darkness around the trees. All he could do was hope that his course hadn't slipped, and that soon, any minute now – any second, *please* – he would see that mass of switchgrass, that wall of wispy sward that heralded an imminent arrival at the trail. Until then, he was simply running and hoping.

After what felt like hours – but could only have been four or five minutes – he arrived at that natural barrier of tall grass. There was no sigh of relief – he didn't have the breath for such a luxury – and no pause for a rest; instead he just ploughed straight into it.

Long blades collapsed before him, some flattened beneath his feet. Others tickled his testicles as he waded through.

He emerged onto the path and grimaced as he set his bare feet down on the gravel. He didn't let this slow him down, his focus shifted to reaching Kenner's old store. He continued sprinting.

Up ahead he saw a form take shape. A shadowy figure with pigtails hopscotching back and forth across the path. He knew who it was, knew *what* it was, but he didn't slow down.

He planned on running straight past her. As he approached her, though, the girl stopped in the middle of the trail and looked toward him, waving. Elwood swerved to the left and moved around her, but as he passed by, he made the mistake of glancing her way, and saw the face of his daughter.

It was Elouise.

His feet collided and he tumbled over himself. For a brief moment, he floated like the astronaut – suspended in mid-air, arms splayed, a single thought booming in his mind as the gravelly path came up to meet him:

Oh, shit.

Then he hit the ground.

It was his shoulder that crashed into the gravel first. A stinging pain like hot pins flared at the top of his arm and spread downwards as he scraped across the rough surface. Jagged stones broke through his skin, drawing blood and peeling back his flesh in tiny curls like pencil shavings. Next came his hip, thigh and part of his left ass cheek, the pointed edges of the gravel grazing the soft tissue and claiming more blood.

The friction of skin on stone brought his agonising slide to a mercifully quick end, leaving him curled up in a heap in the middle of the trail.

He looked back and saw that it wasn't Elouise after all. The girl with pigtails and no eyes stood a few feet behind him, frowning, her head tilted curiously.

'Where are you going, daddy?'

Ignoring her, Elwood climbed to his feet, brushing away stones and specks of dirt that were lodged in his skin. The entire left side of his body felt numb to the touch and he found himself trembling with shock.

He turned away from the girl and hobbled along the trail, his left leg pretty much useless.

'Daddy, don't go,' it was Elouise's voice now and

the sound of it sank his heart. 'We can help you, mom and I can help you, we can take away the pain. You just have to come with us, daddy.'

He didn't look back.

After a few minutes of shambling along the dark path, the feeling returned to his leg and he sped up. The path was on a downward slant now and that helped him maintain some momentum, for the time being at least.

When the end of the trail finally came into view he felt a rush of adrenaline sweep over him, and with it came a lightness of being that encouraged his pace.

He was nearly there.

Once he got across the gravel car park he would hit the smooth, flat tarmac of Crescent Road. Never in his life could he have imagined he'd so desperately crave the feeling of asphalt beneath his bare feet. He didn't want to think of what his soles might look like right now, but he assumed he was probably leaving a trail of bloody footprints in his wake.

There was light up ahead, and that concerned him. He couldn't recall seeing any sort of spotlight or streetlamp in the car park, and the soft glare that emanated from that area now was almost certainly artificial. That could only mean one thing.

As he neared the end of the trail he could smell them; burning marijuana and tobacco laced with cheap perfume. He could hear them, too: something poppy and country, Florida Georgia Line singing about how they did things round here.

He wasn't letting up for anything though. He passed the sign for the trail and continued moving as quickly as he could across the car park.

THOSE YOU KILLED

He saw a line of cars parked along the treeline to his right, smoke drifting out of the windows, shadows jostling inside. There was laughter too, but this ceased when the youths inside noticed the naked man running across the parking lot.

'No. Fucking. Way! Check it out.'

'Hey Trent, get a load of this weirdo.'

'Oh my God. Tiff – Tiff, look.'

Although he felt undeniably ashamed, it wasn't too difficult for Elwood to ignore them. He had more important things to worry about than a bunch of strangers seeing him naked.

There was the monster, Always.

The half-woman-half-axolotl abomination was perched on the roof of Kenner's old store, watching him. When he noticed her, she craned her wide head to the sky and let out another high-pitched, bleating hiss. There was something in that deafening cry, something like feral disappointment and anger, a wild yearning for a seed that she'd been denied. Hell hath no fury like a monster scorned.

Elwood kept his eyes on her as he hit the rain-soaked tarmac of Crescent Road. She wasn't moving from her spot, though, just watching him.

The smooth blacktop felt cool beneath his mangled feet, but he knew this reprieve would likely be short-lived. He heard engines starting up behind him. He thought it highly unlikely those kids just happened to be ready to leave when he'd appeared. No – there was a small chance, of course, but no. They were kids, they were getting high and drunk. They were having a good time, and they'd seen a naked guy appear out of the woods in the middle of the night. They were doing what any other group of youths would do in that same situation; they were going to follow him. They were going to mock him, and they were probably going to take photos of him that would get shared and reposted and re-grammed and retweeted and liked by people on the other side of the fucking world within the next three minutes.

He couldn't risk that sort of exposure. He wasn't exactly front page news anymore – well, he never really had been. Writers never saw the same kind of limelight that rock stars, sporting sensations, Hollywood players, or reality show losers did. He hadn't been a Stephen King – perhaps a Grant or Masterton, at the height of his success, but nothing more than that. Even if you didn't happen to be the flavour of the week though, a downward spiral like being seen naked by some kids in the woods was a sure-fire way to become instantly palatable for the press and masses. If Gracie didn't catch wind of the story herself, somebody she knew would, and that would lay to rest any hope he had of being a father to Elouise again.

He veered off the road and straight into the dense thicket of woodland that separated the Crescent from the lake. All he'd have to do now would be to keep a straight course for a couple of minutes and then he'd hit the shoreline. From there, he'd be able to see the villa, and he hoped that sight would provide the final injection of grit he was so desperately in need of.

His entire left side still ached and tingled. His legs felt like hefty metal pins moving on feet that were nothing more than sacks of splintered wood. And his chest – oh Christ his chest – he imagined the Michelin man, only it was his lungs bulging through the gaps between his ribs. Elwood's breath came and went in raspy croaks that would have surely seen him admitted to the cardio unit on any other day.

He heard the cars slow down behind him, horns blaring, whistling.

'Hey mister, wanna party?'

'Come back here, fucking weirdo.'

'Fucking perv. I say we beat his ass.'

'Fuck that – call your dad, Jess.'

The cars sped off. Screeching tyres drowned out the rest of the jeering and threats, but he was left wondering who they were going to tell. What if this Jess just happened to be the daughter of some gun-toting redneck? Some toothless backwoods nut with a few friends that might relish the opportunity for a human hunt? What if word spread around town and the story found its way to the wrong sort of ear? Not just those who might cause him trouble, but those he respected. He suddenly cringed at the thought of Whiskey or Aubrey hearing of his naked antics.

He let it go, knowing there was nothing he could do about it now. No photos had been taken, that was all that mattered for now. Tomorrow, he'd take the shovel and head back out to the gulley, find that cave entrance and bury it as deep as he could. Then he'd be out of here.

He hit the shoreline and made out the villa through the downpour. The lights inside were turned on and it shone like a lighthouse in the storm. He started along the grassy shore with the water to his left, derelict villas sitting in the darkness to his right.

Through the thunder in the sky and the commotion of his own thoughts, he suddenly felt a strange sense of tranquillity. Whether it was the soft patter of rain rippling the lake, or the fact that he was getting closer to his totem, he couldn't be sure. Maybe it was both.

A loud splash behind him. Something bigger than a raindrop falling into the lake.

He didn't look back; he knew what it was, knew who it was.

The villa was tantalisingly close now. If only he could walk on water like that old carpenter from Nazareth, he'd be there in no time – back inside, back in some clothes, back to the totem.

Something appeared in his peripheral view. Something swimming in the water beside him, dropping above and below the surface as it kept pace with him.

With each jetty he passed, the thing dived up out of the water and over the docks like Free fucking Willy.

'Fuck off,' he screamed. 'Just fuck off, leave me alone!'

He reached the overgrown path that led up to the terrace. Refusing to look back, he dashed up the trail. A loud *thump* behind him; the abomination had landed on the dock instead of diving over. It was right behind him.

Elwood roared. Fear and anticipation gripped him. He needed to get inside. He needed to get the totem.

The French doors were shut. He crashed into the window and tried to slide them open, but they were locked from the inside. He spied the reflection of Always bounding up the path behind him, her hulking form breaking through the rainfall, great plumes of breath rising like steam from those writhing, snake-like gills on her head.

Elwood moved along the outer wall and down the side of the villa, passing by the cutting block where he'd thrown up days before. He slipped in something slimy and coarse but managed to hold his balance. Too preoccupied with staying on his feet, he didn't pay any mind to the possibility that he'd just slid barefooted through his own days-old vomit.

Another bleating hiss from behind, too close.

He emerged from the side of the villa onto the weed-strewn front and began to wade through the overgrowth. As he neared the porch steps he noticed the trunk of his car was open. Stuffed inside were the bodies of the dancing lady and the eyeless girl, awaiting burial. Their heads turned in his direction, both grinning.

The front door of the villa was wide open and a large puddle of rainwater had gathered across the threshold and on the kitchen floor. He slowed down as he came inside, turning just in time to see the beastly, axolotl form of Always crashing through the jungle of weeds and tall grass behind him. He slammed the door shut and locked it just as she was reaching the first porch step; the last thing he saw was her toothless grin, wide and obscene. A smile he was sure would live with him long after he managed to – hopefully – put this place behind him.

The door rattled on its hinges as she thrust her weight against it. Dust and splinters rained down on Elwood as the doorframe itself was torn loose from the wall above his head.

A crackling, distorted noise suddenly erupted behind him and he turned to find the astronaut floating over the dining room table toward him, arms outstretched and ready to seize him.

'Oh, come on,' Elwood cried. 'You've got to be fucking kidding me.'

He dropped to the floor just in time and began crawling toward the entranceway to the hall as Olesk drifted through the air above, arms reaching down.

Elwood clambered to his feet in the hall and broke into an awkward run – his rain-slicken feet making it difficult to pick up speed on the laminate wood surface – as the front door burst open behind him.

When he reached the foot of the stairs he glanced back down the hall and saw it. The hideous, transfigured form of Always Jackson crashed through the entranceway and careened down the hall toward him.

Elwood took the steps three at a time – thighs screaming, his entire body pleading for a respite that he hoped would come soon. He never thought he'd make it back, make it this far, but he had, and he was nearly there, nearly at what he hoped would be the end of this nightmare. It was all on the totem now, his faith placed entirely in a lump of wood given to him by an old lady in a bookstore.

God, he hoped she was right about this thing. Hoped the stories of the Shawnee were true. If not, this nightmare was still going to end, just not in the way he wanted it to.

He took the corner and hit the second set of steps just as the beast arrived at the bottom, pausing to let out another deafening cry of angst and fury before it began its ascent. Elwood reached the landing above and heard it crashing around the corner below him. It was getting close – no time to look back, no time for anything now except hauling ass and hoping for the best. He moved along the upper landing as fast as his slippery feet would allow him. The floor shuddered beneath him and he almost lost his footing as the beast reached the top of the stairs at speed, smashing into the opposite wall and shattering one of the windows that overlooked the front of the property.

He reached the open space at the end of the hall and was glad to see the sofa bed empty. He'd half-expected the rotting corpse of the dancing lady to be lying there waiting for him, legs splayed seductively and Phil Collins playing in the background.

He scrambled over the bed toward the console table. The thing was right behind him now, he could smell it; dank and boggy and wrong in every way.

A heavy weight came down on the bed, snapping it in half as he flung himself forward, diving for the console, *for the totem.* Something wet and slimy grasped at his foot but it was too late, he had it. His fingers curled around the small lump of wood just before he hit the floor and thudded against the balcony windows. He turned and faced the thing, holding the bear up above his head.

He screamed. Bellowed. Roared a guttural, wordless war cry.

The monster retorted with that same deafening bleat, thrashing and bashing the mattress with clenched, webbed fists. The already-broken frame of the bed splintered and cracked beneath her weight and fury.

The rotting mother and eyeless daughter – Meredith and Laney – appeared out of the hallway behind the beast, the young girl holding her mother's hand – both frowning.

Elwood heard a gentle thud over the din, and turned to find the astronaut floating on the balcony. The lip of his shattered visor bumped against the window as he floated back and forth, suit gloves scraping against the glass.

Elwood held the totem up in the air once more. 'I'm sorry,' he screamed. 'I'm sorry,' tears streaming down his face. 'I was never supposed to forget who I was. I fucked up. I got fucked up and *I fucked up* and that's on me. But I remember now. You hear me? I remember all of you, all the parts I killed, all the parts I buried!'

He pointed the totem at the monster Always Jackson, her form flickering.

'You,' he cried. 'My humanity. Christ, I forgot what it was to be a human fucking *being*, but I remember now, I'm claiming you back as my own. You can't scare me or hurt me anymore, because you're me, you're a part of *me* and I'm digging you up right here, right fucking now, and taking you back.'

The monster flickered out once more, and didn't return.

He pointed the totem toward the girls by the entranceway. 'And you two, you –' he spluttered, his tears overwhelming him. 'You're not Meredith and Laney, you never were. You're Gracie and El. I might not have killed them, but I killed you, buried you, and I buried them too. I forgot about them. I forgot about them and it's the worst fucking thing I could've ever done and *I'm sorry...* and I wish I could take it back. I wish I could take it all back, every fucking needle, every spoon, every damn time I chose it all over them.' He was sobbing now, his arms shaking, but still he held the totem high, jabbing it through the air as the words poured out of him with so many tears.

The two dead girls flickered in and out of the room but held their position on the other side of the bed.

'What's done is done, but I remember now, I remember what matters, I remember my family. And that's why you can't scare me. You can't hurt me.'

Another flicker, and they too were gone.

He turned around and shuffled away from the balcony windows until his back was up against the broken sofa bed. Olesk was still floating out there – back and forth, back and forth, his shattered visor thudding against the glass.

'And you,' Elwood cried, holding the totem before him like a dagger. 'You were a crazy, ambitious bastard that's for sure, and that ambition took you over the edge, just like mine took me over the edge. I thought it would help, thought it would amplify my creativity and I was a fool for thinking that. Because it didn't. It made everything shit, turned it all to *shit*; my head, my imagination, my ambition, my work. My fucking life, all of it. Turned to shit. I became like you, something else… something that didn't have ambition, didn't have anything. I lost my fucking mind. I lost everything,' he screamed at the now-flickering Olesk, rain beating down on his suit and falling straight through it at the same time. 'I lost everything. But the writing, the success, the fans, the ambition… I can claim all of that back, I can make that happen again, I know I can. I know I fucking can. And I will,' he yelled.

And with that last promise, the astronaut flickered out a final time.

Elwood let his arms drop, still clutching the totem, rested his back against the smashed timber frame. Exhausted, crying rivers… alone? No, he didn't think so. They were still here, but things had changed, he'd changed.

Whatever that trapped thing out in the forest was, that *dusios*, it had no power over his own demons, because they weren't his demons anymore. They were no longer forgotten, no longer a source of shame and regret. They were parts of him, parts no longer lost but reclaimed. The best of him. And now that he knew that, now that he understood that, they couldn't be twisted, couldn't scare him, couldn't harm him.

They could only make him stronger.

CHAPTER TWENTY
IN WHICH IT ALL GOES TO SHIT

The storm was over.

Both storms, in fact; the one within him had been tamed, and the one outside had turned to a fine drizzle beneath a chalky sky. But there were still ribbons of cloud on the horizon, and still one thing left for him to do, one more incline before the sky cleared and the sun could shine bright in his life again.

All of his demons had been unearthed during his time here, and before he left, there was one he had to bury. The *dusios.*

Today. That was his plan. But later, in the afternoon perhaps. He needed time to rest, more time than he had, but any time was better than none. He didn't like the idea of heading out there when it was dark, and equally, he didn't like the idea of still being here come tomorrow morning. For all he knew, there might already be talk of his naked antics among most of the local kids. It wouldn't be too long until a parent heard something, and once that happened, it would spread like wildfire.

He didn't have much choice, though. Right now, he wasn't sure he'd even be able to lift a shovel, let alone dig. He felt as though his entire body had been smashed apart, the joints haphazardly fixed back together at each junction with a stapler. Ligaments and tendons excessively rigid or concerningly loose; parts of him felt as though they might drop off with the slightest movement, whilst others felt as though they might tear apart in ribbons of red beneath his flesh if he so much as reached for his coffee cup.

After spending a night half-in and half-out of a broken sofa bed, he'd managed to create a biting point in the centre of his back and was now afraid to bend too far in either direction to try and crack it. Chances were, a simple stretch and crack would alleviate much of the discomfort, but he had an idea that attempting such a thing could snap his spine completely. It was ironic that, after finding the strength and courage to confront his own demons last night, he was now submitting to basic irrational fears.

His feet sang a high-pitched tune that didn't ring in his ears, but in his knees. Each chorus sent shockwaves through his legs that tickled and jolted every muscle and nerve. It reminded Elwood of those awful muscle-toning pads he'd tried many years ago, only these pads weren't applied to his non-existent abs, they were the very soles of his feet.

He'd cleared out the first aid box, leaving nothing for a future Casper that might be in need of the support.

Fuck him, Elwood had thought as he'd used the last of the sanitised wipes and moved onto the remnants of his whiskey bottle. Most of the supplies he'd used on his feet – an exercise which had been excruciating, to say the least. The original wound he'd sustained out on the lake had turned from a fine slit to a great river of red, with countless tributaries branching out from it in shades of dirt and crimson. The other foot was pretty much the same, but without the Mississippi running through the middle; just a vast network of fleshy canyons and gulleys of vermillion, pockmarked with the dust and pointed gravel that had broken through the skin, the surface beneath blackened and purple with clotted blood.

Once he'd cleaned out these trenches and managed to pull out all of the stones and splinters that had cut into the soft flesh, he wrapped bandages tightly around his feet – again, using up everything the first aid box had to offer.

He had found a kitchen cloth, soaked it in a bowl of vodka, and wiped down the entire left side of his body, which was covered in shallow grazing from his shoulder down to his ankle. He'd applied a few plasters in areas where sheets of flesh had been peeled back to reveal the moist and reddish under-skin beneath.

And last, but certainly not least, after tending to all of his wounds, he'd finally put some clothes on. The simple act of slipping into some jeans and a shirt had felt almost ceremonious; the final nail in the coffin that had been a far-from-enjoyable encounter of passion, and the naked, nightmarish jaunt that had followed.

He sipped his coffee now and stared out at the lake,

feeling somewhat dignified. Although the sky was overcast, the warm air and gentle morning breeze had tempted him out onto the terrace for breakfast.

He'd taken the time to whip up a hearty portion of boiled eggs and toast, hoping that an injection of carbs and protein might help prepare his body for the arduous task that lay ahead.

The totem, he hoped, would take care of his mind.

He found himself looking down at his phone every so often, expecting Casper to crash the party once again. There was a small part of him – arguably self-destructive – that was almost willing it to happen, hoping the crazy gangster-come-drug dealer would call again. Because things had changed now; he wasn't the same man he'd been yesterday, the day before, or for the last few years. He was cleansed. Reborn. Rejuvenated. Whatever the hell you wanted to call it. He was stronger, and that part of him – the self-destructive part, or perhaps the doubtful part – wanted to test that assertion.

There was no call, though, and probably for the best. When he'd finished his business later today he'd do exactly what Casper had asked: post the keys back through and do his best to steer clear of the man for the rest of his life. That wouldn't be too hard either; he'd decided it was time to find a place back in Illinois, somewhere closer to El and Gracie. He couldn't be a father if he stayed in LA, and he certainly couldn't avoid Casper or any of his associates. The man was a big deal in the city of angels.

He toyed with the idea of never going back to his old apartment. Returning to that place would be like returning a needle to his veins. It just felt like a step in the wrong direction. He'd moved on now, seemingly cured himself and found a better path, and that path didn't lead to LA – it led to Illinois, it led to sobriety, and ultimately, it led to his daughter.

When he thought about it, there wasn't much to tie up which actually required he be there in person. In fact, there was nothing. Nothing but a single room and adjoining shower and toilet on the fifth floor of a decaying complex, nestled somewhere between South Park and Skid Row. A far cry from their townhouse in Brentwood.

At least the girls had never had to see any of the other places, never had to live in them, or walk the questionable neighbourhoods they were situated in. They'd left a few months before the foreclosure. From then on, the standard of Elwood's rented accommodation had gradually declined as his addiction intensified, the cost of his habit increased, and his book sales took a nose-dive. As a writer, you could only rely on your bibliography so much, especially when you hadn't reached the heights of King or Barker. You had to keep writing, had to keep releasing new books, snagging higher advances each time.

Instead, he stopped writing completely, made a fool of himself on more than a few occasions, and ultimately wound up becoming reliant on royalties that barely covered his basic living costs. Possessions were sold, meals were skipped in favour of powdered spoons. A bed eventually became a mattress on the floor; a sofa simply became that floor.

So, no. When he thought about it, there wasn't

anything he needed to go back for. He'd call the management company and give notice as soon as he was on the road to Illinois. If he had to sacrifice his deposit then so be it, he guessed he'd probably left the place in a poor state; cleaning was an exercise the most vehement of junkies rarely engaged in.

There hadn't been any deposit or payment made to Casper in exchange for staying at the villa though, and he wondered what he might have to sacrifice in order to make up for the broken front door and wrecked sofa bed. The cost of fixing them up would be a drop in an ocean of cash for someone like the friendly ghost, but if he saw it as a sign of disrespect, he might come after Elwood, might send some goons to have a little chat.

He needed to lie down, shut his eyes for a few hours. He was letting his mind sprint ahead of him, worrying about things he needn't be worrying about, now, or possibly ever.

An old habit. He'd always been a worrier, a second-guesser, an over-thinker and self-deprecator. The habit he'd just given up had been like a shield against these more-often-than-not toxic inner-reflections.

Well, *shield* was perhaps a little too positive a word; the heroin had been more of a diffuser, a filter. Only it had diffused and filtered out more of his life – more of him – than he'd ever truly wanted it to. He guessed he'd need to find another way though, a healthier way to deal with his self-induced stresses. And he would, in time. Hell, he might even try meditation. Gracie had sworn by it, though he'd never obliged any of the countless invitations to join her.

He set his empty cup down, resigned to the decision

that sleep was the best thing for him right now, for his mind, and for his body. And that was exactly what he got, in a way.

Sleep.

He didn't hear the faint sound of approaching footsteps in the tall grass along the side of the house, nor did he hear the intruder tread carefully across the stony terrace behind him. What he did hear, though – in the split-second before sleep was thrust upon him – was the whoosh of something cutting through the air.

He didn't have time to turn around. There was a brief moment of awful pain at the back of his head; a searing agony that quickly spread across his entire skull. Before it could reach his eyes, though, they were closed. Darkness welcomed him like an old friend, and the bricks of the terrace welcomed his slumped body.

'Eeny, meeny, miny moe, catch a junkie by its toe…'

Elwood stirred. His skull pounded like he'd gone twelve rounds with Jose Cuervo and headbutted the sidewalk.

'If it squeals, stick it good…'

His eyes blinked open; nothing but white, a dirty off-white that was yellowy-brown in parts. A ceiling. It was the lounge ceiling. He was on the sofa.

'*Eeny, meeny, miny moe…*'

He recognised that voice, knew it all too well, but it couldn't be. Surely, he couldn't be here.

'Wakey, wakey, junkie bunny.'

The terrace. That was the last thing he remembered, being out on the terrace. Coffee, he'd finished the cup and set it down. Illinois, getting away…

'Casper?'

'The one and only.'

Still fuzzy from the knock that had put him to sleep, Elwood let his head roll to the side. Through still-hazy eyes he saw him, the friendly ghost himself, perched on the coffee table and grinning down. There was nothing *friendly* about his smile though – this was the smile of a man who knew he was above you in the food chain, the sort of amused and equally patronising grin one might wear at the zoo, whilst looking in on the monkeys or meerkats.

He wore his usual attire, an outfit that screamed nineteen-ninety-two: loose-fitting blue jeans and a baggy, white cotton shirt, tucked in at the waist and with a ludicrously wide V-neck that showed off too much of his broad, ripped chest. His sleeves were rolled up, revealing veiny, pumped forearms that Elwood had always thought looked strangely thicker than his biceps.

His Trump-orange skin glistened with sweat, as did the boot-polish-black hair tied back in an oily bun atop his head.

A stranger might be forgiven for mocking this apparently Mediterranean time-travelling muscle-man, but Elwood knew better, and any who smirked at Casper's appearance soon *learned* better.

'What are you doing here, Casper?'

He already knew the answer though, as absurd as it was. For a sober Elwood it was clear to see; the junkie, however, had been none-the-wiser. He'd been so desperate, so blissfully ignorant that he hadn't thought to question why Casper was offering to help him.

Hadn't wondered why the dealer was essentially taking steps to get rid of one of his most lucrative sources of income. There was nothing special about Elwood, nothing that set him apart from any of the other shambling wrecks that sought out Casper's product – although, in fairness, he likely spent considerably more money than many others – yet he'd somehow earned himself a ticket to the man's private lakeside retreat for a little detox getaway.

As had others just like him.

'Oh, I think you know why I'm here, bunnyman. Don't play dumb now.'

'It's you, isn't it? You're the one *feeding* it.' His head throbbed.

Casper only grinned.

'So, there really is a demon out there. A *dusios*.'

'A *dusios*? Sounds like someone didn't listen to me and took their junkie-ass into town,' he sighed, shaking his head. 'Fucker.'

'So, you know all about it then?' Elwood asked, still feeling hazy and struggling to sit up.

'Yeah,' Casper replied. 'I sat in that stinky store and smiled, listened to the old lady and ate her fucking cookies. So yeah, I know everything you know, and more – so much fucking more.' He laughed.

'How did you find it?'

'What are you, fucking Letterman now? This ain't no interview, Elwood, it doesn't matter how I found it, I just did.' He pulled a cigar from his breast pocket. There was the *chink* of metal on glass as he placed the gun he'd been holding upon the coffee table beside him. Elwood hadn't even realised he'd been wielding a gun, but now he wasn't – now it was out of his hands and sitting on the glass-top. Must have been what had put him to sleep. Sitting beside it was Elwood's phone, the screen shattered, the body almost broken in half. Also, the crumpled pack of cigarettes that had been in his pocket before he'd been knocked unconscious.

Casper caught his glance and grinned. 'Yeah, service can be pretty shitty out here sometimes. I don't think you'll be making any calls.'

There had to be another way out of this, some other way to get help. As much as he'd hated the idea of Sheriff Tims coming out to see him, he figured the guy would be his best bet right now. If this were one of his books, then word of his naked antics would've reached the Sheriff, and the man would already be on his way out here with an itchy trigger-finger. Real life was unfortunately rarely so contrived.

He just hoped Whiskey didn't stop by. The thought of that kindly old man coming face to face with this – this *monster* – well, he didn't want to think about how that might play out.

There had to be some other way.

He glanced at the clock on the wall and saw that he'd been out of it for most of the afternoon, it was close to five o'clock.

Five o'clock. That meant he wasn't entirely alone out here with Casper; there might be someone who could help, someone who might at least get the cops out here, if given a reason to.

The bare bones of a far-fetched plan began to take shape in his mind.

'You know what, fuck it,' a dense cloud of cigar

smoke now filled the air between them. 'I'll indulge you, bunnyman. We got some time to kill until sundown.'

'Why? What happens then, Casper? Are you going to try and feed me to that thing out there? Is that it? Some kind of sacrifice or offering? And for what? What do you get in return?'

'Well, I'll be a fucking padre in a pussy joint,' Casper laughed, coughed. 'You think I'm going to *try*? What, like there's going to be some kind of opposition? Some sort of fucking pushback that's going to result in *me* having to *try*?'

He laughed again, shaking his head in disbelief, releasing dense curls of earthy cigar smoke with each chortle.

'The junkie really has grown some balls. I mean, I caught vibes on the phone, but then you switched back to that blubbering, stumbling mess of a shit you've been over these last few years, the mess of a shit I know so well. And you know why I know it so well?'

He didn't wait for a response.

'Because I fucking *made* you. That's what I *do*. This isn't some side-hustle… this *is* the hustle, and it feeds everything else.'

Elwood dragged himself into a sitting position, still grimacing at the pain he felt in the back of his skull. 'I get it. So, you fuck up people's lives, get them hooked. Then you send the end-of-the-liners here for a little rehab. That about right, Casper? Only they never come back from it, do they?'

He glanced back down at the crumpled pack of cigarettes. He was sure he'd stuffed his lighter in there.

He'd be needing it.

Casper grinned, cigar clamped between his teeth. 'You got it, bunnyman. I take people and I turn them into people nobody'll miss, people nobody will ask about because they have nobody left to care. Nobody, except the friendly ghost. And let me tell you, compared to that thing out there, I really am the fucking friendly one.'

'How many?' Elwood leaned forward. 'How many before me? You son of a bi–'

Casper swung, and he swung hard, his fist connecting just above Elwood's left eye before he could finish the slur. The blow knocked him back into the sofa and left his head reeling, his perception shifted as everything on his left suddenly went black.

'You better watch your mouth. I might need you alive, but that don't mean you have to be in one piece.'

Elwood felt something wet rolling down his cheek. He looked down and saw a red blotch growing across his chest. With his head bowed, the blood that was leaking from his split eyebrow began to fall in droplets into his midriff, and a blackish red stain quickly spread across his crotch.

'Fuck,' he brought his hand up and touched the area around his eye, it was already swollen, and he flinched as his fingers pressed against the tender flesh.

'You try and show me those big balls of yours again and I'll do more than just crack your skull. You hear me?'

'Yes, I hear you, damnit,' Elwood flopped back in the sofa, shooting a quick glance at the clock.

He had two minutes.

CHRISTOPHER BADCOCK

Two minutes until Kenner locked up the old store. If he was lucky, perhaps three minutes until the old man would be passing by the end of the drive in his truck. Whiskey had mentioned that Kenner was friendly with the Sheriff and would surely be keeping an eye on the place, but he wouldn't see much from the road.

That was where the lighter could change things. The lighter, and that butane canister in the back of the closet. It was crazy, it was risky, and it was overblown, but he couldn't think of any other way of catching the old man's attention.

Casper laughed. 'I never really liked you, bunnyman, but I'm starting to. You found some fight in there. Most last a couple of days, max. My buddy out there worms its way in as soon as it senses your sort – starts fucking with you like kitties do with little mice. I ain't ever had to come out here like this, but I send you out here, a sorry sucker like the rest of them, and somehow you resist? I have to park in the next fucking county and trek my ass through the woods... the fucking *woods*, bunnyman,' he puffed his cigar and eyed Elwood searchingly. 'Somehow. And maybe I want to know what that somehow is.'

Elwood thought of the bear totem, still sat on the console upstairs. How it had weaponised his memories, how it had saved him the night before.

He looked back down at the pack of cigarettes. 'Throw me my smokes and I'll be happy to share.'

Casper didn't hesitate. Clearly he needed to know, and he seized the pack and tossed it into Elwood's lap.

'Spill the beans.'

As he began to psych himself up for what needed to

333

come next, Elwood pulled a cigarette out of the pack and the lighter with it. The easy part was out of the way, and now came the hard part; getting to the closet.

He lit his smoke and inhaled deeply, relishing the taste, knowing there was every chance it could be his last.

He'd only have one shot at getting to the closet, and one chance at grabbing the gun before Casper did.

One desperate move.

He'd need to be careful, and make sure he led with the heel of his shoe. His only advantage was Casper wouldn't be expecting him to thrash out or attempt to fight back – not now, not after being put back in his place and left bleeding.

'Well, it was actually quite simple, you might say I made use of the *bare necessities*,' he laughed to himself, glancing at the clock again.

Five.

'I warned you not to fuck with me,' Casper replied. 'And I see you looking at that damn clock too, what are you wait–'

As he turned his head to look at the clock himself, Elwood leaned back into the sofa and lifted his leg as high as he could, before bringing it down heel first on the coffee table, shattering the glass top that Casper was sitting on. The weight of the friendly ghost took him straight through the glass undershelf, an agonised, furious cry escaping him as he landed ass-first in the mess of shards on the carpet beneath.

Elwood kept his eyes on the gun, watching as it dropped through the glass with Casper, landing on the undershelf and remaining there for only a split-second before Casper smashed through it. From there, it hit the carpet barrel-first and bounced in his direction, between his legs, and disappeared beneath the sofa.

Shit.

'You mother fu–' Casper was already trying to get up, his bloody elbows crunching in the shattered remains of the coffee table as he tried to clamber out of the now-glassless frame.

There was no time for Elwood to get down on his hands and knees and reach beneath the sofa, not now. Every second counted; he'd have to leave the gun and hope that Casper hadn't seen where it had wound up. He jumped to his feet and ran through the doorway into the hall, clutching his lighter and praying that Kenner would be leaving the old store on time today.

He stumbled into the closet – still half-blinded by the blood in his eye - and closed the door behind him. He moved straight to the high window against the far wall, reached up and unlatched the iron clasps at either end. It opened towards him from the top, with the hinges fixed in place at the base, leaving a space at the crown that was barely wide enough to fit a young child through.

Without hesitation, Elwood grasped the top of the pane and planted one of his feet against the wall, pulling down with all of his weight. The hinges snapped and the glass shattered and rained down around him. He ignored the stinging pain in his palms and headed back toward the door, brushing glassy fragments from his hair and the back of his neck as he moved.

'You mother-fucking junkie-fuck!' He heard stomping in the next room; Casper was on the move.

Elwood grabbed the shelving unit nearest the door and pulled it forward until it toppled over and crashed into the opposite wall, creating a barricade. The contents of the shelves spilled onto the floor – various tins and cans and aerosols, most of which he guessed would be flammable. He moved to the next unit and began pulling off all the cleaning products, paints and sponges that he could see, tossing them all toward the door. On the third set of shelves there was a supply of rolled kitchen towels; he tore a few packs open and unravelled the three-ply paper onto the pile at the door.

'I can hear you in there, you son of a bitch.'

The handle began to move up and down, but the door remained firmly shut against the fallen shelving unit.

'What are you doing in there, bunnyman?'

Elwood grabbed the last roll of kitchen paper and began searching the ground around him for something to douse it in. He picked up a tub of floor disinfectant and unscrewed the top with his teeth; he then poured a little over the top of the roll and dashed the open container onto the pile with the rest of the cleaning debris.

The door trembled on its hinges as Casper tried to force his way in. 'Open this fucking door, you junkie son of a whore!'

Elwood ignored him. Licking his lips, he held the lighter to the soaking roll of towels and thumbed the serrated edge of the wheel. The flint sparked and he felt a wave of heat smack him in the face as the roll of paper burst into flames.

Casper continued his barrage against the door, singing curses and threats in equal measure as Elwood dropped the flaming roll between the fallen shelves onto the pile of maintenance debris.

The fire spread quickly, and soon enough the flames would burn through the various cans, jugs, tins and aerosols. The room began to fill with smoke.

'What the fuck,' Casper shouted. 'What the fuck are you doing in there?'

Elwood shuffled back toward the window at the far end of the room, picked up the butane canister and hurled it onto the makeshift pyre. It wouldn't take long now – seconds, in fact – so he wasted no time. He pulled the barbeque out from the corner, set it against the wall beneath the window and climbed up onto the open grill. He felt the heat of the blaze against his back as he pulled himself up and through the window. Smoke billowed around him and he could hear something hissing back in the room.

It was either the butane or one of the other countless aerosols he'd thrown onto the bonfire; it quickened his escape regardless. He was halfway through when something popped behind him and he felt the heat suddenly intensify. He had a moment to determine that it hadn't been the butane – surmising that it would've been more of a *boom* than a pop – before he felt a searing pain on the backs of his legs and ankles.

He cried out – not just from the pain, but from an unwelcome awareness of the fact that he was on fire. He squirmed and twisted, frantically shifting the remainder of his upper torso over the window ledge so that gravity would take over.

He fell through the air for a second that felt closer to a minute, only just managing to cross his arms in front of his face before he hit the ground. Smoke poured out of the tiny window above as he rolled back and forth in the overgrown lawn, trying to put himself out. The heat died down after a few seconds, and he stopped rolling for a moment to look down at his legs, dreading what he might see.

His joggers had become three-quarter-lengths, the lower-hems scorched and blackened from the flames. Thin curls of smoke rose up from the fabric. His shins had turned a reddish-pink, and he could see a few blisters rising up on the sore skin; aside from that though, he seemed to be okay.

Elwood climbed to his feet and began to wade through the mess of overgrown lawn and shrubbery toward the side of the villa, rubbing away the now-crusty blood from his eye as he approached the corner of the building. He could still hear Casper inside, banging against the closet door and spouting a multitude of profanities, all of them double-barrelled with *junkie.*

'*You junkie-fuck.*'

He passed the chopping block, picked up the rusty axe from the grass beside it, and moved toward the side-entrance that opened onto the hallway.

'Open up, you junkie-cunt!'

He needed to get upstairs. He needed the totem.

'Junkie-bastard!'

He was also acutely aware of the fact that he now had two monsters to deal with. Shovelling some dirt over an entrance to a cave wasn't going to stop Casper from continuing to do what he was doing. Burning the villa down might stall his efforts, make things awkward, but ultimately, things would carry on as they were.

He needed to kill Casper.

The thought of dispatching the friendly ghost felt – strangely – even more daunting than going up against a demon.

No. Elwood brushed that thought aside. Casper was a man, a human being. Yes, he was dangerous, yes, he'd killed people, and yes, he'd exercised pretty much complete control over Elwood for the last few years.

But he was flesh and bone, and both could burn.

Cautiously, Elwood eased the door open. Just a crack, enough to peer through and watch as Casper continued his barrage against the closet door.

'*Open this fucking door you junkie-prick!*'

The hall was filling with smoke, but the friendly ghost seemed unperturbed by this, blind with rage, his shirt blood-soaked from rolling around in the shattered glass of the coffee table.

A high-pitched whistle suddenly erupted from the closet, cutting through the carnage and profanity and bringing Casper to his knees, his hands clasped over his ears.

'*Fuck,*' he screamed.

The noise reminded Elwood of a kettle on a burner; the pitch quickly rose to excruciating heights and he soon found himself covering his ears, wincing too as the whistle turned to a screech.

Still down on his knees, his hands over his ears, Casper turned away from the door. Their eyes met through the haze of smoke.

'What the fuck did you do, you junk–'

Boom.

THOSE YOU KILLED

***

George Kenner had always been of the opinion that cell phones were bad. Radioactive ringers that grew tumours in your brain whenever you had one stuck to the side of your head. He resisted them for years, but after his third heart attack and first stroke, a co-ordinated intervention from his wife, four daughters and nine grandkids had finally changed that.

The old man was still of the same opinion, and firmly believed that when his time was up, his time was up. Calling someone to let them know wouldn't change that fact.

Begrudgingly, though, he carried the phone around with him whenever he was out and about on his own.

He still hadn't mastered text-messaging, and had no inclination to either, no matter how much Eric – his eldest grandson – showed him how easy it was. He occasionally took calls from Rita – his wife – but he never made calls himself.

And that was exactly what he was trying to work out how to do now.

Eric had shown him how to make calls, but he'd only been half-listening; his other ear – and both eyes – had been on the NC State game.

'Dang it. Stupid ringer.'

Smoke drifted across the road in front of his parked truck.

He'd locked up for the night and was heading back toward town when he'd noticed it rolling in from the trees on the left. It hadn't taken him long to determine the source; the clouds grew thicker as he passed the turnoff for villa No.10, then thinner as he approached the turnoff for No.8.

It was No.9.

Made sense too. That was where the sick boy was staying – well, he'd looked sick anyway, that night he'd come to the store looking for liquor and the like. Sheriff Tims said he used to be some kind of writer, but not anymore. Now he was a deadbeat, like all the others who came to No.9. A deadbeat that could cause trouble for the town, a deadbeat they needed to keep a close eye on.

Kenner had Tims' number in the phone, or at least he thought he did. Eric had asked for a list of all the people he wanted to put into his contacts and Kenner had provided a handwritten list scrawled on the back of a gas station receipt. His grandson had then gathered the numbers of everybody on the list – he ran a convenience store in town so regularly saw most of them anyway – which included Sheriff Tims. But now it appeared that Eric had only added his wife, Rita, and he'd added her at least forty times, forty one, forty two, forty three. Kenner continued scrolling but all he saw was her name, over and over again.

He didn't realise he was looking at his call log.

'Piece of shit,' he shook the phone, as if that might help in some way; maybe the screen would change like one of those Magic 8-Balls.

It didn't.

The smoke was a dense cloud of grey now, blocking any view of the road ahead and growing so pungent that he was forced to roll up his windows.

He poked Rita's name and the screen turned to a full

image of her in close-up, smiling beneath the white fedora she always wore on sunny days in the yard. A green telephone icon pulsated in the middle of the screen, which he believed indicated that a call was being made. He held the phone to his ear and only caught a brief second of the dial tone before his wife answered.

'George? Is everything okay my love?'

He sighed. 'I'm fine, Reet, I'm fine. I just can't figure this damn ringer. Do me a favour would you, holla at Tims and let him know there's some kind of fire out here at Chance, I thi–'

'Fire? What do you mean, George? Are you ok?'

'Would you let me talk, Reet? Okay. Fire. There's a fire out at Chance, it looks like it's coming from number nine. Yeah, the one I told you about, that's right. I can't see it through the trees and this damn smoke, but you let him know to call Andy over at Nils FD, think we'll need those boys over here.'

'I'll do that, but you come straight home right now, you hear?'

He sighed again. 'Yeah, yeah, I hear you, Reet. But you make sure to call him soon as you're off the ringer. He'll want to come out here for himself and see –'

Boom.

CHAPTER TWENTY-ONE
A CONFLAGRATION

The closet door was ripped from its hinges by the force
of the explosion on the other side. A hail of scorched
splinters scattered throughout the air and the shockwave
blew out all of the windows that lined the hallway. The
ceiling in the closet and across the threshold directly
above Casper's position – as well as the walls on either
side of the doorway – burned for only a brief moment
before they were obliterated and reduced to charred
framework. The gaping maw that appeared above
Casper's head cut across the ceiling and cracked open
the outer wall, all the way up into the eaves and as far
down as the foundations. As the window to his left
shattered, the surrounding frame split down the middle
and peeled back like cardboard. The wall above and
below cracked open like an egg and in less than a
second the window had turned to a jagged cavity of
burnt timber and crumbling brick that extended from
ground to gutter, ultimately splitting the front of the

villa in half.

It was through this opening that Casper was propelled, the entire right side of his body pitted with fiery splinters and his head a blaze of combustible hair product. His limp form moved through the air like a daredevil over the tall weeds in the front yard, overshooting them completely and landing on the trunk of Elwood's car.

Elwood instinctively turned his head away, raising his arm to shield his face before the windowpanes in the door shattered outwards. He felt a prickly, searing pain across the back of his hand and lower arm, and then the weight of the door crashed into him and knocked him back into the weedy lawn amid a flurry of glass and splinters.

The world suddenly turned shady. It took him a minute or so to regain his senses and realise he was lying face down in the grass, with the door on top of him. He shifted his body; the remains of the door fell away and the day brightened once again. He turned over, ears ringing, and looked through the now-empty doorframe into the hall. Thick columns of smoke wafted outwards and rose into the sky above. If Kenner had somehow missed all this, Elwood guessed that people in town would at least be able to see it.

He climbed to his feet, wincing as he pushed himself up. He looked down and saw that his arm was dotted with specks and shards of glass from the door. Blood trickled down over his wrist, dripping from his fingers into the grass at his feet. He began to pull out some of the larger chunks, grimacing as he eased each jagged piece out from beneath his skin. Once he'd removed the longer shards, he turned his attention back to the doorway. He needed to get upstairs. He needed the totem.

He moved to the corner of the building and glanced out across the front yard. He noticed the huge, blood-stained dent in the trunk of his car, and the rear window that was now a spiderweb of hairline cracks. Casper was lying on the ground beside the exhaust; he wasn't moving, and from his current vantage point Elwood was unable to tell if he was even still breathing.

He thought of all the movies he'd ever seen where the hero had a good chance to finish off the villain, to make sure he was dead, and didn't. There wasn't anything heroic about it; audiences didn't cheer for the person who took an opportunity like that. But there was no audience here. Just him, and Casper. And that thing out in the woods.

He could walk over there right now and make sure he was dead. Crush his windpipe while he was still unconscious, pick up one of the shards of glass and slice his throat and wrists, jump up and down on his face – whatever it took to finish him off, to put an end to the game he was playing.

But he'd still need the totem, he'd still need to try and seal away that thing out in the woods. And the villa was burning. He couldn't risk losing what might be his only defence.

Elwood moved back toward the doorway. Smoke billowed out in great plumes; already, he could feel the heat.

Shit, he thought, it might already be too late.

He decided it would do no good to waste any more

time hesitating. He pulled his collar up to cover the lower half of his face, and stepped into the hall.

Closing his eyes against the smoke, he began to feel his way along the interior wall, moving as quickly as he could until he reached the stairs. The heat was intense here; he blinked his eyes open for a second and saw flames dancing in and out of the closet doorway, spreading up and down the exposed framework on either side and licking the ceiling.

He turned left and made his way up the stairs. As he neared the U-bend on the middle landing the heat became almost unbearable. He squinted through the miasma, saw that the left wall – the one that bordered the closet – had been blown apart by the explosion. Broken timber and scorched wallpaper littered the way forward; he could see the inferno below through the breach in the wall. The flames hadn't yet spread onto the stairway, but they would soon. Elwood skipped up the remaining steps as quickly as he could, hearing the weakened wood creak beneath his weight.

He wouldn't be coming back this way.

As he reached the hallway above, this thought was confirmed. The creaking suddenly turned to a loud, drawn-out yawn, culminating in a crescendo of cracking lumber. The stairway collapsed in on itself, leaving nothing but dust and fire and smoke in its wake.

Elwood stepped back and looked upon the destruction, oddly detached for a moment, watching the flames rise as the inferno below continued to grow.

Would it just be easier to end it all now? he thought. He could do that. The uncertainty, the pain, the sadness – all of it – with just one step. That was all it would take.

One step. He'd die in pain, of course, but it wouldn't last long, wouldn't be nearly as rough as he expected the road ahead to be. He was sure he'd read somewhere that after a few seconds in intense heat, your nerve-endings fried and you began to feel cold, rather than hot. That would be nice, to do away with all this heat and just… *chill*, just for a moment, before peaceful oblivion.

It was the painful sting of smoke in his eyes that tugged him back from this *l'appel du vide*. He'd left them open a little too long and floods of tears streamed down his ash-blackened cheeks. He glanced to his right and saw the crack in the floor, now a fiery fissure at least three feet wide. Flames whipped through the opening, charring the jagged edges of laminate wood on either side. He hopped over this and continued down the hall toward the balcony doors, closing his eyes once again and feeling his way along the wall.

He reached the corner and stumbled forward, not wanting to slow down now. His foot struck the broken sofa bed and he fell forward onto the mattress. Unperturbed, he scrambled forward across the bed, blind. He reached the other side and crawled onto the floor, his hands outstretched, feeling for the console table.

It wasn't there.

He paused for a moment, trying not to panic. He opened his eyes for a second, but that was all he could manage – the smoke was too thick, and he couldn't see anything but grey. He wondered if he'd lost his bearings when he'd fallen onto the mattress; for all he knew he was on the wrong side of the room completely.

'Fuck.'

He was coughing now, choking on the noxious cloud of smoke swirling around him. He shuffled forward on his hands and knees. Once he found a wall he could follow it back to the corner of the hall and work out where he was –

He flinched as his head bumped against glass.

Glass. He was at the balcony doors. He was close.

Staying near to the floor, he moved right and found the latch, flicked it down and slid the door open. The smoke collecting in the room began to slowly dissipate, flowing around him and out through the open balcony door. He laid low for a few moments while the room cleared and visibility improved. Smoke was still drifting in from the fire – still spreading, now raging in the hallway – but most of it was now passing through instead of lingering.

The console table was just a few feet away to his right, the totem in the same spot where he'd left it – the bear looking right at him.

He rolled over and reached for it. He felt more than just the weight of the wood in his palm when he picked it up; an immediate sense of calm settled over him. He was still coughing, and the villa creaked and groaned under the pressure of the blaze, but it had all been dialled down, like music in a nightclub when you stepped outside.

The world around him had quieted.

Still lying on the floor, he brought the totem close to his face and looked into the bear's eyes. Those black dots that had been scorched into its face stared right back at him, spoke to him. The bear had been burned before, his eyes and nose forged in flame. He wasn't scared, he didn't fear the fire, and Elwood didn't need to either. The flames, the *dusios*, Casper. The heroin. He could conquer it all. He had the strength of a bear behind him, the memory of who he was.

And for just a second, he was sure he could hear a growl. A low, rumbling snarl that was undeniably grizzly.

Volume suddenly returned to the world and he realised it was him. He was the one growling, psyching himself up for what he knew had to come next.

He scrambled through the open door and onto the balcony. The smoke cloud above the lake was a massive murky stain in the sky that could surely be seen for miles. He could hear sirens on the wind – distant, but heading this way.

He looked over the railing at the stone terrace below. Smoke poured out from the dining room, but he could see it wasn't too high. Once he'd climbed over and lowered himself into a hanging position, the drop was less than his own height.

He let his fingers slip from the surface of the balcony and landed squarely on his feet.

The shovel was still propped up against the wall beside the open French doors. Inside, the fire had spread to the kitchen and dining area. Flames danced across the surface of the table and the worktops, the curtains above the sink now a conflagration.

Elwood snatched up the shovel and moved out of the smoke cloud into the tall grass bordering the terrace. He took the corner and paced along the trail he'd already beaten along the west wall, veering away from the villa as he passed by the open doorway near the old chopping block. The route inside was completely impassable; where only minutes before he'd been able to enter and reach the stairs, a hellish inferno now raged. The blaze had reached the weeds nearest the villa too, and thin tendrils of smoke wound up from the ground. The green grass was dotted with the orange of embers that foreshadowed a wildfire.

Elwood wondered if that might be for the best. Maybe that was exactly what this entire place needed. To just... burn.

He gripped the shovel tightly in both hands as he reached the corner of the building. This was what he would use – not just to bury the *dusios*, but to finish off Casper as well, if he needed to. He hadn't planned on killing anyone today; he'd never planned on killing anyone, other than those who existed in the pages of his books. He could feel the weight of the totem in his pocket though, and with it, the resolve to do whatever was needed. And if he needed to bash Casper's skull in with a shovel as old as Billy the Kid, then so be it.

He scanned the front yard; saw his car and the blood-stained dent, saw that the mass of overgrown lawn and weeds were now on fire too, saw all of this through the haze that covered the whole area like a veil of grey.

But he couldn't see Casper.

Shit.

Elwood tensed, eyes narrowed as he surveyed the area again, slower this time. He pressed his shoulder against the warm brickwork – not wanting to move from his current position, not wanting to venture out into open ground. Casper wouldn't have just left, he wasn't the retreating type. In this situation, Elwood guessed he was either the search-and-destroy type, or the *wait-and-watch* type.

He glanced behind him. Nothing. Casper had last seen him on the other side of the villa – if he was searching, it was likely he'd gone that way and planned on circling the building before he expanded his search any further into the surrounding woodland. The villa itself was completely inaccessible now; he wouldn't be in there.

Which means he's out here. Somewhere.

For all Elwood knew, Casper might already have eyes on him. Might be watching him right now, just waiting for his moment to pounce.

He looked to his left. The treeline was close to the villa on this side of the building. Only a few feet separated him from dense foliage, and he didn't like it. Maybe it would be better to get out in the open, he thought. At least then he'd be able to see Casper coming, be able to prepare himself. He wasn't sure if he'd even be able to swing the shovel here, not effectively anyway.

The car felt like his best bet. It was out in the open, but at least it still provided some cover if he needed it. For all he knew, Casper had managed to retrieve his gun before giving chase; Elwood hoped to God that he hadn't.

He didn't want to be the guy who brought a spade to a gunfight.

Stepping away from the villa, he moved toward the car, glancing back at the porch as he did so. He hadn't been able to see the front door before and he half-expected Casper to be there, crouched on the wooden rail like some tanked-up toad ready to hop onto its prey. The porch stood empty though, smoke filtering through the cracks around the door and joining the smog that lingered in the air.

He reached the front of the car and knelt down, glancing around him. Still no sign of Casper.

The sirens were getting closer.

He didn't want to be here when they arrived – didn't want to have to answer the questions, deal with the suspicion, or wind up handcuffed in the back of a PD cruiser. Not yet. There were things he needed to take care of first. Casper was probably thinking the same thing. If Elwood could hear the sirens, then so could he.

Any moment now, Elwood thought. He'd show himself. He'd make his move.

And then he did.

The car engine fired up.

Startled, Elwood stood up and pushed himself away from the hood. He saw Casper rise up in the driver's seat, hands fixed on the wheel, his face a picture of soundless laughter.

Before Elwood could even think about moving out of the way, the car pitched forward at speed, wheels skidding across gravel and kicking up dust. There was nothing he could do but jump and hope for the best, so that's what he did.

Stars like Arnie and Bruce made it look so easy in the movies: jump and roll; hit the ground and get back up. But real life was nothing like the movies, and Elwood was nothing like Arnie. He managed the jump, but didn't get nearly high enough. The car lurched forward and the fender crashed into his ankles – low enough to prevent him from being taken under the car, but not enough to stop the counterforce from flipping his entire body like a ragdoll.

The world spun like a night with too much liquor on fast forward – only it didn't rock back, it just kept going forward at breakneck speed until the world became nothing but hood. His head was the first thing to hit the fibreglass surface.

Then everything went dark. He didn't feel himself roll up the windscreen. His right elbow and ass crashed into the window and shattered the glass before he was taken up onto the roof.

He regained consciousness a second later and found himself in the air, the world still spinning; trees, sky, smoke, *fire*. Only this time it was gravel that greeted him. He hit the ground face-first and heard his nose crack on impact. He didn't feel it – there was too much going on and he was too out of it – but the sound it made was sufficiently awful to cause him to cry out in dismay.

He rolled onto his back, feeling the warm flow of blood over his top lip. Only for a moment though, then his entire face became numb to all feeling.

The smoke-filled sky danced, undulating as though he was viewing its reflection in the lake. As his eyes grew heavier, everything blurred. The world began to darken. He heard a car door open.

'You're one crazy son of a fucking whore, bunnyman. I'll give you that much.'

Almost black, now.

A sound. Shoes on gravel.

'But I'm the daddy-o. Nobody wins this game but

me.'

The voice begins to fade out.

A hand grips his ankle.

He's moving.

He's gone.

A blur of green. Trees. The world's moving quicker, or he is. Yes, he is. He's sitting up. Sirens, much closer now.

Darkness.

More trees, still moving. Sirens, still blaring, but fading.

'That's all you've got left now, bunnyman. Thirty minutes. Thirty minutes of regret for bringing this shitstorm down on my racket, you junkie-fuck.'

No more trees.

Only black.

Tyres on gravel. Trees again. Moving slower, though.

No more sirens.

'All over my ass, that's where they'll be, thanks to you.'

A car door opening.

Darkness.

Shoes on gravel, getting closer. Trees, but still. No longer moving. A sign. The trail sign. The world's coming into focus. So is the pain.

A car door opens again, closer this time. Cold air against his skin.

'Out.'

A hand grips his shoulder and drags him sideways.

He's flying again, weightless. Olesk, the dead astronaut, he's floating. Then he hits the ground.

The dark returns.

He sees the early evening sky above. A face enters. Stage right.

Freddy?

No, wait, it's not that man from Elm Street. It's Casper. His face red and blistering, patches of skin charred and blackened from the explosion.

'Look what you did. Look what you did to me, you junkie-bum-fuck.'

Where's the shovel?

Casper laughs, a coarse chortle that turns into a coughing fit.

'Well, fuck me. You still got some fight in you? Huh? Junkie-fuck. You looking for something? That shovel you were holding?'

More laughter.

'Bunnyman, this isn't a fight. It never was,' he raises his hand. 'It's feeding time.'

No more sky. Only knuckles. Then pain.

Lights out.

A gravel path.

He can feel all of his weight centred in his midriff. His vision rocks as his head bobs back and forth in step with the shoes that he can see treading the path below.

He's being carried.

But that's his only thought, as darkness sweeps over him once again.

Flashes of dirt and undergrowth. The sound of twigs

snapping underfoot. But everything's darker now.

He arches his neck and sees a canopy of leaves above, blocking out the last of the sun as early evening makes way for the night.

No path.

No sirens.

No smoke.

He can feel blood clotting and crusting across the lower half of his face. And pain. A dull ache stretching across his nose and beneath his eyes. He doesn't know why, though. The last thing he remembers is an engine, and Casper behind the wheel.

The shovel. He's lost the damn shovel.

Roots. He can see roots now, either side of him, walls of dirt rising up like a trench. It *is* a trench.

It's *that* trench.

The trench where the old man had found him. The one where Always had been. Always, the monster.

The trench that had been calling out to him. Tempting him.

No. It wasn't the trench. It was something *in* the trench.

The demon. The, *dusios*.

No. Not like this. This isn't how it was supposed to go. This isn't the plan –

He reaches out, clawing at the exposed roots, desperate to find some purchase.

It's no good, though.

Casper's stride is firm. With each root Elwood manages to grip, another step tugs him onwards.

He's starting to feel better though. His vision is narrowed, eyes swollen from the fallout of his smashed nose, but he remains conscious, the grogginess fading.

No more blackouts.

But Casper doesn't know that.

And right now, that's all Elwood has.

The trench meandered through the woods for what felt like miles. Elwood had no way of judging exactly how far, though; he'd lost all sense of time and distance. Moonlight now poured through the leafy ceiling above them – day had become night. All he knew was that it had been long enough for him to ponder his current predicament and fail to reach any conclusion other than the tried-and-tested *wait and see* approach.

This strategy did hold some promise, though, because they'd also been on the move long enough for him to notice they were being followed.

Afraid to arch his head too much for fear of alerting Casper to the fact that he was awake again, the person remained a peripheral form only, moving quietly along the top of the trench. He couldn't see well enough to determine who it might be, but he prayed to any god who might be listening that whoever it was might be real, and not just a figment of his imagination. Casper appeared oblivious, focused on his march and making too much noise himself.

They came to an abrupt stop at another bend in the ditch. Without warning, Casper grabbed Elwood's ankles and pushed his legs up and over his shoulder. Sufficiently conscious by now, Elwood had the wherewithal – and just enough time – to cross his arms in front of his head before hitting the dirt like a scorpion.

It knocked the wind out of him, but he didn't complain. Instead, he played possum and remained on his back in the soil that was still sludgy from the storm the night before.

'You awake yet, bunnyman?' he felt Casper's boot nudge his leg. 'Oh, come on now, don't play dead. You've brought a shower of shit down on the racket I got going on here, you junkie-fuck, so I'm going to enjoy this, and you're going to let me. You're going to be awake for the whole damn thing,' another kick, this one a little harder, and higher up. 'Rise and shine.'

Elwood remained prone.

'I said rise and fucking shine,' the boot came in much harder this time, straight to the gut and too much to ignore. Elwood doubled over, clutching at his stomach and wheezing uncontrollably. He opened his eyes.

Casper loomed over him. His face looked like almost-raw steak, his skin red and seared, dotted with swathes of black and purple where the skin had charred. Only a few small tufts of singed hair remained on a scalp that was now inflamed and blistered, gleaming brightly in what little moonlight penetrated the dense cover of foliage above them.

'There he is,' Casper grinned. An enraged, berserker grin that portended the imminent arrival of some hideous fever. His cotton shirt, now more grey than white, was soaked in sweat and clung to his massive chest, swelling with every breath, his shoulders rising and falling in unison.

'Shit, Casper, you look worse than I feel.'

'Fixable,' Casper replied. Still smiling, eyes wide and furious, he raised his leg and brought the heel of his boot down on Elwood's wrist.

He howled. Loud enough to disturb a flock of birds from a nearby tree, but not loud enough to block out the sound of his bones snapping beneath Casper's weight.

'How'd you like that, huh?'

Elwood rolled onto his side, holding his floppy hand close to this chest.

'Fuck. Fuck. Fuck you,' he screamed, the pain almost unbearable. He could feel that darkness creeping in again.

'Another word and you get it in the balls,' Casper warned, his tone suggesting a deep desire on his part for Elwood to oblige, to speak again and greenlight his threat.

Elwood forced himself to sit up, breathing deeply of the evening air and employing all of his remaining will and energy to remain conscious. He leant back against the wall of the trench and looked up at Casper.

'Alright. Alright. You're the boss.'

He noticed it, then. The dark hole behind Casper. Little more than a crawl space, set into the sandstone that was buried beneath the dirt of the forest.

The entrance to the cave. It had to be. That was why they'd stopped here.

Elwood's first thought was that the shovel would've been sufficient. The hole was small, and positioned close enough to the ground so that burying it completely wouldn't have been much of a problem.

His second thought was that he'd be going down there. That had never been part of his plan – it didn't need to be, he didn't need to get close to whatever it was that lived in there – he just needed to bury it. But now…

now he was going to be taken through that black hole and brought to the thing that was being held prisoner down there. He let his hand drop to his side and brush by his pocket, breathing a sigh of relief when he felt the tiny bulge there. The totem.

Only it wasn't going to help him against a crazed Casper Stevens. It was starting to feel as though that particular boat had set sail, and he was left standing on the dock, waving goodbye to the only chance he'd ever have at killing the man. He looked down at his mangled wrist and limp hand, his head still heavy from the kiss he'd shared with the gravel driveway back at the villa, not to mention the various blows Casper had dealt him since showing up on the scene.

He wouldn't stand a chance against him, not now.

As if to compound that dreadful comprehension, Casper reached into his trouser pocket and produced a gun. It wasn't the same one that Elwood guessed was still lying under the sofa back at the villa. This one was tiny in comparison. A Glock 26. Still capable of achieving the same outcome, though: sending a hunk of lead straight through a human body.

Elwood stiffened at the sight of it. He drew up his knees and tried to back away, but he was already pressed against the wall of the trench. There was nowhere to go.

Casper was visibly thrilled by the reaction; laughing, he began to toss the gun back and forth like some demented juggler.

'Here's how we're going to do this, bunnyman.' He crouched down next to the hole and pointed the gun toward the darkness. 'This hole right here. You're going in it. No questions. No fucking complaints. You understand?'

'Yes.'

'Good. Because for every question, or fucking complaint, I'm going to pull this trigger. And when I pull this trigger, this other itty bitty *little* hole is going to be facing *your* way, and I'll make sure that whatever comes out doesn't kill you – just leaves you in a world of hurt. You hear?'

'Yes.'

Casper grinned and nodded toward the hole. 'Feet first. I'll be right behind you. So will this guy,' he pointed the gun at Elwood, who, without hesitation, began shuffling forward across the wet dirt toward the opening. Arguing wouldn't do him any good now.

He imagined teeth. Razor-sharp, more grey than white. Rows upon rows of them, circling the rim of the hole. As much as he was sure that the *dusios* would be trapped much deeper, he couldn't help but feel as though crawling through this hole was like crawling into the mouth of the beast. He pushed on regardless, reassured by the thought that Casper wouldn't be following if that was the case.

For a brief moment he thought of Jud Kennishaw. This was surely the same tunnel that young man had found back in the sixties. The tunnel he had probably crawled into, and never come out of.

Non Gratum Anus Rodentum.

He reached into the darkness with both hands, finding a dusty outcrop of stone above the opening which he used to pull himself through. He was forced to put his back to the ground as he moved inside, and the dim canopy of rustling leaves above was swiftly replaced with nothing. He could barely see his own hands just a few feet above him, feeling for any tiny crags that he could use to pull himself along.

The air quickly turned dense and musty. An earthy, mouldy aroma clawed at his throat and felt heavy in his already-restricted nostrils.

He could hear Casper panting and grunting just behind him. He was surprised the man could even fit in such a tight space.

It was getting tighter, too; he was sure of it. His arms were gradually folding into his body as he moved deeper, his knees scraping the roof of the tunnel more frequently.

It was becoming harder to breathe.

As the tunnel grew tighter, so too did the imagined hold around his throat.

'Calm the fuck down,' Casper grumbled. 'If you pass out on me, I'll drag your ass back out there and kick the living shit out of you. Keep going. We're nearly there.'

Nearly there. Nearly there. Elwood held onto those words, repeated them in his head like some mantra.

'When you come out the other end, don't move. The place is rigged like some Indy-fucking-Jones shit. You touch the wrong stone and we're pancakes. Don't touch a fucking thing, you hear me?'

'Yes, I hear you,' Elwood replied, just as he felt the stone above give way to empty space, a reprieve for his knees which he was sure were grazed and bloodied by now.

He continued shuffling forward until he felt the lip of the tunnel above him, and with one final heave, he pulled himself out and into the open cavern.

It was pitch black, but the distinct feeling of being in an enclosed space was now gone. He could breathe again, though the air was still musty and dank.

As instructed, he remained on his back, waiting for Casper to catch up.

'Twenty years. It's been more than twenty fucking years since I've had to crawl through that asshole.'

As Casper climbed to his feet, the cave was suddenly illuminated in what little moonlight was able to find its way through the roof of the forest and along the shaft. Reflecting off of the cold, rocky interior, it provided Elwood with a faint, first view of his surroundings.

'On your feet.' He felt Casper's boot tap roughly against his shoulder, and stood up as quickly as he could without any audible complaint. His aching body protested every move.

The cave stretched out before them – barely fifteen feet wide, but much longer, and gradually sloping downward. The walls were much like those of the ditch outside; sandstone made up the majority of everything below shoulder-height, followed by a mixture of clay. Dirt and old roots that curled in and out of the earth, hanging down from the roof at points, as though desperately trying to assert their hold within the cave floor below. Toward the far end of the cavern, the sides drew inward, eventually culminating in a shadowy fissure, which he guessed was the way forward. The top was only a few feet above their heads; wooden beams were set into it at various intervals along the passage, reminding Elwood of an old mining shaft. Some of these beams had fallen down, releasing dirt and rock and thick clumps of clay that were strewn across the ground and piled up in banks of debris throughout the length of the cavern.

He noticed one of these piles just to his right: boulders of varying sizes were stacked in a mound against the cave wall; a wooden beam, identical to those along the ceiling, lay on the ground next to them.

'Every beam you see on the ground is there because some wise guy touched the wrong fucking stone and caused a cave-in. When I tell you to, you walk forward and you keep your hands in your damn pockets. You hear me, bunnyman?'

'I hear you,' Elwood tucked his hands into his pockets.

Casper moved to the nearest pile of rubble and reached behind the stones. A moment later he produced what looked like a rucksack and set it on top of the mound. Still pointing the Glock at Elwood, he unzipped the backpack and pulled out a large torch, laughing quietly to himself. This laughter turned to a hysterical fit of mirth as he flicked the switch. Bright LED light washed over the cavern.

'It works. It still fucking works,' he looked at Elwood, grinning like a madman. 'This thing's been lying here since before you even had hair on your balls.' He flicked his wrist and Elwood was blinded by the intense light. Casper laughed some more; this time it turned to that same hacked cough and the beam began to sway in the dark as he doubled over and worked to clear his throat.

'Don't be shy, bunnyman. Lead the way.' He indicated with his gun for Elwood to proceed forward.

As they walked, the light revealed petroglyphs carved into the sandstone on either side of the passage. Vast tapestries depicted groups of stick men wielding spears and loosing arrows at animals that looked like woolly mammoths. Hands and stars and moons, trees and flowers and other extinct animals that Elwood couldn't identify. Mingled in with these ancient carvings were noticeably fresher pictograms: symbols of varying size and colour, none of which Elwood recognised, but which he guessed were possibly left by the Shawnee that Aubrey had spoken of. He noticed one particular image repeated at regular intervals; a line of thick rope, laid horizontally and painted in faded yellow. It appeared only on individual rocks that were wedged into the earth above the sandstone borderline, wherever there was a wooden beam set into the roof.

Wherever a beam had fallen down, there was no stone.

It was quite clear to Elwood what purpose these rocks served, but that didn't change anything; he was on the wrong side of Casper for them to be of any use.

Wait and see. That was still his plan, for now.

The walls of the passage closed in as they neared the next opening – a jagged crevice from floor to ceiling, barely wide enough to sidestep through.

Elwood hesitated when they reached the gap, noticing more paintings that dotted the stone on either side. Here the same pictogram was repeated over and over again – two feathered arrows pointing inward at a small circle – though he had no idea what it might mean.

He clambered over a small crest of rubble that lay before the opening, brushing aside exposed roots as he stepped over.

'This one was me. Took a smoke break, leaned back against that wall there and damn near killed myself,' Casper laughed. 'Took me half a fucking day to clear all this shit out of the way.'

He jabbed the gun into Elwood's back and the two of them moved forward into the crevice.

'Worth it, though,' he continued. 'Every time I send some junkie-fuck down here and feed that thing, my life gets sweeter. The bets all come through, deals play out smooth; cops can't catch a sniff, even when I shit in their laps,' he laughed. 'The planets align, man, they fucking *align*, and I turn into the luckiest son of a bitch on this whole fucking rock.'

Elwood didn't answer – just continued forward, sidestepping his way along the winding path, losing all sense of direction as they shifted one way, shuffled another, ducked beneath outcrops and clambered over ridges. What he was acutely aware of, though, was their general direction downward; the tunnel was leading them deeper into the Earth. As they continued the air grew danker, and the walls turned from sandstone to something else, something colder and older and black as the night.

'Fuck. This is bullshit. You're supposed to be in a trance or something, coming down here on your own right now. How the fuck are you not under its control?'

Elwood remembered being susceptible to its power – how he'd walked, alone and naked, out into the forest at night, trying to reach this very spot and beyond. The thought of him wandering like that had chilled him to his core. But this – the thought of him making it all this way on his own, unaware of what was happening, just moving through the dark – was profoundly unnerving.

He let his hand fall to the totem that was still safely tucked away in his pocket.

'I have no idea,' he replied.

'Bullshit. I remember what you said on the phone. But fuck it. You don't want to talk, that's fine with me, I don't need to know. You're a blip, bunnyman, one single carriage on this junkie train that derailed, and this junkie train's been chugging along for over twenty fucking years now. For all the shit that thing does for me, I'm cool dealing with a bunnyman once every few decades,' he laughed.

The passage was growing wider, and Elwood found he was soon able to turn his body forward and begin walking normally again.

Without warning, Casper turned off the torch and they were once again plunged into darkness – only this time it wasn't completely dark. The brightness of the LED had been hiding a faint light that was pouring into the passageway at some point further ahead, reflecting off the cold stone and creating an incandescence that crept around corners and penetrated deeper into the shaft.

'Nearly there,' Casper advised, almost certainly through that same demented grin. 'Bet you're wondering where the light's coming from,' he laughed. 'Wait till you see it, bunnyman. Fucking thing's lit up like a damn Christmas tree.'

Elwood remained silent, equal parts intrigued and scared shitless. He was about to see a demon, an actual demon – not some depiction in a movie, or words on a page – a real *demon*. Images flittered through his mind. Baphomet, black sheep, things with animal legs and human torsos; gargoyle-looking things, shadowy humanoids with abnormally long fingers, vampiric beings; armour-clad warriors the like of Lucifer Morningstar; towering grotesques and revolting masses. Every demonic incarnation he could ever remember being exposed to flashed before his eyes like life before death. Maybe that's what happens before you're confronted with evil you know is coming, he thought. You see it before you see it. See every version of it in your mind's eye.

As they continued down, the light grew stronger, brighter. Soon enough, the winding passageway was suffused in luminous white light the like of which Elwood had never seen. Oddly, as he approached the resting place of this demonic entity, the word which came to mind was *heavenly*; the light felt pure. There was a warmth to it, but not the sort of warmth you felt on your skin. He imagined that if a place such as heaven truly did exist, its days would shine just as this light did.

It was divine.

Elwood rounded the final bend and passed beneath a stone archway carved out of the rock above. The same inwardly-pointing arrows were etched into its black surface. Beyond this entranceway lay a colossal cavern: a circular, subterranean cathedral at least three hundred feet wide and twice as deep. Crimped draperies and thick stalactites in shades of amber and brown hung from the ceiling, dripping with whatever moisture had permeated the layers of earth above. This multitude of precipitation – which Elwood assumed was a result of the storm the night before – gave the illusion of rain within the chamber. Thousands of tiny droplets ran off the tips of these rocky pillars, falling into the cavern below and creating thin streams and rippling pools of water throughout a field of tall columns, lofty stalagmites and vast flowstones that glistened silvery in the light of the *dusios*.

CHAPTER TWENTY-TWO
THE DUSIOS

A rough path zig-zagged ahead of them, cutting back and forth across the sloping side of the chamber and leading all the way down. It was there, at the cave's core, where the jungle of rocky columns gave way to a substantial area of flat stone in the shape of a malformed circle.

Elwood once again felt the familiar touch of a gun at his spine.

'Feeding time. Let's go.'

He stumbled over tiny ridges and slipped through ankle-deep fords as they made their way down toward the centre, unable to tear his eyes away from what was down there.

A ring of stone pillars created a boundary around the open area; they were clearly manmade and stood in stark contrast to the stalagmites that surrounded them. They'd been chiselled into perfect rectangles, their angles true and their heights identical. Twenty-two of them, spaced evenly, with intricate patterns and pictograms etched into each.

Elwood thought of them as bars – the kind you'd have in a prison cell – only these bars were arranged in a circle, keeping that thing trapped in the middle.

The *dusios.*

It looked like nothing he'd imagined in his mind's eye, nothing he could ever recall seeing in his entire life.

Fools, he thought. Humans really were such fools to presume their minds had anywhere near the capacity to imagine what *demonic* might look like.

The thing trapped at the centre of the ring was a legion. As he gazed upon it, he saw that it was never just one thing, but many. It was a storm cloud, grey and silent and filled with white lightning, but at its core there was a star that shone so brightly, Elwood was afraid his eyeballs might boil and pop in their sockets if he looked upon it a second too long. Within this cloud, something writhed and flexed, a beast that was nothing but limbs and malevolence. As they neared the circular prison, he noticed fur, noticed hairy extremities of indiscernible length, with no visible beginning or end. Slimy, scaly tentacles that coiled to forever, like some nightmarish version of a living Escher staircase. Jet-black arachnid appendages that flicked and curled and pointed.

There was no torso – no head, no eyes – because it didn't need eyes; its entire form saw all things. The endless skin, the haze that it lived within, the light, *all* of it, it all *saw*, and Elwood was sure, as they reached the perimeter of the enclosure, that it saw *him*, that it was looking right at him. Hungry, ready to welcome him into its fold, into the mist and light and swallow him up.

They reached the perimeter of the enclosure. The basin of the cavern was flooded, and they were now almost knee-deep in rainwater.

Elwood stopped in his tracks. This was it; whatever was going to happen needed to happen now. There was only one thing he was sure of, and that was that he wasn't going to just step into that circle and be devoured. No way, not without a fight. Not when he had a little girl almost half a continent away who called him daddy, a little girl with a laugh so sweet that the memory had of it had saved his ass once before.

He turned on Casper.

'Well, I guess this is it.'

Casper grinned, his gun aimed at Elwood's neck. 'You guess right, bunnyman,' he laughed. 'Now, just take a few steps back and it'll all be over, we can all go home.'

'I don't think so, Casper. See, I think your orders and your bullets are worth shit all compared to this son of a bitch behind me.'

'Well, well, well. Here we go. The junkie-fuck showing off his balls again. Are you forgetting we ain't on the phone this time? That I've got a fucking piece pointed right at your *throat* this time?'

'If you think I'm just going to walk into that thing's mouth – or whatever the fuck it uses to eat the poor bastards you've sent here before – you've been getting high on your own supply, man,' Elwood replied firmly.

'I don't need you to walk in there, bunnyman. I'll shoot your damn kneecaps off and throw you in there myself if I have to.'

Figures. Two of them – no, three. Actually, he couldn't be sure. Definitely two – and something else, something smaller – standing at the top of the cavern, at the archway he and Casper had passed through only minutes before.

The bark echoed throughout the entire chamber.

Both annoyed and bemused, Casper turned his head to investigate the source of the unexpected yapping.

Elwood didn't waste the opportunity. As soon as Casper's eyes left his, he lunged forward, reaching for the gun as he drove his shoulder into the big man's chest.

He heard Casper wheeze loudly as he barrelled into the centre of his ribcage, making no effort to stay on his feet. He felt cold metal at his fingertips for only a brief moment before the two of them hit the water.

Elwood suddenly found himself on top of the man, whose head was now submerged in the flooded basin, arms flapping wildly.

Next came a deafening report as the drowning man blindly fired off a round into the air. Elwood pounced on the gun with both hands, trying to pry it free of Casper's grip – meanwhile Casper's free hand clawed at Elwood's collar, then his neck.

Casper's face suddenly appeared out of the dark water, eyes wide and wild. He was choking, coughing, fighting for breath, but laughing. Laughing feverishly as he tightened his hold around Elwood's neck and tore his other hand free. Before Elwood could even consider what his next move might be, Casper brought an arm up and smashed the butt of the gun into the side of his head.

The blow sent Elwood sprawling off to the side, his head suddenly heavy, his vision dulled. He landed on his back and his eyes fell once again onto the *dusios*; the cloud was behaving differently now, shifting inward and outward in swift jerks, growing in parts and constricting in others.

It's excited, he thought.

It knew it was going to be fed soon. And it didn't care who it consumed.

Casper was quick. Before Elwood knew what was happening, the man was on top of him – no gun now, only his hands, both of them – wrapped around Elwood's neck and pressing down on his windpipe.

'Game over, bunnyman.'

This was it. This was how he was going to die. Drowned in rainwater and fed to a fucking demon.

'Get him, Bullseye.'

The last thing Elwood heard before Casper forced his head beneath the surface and everything went dark.

He clamped his one good hand around Casper's wrist and tried to break free of his grip, but it was no use, Casper was just too strong, and he could feel what little fight he had left being swiftly choked out of him. He tried to push himself up, but Casper had him pinned down.

He saw El, then. Saw his daughter. Saw her lying in the hospital crib beneath the green blanket. Saw her crying for her midnight milk. Saw her taking her first steps, laughing.

Baloo.

That memory again. His memory, but not his life. Now that death felt so close, it wasn't his life he was seeing – it was her life, his daughter's life, the one he loved and had left behind. And now… now he'd never return, now he'd never have the chance to be there again.

At least he'd tried. Tried and finally succeeded in getting the monkey off his back. Tried, and *failed*, at doing something that went beyond his own life, something selfless and good.

His hands fell away from Casper's, then. He wasn't giving up though, no – now he was dying.

But as his hands fell away, so too did Casper's.

Desperate for air and forgetting he was still submerged, Elwood opened his mouth to breathe and cold water rushed into his lungs.

He still had just enough fight left in him to force himself upright and out of the water.

'Get him, Bullseye. Get him.'

As he doubled over, coughing up water and struggling for breath, Elwood was vaguely aware of Casper screaming beside him – could feel water splashing against him as the man thrashed about on the shore of the basin, wrestling with something that was fixed to his arm.

'Get off me. Get off me. Fucking mutt!'

Still dazed and coming to terms with not being dead, Elwood climbed to his knees and began searching the water around him, hoping Casper had simply dropped it to one side and not tossed it away. He saw Whiskey to his right. Whiskey? What was he doing down here? And someone else…

The Sheriff. It must've been one or both of them he'd seen following them along the trench earlier. He ignored them for now though, moving in circles and feeling beneath the water.

Meanwhile, Casper was backed up against one of the stone pillars to his right, still screaming as the dog tore through his forearm, spraying blood across the carved symbols etched into the rocky monolith.

'Son of a bitch,' he thrust Bullseye against the stone, once, twice. On the third impact Bullseye yelped and released his grip on Casper's arm, falling into the water and landing on his back.

Elwood's hands finally fell upon cold metal. He drew the gun up out of the water and pointed it at Casper as Bullseye rolled over and jumped to his feet.

'Here, Bullseye. To me, boy.' Whiskey again. The dog obeyed and began retreating away from Casper, who was now clutching his bleeding forearm and propping himself up against the pillar.

He looked at Elwood and smiled. Looked at the gun, and his smile broadened.

'Bunnym–'

Two reports in quick succession.

Elwood had never fired a gun in his life. It turned out he wasn't hopeless at it, either.

Two holes appeared in Casper. One at the tip of the sternum, the other in his neck.

The smile began to falter. His eyes blazed with disbelief as he brought his hands up to his neck in an attempt to stem the already-profuse flow of blood staining the water around him like an oil spill.

'Junkie-fu–' his speech became gargled as he stumbled away from the pillar and, without realising it, strayed into the confines of the circle.

The *dusios* began spinning like a cyclone; the cloud grew toward the outer reaches of the stone ring as the shapeless thing at its vortex thrashed and jerked.

Elwood wasn't sure what was more terrifying; its unfathomable appearance, or the fact that it remained completely silent.

Casper stiffened as he noticed the position of the nearest pillar and realised where he was. Elwood would later feel somewhat ashamed of himself, but in that moment, that second, he took great joy in the fear he saw in Casper's eyes, the terrified realisation of what was about to happen, and the knowledge that Elwood Cathis, the junkie-fuck, had beaten him.

The last thing Casper saw was Elwood's middle finger, then the cloud reached him and his body was eviscerated. Fragments of what had once been Casper Stevens were carried into the storm like red autumn leaves in the wind. The cloud turned blood-red for the briefest of moments, before every piece of him was drawn into the living vortex at its core.

Elwood flinched as a hand came to rest on his shoulder.

'Easy. Easy now,' Whiskey stood at his side, eyes fixed on the *dusios*. 'Unbelievable.'

'Once upon a time, but not anymore,' Elwood replied.

'I knew there was something going on up here, but this… this is… I don't know. What is this?'

'Aubrey Christie was right. It creates good fortune for whoever feeds it. But that's only the cherry on top of this crazy-ass sundae,' Elwood began to slump forward, the weight of everything he'd been through suddenly making itself known.

'Whoa there – come on, now, let's get you out of this water. Need to rest up a minute.' Whiskey grabbed him before he collapsed, ushering him out of the water and setting him down to rest on a nearby flowstone.

'That's twice now, Whiskey. Two times you've saved my ass,' Elwood drifted back and let himself lie down for a moment.

Whiskey sat down beside him, his hand now fixed gently around Bullseyes shoulders, who was clearly keen to leap up onto Elwood and lick his wounds.

'No need to thank me. I think this stinky mutt here deserves all the thanks,' he laughed.

Elwood grinned, and let his hand slide down and find the dog's ear.

'Good boy. How did you know?'

'What do you mean?' Whiskey asked.

'How did you know to come here?'

'Son, half the damn town are down at the lake right now. Whatever happened back there at the villa, it caught everyone's attention. Soon as I saw that smoke, I knew exactly where it was coming from. I got there just after the Sheriff arrived; Kenner said your car came speeding out of there only a minute or two before and you weren't driving it. Sheriff fixed to follow you, and I knew whatever was going on was probably leading you back to where I found you, so I offered to show him. And sure enough, we caught up with you and whoever the hell that other guy was before you even left the trail.'

Elwood smiled to himself. The fire had brought more help than he could've possibly imagined.

THOSE YOU KILLED

The Sheriff.

Elwood groaned as he sat up. 'Sheriff?'

He and Whiskey looked back and found Sheriff Jo Tims standing only a few feet behind them, his jaw working a clump of tobacco between his teeth and gum, the reflection of the *dusios* floating across his shades.

It was hard to tell if he was looking at them or the demon. He remained completely still, one hand resting on the butt of his holstered Colt. 'Tell me everything you know.'

'Can we do this someplace else?' Elwood replied. 'I don't mind where, even the station – just, anywhere bu–'

'Everything. Right here, right now.'

'Hey, ease up a little Sheriff. The boy's beat to shit, can't we at least get him to a doctor –'

'Bob. Enough. Let the man speak.'

There was no point arguing, Elwood could see that. So, he proceeded to tell Sheriff Tims everything he knew, starting with the information he'd gotten from Aubrey Christie. A brief mention of the fact he had suffered hauntings orchestrated by the thing behind them – the details of which he kept to himself. Finally, he explained who Casper was, and the racket he'd been running for at least the past twenty years, sending vulnerable people to a place where he knew they'd succumb to the call of the *dusios*. People who'd left their old lives behind in exchange for one that he nurtured and controlled, one where he was the dealer and where, for junkies, he was God.

He would giveth, and ultimately, he would taketh away.

Tims listened unflinchingly and without a word, never even nodding, just looking forward, watching the thing at the centre of the stone circle.

'So, what now?' Whiskey asked. 'How do we get rid of this thing?'

'We don't,' Elwood replied. 'Natives with hundreds, maybe even thousands of years of spiritual knowledge behind them, were only able to trap it. Which is a hell of a lot more than anything we might be capable of.'

'What if we got a Priest down here?' Whiskey suggested. 'One of those Exorcisers.'

Elwood shook his head. 'Useless. This thing's probably older than the bible. It needs to be buried. Sealed up good so nobody can find their way down here again. If we're lucky, maybe it'll starve. Fuck knows how long that might take, though.'

They stood in silence for a moment, the gentle pattering of rainfall echoing around them.

'You can both leave now,' the Sheriff shifted his head toward them. 'I'll take it from here. Bob, not a word about this to anyone, you hear?'

'But, Sheriff –'

'Same applies to you, Mr Cathis. And I want you out of this town, today. You get in your car and you drive back to wherever it was you came from. You don't look back, and you don't ever come back. Understand?'

Elwood couldn't believe it; he didn't know where this was going, but he didn't like it. 'We need to seal this place up, Sheriff.'

'This ain't an argument. You want to keep your asses out of jail, I suggest you do as I fucking tell you.'

'Hey Jo, come on now –'

'Don't you fucking *Jo* me, Bob, you knew my pap
and his too, but you don't know me. Way I see it, our
town's gone to shit. Been rotten since before I was even
born, and now... well, now we know why. Damn
outsiders benefiting off of what we got here. Not
anymore. This shit stops today. This town could use
some help, use some luck or fortune or whatever the
fuck you want to call it. That thing right there can help
us make this town a better place. And all I have to do is
help a few bad people find their way down here,' he
laughed. 'Shit, we got kiddie-fiddlers and murderers up
in Polsey Correctional. Scumbags I've cuffed myself
and dropped into a system that gives them three meals
a day and TV,' he spat brown mucus into the water.

Elwood didn't know what to say. This wasn't right.

'Sheriff, please, you can't just keep feeding this
thing, you can't ju–'

'One more time. I'll ask you both, one more time, to
forget everything you saw here today and get the fuck
out of this cave.' He looked at Elwood. 'I just watched
you shoot and kill an unarmed man.' He looked at
Whiskey. 'And you, Bob, you were a damn accomplice
– you set your mutt on the asshole and helped this son
of a bitch right here kill the man in cold blood. Now, if
you both keep your mouths shut about this whole thing,
so will I. Is that too hard for you to understand? Do I
need to explain again? Because I said one last time and
we just did all that, so maybe I don't say another word
– maybe I just cuff you and haul your asses off to jail.

'Or maybe I make it easier on myself and just stick a
bullet between your eyes right here and now,' he drew
his gun from the holster and pointed it straight at them.

Elwood climbed to his feet. 'Okay, Sheriff. You win. Nobody else has to die here today. You want me out of town, fine. I wasn't planning on sticking around anyway, I have a life I want to get back to. I'm sure Whiskey and I can forget everything that happened here today, right?'

He looked at Whiskey, who appeared flabbergasted by this new development. Elwood nodded, his eyes pleading with him. *Just agree, so we can both walk out of here.*

The old man's features eased a little, and he nodded his agreement. 'Alright, Sheriff, we can do it your way. For the town.'

Tims grinned. 'Well, I'm real glad we reached an understanding here, gentleman. Now, get the fuck out of here,' he motioned with his gun for them to move along and they quickly obliged, Bullseye in tow.

When they reached the archway leading out of the cavern, Elwood turned back and took one final look upon the place. One last glance at the circle of stones and the prisoner held within it. The Sheriff had moved into the water and was leaning against one of the pillars, staring at the *dusios*. Perhaps even talking to it, for all Elwood knew. Maybe some strange initiation was taking place, some dark deal between supplier and consumer. It didn't matter anyway; he knew what needed to happen next, and hoped Whiskey would understand.

***

The old man *did* understand.

Once they'd traversed the winding passageway, walked the length of the tunnel at the summit, and reached the crawlspace that led outside, Whiskey and Bullseye exited the cave completely, and waited outside in the ditch whilst Elwood returned to the other end of the tunnel.

Once there, he turned back on himself and, one by one, removed each of the keystones that were set into the walls.

He was nearly crushed to death more than once in the five minutes it took him to complete the task. He was far from being in the best shape, still half-blind and riddled with injuries he knew would ail him for months to come, but he managed to do what was needed. The sequence of cave-ins unleashed tonnes of earth and clay and sandstone rock into the shaft, blocking the path completely and leaving it impassable at both ends.

Before they returned to the burned-out villa, Elwood and Whiskey set their story straight and agreed to never tell anyone about what had truly occurred that day.

They kept it simple and sprinkled it with enough truth to make it plausible. Casper had allowed Elwood to stay at the villa in an attempt to recover from his addiction, an offer which Casper had afforded to others in the past. This was all a ruse though, as Casper was a sick man, the sort of sick man who got his kicks murdering people and dumping their bodies in a secluded cave out in the woods. Elwood put up a fight though, and in his desperation, set the villa on fire to try and signal for help. Which worked.

The Sheriff caught up with them at the cave; a

gunfight ensued. There was a cave-in.

Casper and the Sheriff both perished.

Neat and tidy.

Rescue workers visited the site with Whiskey as a guide, but no effort was made to recover any bodies; the ground north of the ditch showed signs of sinking, and an investigation of the hole confirmed there was no safe way to mount such a recovery exercise. In fact, the place was deemed so unstable that work was carried out to reinforce the whole patch of land with more dirt. The ditch was filled in with concrete to ensure nobody ever put themselves in any danger by trying to explore the cave.

And a memorial to *Sheriff Jo Tims, killed in the line of duty* was erected on the site some months later.

Elwood took the time to retrieve the old shovel from the front yard of the villa and return it – along with the bear totem and his thanks – to Aubrey Christie. He told her the same story he and Whiskey had sold to the local PD, but maybe – just maybe – his eyes told her something different.

He left the town and never looked back.

He used what little royalties he still had in his savings account on a rent bond for a place in Rockford, Illinois, a quiet neighbourhood less than half an hour away from where his daughter now lived.

He started with supervised meetings in public places.

Within a year, he was allowed to have El stay over on Saturdays and Sundays.

They went to the movies, visited old bookstores, ate too much ice-cream, laughed – and cried – together, but most importantly, they shared precious moments.

Moments that mattered, moments that would become memories, moments that warmed the soul more than any superficial injection ever could.

How wonderful it was to be a father again.

Gracie had moved on, and that was okay, that was life. But the ease with which Elwood came to terms with that, and was able to feel sincerely happy for her, surprised him.

Before long, he found himself moving on too; her name was Evelyn. She taught art at the same school where Elwood had begun to teach English. Things were going great.

He made peace with his former agent and began work on a new novel; hopefully it wouldn't be another *Cathistrophe,* but only time would tell.

He spoke to Whiskey from time to time. They talked football and politics, but never about what happened that day. They didn't need to.

Another dark chapter in the history of Misstonville and Lake Chance had been brought to a close; only this time, perhaps it was the final chapter. Perhaps the *dusios* was buried for good, this time.

Or perhaps not.

And did it matter? This was never a story about Misstonville or Lake Chance and the demon that was trapped there. This was the story of Elwood Cathis. The story of a man finding himself again, reclaiming who he was. That's what you do when you overcome addiction: you remember the parts of yourself you lost along the way.

You remember *those you killed.*

But those parts, those morals and virtues and

passions, they had never truly been killed; Elwood understood that now more than ever. They'd never died like the characters from his books which had seemingly come to symbolise them. They'd only been buried, left to wait beneath the surface until he found the strength to pick up a shovel.

Addiction was the same, once you got over it. You didn't kill it, you could *never* kill it – only bury it. Like a bad thought you chose to stop feeding, or a demon you buried and left to starve.

Good and evil, whether they existed within you or in the world around you, were similar in that way. Neither could ever be truly killed, only buried.

And where evil was concerned, sometimes – actually, most of the time – that was enough.

ACKNOWLEDGEMENTS

It might be my name on the cover, but a story never gets this far without a little help. First of all, you, avid reader. Have you ever pondered the question – If a tree falls in the forest and nobody is around to hear it, does it make a sound? Well, I think of stories like that sometimes, can a story even exist if nobody reads it? Are they not just words on a page, waiting for you, the intrepid reader, to connect them all and bring them to life? I think so, and for this reason you have my undying gratitude for making it this far, even if you think it's shit.

My family. I'm lucky enough to have their support and encouragement, which means the world to me. My brother promised to buy twenty copies of this book and I'm holding you to that, Tim.

My brother from another mother, Keith. Thank you for being my best friend and for telling everyone and their dogs about the release of this book.

To the #bookstagram community and everyone in the Blood Rites Writer's Circle, I've never found myself surrounded by so many kind, supportive, sincerely friendly and like-minded people in all my days. Special thanks to Nick Harper, and Jess Villafane, for being tremendously supportive, it makes a huge difference.

James Wright, fellow author, colleague and good friend. The back and forth we've had over the years, the honest feedback you give, your unique *horror novel virgin* perspective, and more importantly, your friendship, have been incredibly valuable. Thank you.

And to all those who've shared words of encouragement and support whenever I've mentioned this endeavour, you know who you are, thank you so much.

Until next time, stay scared.

Lightning Source UK Ltd.
Milton Keynes UK
UKHW010636280321
381106UK00001B/10